THE DUEL

THE DUEL

ALEXANDER KUPRIN

TRANSLATED BY JOSH BILLINGS

MELVILLEHOUSE
BROOKLYN, NEW YORK

THE DUEL BY ALEXANDER KUPRIN

ORIGINALLY PUBLISHED IN RUSSIAN BY ZNANIE
(UNDER THE DIRECTION OF MAXIM GORKY) AS
POEDINOK, ST. PETERSBURG, 1905

© 2011 MELVILLE HOUSE PUBLISHING
TRANSLATION © 2011 BY JOSH BILLINGS

FIRST MELVILLE HOUSE PRINTING: JUNE 2011

MELVILLE HOUSE PUBLISHING
145 PLYMOUTH STREET
BROOKLYN, NY 11201

WWW.MHPBOOKS.COM

ISBN: 978-1-935554-52-3

BOOK DESIGN: CHRISTOPHER KING, BASED ON
A SERIES DESIGN BY DAVID KONOPKA

PRINTED IN THE UNITED STATES OF AMERICA

1 2 3 4 5 6 7 8 9 10

LIBRARY OF CONGRESS CATALOGING-IN-PUBLICATION DATA

KUPRIN, A. I. (ALEXANDER IVANOVICH), 1870-1938.
[POEDINOK. ENGLISH]
THE DUEL / ALEXANDER KUPRIN ; TRANSLATED BY JOSH BILLINGS.
    P. CM.
ISBN 978-1-935554-52-3
1. DUELING--RUSSIA--FICTION. I. BILLINGS, JOSH. II. TITLE.
PG3467.K8P613 2011
891.73'3--DC23
                                        2011022609

THE DUEL

I

The sixth company's evening maneuvers were winding down, and the junior officers were checking their watches more frequently and with greater impatience. Today's topic had been guard duty. The soldiers were assigned to different points on the parade grounds: around the poplars, along the side of the road, near the exercise equipment, next to the door of the regimental schoolhouse, on the rifle range. Each of these spots stood for a real post, for example the one at the gunpowder cellar, or under the regimental flag, at the guard house, by the cash box. Sentries were established—and then every so often there was a changing of the guard, at which point non—commissioned officers went around verifying the post locations and testing the soldiers' knowledge by trying to trick them into giving up their rifles, or leaving their places, or agreeing to hold on to some object for a little while, most often the non-com's own cap. Those men who had spent some time in the service and therefore knew all about this kind of joshing answered their demands with exaggerated brio: "Go away! I have no right to give up my rifle unless the tsar himself orders me to do so." But the younger ones were confused. They couldn't tell which orders were meant as jokes and which ones were sincere, and because of this they responded with either too much seriousness or not enough.

"Khlebnikov! You butterfingered buffoon!" shouted Lance Corporal Shapovalenko, a smart-looking, round little man, in whose voice one could hear the patient suffering of authority. "We've gone through this over and over again. Who gave you that order? Your prisoner? What's the matter with you? Answer me: why are you at this post?"

Over in the third platoon, a more serious situation was developing. A young Tartar named Muhamedzhinov, who could barely speak or understand Russian, was being driven completely out of his mind by his commanding officers—some of whom actually were his commanding officers, and some of whom were only playing the part. Suddenly he snapped, took up his rifle, and began answering all commands and attempts at persuasion with a single resolute phrase:

"I s-stab you!"

"All right, stop that . . . Yes, you fool. . . ." Sergeant Bobil said. "And do you know who I am? I'm your sentry boss, remember?"

"I s-stab you!" the Tartar cried in terrified rage, thrusting his bayonet anxiously at anyone who approached him. His eyes were bloodshot, and a small group of soldiers had gathered around him, glad for anything that might momentarily interrupt their monotonous training.

Captain Sliva, the company commander, came over to break things up. As he trundled sluggishly along, dragging his legs, a handful of junior officers on the other side of the parade ground went off to talk and smoke. There were three of them: Lieutenant Vetkin, a bald, mustachioed man of thirty-three years, who was merry, talkative, and a drunk; Sub-lieutenant Romashov, who was serving his second year in the regiment; and Sub-ensign Lyubov, a lively, well-built boy with crafty, affectionate, stupid eyes, whose fat naïve lips were constantly smiling. All three of them started talking about the senior officers.

"That swine," Vetkin said. He looked at his watch and then snapped the cover down angrily. "Why the hell is he holding his company this long? It's barbaric!"

"Perhaps you'd like to explain your view of the situation to him, Pavel Pavlovich?" Lyubov said slyly.

"You can go to hell too. Explain it to him yourself. What are we doing here? Simple: we're not doing anything. They always dig into the men before inspections. And they always overdo it. They pester a man—they bully him, and when inspection comes he just stands there like a stump. Ever hear the story about the two company commanders who bet on whose man could eat the most bread? They both chose the biggest gluttons they could find. The bet was enormous—something like a hundred rubles. One soldier ate seven pounds before pushing his plate away: he couldn't eat any more. The commander dressed down his sergeant-major: 'What's the matter with you, I thought he was a ringer?' The officer bugged his eyes out: 'I don't know what happened, sir. This morning we practiced it: he put down eight pounds in a single sitting . . .' That's how we do it. Lather rinse repeat, and then when the inspection finally comes they wilt in their galoshes."

"Last night . . ." Lyubov said, between bursts of laughter. "Yesterday, all the drills were over in all the companies, so I go to my room, it's eight already, or around then, anyway totally dark. But then what do I see but the eleventh company practicing their signals! A veritable choir: 'Rea-dy-aim, for-ward-thrust, down-he-goes!' I ask Lieutenant Andrusevich, 'What's with the late night serenading?' And he says, 'Like dogs, we howl at the moon.'"

"A dog's life, yes . . . talk about boring!" Vetkin said, and yawned. "Hold on, who's that riding up there? Bek, maybe?"

"Yes. Bek-Agamalov," said the sharp-sighted Lyubov. "He sits in his saddle well."

"Very well," Romashov agreed. "In my opinion, he rides better than any of the cavalrymen. Ho-ho-ho—look at that! He's making her dance. He's showing off."

An officer in white pants and an adjunct's uniform was slowly making his way along the main road, on a tall, golden horse whose tail had been cropped in the English manner. She was in a feisty mood, and kept impatiently shaking her tightly reigned neck and rearing her slender legs.

"Is it true that he's a native Circissan?" Romashov asked Vetkin.

"I think so. Sometimes Armenians do pass themselves off as Circissans and Caucasians, but Bek doesn't seem like the lying type to me. Just look at how he handles his horse!"

"Wait a second, I'll call to him," said Lyubov.

He cupped his hands around his mouth and called out in a restrained voice, so that the company commander wouldn't hear:

"Lieutenant Agamalov! Bek!"

The officer riding along the ridge pulled on his reins, stopping for a second before turning to his right. After he had pulled his horse around he hunched slightly in the saddle; he coaxed her to jump over a ditch with a few subtle movements and then rode up to the officers at a gallop.

He was below-average height, with a lean, wiry, and very strong body. His face, with its sloping forehead, bulbous, hooked nose and strong, decisive-looking lips, was manly and handsome, with a sort of Asiatic paleness to it that, at that time, was still quite prevalent: a coloring that made his skin seem simultaneously both thick and glossy.

"Hello, Bek," Vetkin said. "Who was all that prancing for? Girls?"

Bek-Agamalov shook hands with the officers, bending low and carelessly in his saddle. He smiled, and it seemed as if his row of white teeth cast its reflected light on the entire lower half of his face, not to mention the small, black, well-groomed mustache hanging over it.

"Two fine little Jewish girls were walking along up there. But what's that to me? I didn't pay any attention to them."

"We know all about your swordplay," Vetkin said, shaking his head.

"Listen, gentlemen," Lyubov said, smiling, as usual, before he'd even said anything, "Do you know what General Doxturov said about infantry adjutants? This concerns you, Bek. He said that they are the most reckless riders on earth . . ."

"Hold your tongue, ensign!" Bek-Agamalov said.

He jogged his horse forward and made as if to run Lybov over.

"No—I swear! All of them, he said, rode not horses but something like guitars, or steamer trunks: lame, bloody-eyed, excitable nags, and with short fuses too. Give one of these characters an order, he said, no matter where to, and they rush off at full gallop. They see a fence—they jump it. A ravine—jump it. Shrubs fly left and right. They drop the reins, lose the stirrups, their cap flies to the devil! Wild riders!"

"So anyway, Bek, what's new?"

"What's new? Nothing's new. Just this minute the regimental commander discovered Sub-lieutenant Lekh loitering in the officers' club. He bawled him out so loudly that you could hear it in the church square. And there's Lekh, drunk as a skunk: he couldn't have pronounced the words 'mama' or 'dada' in his condition. He stands in place and rocks back and forth, his hands behind his back. And Shuglovich bellows at him: 'When addressing your regiment commander, please be so kind as to keep your hands off your ass!' This in front of the servants."

"Nicely put!" Vetkin said with a smile. His voice sounded neither completely sarcastic nor totally sincere. "Yesterday he started shouting at the Fourth Company: 'Why are you holding the rule book up under my nose? I know it better than you—and anyway, I'm the law in this regiment!'"

Lyubov smiled suddenly at something he was thinking.

"And one more thing, gentlemen: what about what happened with the adjutant in N company . . ."

"Jesus, Lyubov," Vetkin snapped sternly. "Give it a rest. Your own echoes are going to start interrupting you."

"There's more news," Bek-Agamalov continued. He pointed his horse at Lyubov again and once more jokingly made as if to run him over. The horse shook its head and snorted, spraying foam everywhere. "There's more. The commander is demanding that every company start practicing with sabers on dummies. Nobody in ninth company liked this: their temperatures rose as soon as they heard—and not in a good way. Epifanov was put under house arrest because his saber wasn't sharp enough . . . Well what are you afraid of now, ensign?" Bek-Agamalov shouted suddenly at Lyubov. "Don't get so upset. Someday you'll be an adjunct yourself. Then you can sit on your horse like a fried sparrow on a plate."

"You Asiatic . . . Get that worthless nag out of my face," Lyubov said, waving his hands at the horse's muzzle. "Hey, Bek—did you ever hear about the time one of the adjutants from N company bought a circus horse? He rode her around to show off, until suddenly, right in front of the commander, she began to parade using Spanish steps. You know Spanish steps, right? Hoofs high, like this, from side to side. Finally he forced his way to the head of the company—everyone was shouting, it was total chaos. But the horse didn't care: she just kept on doing those Spanish steps. At last Dragomirov put his hands up like this and shouted, 'Very good Lieu-tenant! Now just continue your marching, exactly like that if you will, all the way to the guardhouse—for twenty-one days' house arrest! Throw him in the brig!'"

"Idiot," Vetkin said, rolling his eyes. "Listen, Bek, this business about the saber practice is news to me. What does it mean? Are we supposed to have absolutely no free time at all? At least now we know why they brought that freak in yesterday."

He pointed to the center of the plaza, where the practice dummy stood. It was made out of gray clay and looked something like a man, except without any arms or legs.

"What do you mean—haven't you had a whack at him yet?" Bek-Agamalov asked curiously. "Romashov, have you tried it?"

"Not yet."

"Are you kidding—with all I have to do," Vetkin muttered. "When am I supposed to find time for saber practice? We hang around here from nine in the morning to six at night. There's barely a minute to catch a bite or have a sip of vodka. Now they've given us dolls so we can play like good little children . . ."

"Don't be stupid. An officer has to know how to handle his saber."

"Oh yes? And why is that, if I might ask? For battle? You couldn't get within a hundred paces of today's firearms. Who cares about your damned sabers? I'm not in the cavalry. And if I had to fight, I'd be better off grabbing a rifle butt—bam, bam, right on the skull. More accurate."

"All right, then, what about during peacetime? Plenty of opportunities for use there. A rebellion, or a revolt somewhere . . ."

"But how is that any different? Again, why a saber? No way in hell I'm going to get my hands dirty separating men's heads from their shoulders. 'Open . . . fire!'—and it's in the bag . . ."

Bek-Agamalov made a dissatisfied face.

"Ahhh, you're only joking, Pavel Pavlich. Answer me seriously—suppose you're out walking somewhere, or at the theater, or let's say you're in a restaurant, and some siv insults you . . . we'll take an extreme case. Let's say this siv gives you some sort of slap in the face. What would you do?"

Vetkin shrugged his shoulders and pressed his lips together scornfully. "All right: first of all, a siv would never slap my face, because they only start fights with people they know are afraid to fight back. And secondly—actually, you know what I'd do? I'd give him a crack with my revolver."

"And if you'd left your revolver at home?" Lyubov asked.

"Well, then, what the hell, I'd go get it . . . This is stupid. I remember the time a certain captain was insulted in a *café chantante*. He took a carriage home, got his revolver, and then came back and killed the bastards. And that was that! . . ."

Bek-Agamalov shook his head.

"I know, I heard all about it. But the court decided that he had acted with murderous intent, and found him guilty. So how was that a good idea? As for me, if I'd been the one insulted or struck . . ."

Instead of saying anything else, he clenched his small hand into a fist that was so tight, the reins it was holding began to tremble. Lyubov suddenly doubled up with mirth and burst out laughing.

"Again—that's enough out of you!" Vetkin snapped.

"Gentlemen . . . Please . . . Hee-hee-hee! A funny thing happened in M company: sub-ensign Krauss was making a scene at one of their respectable get-togethers, and the bartender grabbed him by the shoulder strap so hard that he almost tore it off. So Krauss pulls out his revolver—one sh-shot, right in the head! Where he stood! When a second man—some sort of lawyer—threw himself on him, Krauss shot him too. Well, as you can imagine, everybody ran for the exits. And then Krauss went calmly back to his camp, to his old barracks. The watchman shouted 'Who goes there?' 'Sub-ensign Krauss, come to die beneath the flag!' He lay down and shot himself in the arm. Afterward the courts let him off."

"Nicely done!" said Bek-Agamalov.

At this point they began talking about one of the junior officers' favorite topics, that is, outbreaks of unexpected violence and how they almost always tended to go unpunished. In one small town, a drunken cavalryman—who was so young that he didn't even have a beard yet—cut into a crowd of Jews with his saber, leaving them each with "a mark for Passover." In Kiev, an infantry sub-ensign had cut down a student in a dancing hall because he'd elbowed him at the refreshment counter. In one of the big cities (either Moscow or St. Petersburg) an officer had "shot like a dog" a civilian who, in a restaurant, had made the remark to him that proper people didn't act that way with women they didn't know.

Romashov, who had kept quiet up to this point, and who was blushing more and more from confusion, suddenly adjusted his glasses for no reason and coughed, interrupting the conversation.

"Well, gentlemen, here's how I see it. Let's disregard the situation with the bartender . . . alright . . . But if a civilian . . . How can one put it? . . . Yes . . . Well, if he's a proper man, a nobleman and so on . . . Why would I attack him—an unarmed man—with my saber? Why shouldn't I be able to demand satisfaction from him? After all, we're civilized men, as they say."

"What kind of garbage are you talking, Romashov?" Vetkin interrupted him. "Well, all right, so you demand satisfaction, and he replies, 'Well . . . er, er, er . . . I, don't you see, I usually don't . . . you see . . . I don't acknowledge challenges to duel. I'm against bloodshed . . . And what's more, I, er . . . there's the law to consider . . .' And you get to spend the rest of your life with a broken nose."

Bek-Agamalov flashed his bright smile.

"Aha! So you agree with me? I'm telling you, Vetkin: learn the sword. In Kafkaz, we start studying when we're children. We practice on stumps, on sheep carcasses, on waterfalls . . ."

"How about on people?"

"On people too," Bek-Agamalov answered calmly. "Just imagine how they cut! With one stroke you can slice a man from shoulder to hip, diagonally. Now that's a blow! Why would you do it any other way?"

"And you, Bek—can you do that?"

Bek-Agamalov sighed regretfully:

"No, I can't . . . I can cut a young ram in half . . . I even tried cutting a calf carcass up once . . . But probably not a person, no . . . I've never cut a man in half. I could behead him, that I know, but to cut in twain? . . . No. My father could do it easily."

"Well, then, come on, let's try it," Lyubov begged, though his eyes were burning. "Please, Bek—come on."

The officers went over to one of the dummies. Vetkin cut first. After twisting his kind and simple face into a ferocious mask, he fell on the dummy with all his strength, executing a huge and ungainly stroke. At the same time, he unintentionally produced the sort of loud noise that a butcher makes when he cuts into a calf. *Hrass!* The blade entered the clay about a foot deep, and it was difficult for Vetkin to pull it out again.

"A bad hit!" Bek-Agamalov remarked, shaking his head. "Now you, Romashov . . ."

Romashov withdrew his saber from its sheath and adjusted his glasses with some confusion. He was average height, thin, and though strong enough for his build still awkward from his great shyness. Even in the academy he had been ungainly with flat-bladed swords, and after a half a year in the service he had lost completely whatever knowledge he'd once had. Raising his weapon high above his head, he instinctively held his left arm out in front of him.

"Hand!" shouted Bek-Agamalov.

But it was too late. The end of the saber only barely scratched the clay. Romashov, whose body had been expecting more resistance from the material, lost his balance and staggered forward. The edge of the saber struck his outstretched hand, tearing a scrap of skin from the index finger. Blood began gushing out.

"There, now—if you keep that up you'll cut your arm off!" Bek-Agamalov shouted angrily, sliding off his horse. "Did you really think that was the way to do it? Well, never mind, it's just foolishness, wrap a bandage around it. Looks like you're one of those Institute girls. Hold my horse, ensign. Here, watch. The essential strength of the blow comes not from shoulders, and not from elbow, but right here, in the flick of the wrist." He made a few quick, sharp-cornered movements with the fist of his right hand, and then raised the saber blade above his head in a single smooth, sharp arc. "Now look: I hold my left hand behind me, on my back. When you deliver the blow, don't beat or slash at your target: tear at him, as if you're sawing. Then pull the saber back . . . Understand? More than anything, make sure to remember this: the plane of the sabre should be at an angle to the plane of the cut—absolutely at an angle. This will make your cut sharper. Here, watch me."

Bek-Agamalov took two steps back, sighting the clay dummy and then flashing his saber high into the air with a series of swift and subtle movements, after which he threw himself forward to strike. Romashov only barely had time to hear the piercing whistle of the parted air before the top half of the dummy slid to the ground with a heavy plop.

The surface of the cut was smooth, even polished.

"Good lord! Now that's a blow!" Lyubov cried admiringly. "Bek, you devil, let's have another!"

"Yes, Bek—again, please," Vetkin asked.

But, as if to preserve the effect, Bek-Agamalov only smiled and returned his saber to its sheath. He sighed heavily: at that moment, with his fierce, widened eyes, his hooked nose, and his bared teeth, he looked less like a man and more like some sort of vicious, proud, predatory bird.

"A blow? Please. Can we really call that a blow?" he said, with affected disdain. "In Kafkaz my father, who was sixty years old, could cut a horse's head off. Clean off! Continual practice, my boys, is an absolute must. Here's how we do it back home: we stand a willow switch on its end and strike at it, or we stand beneath a thin stream of water and strike at it. If there's no splash, we know it's a clean blow. All right, Lyubov, your turn."

Just then Bobilyev, a non-com, came running up to Vetkin with a frightened expression on his face.

"Your excellency . . . The regiment commander is coming!"

"A-ten-shun!" Captain Sliva drawled, severely and with great annoyance, at the other end of the square.

The officers quickly went to join their platoons.

A large, clumsy-looking carriage made its way slowly down the road to the plaza, and then stopped. From one of its sides the regiment commander crawled (he was so heavy that he caused the carriage to tip) while from the other emerged Lieutenant Fedorovsky, the regimental adjutant: a tall foppish officer who jumped to the ground in a single hop.

"Good morning, Sixth!" came the colonel's calm, deep voice.

The soldiers began shouting loudly and raggedly from the various corners of the plazza:

"To your he-alth, sir-r-r!"

The officers brought their hands up to the brims of their caps.

"Please, carry on with the maneuvers," the regiment commander said, as he made his way toward the nearest platoon.

Colonel Shuglovich was in a terrible mood. He walked from platoon to platoon, directing his questions at the garrison soldiers, and letting loose, occasionally, with the supremely virtuosic cursing that is so frequently a hallmark of veterans of front-line service. The steely and unyielding expression of his old, white, faded stern eyes completely hypnotized whatever soldier he addressed, causing them to stare straight ahead without blinking or even breathing, practically, as their bodies shriveled in fear. He was a huge old man: obese, and immensely rotund. His fleshy face, with its broad skull, narrowed at its peak right at the forehead, while its bottom—whose rhombus shape resembled nothing so much as a large, heavy shovel—was gradually overrun by a thick silver beard. His eyebrows were gray, unkempt, and intimidating. He spoke in an almost complete monotone, but every inflection of his unusual voice (which was legendary in the division and to which he owed, by the way, his entire military career) resounded clearly over the farthest corners of the vast plaza, and even on the road.

The colonel stopped suddenly in front of Sharafudinov, a young soldier who was standing near the gymnastics equipment. "Name and rank!" he said.

"Private Sharafudinov, of the sixth regiment, sir!" the tartar cried diligently, his voice hoarse.

"Idiot! I'm asking what post you're assigned to."

The soldier, who was losing his nerve under the commander's shouting and angry look, kept quiet, only blinking his eyelids.

"We-ll?" Shuglovich's voice rose.

"To keep the sentry post . . . safe from enemies . . ." the tartar began to babble at random. Finally he concluded, in a quiet and firm voice, "I don't know, your excellency."

The commander's whole face flushed a deep brick color, and his bushy eyebrows crowded together angrily. He turned around and inquired sharply:

"Who is the junior officer of this plattoon?"

Romashov forced himself forward and put his hand to his cap.

"I am, Colonel."

"A-ha! Sub-lieutenant Romashov, naturally—an excellent drill instructor! Knees together!" Shuglovoich barked suddenly, bugging his eyes out. "Is that any way to stand in the presence of your regiment commander? Captain Sliva, I'm holding you responsible as well from the fact that your subaltern-officer is unable to carry out his military duties in the presence of his commanding officers . . . You, dog-face"—Shuglovich turned to Sharafudinov—"who's your regiment commander."

"I can't say," the tartar answered dolefully, though without hesitation.

"You can't s— . . . I'm asking you who your regiment commander is! You want to know who? Me, that's who! Get it: me, me, me, me, me!" Shuglovich struck his palm fiercely against his chest a few times in succession.

"I can't say . . ."

Here the Colonel launched into a twenty-word-long string of intricate and crude curses. "Captain Silva, this son of a bitch is going stand here in full dress. Let him rot: full gear, with his gun. You, sub-lieutenant: clearly you think about chasing tail than you do about the service. You dance the waltz? Read Paul de Koch? What does that make you—a soldier? Is that what you think?" He poked Sharafudinov in the lips. "This is a disgrace, an outrage, a shame—not a soldier. You don't even know the name of your regiment commander. I'm astonished, sub-lieutenant."

Romashov stared at the angry redhead with its gray hair and felt his insulted heart thump with rage as his sight grew dim . . . At which point he suddenly heard himself say, in a muffled voice that came as a surprise even to him.

"He's a tartar, Colonel. He doesn't understand Russian, and what's more . . ."

For a second, Shuglovich's face grew pale; his flabby cheeks began to jiggle and his eyes grew vacant and terrifying.

"What?!" he roared, in such an unnaturally loud voice that the Jewish boys who had been sitting against a fence near the road jumped like sparrows to the other side of it. "What? Who gave you permission to speak? Si-lence! This greenhorn, this second lieutenant has permitted himself . . . Lieutenant Fedorovski, please publish, in today's report, the fact that I am placing Romashov under house arrest for four days due to an incomprehension of military discipline. And I am officially reprimanding Captain Sliva for failing to instill a true understanding of their military duty in his junior officers."

The adjutant gave a dispassionate and deferential salute. Sliva, who had been standing hunched over with a wooden and expressionless face the whole time, held a shaking hand to his cap.

"Shame on you, Captain Sliva," growled Shuglovich, who was calming gradually down "One of the regiment's best officers, an old soldier—allowing his juniors to regress. Rough them up, keep at them—don't hold yourself back. You'll get nothing by holding yourself back. They're not young ladies, they won't go to pieces on you . . ."

He turned sharply and returned to the carriage, with the adjutant following close behind. And as he took his seat—while the carriage made its way back to the road and then disappeared behind the regimental schoolhouse—a tentative, bewildered silence settled over the plaza.

"Oh, well done," Sliva said, dryly and spitefully, after a minute had passed and the officers had begun returning to their rooms. "Next time, you stand there with your mouth shut—even if God himself dies. Now I'm being punished for your remark. And why the hell did they send you to my company anyway? I need you like a dog needs a fifth leg. You should be back home with the other striplings, but instead you're . . ."

He stopped mid-sentence, waving his hands exhaustedly and turning his back on the young officer. His hunch-backed body dragged itself towards his dirty old bachelor's apartment, as Romashov watched him go. The sight of his long, weak, narrow spine dulled the rage he felt over the public embarrassment that he had just endured, stirring in him instead a feeling of pity for this solitary, coarse, and unloved man, to whom only two things still mattered in the world: the beauty of a well-ordered regiment, and the quiet, solitary stupor of his nightly drinking (which bouts usually lasted, as the regiment's chronic old bourbon drinkers put it, "all the way to the pillow").

And because Romashov had the naïve and slightly funny habit of thinking of himself in the third person—a characteristic trait of young men—he spoke the following words in his head:

"His fine, expressive eyes were veiled by clouds of sorrow . . ."

II

The platoons were dismissed one after another, and the soldiers returned to their quarters. The plaza emptied out. Romashov stood in the road for another few minutes, unsure of what to do next. It wasn't the first time in his half year of service that he'd felt a terrible consciousness of how stranded and alone he was in the middle of these strange, malicious, or at best indifferent people: a depressing feeling that always left him without any idea what to do with his evening. The thought of going back to his room at the officers' club was loathsome to him. The club would be empty right now, anyway; at best, two sub-ensigns would be playing billiards at the small table, smoking and drinking beer, cursing facetiously over every shot. The stale smell of bad country cooking would be spreading through the rooms—horrible! . . .

"Might as well go to the station, then," Romashov told himself. "Why not?"

There wasn't a single restaurant in the poor Jewish settlement. Both the military and the civilian's clubs looked utterly pitiful and neglected; because of this the train station was pretty much the only place where the locals could go no matter what the hour, to drink and carouse and even play some cards. Women went there too, to greet whatever incoming trains were going to inject a little variety into the profound boredom of their provincial lives.

Romashov loved going to the station in the evening. He especially liked to see the express train, which stopped here for the final time before crossing the Prussian border. He watched with a strange sort of excited fascination as the train—which consisted of five sparkling new wagons—leaped around the corner and then flew into the station at full steam, its fiery eyes dilating and then flaring up, casting their bright patch of light on the rails in front of them while the train itself, which seemed as if it were about to tear right through the station, stopped suddenly with a hiss and a groan—"like a giant catching himself at the edge of a cliff," Romashov thought. The insides of the wagons, which were lit up with bright and festive lights, opened to release beautiful, wonderfully groomed women in incredible hats and supremely elegant dresses, as well as men, civilians, all of whom were decked out marvelously and with imperturbable self-assurance, with great, lordly voices that spoke French and German, easy gestures, and idle smiles. Not one of them directed even a fleeting glance toward Romashov; nevertheless, he recognized in them a fragment of a sort of inaccessible, refined, and marvelous world, where life was a never-ending holiday and delight . . .

After eight minutes a bell sounded, and the engine whistled, and the glittering train left the station. The lights on the platform and at the buffet were extinguished almost immediately. All at once, a feeling of dull regularity settled over the scene. Romashov, who by this point had usually become overwhelmed by a dreamy and melancholy mood, liked to watch the red lantern as it rocked gently behind the final wagon, dwindling farther and farther into the dark night until it shrunk into a tiny, barely visible spark.

"I'll go to the station," thought Romashov. But just then he looked down at his boots, and blushed with a sharp feeling of shame. They were heavy, calf-high boots plastered to the brims with a coat of doughy black mud. All the officers in the regiment were issued boots like these. He examined his overcoat, which was cut short at the knees (again, because of the mud), with its frayed bottom hem and stretched-out button holes. He sighed. The week before, as he had been walking the platform alongside the same express car that always captivated him, he had caught sight of a tall, shapely, extraordinarily beautiful woman in a black dress standing in the doorway of the first class wagon. She had been hatless, and Romashov had been able to get a quick but clear look at her thin, straight nose, her full and charmingly small lips, and her long, flashing black hair, which fell across her cheek from a part directly in the middle of her head, covering her temple, the tips of her eyebrows, and her ears. Beside her, peeking out from behind her shoulder, stood a strapping young man in a light two-piece suit, with an arrogant face and a long, upward-tilting moustache like Emperor Wilhelm—he looked quite a bit like Wilhelm, actually. The woman was staring at Romashov too, and—or so it seemed to him—examining him with intense interest. Passing her, the sub-lieutenant thought to himself, as was his wont: *"The beautiful stranger's eyes lingered with pleasure on the lean, well-built figure of the young officer."* But when, after another ten steps he turned suddenly in order to catch this beautiful woman's eyes one more time, he saw that she and her young companion were laughing distractedly as they watched him walk away. Suddenly, and with overwhelming clarity, he saw himself as he must have looked to them: his boots, overcoat, paleface, and glasses, all of which were disheveled and awkward as usual. He recalled the elegant sentence that had just now passed through his head and blushed with an acute pain, at the unbearable shame of it. Even now, walking alone through the half-lit spring evening, he blushed once more from his previous embarrassment.

"No, no need to go to the station," Romashov whispered, with bitter hopelessness. "I'll just go a little further and then turn around."

It was the beginning of April. The night was growing imperceptibly darker. The row of poplars, the narrow white houses with tiled roofs facing the road, the occasional passing figure— all of these were darkening, losing their color and dimensions; everything was becoming flat dark silhouettes, whose outlines nevertheless stood out wonderfully against the murky air. In the east, the sun was rising over the city. Blue-gray clouds descended into the bloodred, amber, and violet fires that burnt, as if on the surface of a kind of golden liquid, at the mouth of its scorching volcano. And above this volcano a high dome rose: the green, mild, turquoise, and aquamarine-colored sky of a spring evening.

Romashov stared unblinkingly at this enchanted fire as he walked slowly down the road, dragging his feet in their huge boots. As had been the case since he was a child, the sight of this bright evening glow made him dream of a secret and radiant life that he imagined lay hidden somewhere on the other side of it. Just there, far, far beyond the clouds and the horizon, beneath a sun which was invisible from where he stood, a wonderful, dazzlingly beautiful, cloud-hidden city stood, burning with inner fire. An unbearable splendor of bridges and golden cobblestones glittered there, along with massive, intricate cupolas and purple-roofed towers, with gems sparkling in the windows and bright, multicolored flags fluttering in the breeze. And it seemed to him that in that distant, enchanted city a happy, triumphant people lived, whose lives passed like sweet music, and to whom everything pensive and melancholy was tender and beautiful.

These people walked through glistening squares, in shady gardens, between flower beds and fountains; they strolled, godlike, light and full of indescribable happiness, knowing no obstacles to their joy and desire, their lives unshadowed by embarrassment, shame, or worry . . .

Suddenly, Romashov recalled the scene that had just occurred in the plaza: the coarse cries of the regiment commander, the feeling of being insulted, the embarrassment at being reprimanded in front of the soldiers. The worst part of it all was the fact that he sometimes shouted at those witnesses of his recent shaming in the exact same way that Shulgovich had just shouted at him—and for some reason this knowledge contained something even more humbling to his existence as an officer and, he decided, as a human being.

And immediately, as with a child (for indeed, there was still something quite childish about him), vindictive, fantastic, intoxicated dreams began to boil up inside him. "Stupidity! With my whole life in front of me!" Romashov thought. Under the spell of this idea, he began to step more lightly and breathe more deeply. "I'll show them: tomorrow first thing I'll sit down with a book— I'll prepare myself to join the academy. Work! Well, everyone has to work, what kind of a world do you think this is? Only the trick is to work on one's own self . . . I'll whittle away at myself like a madman . . . And then, to everyone's surprise, I'll post a brilliant exam score. At that point people will naturally say: 'Who's surprised? We knew about that long ago. Such a capable, well-liked, talented young man.'"

With overwhelming vividness Romashov imagined himself among the student officers of the general headquarters, achieving his great hopes. His name was written at the academy on a golden plaque. His professors predicted a dazzling future; they wanted him to stay in the academy—but no! He would enter the service. It was necessary to spend some time as a company commander. This would be in his current company—of course it would. Here he is arriving: elegant, condescending, unimpressed, correct, and impertinently polite, like those officers from the general headquarters whom he had seen at last year's big maneuver and the inspection. He keeps aloof from the company of the officers. Crude military habits, familiarity, cards, binges—no, these are not for him. For he understands that his current position is only a way station on the long road of his military career.

Maneuvers. A large battle between two opposing forces. Lieutenant Shulgovich does not understand the situation; he grows confused; he shuffles people around and loses his head: the corps commander has already reprimanded him twice in front of the orderlies. "Come now, Captain, help me out," he says, turning to Romashov. "For old times' sake? Do you remember, he-he-he, how we used to bicker! But please . . ." His confused face attempts an ingratiating smile, but Romashov, saluting flawlessly and leaning forward on his saddle, answers him in a calm and dignified manner: "I'm sorry, Lieutenant . . . it's your duty to give the unit its orders to move. My job is to receive those orders and then execute them . . ." And so a third orderly flies from the corps commander with a new rebuke.

Romashov, the brilliant officer of the general staff, rises higher and higher through the ranks . . . A riot of fiery indignation bursts out amongst the workers at a steel mill; the company immediately demands Romashov. Night . . . the fire's glow . . . a huge roaring crowd, bricks flying . . . A handsome, well-built captain at the head of his company. It's Romashov. "Brothers," he says, turning to the workers, "for the third and final time, I warn you: we will shoot!" Cries, whistles, laughter . . . A brick strikes Romashov's shoulder, but his earnest and manly face remains calm. He turns to the soldiers, whose eyes are ablaze with rage, for the crowd has harmed their beloved commander. "Straight into the crowd, company, prepare to fire . . . Company, fire!" A hundred shots resound as one . . . a roar of terror. The tens of dead and wounded fall into a pile . . . The rest run confusedly, a few remain on their knees, begging for mercy. The revolt has been suppressed. Romashov awaits the gratitude and rewards of his superiors for his courageous example.

And then, war . . . No, it would be better for Romashov to leave for Germany before war breaks out, as a spy. He learns to speak fluent German and then heads off. What exquisite courage! Alone, completely alone, a German passport in his pocket and a barrel organ around his neck. It absolutely must be a barrel organ. He travels from town to town, hands in his pockets, scrounging for pfennigs, playing the fool while at the same time secretly procuring the blueprints of fortifications, warehouses, barracks, camps. Surrounded by constant danger. His government has given up on him: he is outside the law. If he succeeds in sending the desired information, he'll win money, accolades, situations, fame; if not, they'll shoot him without a trial, without any of the usual formalities, early in the morning courtyard of some slanting caponnierre. They offer him a hankerchief to cover his eyes out of sympathy, but he throws it proudly to the ground. "Do you really think a true officer would be afraid to look death in the face?" The elderly colonel speaks sympathetically: "Listen, you're young, my son is the same age as you. Tell us your last name, tell us your nationality at least, and we will change your sentence of execution to one of imprisonment." But Romashov cuts him short him with icy politeness: "Thank you, Colonel, but your words are in vain. Do what you must." Then he turns to the platoon of riflemen. "Gentlemen," he says with a strong voice—in German, naturally—"I beseech you as a fellow soldier: aim for the heart!" The sensitive lieutenant, only just managing to cover his eyes, waves the white handkerchief. The volley . . .

This picture entered his imagination so clearly and with such force that Romashov, whose long, vigorous strides and deep breaths had already taken him quite a long way, stopped suddenly and shuddered in horror, his fists clenched and convulsing and his heart pounding. Then he gathered himself together and, smiling weakly and guiltily in the dark, continued down the path.

Soon, however, the stream of swift and invincible thoughts overwhelmed him once again. A bitter, bloodthirsty war with Prussia and Austria breaks out; a gigantic battlefield, troops, grenades, blood, death! A grand battle, during which the fates of both companies will be decided. The last reserves are sent up, they wait from moment to moment for the enemies of the dispersed Russian columns to appear and outflank them. The enemy's terrible onslaught must be withstood—they must hold their position as if made of steel. And the most terrible fire, the most furiously strong resistance of the enemy is in the Kerensky unit. The soldiers hold out, like lions, they don't waver once, though their rows weaken more every second under the hail of enemy bullets. A historic moment! To hold out for one more minute, two—and the battle will be won for the enemy. But Lieutenant Shugolvich is confused; he is brave—no one would argue that— but his nerves cannot hold up under such terror. He closes his eyes, shudders, pales . . . Here he has already given the buglers the sign to sound the retreat; already the soldier has put the horn to his lips, but just then, from behind the hill, riding a frothing Arabian horse, flies the head of the division staff, Lieutenant Romashov. "Lieutenant, don't you dare retreat! The fate of Russia will be decided here!" Shuglovich's temper flares: "Lieutenant! I'm in command here, and I answer only to God and the government! Trumpeter, sound!" But Romashov has already taken the trumpet out of the trumpeter's hand. "Forward, brothers! The Tsar and the motherland are watching you! Hoorah!" Madly, with a stupendous cry the soldiers dash forward after Romashov. Everyone blends together, obscured by the fog, as they tear off toward the abyss. The enemy rows tremble and disperse in disarray. And behind them, far over the hills, the bayonets of a fresh reinforcements. "Hooray brothers! Victory!"

Romashov—who at this point was not walking, but running, his hands moving excitedly—stopped suddenly and slowly came to himself. He felt something running like cold fingers along his back, along his hands and feet, his clothes, his bare body, the hair on his head stirred, his eyes felt the pain of passionate tears. He hadn't even realized that he had reached his house, and now, squinting from the dust, he looked with surprise on the gates he knew so well, on the sparsely—populated fruit gardens behind them and on the tiny white outhouse in the center of the yard.

"What nonsense lies around in one's noodle!" he whispered disconcertedly. And his head straightened shyly over his shoulders.

III

After he got home Romashov lay down on his bed without taking off his coat or even removing his saber, and then stayed there for a long time, not moving but only staring, blankly and fixedly, at the ceiling. His head hurt and his back ached, and there was a kind of emptiness in his heart: a place where no thoughts were being formed, or memories or feelings; where he experienced neither annoyance nor boredom, but simply the sensation of something lying there inside him, large, dark, and indifferent.

Outside the window a melancholy and delicately green dusk was extinguishing itself mildly. Clanging noises were coming from the hallway, where the batman was quietly going about his business.

"That's strange," Romashov said to himself, "I read somewhere that it was impossible for a man to go a single second without thinking of something. And yet here I am lying around not thinking of anything at all. Is that true? No, just now I thought about the fact that I wasn't thinking about anything— it's like there's a kind of wheel turning in my brain. And now I'm examining myself: therefore, once again, I'm thinking . . ."

He continued to mull this tedious and convoluted idea over, until suddenly it came to seem almost physically repulsive to him: as if a dirty gray web, from which nothing could escape, had spread itself beneath his skull. He raised his head from the pillow and shouted:

"Gainan!"

Out in the hallway something crashed and began to roll across the floor—a samovar chimney, probably. The batman burst into the room, opening and shutting the door quickly and noisily, as if he were being pursued.

"Here, sir!" cried Gainan in a terrified voice.

"Nothing from Lieutenant Nikolaev yet?"

"No, sir!"

The officer and his batmen had long ago developed a simple, trusting, and even somewhat affectionate relationship. But when a question required a definite response—something along the lines of "Yes, sir!" "No, sir!" "Good day, sir!" or "No idea, sir!"—Gainan involuntarily shouted his answer out in the untutored, anxious, empty-headed tone that soldiers always use when addressing officers. It was an unconscious habit, one that had been impressed on him during his first days as a recruit and would probably remain with him for the rest of his life.

Gainan was a Cheremis by birth, and by religon—an idolator. For some reason, this latter characteristic pleased Romashov very much. The ridiculously, immature, and slightly childish pastime of teaching one's batman to act in various strange and unnatural ways had become fashionable among the junior officers of the regiment. Vetkin, for example, regularly asked his Moldavian batman in front of guests, "So, Bezuskal, have we got any champagne left in the cellar?" To which Bezuskal would answer, with complete seriousness: "None at all, your excellency: last night it pleased you to polish off the last dozen bottles." Another officer, Sub-lieutenant Epifanov, loved to ask his batman questions that were so difficult, he himself had no idea what they meant. "What's your opinion, my friend," he would ask, "on the restoration of the monarchy that is currently going on in France?" At which point the batman would answer without batting an eyelid: "Just this, your excellency: that it will meet with great success." Lieutenant Bobetinski taught his batman the catechism, so that he could answer the most surprising and unrelated questions without hesitation: "What is the significance in the third place?"—"In the third place, it is not significant," or, "What is the opinion of the Holy Church on this?"—"The Holy Church is silent on this matter." He could even recite, with absurdly tragic gestures, Pimen's monologue from *Boris Gudonov*. Particularly popular was the fad of getting the batment to speak in French: bonjoor, messyoor; bon nuweet, messyoor; voolay voos dweet. And so on and so on: whatever they could think up as a stay against boredom, the restrictions of their isolated lives, and their absence of nonmilitary interests.

Romashov talked frequently with Gainan about his religon—this despite the fact that the Cheremiss himself had quite a vague and meager understanding of it. He particularly liked to hear Gainan talk about his vow of service. Apparently, the batman had taken this oath in a very original way. It had been read out, simultaneously, by a priest to True Slavs, by a priest to the Catholics, by a rabbi to the Jews, by Captain Deitz to the Protestants (as there was no pastor), and by Lieutenant Bek-Agamalov to the Moslems . . . With Gainan, a completely different procedure had been arranged. The militarty adjutant had held out a piece of salted bread impaled on a saber point to him and two of his countrymen in turn, and they—without touching the bread with their hands—had taken it in their mouths and eaten it, right then and there. The symbolic idea behind this ritual was as follows: *here I eat this salted bread in the service of my new master, and may I be punished with the sword if I prove unfaithful.* Gainan, apparently, was more than a little proud of this fantastic ritual and spoke about it often. And each time he did so he inserted a few more details into the story, to the point that finally it became a kind of fantastic, unbelievably absurd, and truly funny tale, which entertained Romashov, and whatever second lieutenants who came to visit him, to no end.

Gainan thought that the lieutenant was about to engage him in a sincere discussion on gods and oathtaking, and so stood there smiling expectantly to himself. But Romashov spoke sharply.

"All right, that will be all . . ."

"Should I get lay out a new jacket, sir?" Gainan suggested.

Romashov kept quiet, vacillating. At first he wanted to say yes . . . then he wanted to say no . . . then again, yes. He sighed deeply, drawing the sound out with a series of childish modulations, and then said despondently:

"No, Gainan . . . why bother . . . To hell with it . . . 'Tea time, everyone!' . . . Then it's off to the club to get some dinner. But who cares?"

He came to a final, unenthusiastic decision. "Tonight, I'll stay away for sure," he thought. "You can't just go around constantly boring people. . . . anyway, no one is ever happy to see me there."

This last statement sounded solid enough—but then somewhere deep inside his heart, in a place whose presence he himself barely even recognized, the awareness stirred that today, like yesterday, like almost every day over the past three months, he would go see the Nikolaevs anyway. Every night he left their house at midnight, filled with shame and annoyance at his essential lack of character; he told himself that he would put a stop to this for a few weeks, or even stop going at all. He believed, as he walked home, and lay down in bed, and fell asleep, that it would be easy for him to keep his word. But the night passed, and the day dragged along slowly with all its frustrations, and the evening arrived and then there he was, reclining once more in that clean, bright house, in those cozy rooms, with those calm and happy people, and, most important, in the company of the sweet, gratifying, provocative charms of feminine beauty.

Romashov sat on the bed. It was growing dark, but he could still see around his entire room. Oh, how it annoyed him to see, day after day, the poor, sparse furnishings that made up his "décor." The lamp with its pink tulip shade on the minuscule writing desk, next to the round, quickly beating alarm clock and the ink stand that looked like a pug dog. On the wall next to the bed there was a felt blanket with a tiger on it, as well as an Arab riding a horse, lance in hand; a rickety bookshelf with books stood in one corner, while the other was taken up by the fantastic silhouette of a cello case. Above the lone window there was a straw blind, which rolled up into a tube; near the door, a sheet covering a coat rack. Every unmarried officer and sub-ensign possessed these exact same items, with the exception, perhaps, of the cello, which Romashov had acquired from the regimental orchestra where it had not been needed. But he had given up music over a year ago, having failed to learn even the major chords.

A year ago the younger Romashov, who had just completed his regimental training, had installed these banal objects with delight and pride. His room, his own things, the ability to purchase them, to choose what he wished, to arrange things according to his taste: all this was suffused, as was only natural, with the passionate narcissism of a twenty-year-old boy who only yesterday had been sitting on a mess-hall bench drinking tea and eating breakfast with his classmates. And how vigorously he had hoped and dreamed while purchasing all those pathetically luxurious items! . . . How carefully he had worked out how his life would proceed! During the first two years: a foundational knowledge of classical literature, the systematic study of French and German, plus he would take up music. In the last year: preparation for the academy. It was necessary to follow what was going on in the world, in literature and science, and in order to do this Romashov had subscribed to the newspaper and to a popular monthly journal. He acquired self-improvement manuals: Wundt's *Psychology*, Louis's *Physiology*, Smiles's *Self-Help* . . .

And now these books had stood for nine months on the bookshelf (which Gainan forgot to dust), the newspapers lay in unopened wrappers under the writing desk, the journal had stopped coming after a half a year of unpaid subscriptions; as for himself, Lieutenant Romashov drank plenty of vodka at the officers' club, indulged in a long, sordid, boring affair with a woman of the regiment, deceived, along with her, her feeble and jealous husband, and played cards, as the service, his fellow men, and his own life burdened him more and more.

"I'm sorry, sir!" the batman shouted suddenly, thrusting himself forward with a grumble. But then he began to speak in a completely different way, in a simple, and good-hearted tone of voice. "I forgot to tell you. A letter from Mrs. Peterson came for you. A batman brought it, and asked if you would write a reply."

Romashov screwed his eyes up, and tore open the long, thin, pink envelope, on the corner of which a pigeon was flying with a letter in its beak.

"Light the lamp, Gainan," he ordered.

"My dear, beloved, mustachied Georgie," Romashov read. He recognized the untidy handwriting, which curled the ends of the individual letters into little flourishes.

> You've been away from us a whole week already, and I miss you so much that I cried all last night. Remember at least, if you want to laugh at me, that I that cannot bear such a betrayal. A single swallow from this vial of morphine will end my suffering forever, and your conscience will chew you up. Come today without fail at one half past seven in the evening. <u>He</u> will not be home, <u>he</u> will be occupied with tactics, and I will kiss you hard, hard, hard, as only I can. Come. I will kiss you 1,000,000,000 times. Yours forever, Raisa.

> p.s.: 'Remember, darling, the mighty branches
>   Of the river willows,
>   You left burning kisses,
>   I left extinguished.'

- R.P

> p.p.s: You absolutely, absolutely must come to the officers' next Saturday night. I will promise you the third quadrille. I swear it!!!!!!

R.P.

Finally, at the very bottom of the fourth page ran the message: "Here, I have kissed."

The familiar scent of Persian lilac wafted up from the letter; the droplets of this perfume had left yellow spots all over the paper, and many of the letters they touched had started to run in various directions. That cloying smell, in addition to the letter's playful and kitschy tone, and the small, red-haired, freckled face that it brought to mind, filled Romashov with a sudden and unbearable revulsion. He tore the letter in half with wicked satisfaction, then lay the pieces together and tore them into four pieces, and again, and again—until finally, when it became too difficult for his hands to tear anymore, he threw the scraps under the desk. His clenched teeth were bared. And yet, despite all this Romashov was able at that point to imagine himself in the usual third person:

"And he smiled a bitter, contemptuous smile."

He knew now, without a doubt, that he would go to the Nikolaevs' house. "But really, this is the last, the very last time!" he added, to convince himself. And immediately he grew happy and calm.

"Gainan, my clothes!"

He washed himself hurriedly, put on a new frock coat, and sprayed a clean handkerchief with floral eau-de-cologne. But just as he had finished dressing and was preparing to go, Gainan stopped him unexpectedly.

"Sir!" the Cheremiss said in an unusually soft and pleading tone. Suddenly, he began dancing in place. He always danced like this when he was upset or troubled about something: he stuck his kness out one after the other, hugged his shoulders, thrust his neck forward, and flapped his limp hands nervously.

"What else do you want?"

"Sir, I would so like, if you can, I beg you . . . Give me the white man."

"What are you talking about? What white man?"

"The one you ordered me to throw out. That one, the one here . . ."

He pointed to the stove, where a bust of Pushkin stood on a little mat. Romashov had acquired it somehow from a passing peddler. Despite its label, the bust's model was an old Jewish broker, and not the great Russian poet; it was very worn, and spotted with dead flies; its presence bothered Romashov so much that earlier that day he really had ordered Gainan to throw it out.

"What is he to you?" the lieutenant asked with a smile. "All right, take it, go ahead, do what you want. I'll be very glad to get rid of it. I don't need it. Only, why do you want it?"

Gainan shifted quietly from one foot to another.

"Well, all right, God be with you," Romashov said. "Only, you know who that is?"

Gainan smiled a bashful smile, and began dancing as he had before.

"I don't know . . ." he said, wiping his lips with his hand.

"You don't know—I'll tell you, then. This—is Pushkin. Alexander Sergeyevich Pushkin. You understand? Repeat after me: Alexander Sergeyevich . . ."

"Besyev," Gainan repeated firmly.

"Besyev? Ok, let him be Besyev," Romashov said. "I, however, am leaving. If anyone comes from the Petersons, tell them that the sub-lieutenant has gone out, you don't know where. You understand? And if there's any regimental business, run and get me at Lieutenant Nikolaev's house. Goodbye, my friend! If you get my dinner from the officer's club, you may eat it."

He gave the Cheremiss a friendly clap on the shoulders, in answer to which Gainan flashed a broad, familiar, contented smile.

IV

The night had grown black and impenetrable by the time Romashov, who was rendered practically blind by the darkness, began to grope his way along the road. His feet in their gigantic galoshes sunk deep into mud that was thick as Turkish delight, emerging with a squish and a whistle. Every once in a while one of the galoshes stuck so firmly that his foot leapt out of it—and when this happened Romashov had to hop back and search around with one leg for the invisible galosh, as he stood balancing on the other.

The small town was deserted; not even the dogs were barking. A fog-striped light was tumbling from the windows of the humble white houses to where it lay, in glittering bars, on the brownish-yellow ground. But from the damp bark of the poplars and the muddy road, from the wet and sticky fence, which Romashov had been following the whole time, came the smell of something fresh, vital, and happy, something cheerfully and joyously aroused. Even the strong wind, which was making its way rapidly down the road, blew roughly, like a spring breeze, and haltingly too: trembling at points where it became tangled or began playing tricks.

The sub-lieutenant stopped in front of the Nikolaevs' house, struck by a momentary bout of weakness and indecision. The house's small windows were covered by square brown shutters, but behind them a bright and steady light was shining. In one place, a heavy curtain was parted, to reveal a long, narrow crack. Romashov pressed his face to the glass excitedly; he breathed quietly, as if afraid that they might hear his thoughts inside the room itself.

He caught a glimpse of the face and shoulders of Alexandra, who was sitting stooped at the back of the familiar green repp divan. By her pose and the light movements of her body, not to mention the low tilt of her head, it was clear that she was occupied with her needlework.

Suddenly she straightened, picked her head up, and sighed deeply . . . Her lips moved . . . "What's she saying?" Romashov thought. "Now she's smiling. How strange it is to watch someone speak through a window and not be able to hear her!"

The smile suddenly vanished from Alexandra Petrovna's face, and her forehead furrowed. Her lips moved again, making the same quick expression, after which she flashed the usual playful and humorous smile. Her head shook in slow denial. "Perhaps, she means this for me?" Romashov thought shyly. Some quiet, pure, and sincerely calming influence flowed into him from this young woman, whom he watched now as if she were the embodiment of some favorite picture that was being drawn now in front of his eyes. "Shurochka!" he whispered tenderly.

Alexandra Petrovna lifted her head up unexpectedly from her work and turned it toward the window. She had an agitated expression on her face. Romashov felt like she was looking directly into his eyes. His heart constricted and grew cold from fear, and he quickly hid himself beneath the window ledge. For a minute, he felt ashamed. He was on the verge of returning home again; but then he overcame his feeling and went through the gate into the kitchen.

Nikolaev's batman cleaned his galoshes with a kitchen rag, as he himself wiped his glasses clean of the moisture that had appeared on them in the warm room, and returned them to his nearsighted eyes. At which moment he heard the sound of Alexandra Petrovna's voice coming from the living room:

"Stepan, has an order just arrived?"

"That's on purpose!" the sub-lieutenant thought, as if to torture himself. "She knows that I always come at this time of night."

"No, it's me, Alexandra Petrovna!" he cried through the door, in a false-sounding voice.

"Ah! Rommy! Well, come in, then, come in. What are you lurking around in here for? Volodya, Romashov's here."

Romashov came in, embarrassed and awkwardly hunched over, rubbing his hands together for no reason.

"What a pest I've become, eh, Alexandra Petrovna?"

He made this remark thinking that it would come out carefree and dashing, but as soon as he said it, he realized how inappropriate it was.

"Not this nonsense again!" exclaimed Alexandra Petrovna. "Sit down, let's have some tea."

Looking clearly and perceptively into his eyes, and with her usual energy, she took his cold hand in her small, pleasantly warm one.

Nikolaev sat with his back to him, at his desk, surrounded by books and drawings. He would have to take the exam at the general military academy, and he had been preparing himself for some time, stubbornly and without rest. He was taking the exam for the third year in a row, having failed the last two times.

Without turning around, or even tearing his eyes from the book that was lying open in front of him, Nikolaev gave Romashov his hand over his shoulder and said, in a calm, deep voice:

"Hello, Yuri Alexeyich. No news? Shurochka! Give him some tea. If you'll excuse me, I'm busy at the moment."

"I've come in vain, of course," Romashov thought, once more in despair. "Oh, what a fool I am!"

"Well, let's see, what news do I have . . . The Centaur really lit into Sub-lieutenant Lekh at the officers' club. Apparently, he was totally soused. Now they're making us practice with training dummies . . . Epifan was put on house arrest . . ."

"Really?" Nikolaev said absent-mindedly. "Please, go on."

"I also caught hell, for four days. But that's old news."

It seemed to Romashov that there was something strange and constrained in his voice—as if something had gotten stuck in his throat. "How pitiful I must seem!" he thought, though he calmed himself immediately with the commonplace idea, to which awkward people so frequently turn, that "It's always like that when you're confused: you think that everyone can see right through you, though of course you're the only one who notices anything out of the ordinary, and to everyone else, it's as if nothing has happened."

He sat on the armchair across from Shurochka, whose hooks were now flashing rapidly over some piece of lace she had taken up. She never sat down without some sort of busywork; she had made, by hand, all of the tablecloths, napkins, lampshades, and curtains in the house.

Romashov carefully picked up the end of the thread that ran from the ball to her hands, and asked:

"What kind of lace is this?"

"Guipure. That's the tenth time you've asked me."

Shurochka glanced perceptively at the sub-lieutenant, and then just as quickly returned her eyes to her knitting. But then she lifted her eyes again and smiled.

"Don't worry, Yuri Alexeyich . . . just sit here and relax for a little while. 'At ease!' Isn't that what you say in the regiment?"

Romashov sighed and squinted at Nikolaev's powerful neck, which was stark white above the gray collar of his jacket.

"Vladimir Efimich is a lucky man," he said. "Next summer he'll be in Petersburg, at the academy."

"We'll see about that!" Shurochka cried fervently in her husband's direction. "We've come back to the regiment in failure twice already. This is our last chance."

Nikolaev turned around. His respectable soldier's face blushed under its fluffy mustache, and his large, dark, fiercely powerful eyes flashed angrily.

"Don't talk nonsense, Shurochka! It's like I said: I work— and I'll pass." He banged his hand down loudly on the edge of the desk. "All you do is sit and gab. I've said it before . . ."

"It's like you said!" his wife said, slamming her dark-complexioned little hand against her knee, just as he had. "Maybe it would be better if you said under what conditions a unit formation must comply with?" Her eyes smiled, slyly and keenly, at Romashov. "You know, I know his tactics better than he does. Well, then, Volodya, let's hear it, officer of the general staff: What are the conditions?"

"Enough, Shurochka, this is ridiculous," Nikolaev growled unhappily.

But suddenly he turned in his chair toward his wife, and in his wide open, handsome, and somewhat stupid eyes there seemed to be a perplexed confusion, almost a fear.

"Enough, girl—so what if I don't know everything. A unit formation? Unit formations ensure, first, that the least amount of men are lost under fire; second, that it is easier to deliver orders . . . And third . . . Hold on . . ."

"And third, to give the commanding officer time to think of what unit formations are for," Shurochka interrupted.

At this point she began speaking very quickly, lowering her eyes and rocking slightly, like a star student:

"A unit formation must satisfy the following conditions: maneuverability, mobility, versatiliy, the convenience of command, adaptability to place; it must expose itself to the least possible amount of enemy fire; it must be easily assembled and dissasembled, and must be able to adapt quickly to a marching order . . . That's it! . . ."

She opened her eyes, took a deep breath, and, turning her smiling, expressive face toward Romashov, asked:

"How was that?"

"Good lord, what a memory!" Nikolaev cried—enviously, but with admiration. He plunged back into his notebook.

"I always study with him," Shurochka explained. "Frankly I could take the exam today if I had to. The most important thing"—she raised her crocheting hook into the air—"The most important thing is to have a system. Our system is my own invention, my pride. Every day we do one part mathematics, one part military science—ballistics, however, are difficult for me: it's all a bunch of wretched formulas—then we finish up with a lesson on regulations. After that we do either languages or geography and history, depending on the day."

"What about Russian?" Romashov asked out of politeness.

"Russian? Who cares about Russian—we can spell, can't we? And everyone knows about the essay. Every year it's one or the other: either '*Para pacem, para bellum*'or 'Onegin's character in relation to his times.'"

She perked up suddenly and grabbed the thread from the sub-lieutenant's hand, as if she wanted to ensure that it wouldn't distract him, and then began talking passionately about the subject which absorbed her every interest—which was the very essence of her current life.

"I can't, I simply can't stay, Rommy! You must understand! To stay here—that means to lose myself, to become a regimental wife, to attend your barbaric nights out, to gossip, to plot and scheme after stipends and travel allowances . . . half-kopek pieces! . . . Brrr . . . To take turns with my friends planning those ridiculous 'balls,' to play Boston . . . You like to say how cozy our house is. But just look, for the love of God, at all this pettines! All these doilies and needlepoints—I made it all myself—this dress, which I altered, that loathsome shaggy carpet made out of scraps . . . It's junk—all of it! Rommy my dear, don't you see that I need society, a real, large society, light, music, bows, and subtle flattery, intelligent company. All right, I'll grant you that Volodya isn't exactly inventing gunpowder here, but he's an honorable, brave, hardworking man. If he made it to the official ranks, I swear I could make him a sparkling success. I know languages, I can carry myself in that kind of pleasant society, and then there's something else—I don't know how to put it exactly—my soul is flexible enough to fit in anywhere: I can adapt myself to anything . . . I mean, look at me, Rommy: look closely. Am I really such an uninteresting person, such an ugly woman, that the whole of my life must be wasted away in this hole, this wretched swamp, which you can't even find on a single map?"

She covered her eyes with a hurried gesture and broke suddenly into fierce, proud, self-pitying tears.

Her husband, who was upset by all this, rushed to her immediately, with a confused look on his face. But Shurochka, who had already managed to compose herself, removed the handkerchief from her face. Her tears had stopped—though an intense and furious fire now glittered in her eyes.

"It's nothing, Volodya, it's nothing, my dear," she said, pushing him away.

And, handing the thread back to Romashov, she inquired, with a capricious and coquettish smile:

"How do I look, Rommy? If a woman gives you the opportunity to compliment her, and you hesitate—now that's the height of impoliteness!"

"Shurochka, aren't you ashamed of yourself?" Nikolaev remarked from his corner.

Romashov attempted a shy and suffering smile, but answered in a somewhat trembling voice, seriously and sadly:

"Very beautiful!"

Shurochka screwed up her eyes and shook her head playfully, as if to get the hair out of her eyes.

"Ro-mmy, how fun-ny you are!" she sang in a thin and childlike voice.

The sub-lieutenant blushed, thinking to himself: *"His heart had been cruelly broken . . ."*

They fell silent. Shurochka's hook flashed. Nikolaev, who was translating some German phrases from Tussen and Lagenshteid's manual, muttered quietly to himself under his nose. The lamp flame hissed and crackled under its yellow silk lampshade, which looked like a tent. Romashov picked up the thread again and quietly, almost imperceptibly to himself even, pulled it from the hand of the young woman. It gave him a subtle and tender pleasure to feel how Shurochka's hands unconsciously resisted his careful tug. It seemed as if a kind of secret, mutually disturbing current was flowing through that thread.

He looked at her bent head—imperceptibly and out of the corner of his eye, though without lowering his eyes—and thought, moving his lips just slightly, whispering the words to himself quietly, as if he were having an intimate and heartfelt conversation with Shurochka:

"How dare she ask how she looks? Oh, my darling! You're beautiful! What happiness, and all I'm doing is sitting here staring at you! Listen: I'll tell you how beautiful you are. Listen to me. You have a pale and shadow-haunted face: an ardent face. Red, burning lips—how they want to be kissed! And your eyes, with their yellowish rings . . . When you look straight ahead the whites look almost indigo, and a deep, cloudy blue swims in your pupils. You aren't a brunette, but nevertheless, there's something of the Gypsy about you. On the other hand, your hair is so clean and thin, and it falls from its knot with such a precise and natural divide, that one can't help but want to quietly run one's fingers through it. You are small, you are light, I could pick you up by the hand as if you were a child. But you're lithe and strong too, you have breasts like a woman, and you move . . . impulsively. On your left ear, right at the bottom, there's a tiny birthmark like the hole where an earring goes—it's exquisite! . . ."

"Did you read in the newspaper about the officers' duel?" Shurochka asked suddenly.

Romashov gave a start and tore his eyes from her.

"No, I didn't. But I heard about it. Why do you ask?"

"Of course you haven't read about it—you never read about anything. Really, Yuri Alexeyevich, you're really letting yourself go. In my opinion it was absurd. I get what everyone says: a duel between officers is a necessary and rational thing." Shurochka clasped her knitting to her breasts with conviction. "But why such tactlessness? Think about it: one lieutenant insults another. It's a serious insult, and as usual the officers decide to have a duel. But from this point on, everything devolves into stupidity and nonsense. The conditions practically ensure death: fifteen paces, and the shooting continues until someone is heavily wounded . . . So long as both opponents remain upright they keep shooting. But it's such . . . slaughter—I don't know what else to call it! And this is just the tip of the iceberg. All the officers of the regiment, even a few of the regimental wives, gathered at the site of the duel—some took photographs! Isn't that terrible, Rommy! And the unlucky sub-lieutenant, an ensign like you, as Volodya noted, and moreover the aggrieved, and not the offended party, takes three shots before receiving a terrible wound in the stomach, and dies that night in pain. And now it turns out that he has an old mother and sister, an old Barishnya, who lived with him, much like our Mihin . . . Now let me ask you: was it really necessary to turn this duel into such bloodthirsty buffoonery? And this is just the first time such a thing has happened since dueling was made official. Now you watch, just watch!" Shurochka cried, her bright eyes blazing. "Now the sentimental opponents of an officers' duel—Oh, I know about these contemptible liberal truce-mongers!—now they'll start crowing: 'Ah, how barbaric! Ah, the remnant of a distant age! Ah, fratricide!'"

"You, on the other hand, are bloodthirsty, Alexandra Petrovna," Romashov cut in.

"Not bloodthirsty—no!" she retorted with a shout. "I am compassionate. I'm a house cat, I try never to bite anyone who scratches my neck. But try to understand, Romashov—it's a matter of simple logic. What is the purpose of an officer? Battle. What does battle demand above all else? Bravery, pride, the ability to look death in the face without blinking. Where can these qualities be most clearly seen in times of peace? Duels. That's it. It seems obvious enough to me. French officers don't need to duel—because an understanding of honor, even to the point of exaggeration, is in every Frenchman's blood. Neither do the Germans, because every German is disciplined and law-abiding from birth. But we—oh yes, we do! If proper dueling etiquette were in place, we wouldn't find swindlers and cardsharks like Archakovsky in the officers' ranks, or drunks like your friend Nazanski; then we'd have less of this hypocritical amicability, this familiar foul language, in front of the servants, less bottles thrown at one another's heads with the intention, despite all appearances, not to hit the target, but to miss him. Then you'd talk less behind one another's backs. An officer must consider every word he says. An officer should be a model of correctness. And as for all this tenderness: it's nothing more than the fear of taking a shot! Your profession is to risk your life. That's the point exactly!"

She cut her speech short with capricious flourish, and returned heatedly to her work. Once again, everything became quiet.

"Shurochka, how do you say 'opponent' in German?" Nikolaev asked, raising his head from his books.

"'Opponent?'" Shurochka thoughtfully pulled a hook through the part of her soft hair. "Let's hear the whole phrase."

"It's right here . . . Just a minute . . . 'Our foreign opponent' . . ."

"*Unser auslandischer Nebenbuhler*," Shurochka interrupted quickly.

"*Unser*," Romashov repeated in a whisper, gazing dreamily into the lamp. "When she gets excited about something," he thought, "the words fly out of her mouth swiftly, clearly, and distinctly, like shot pouring onto a silver tray. *Unser*—what a funny word . . . *Unser, unser, unser* . . ."

"What are you muttering about, Rommy," Alexandra Petrovna asked sternly. "How dare you rave like that in front of me."

He gave her a vacant smile.

"I'm not raving . . . I'm just saying it to myself: *unser, unser.* What a funny word . . ."

"What kind of stupidity is this . . . *Unser*? Why is that funny?"

"Well, if you think about it . . ." He concentrated hard, trying to explain what he was thinking. "If you repeat any single word and think hard about it, then all at once it loses its sense and becomes . . . How to put it?"

"Ah, I know, I know!" Shurochka said, briskly and delightedly interrupting him. "Only now it's not as easy to do as it used to be when I was a child—ah, how much fun it was!"

"Yes, yes, precisely, in childhood. Yes."

"I remember it perfectly. I even remember the word that especially struck me: 'maybe.' I shook all over and closed my eyes and repeated it: '*maybe, may-be.*' And suddenly, I completely forgot what it meant. Then I tried to remember, and couldn't. It seemed to me that it was something brown, with reddish spots— and two tails. Doesn't that sound like what it would be?"

Romashov looked at her affectionately.

"How strange, that we were thinking the same thing," he said quietly. "And *unser*, as far as I see it, is very tall, lean, and ridiculous. Something like a long, thin insect—a very ugly one."

"*Unser?*" Shurochka raised her head and, scrunching up her eyes, looked away into a dark corner of the room, trying to understand what Romashov was saying. "No, wait a second: it's something green, and sharp. Yes, oh yes, of course—an insect! Like a grasshopper, only more despicable and vile . . . Pfff, how silly we get together, Rommy."

"And there's something else," Romashov began, as if telling a secret. "When I was a child, it was much clearer. I would say some word and try to stretch it out as far as it would go. I stretched each letter out endlessly. And then suddenly, in a second something strange, something very strange happened. It was as if everything around me had disappeared. And then it came to seem surprising to me that I was speaking, that I was alive, that I was thinking."

"I know what you mean!" Shurochka added happily. Only not exactly like that. I would hold my breath, as hard as I could, and think: I'm not breathing, and now I'm still not breathing, and now I'm still not, and now, and now . . . And then the strangeness began. I felt that time was going past me. No, that's not it exactly: maybe it was more that there wasn't any time at all. I can't explain it."

Romashov gazed at her rapturously, and repeated in a deep, happy, and quiet voice:

"Yes, yes . . . I can't explain it . . . It's strange . . . inexplicable . . ."

"Nevertheless, my little psychologists—or whatever you are—that's enough: it's time for dinner," Nikolaev said, standing up from his desk.

His back hurt and his feet had begun to swell from sitting for so long. Stretching himself up to full hight, he reaching his arms up above his head and thrust his chest out, and all of his large, muscular body crunched under the powerful movement.

Cold hors d'oeuvres had been laid out in the tiny but pleasant drawing room, which was brightly lit by hanging porcelain lanterns made from white matte. Nikolaev did not drink, but a small decanter of vodka was brought out for Romashov. Shurochka screwed her pretty face into a fastidious grimace and asked brashly, as she asked everything:

"You can't really be serious about that muck?"

Romashov smiled guiltily and choked on the vodka from embarrassment. He coughed.

"You should be ashamed of yourself!" his hostess remarked insistently. "You drink even when it makes you choke . . . I understand that it's acceptable to your beloved Nazanski—he's a complete lout. But why should you drink? Such a splendid and capable young man, and yet you can't even sit down to eat without some vodka . . . But why? This is Nazanski's influence."

Her husband, who was reading an order that he had just received at that moment, suddenly cried:

"Well, look at that: Nazanski just took a month's leave to take care of some domestic matters. In other words, he's been caught in the middle of one of his binges. You saw him, no doubt, Yuri Alexeyich? What did he do—go on a binge?"

Romashov blinked awkwardly.

"No, I didn't see anything. I suppose there may have been some drinking . . ."

"That Nazinski of yours—what a wretch!" Shurochka said, in a pinched and angry voice. "If it were up to me, I'd have people like that shot like wild dogs. Such officers are a disgrace to their unit—an outrage!"

After dinner Nikolaev, who had eaten just as copiously and zealously as he had been studying, began to yawn. At last he said frankly:

"Well, my friends, do you know what would happen if I lay my head down for a minute? I would 'collapse into a stupor,' as they say in the good old books."

"Fair enough, Vladimir Efimich," Romashov said, with a familiarity that even he found obsequious. As he stood up from his chair he thought despondently: "No, they don't stand on ceremony with me in this house. So why did I clamber up here in the first place?"

He got the impression that Nikolaev took great pleasure in ushering him out of his house. But even while he was shaking his host's hand, he continued to think, with no less pleasure, about Shurochka's firm, tender, and feminine grip. He always thought about this while he was taking his leave. And by the time the moment to leave had arrived, he had been transported to such heights by that wonderful embrace that he didn't hear Shurochka say to him:

"Make sure you don't forget about us. We always love to have you here. Instead of drinking yourself stupid with Nazanski, come by and we'll pull up a chair. But remember: we don't stand on ceremony with you."

He heard these words, but consciously understood them only as he was making his way out onto the street.

"No, they don't stand on ceremony with me," he whispered, with the bitter sensitivity that one finds so often in young, self-involved people.

V

Romashov stepped off the porch. The night had grown even thicker by now, as well as blacker and warmer. The sub-lieutenant groped his way along the wattle fence, holding on to it with his hands as he waited for his eyes to adjust to the gloom. While he was doing this, the door to the Nikolaevs' kitchen suddenly opened, throwing a large stripe of hazy yellow light out into the darkness. Someone stomped out onto the mud, and Romashov heard the angry voice of the Nikolaevs' servant, Stepan:

"He comes, he comes: every day he comes. But only the devil knows why!"

A second voice, a soldier's, which the sub-lieutenant did not recognize, answered with a lazy, drawn-out, and indifferent yawn.

"That's the way it goes, my brother . . . It's all a mess. But anyway, good night, Stepan."

"Good night, Baulin. Come again sometime."

Romashov stood beside the fence as if rooted there. An acute feeling of shame made him blush invisibly in the darkness; suddenly his entire body was covered in sweat; he felt as if a thousand tiny needles were being nailed into the skin of his feet and back. "Naturally! Even the servants are laughing at me," he thought despairingly. He went back over the evening in his mind, recognizing many small things that he had not noticed before, in certain of the words, phrases, and looks that his hosts had exchanged with one another, which now seemed to bear withness to a certain casual mockery, to an impatient irritation with their tiresome guest.

"Disgraceful—disgraceful!" the sub-lieutenant whispered, without moving a muscle. "To willingly spend time in a place where your presence is barely tolerated . . . No, that's enough. Now I'm sure of it: I've had enough!"

The lights in the Nikolaevs' dining room were being extinguished. "They've already gone to their bedroom," Romashov thought, at which point he imagined, with particular vividness, what the two of them must look like preparing for bed, undressing in front of one another with the habitual indifference and unself-consciousness of people who have been married for a long time, as they discussed him. She, dressed only in her slip, gave her hair its nightly brushing. Nikolaev, who was sitting on the bed in his underclothes, took his boots off and, flushed from the effort, said with angry drowsiness: "You know, Shurochka, your Romashov continues to annoy me. I'm curious: why do you waste so much time with him?" And Shurochka, without taking the hairpin out of her mouth, and without turning around, answered his image in the mirror with exasperation: "*My Romashov*? Really! He's not my Romashov—he's yours!"

Five minutes passed, durning which Romashov, tormented by these agonizing and bitter thoughts, made up his mind to go on. He proceeded stealthily along the length of the wattled fencing that surrounded the Nikolaevs' house, picking his feet carefully out of the mud, as if they might hear him and find something untoward in what he was doing. He did not want to go back home: he found it terrible and unpleasant to think about his cramped and narrow room, with its single window, and its contents, which had become odious to him. "I'll go see Nazanski, just to spite her," he said suddenly, feeling immediately a sort of vengeful relish in the decision. "She scolded me for being friends with Nazanski—that was to spite me, no doubt! So I'll just go! . . ."

He raised his eyes to the sky and clutched his hands to his chest vigorously. "I swear, I swear that I have come here for the last time. I do not want to experience that humiliation again. I swear!" he said.

And now, as was his wont, he added:

"His expressive black eyes flashed with scorn and resolution!"

This despite the fact that his eyes were not black at all but rather yellowish, with green rims: quite ordinary-looking, in other words.

Nazanski rented a room from his friend Lieutenant Zegerzht. Despite an impeccable service record in the Turkish campaign, this Zegerzht was, most likely, the oldest lieutenant in the entire Russian army. His failure to advance in rank had a fateful and mysterious feeling to it. He was a widower, with four small children, and yet managed to support himself on a forty-eight-ruble-a-month salary. He took possession of large houses and then rented them out by the room to unmarried officers; he hired someone to cook, cultivated chicken and turkeys, and managed, somehow, to get his hands on timely and exceptionally cheap supplies of firewood. As for his own children, he bathed them in troughs, treated them with his own home remedies and sewed their blouses, pants, and shirts on a sewing machine. Before he was married, Zegerzht, like many unmarried officers, had developed a passion for various feminine handcrafts; now he tried to make use of these talents out of the sharp necessity. Malicious tongues held that he secretly sold his wares at one of the area markets.

But none of these breezy domestic finaglings helped Zegerzht much. The fowl were struck by an epidemic of some kind, the rooms stood empty, what boarders there were cursed the poor meals and didn't pay their bills, which meant that periodically, four times a year or so, one could see the thin, tall figure of Zegerzht, his face confused and sweaty beneath its beard, wandering around town in hopes of receiving money from somewhere, while his service cap, which looked like a pancake, sat on to his head at a precarious tilt and his peasant jacket, which he had worn since the time of Nikolai I, trembled and fluttered around his shoulders like a pair of wings.

A fire was burning in his room when Romashov, approaching the window, made out Zegerzht himself. He was sitting on a round stool beneath a hanging lamp, bending his bald head, with its dirty, wrinkled, and mild face, as he embroidered some kind of linen square with a piece of red cotton—most likely the breast of a Ukranian shirt. Romashov knocked on the window. Zegerzht flinched, put his work down, and came to the window.

"It's me, Adam Ivanovich. Open up for a second," Romashov said.

Zegerzht climbed up onto the windowsill and stuck his hairless forehead and straggly beard (which was tangled on one side) against the little ventilation window.

"Is that you, Sub-lieutenant Romashov? What's going on?"

"Is Nazanski home?"

"He's home, he's home. When is he ever not? Ach, good heavens." Zegerzht's beard began to shake in the breeze coming through the ventilation window. "That Nazanski of yours is trying to pull a fast one on me. For the second month in a row, I've been sending him supper—and all he ever does is promise to pay. When he moved in, I told him clearly, in order to avoid a misunderstanding . . ."

"Yes, yes, yes . . . that's . . . Indeed . . ." Romashov interrupted distractedly. "But tell me—how is he? Is it possible to see him?"

"I think so . . . He walks about in his room all the time." Zegerzht listened for a second. "That's him now. You understand that I explained it to him clearly: In order to avoid a misunderstanding we will agree that you pay . . ."

"Excuse me, Abram Ivanovich, I have to go," Romashov interrupted. "I'll come back another time, if that's all right. I have very urgent business . . ."

He kept walking until he turned the corner of the house. Behind the thicket of the back garden, Nazanski's fire was lit. One of his windows was wide open. Nazanski himself was pacing rapidly around the room, without his jacket on, in an undershirt whose collar was unbuttoned. His blonde head and white body flashed in front of the firelight and then disappeared behind the wall. Romashov climbed over the garden fence and called out to him.

"Who is it?" Nazanski asked quietly, as if he had been expecting the call. He leaned over the windowsill. "Is that you, Georgie Alexeyich? Hold on a second: the door is hard to find in the dark. Come in through the window. Here, give me your hand."

Nazanski's room was even shabbier than Romashov's. Along the wall with the window in it there was a narrow, humble-looking bed—which was so warped that it looked more like a hammock—covered by only a single pink quilt. A simple unpainted desk and two rough stools stood against the other wall. In one of the room's corners, a dish cupboard was set into the wall, in the manner of an iconostasis. At the foot of the bed there was a red leather suitcase, which was covered all over in railway stickers. Other than these objects, amd the lamp on the table, there was not a single other thing in the room.

"Hello, my friend," Nazanski said, gripping Romashov's hand tightly and shaking it, as he looked straight at him with his thoughtful, handsome blue eyes. "Come, have a seat on the bed. You've heard that I'm on sick leave."

"Yes. Nikolaev told me about it."

Romashov recalled the awful words of the servant Stepan, and his face wrinkled with pain.

"Ah! You were at the Nikolaevs' house?" Nazansky asked suddenly, his interest clearly piqued. "You visit them a lot?"

Some kind of vague and instinctual wariness, provoked by the unusual tone of the question, compelled Romashov to lie, and he answered offhandedly:

"No, not that often. I just happened to be there."

Nazanski, who was pacing back and forth, stopped next to the cupboard and opened it. A decanter of vodka stood on the shelf, next to an apple that had been divided into thin, precisely cut pieces. Standing with his back to his guest, he hurriedly poured himself a glass and drank it. Romashov watched his back shudder convulsively beneath the linen shirt.

"Would you like some?" Nazanski offered, pointing to the cupboard. "It's not a feast, but if we're hungry, we can whip up some eggs. We could ask Zegerzht to make us something."

"Thank you. I'll eat later, I think."

Nazanski thrust his hands in his pockets and began walking around the room again. When he had completed two circuits he began to speak as if he were continuing a conversation that had just been interrupted.

"Yes. I've thought it all over. And you know, Romashov, I'm happy. Tomorrow everyone in the regiment will say that I've been on a binge. Which is, I grant you, true—though not entirely so. I'm happy right now: I'm not feeling any pain, nor am I suffering. Most of the time both my mind and my will feel depressed. My hunger and my cowardice blend together into a prudent and banal mixture that, quite honestly, bores me to tears. I loathe, for example, military service; yet I serve. Why do I serve? The devil only knows! Because from my earliest years, it was drummed into me—and now everyone around me repeats it—that the most important thing in life is to serve and to be sufficiently well dressed. And philosophy, these same people say, is nonsense, good only for those who have nothing better to do, whose mommies have left them an inheritance. And as I go around doing these things that my heart hates, I fulfill, through the joy of human suffering, the commands of life, which seem to me difficult at some times and senseless at others. My life is monotonous as a fence and gray as a soldier's uniform. I don't dare to think—I don't dare speak up, in order to think it all over out in the open: love, beauty, my relationship to the rest of humankind, nature, the wounds and happiness of man, poetry, God. They laugh: ha ha ha, it's all philosophy! . . . It's funny, and stupid, and impermissible for infantry officers to think about elevated things. That's philosophy, devil take it, therefore foolishness: absurd and idle chatter."

"But that's the most important thing in life," Romashov said thoughtfully.

"And so the time is here for me, which people call by such a severe name," Nazanski continued, without hearing him. He had been pacing the whole time, making gestures full of conviction that were directed, it seemed, not at Romashov but toward the two opposite corners between which he walked. "This is the time of my freedom, Romashov, the freedom of my heart, will, and mind! The life that I am living within myself is strange, perhaps, but deep and wonderful. Such a full life! Everything that I see, that I read about or hear—all of it is reborn again inside me, where it takes on an unusually clear light and deep, fathomless meanings. My memory is like a museum full of rare treasures. You understand—I am its Rothschild! I take the first idea that comes into my head and reflect on it for a long time, sincerely and with pleasure. I think about faces, meetings, characters, books, women—ah, especially about women, and about women's love! Sometimes I think about great men of the past, about the martyrs to science, about wise men and heroes and about the astonishing things they have said. I do not believe in

God, Romashov, but sometimes I think about saints, the zealots, and true believers, and I go over the history of the canons and immortal poetry of the acathistus. I studied at the seminary, my friend, and I have a wonderful memory. I think over everything, and sometimes, as I'm doing this, I begin to feel a terrible and wonderful joy, or wonderful sorrow, or the immortal beauty of some action, which makes me want to go off alone and cry . . . hot, bitter tears . . ."

Romashov got up quietly from the bed and sat with his legs up on the open window, so that his back and the soles of his feet were propped against opposite sides of the frame. From where he was sitting inside the illuminated room the night seemed even darker, deeper, and more mysterious than it had before. A warm, spasmodic yet noiseless wind shook the black leaves of some low-hanging branch above the window. In the thick air, which was full of strange spring aromas, in the quiet, the darkness, in those wonderfully bright stars, which looked almost warm, one could feel some kind of secret and passionate ferment, the maternal thirst of the extravagantly voluptuous earth, the plants, the trees—the entire world.

Nazanski did another circuit and spoke without looking at Romashov, as if addressing himself to the walls and four corners of his room:

"At these times, my thoughts run by so fancifully—so unexpectedly, and in so many colors. My mind becomes sharp and bright; my imagination, a veritable current! All of the things and faces that I summon stand before me as if in relief, so hypnotically clear that it's as if I were watching them in a camera obscura. I know, I know, my friend, that this feeling of intensification, all this illumination of the soul is—alas!—nothing more than the physiological effects of alcohol on the nervous system. When I first experienced this wonderous elevation of my internal life, I thought that it was the result of true inspiration. But no: there's nothing creative about it, let alone anything lasting. It's simply a morbid process. These 'inspirations' are sudden influxes, which eat away at the bottom more and more each time they come. Yes. Still, this madness is sweet to me and . . . may the devil take all thoughts of redemptive thriftiness, not to mention the foolish hope that I might live a hundred and ten years and be made into newspaper pulp, as so often happens to examples of longevity . . . I'm happy, and that's everything now!

Nazanski walked up to the cupboard again and, after taking a drink, carefully closed its doors. Romashov got up and did the same thing, though without paying as much attention.

"What were you thinking about before I got here, Vasily Nilich?" he asked, resuming his seat on the windowsill.

But Nazanski barely heard his question.

"What pleasure can be had, for example, in dreaming about women!" he cried, walking up to the furthermost corner of the room and then addressing it with a sharp, earnest gesture. "No, it's not degrading to think about such things. Why would it be? You should never make a man do evil things, let alone dirty ones—not even in your own thoughts. I often think of sweet, clean, graceful women, of their bright and charming smiles; I think about young, chaste mothers, of lovers, following their joy of love towards death, of beautiful, innocent, and proud girls with hearts as white as snow, who know everything and are afraid of nothing. These women do not exist. But this isn't exactly true. No doubt, Romashov, these women do exist, but we will never see them. You will maybe see them—but as for me? Never."

He stopped in front of Romashov now and looked him straight in the face, but by the dreamy expression of his eyes, and the vague smile playing on his lips, it was clear that he couldn't see who he was talking to. Even during its best and most sober moments, Nazanski's face had never seemed so beautiful and interesting to Romashov. His golden hair fell in thick, unbroken locks around his high, clear forehead; his thick, red, four-sided beard, which was not large, lay as if crimped; his large and elegant head, with its fine neck, resembled the head of one of those Greek heroes or wise men, whose magnificent busts Romashov had seen in various engravings. His clear, almost moist blue eyes gazed ahead vividly, intelligently, and gently. Even the color of that handsome, well-proportioned face overcame its even, delicate, pinkish tone, and only a very experienced eye could discern, beneath that appearance of freshness, a few swollen lines, which were the result of blood inflamed by alcohol.

"Love! For a woman: what an abyss of secrets! What delights—what sharp, sweet sufferings!" Nazanski cried, suddenly and passionately.

He tore fitfully at his hair and turned again toward the corner—but when he reached it he stopped, turned his face again toward Romashov and laughed happily. The sub-lieutenant watched him, feeling a little alarmed.

"That reminds me of a funny story," Nazanski began, simply and genially. "How the thoughts jump around inside me! . . . One day I was in Ryazan, at the Oka station, waiting for the steamer to come in. I'd been there, if you can believe it, almost a full day and night—it was during the spring flood—and I—you understand this of course—I had made myself a little nest at the bar there. And there was a barmaid there, maybe eighteen years old—the sort of girl, if you know what I mean, who is pockmarked and hardly beautiful, but lively, with black eyes and a wonderful smile: quite a darling, to be totally honest. There were only three of us at the station: she, myself, and a little fair-haired telegraph operator. Her father was there too, of course: a fat old man with the red snout of a ferocious bulldog. But it felt like he was behind the scenes, for some reason. For two minutes he'd go behind the bar and stand yawning at everyone, scratching his belly beneath his waistcoat, his eyes barely keeping open. Then he left again to go to sleep. But the telegraph operator stuck around. I remember, he leaned his arms on the bar up to the elbow, without saying anything. And she didn't say anything either; she just looked out the window, at the flooding. And then the young man started singing, softly:

> Love—what is it?
> What is love?
> An unearthly feeling,
> That sets our blood reeling.

"And then he was quiet again. Five minutes later she began purring: 'Love—what is it? What is love? . . .' You know, that ridiculous, ridiculous song. Most likely both of them had heard it at some operetta or on the stage . . . I daresay they had walked into town just for that. Yes. They sang it all the way through and were quiet again. And then the young woman looked out the little window almost imperceptibly, and put her hand on the counter, and he took her hand in his and began rubbing her palm. And once more: "Love—what is it? . . .' Out in the yard: spring, the flood. Languor. And in this way they passed the entire day and night. At the time their 'love' really annoyed me, but now, you know, I recall it with affection. For this must have been the way they paid court to one another for the whole two weeks before I had gotten there and for another month after I left. And it was only after I'd left that I understood what joy they had, what a ray of light their lobe was in their poor, narrow little lives, which were after all even more limited than our own ridiculous existences—oh, so much more! A hundred times! But then . . . wait a second, Romashov. My thoughts are becoming confused. Why did I start talking about the telegraph operator?"

Nazanski went up to the cabinet again. But instead of turning around, he kept his back to Romashov, rubbing his forehead cruelly and furiously clutching his temple with the palm of his right hand. And there was something pitiful, helpless, humiliated in the nervous gesture.

"You were talking about women's love—about misfortune, about secrets and joy," Romashov reminded him.

"Yes, love!" Nazanski shouted exultantly. He drained his glass quickly, turned with burning eyes from the wall cabinet and hurriedly wiped his lips on the sleeve of his shirt. "Love! Who understands her? They mine her for the themes of dirty, trashy operas, for smutty paintings, for foul anecdotes, for filthy, filthy poems. We officers do this. Yesterday, Deitz came to see me. He sat in exactly the same place that you're sitting now. He played with his golden pince-nez and talked about women. Romashov, my friend, if animals, a dog, for example, were given the gift of being able to understand human speech and if one of them could have overheard Deitz talking last night, my God, it would have left the room in shame. Deitz is a good man, you know; actually they're all good, Romashov: there are no bad people. But he is ashamed to speak in any other way about women, ashamed out of the fear of losing his reputation as a cynic, libertine, and conqueror. This is a usual sort of attitude, the atmosphere of male adolescence, this boastful disdain for women. And all because of the fact that, for the majority of people there is something in love, in the possession of a woman, you understand, in the ultimate posession of her—there is something creudly bestial hidden in it, something egotistical, for oneself only: something secretly base, thieving, and shameful—devil take it, I'm not saying it right! And because of this, for the majority of men, this possession results in coldness, disgust, hostility. Because of this, men conduct their affairs at night, like bandits and murderers . . . Now, my friend, nature sets a sort of trap for people, complete with bait and noose."

"It's true," Romashov agreed, quietly and sadly.

"No, it's not true!" Nazavski cried out loudly. "I tell you, it's not true. Nature, like everything, arranges her affairs genially. That's why for Lieutenant Ditz, love is followed by squeamishness and a feeling of being stuffed, whereas for Dante all of love is charm, wonder, spring! No, no, here I'm using the word 'love' in its common, physical sense. As for true love—she's the destiny of a select few. I'll put it like this: all men possess an ear for music, but for millions of people this sense is like a carp's, or Sub-Cabtain Vasilchesky's. But one out of these millions is a Beethoven. It's the same way with everything: in poetry, in painting, in wisdom . . . and love, I tell you, has its heights too, which can be reached only by one in a million."

He went up to the window, leaned his forehead against the corner directly across from Romashov, and, staring thoughtfully out at the warm darkness of the spring night, began speaking in a trembling, deep, insistent voice:

"Oh, how little we are capable of appraising her fine, elusive charms—we who are coarse, lazy, and shortsighted. Can you understand how many various joys and wonders there are in unrequited and hopeless love? When I was younger, I had a single dream: to fall in love with an unattainable, unusual woman, the kind, you know, with whom I could have absolutely nothing in common. To be in love my whole life, to dedicate all my thoughts to her. I would do whatever it took: I would hire myself out as her servant, become her footman, her coachman—I would disguise myself, dissemble, in order that I might one time a year see her by chance, kiss where her feet had walked on the stairs, in order to—oh, what unimaginable bliss!—to brush against her dress, if only for one time in my entire life."

"And then, to go mad," Romashov said darkly.

"Ah, my friend, don't say that!" Nazansky retorted fiercely, and again ran nervously up to the window. "Maybe—who knows?—you will get a chance to enter into that blessed, fairy-tale life. Very well, then: you lose your mind from an amazing, unbelievable love, and Lieutenant Deitz loses his mind from progressive paralysis and terrible pain. Who can say which is better? Only think, what happiness it must be to stand all night on the opposite side of a street, in the shadows, and to see in the window the woman you worship. The inside of the room is lit, shadows move across the curtains. Could that be her? What is she doing? What is she thinking? The light goes out. Sleep well, my joy, sleep, my beloved! . . . Already, the day is a complete victory! Days, weeks, years to use all strength of inventiveness and persistence, and there you have it—a great, stupendous passion:

you have her handkerchief in your hands, a candy wrapper, a dropped playbill. She knows nothing about you, has never heard of you, her eyes skate over you, unseeing, but you are there all the same, beside her, always worshipful, always ready to give her—no, why just her?—to give her caprices, her husband, her lovers, her most beloved dog—to give your life, your honor, everything, in other words, that you are able to give! Romashov, this kind of happiness is unknown to beauties and winners."

"Oh, how true, how good everything you say is!" cried Romashov rapturously. He had already stood up from the windowsill a long time ago and now, like Nazanski, he walked back and forth across the long and narrow room, colliding with him and stopping every minute. "What ideas enter your head! I'll tell you about myself. I was in love with a . . . woman. This was elsewhere, elsewhere . . . I was still in Moscow . . . I was . . . a junker. But she didn't know anything about that. And it was an exquisite pleasure for me to sit next to her and, while she was working on something, to take her thread and lightly pull it from her hands. That was all. She never noticed it, never noticed it at all, but I was driven out of my mind by happiness."

"Yes, yes, I understand." Nazanski nodded his head and smiled, joyfully and tenderly. "I understand what you're saying. Something like a wire, an electric current? Right? Some kind of fine, pleasing connection? Ah, my friend, life is beautiful! . . ."

Nazanski was quiet, touched by his own thoughts, and his blue eyes, which were filled with tears, sparkled. Romashov was seized by a kind of tender and indefininte pity, and a mildly hysterical tenderness—which feelings were aroused by both Nazanski and himself.

"Vasily Nilich, you surprise me," he said, taking both Nazanski's hands in his and squeezing them tightly. "You're such a talented, wonderful, broad-minded person, and here you are, destroying yourself for nothing. Oh no, no, I wouldn't dare read you a ridiculous morality tale . . . I myself . . . But what if a woman were to enter your life who you could value and who would be good enough for you. I think about that often . . ."

Nazanski stood still and looked for a long time out the open window.

"A woman . . ." he said, stretching the word out thoughtfully. "Yes! I'll tell you!" he shouted decisively. "Once in my life—and only once—I did meet a remarkable, unusual woman. A girl . . . But you know, as Heine says: 'She was suitable to be loved, and so he loved her, but he was unsuitable to be loved, and so she did not love him.' She stopped loving me because I drank . . . However, I don't know, perhaps I began drinking because she stopped loving me. She . . . she's no longer here, this was a long time ago. I was in the service for three years at first, you know, then the reserves for four years, after which, three years ago, I entered the regiment again. There was never any romance between us. We met all of ten or maybe fifteen times, had five or six close conversations. But do you ever stop to consider the fascinating and irresistible influence that the past has on us? I consider these innocent trifles to be the most precious things I have. I've loved her, up to this day. Wait, Romashov . . . you deserve to hear this . . . I'll read you her only letter—the first and the last one that she wrote me."

He squatted in front of the suitcase and began patiently turning over some of the papers that were inside it. As he did this, he continued to speak:

"To be honest, I don't think she ever loved anyone other than herself. Something power-hungry, some evil and proud strength was in her. But at the same time she was good, womanly, unceasingly kind. It was as if she were two people: one, which possessed a dry, egotistical mind, and the other, who had a sweet and passionate heart. Here it is, read it, Romashov. That part at the top there isn't important." Nazanski folded over a few lines at the top. "From here. Go ahead—read it."

Romashov felt as if something had struck him on the head, causing all the room to shake in front of his eyes. The letter was written in a large, thin, nervous hand, which could only belong to Alexandra Petrovna—it was so original, irregular, and elegant. Romashov, who had frequently received invitations from her to dinner or to a card party, could have picked that handwriting out of a thousand other samples.

". . . It's bitter and difficult for me to say this," he read, beneath Nazanski's hand. "But you yourself did everything you could to bring our acquaintance to this sad end. I refuse to lie to you: more than anything else in life I am ashamed of lying, which is always the result of cowardice and weakness. I loved you and still love you now; I know that this feeling will not soon nor easily leave me. But at the end of the day, I have control over this feeling. What would have happened if I had acted differently? It's true, there is sufficient strength and selflessness in me to be the guide, nanny, sister of mercy to a willess, wasteful, dissolute man—but I loathe feeling pity and the humiliation of perpetual forgiveness, and do not want *you* to cause these feelings in me. I do not want you to nourish yourself on the alms of pity and dog-like devotion. But you cannot be otherwise, regardless of your mind and beautiful soul. Tell me honestly, sincerely, is this true?

Ah, my dear Vasily Nilich, if you could only be different! If only! All my heart, all my wishes would rush to you. I love you. But you yourself do not want me. For it should be possible to change the whole world for a beloved person—and I am asking so little! Can you really not do it?

"Farewell. In my mind, I am kissing you on the forehead . . . as if you were a corpse, since you are dead to me now. I advise you to destroy this letter. Not because I am afraid of anything, but because in time it will become a source of suffering and painful memories. Again, I repeat . . ."

"The rest wouldn't interest you," Nazanski said, taking the letter out of Romashov's hand. "It's the only one she ever sent me."

"What happened after this?" Romashov asked, with difficulty.

"After this? After this we never saw each other again. She . . . she went off somewhere and got married, it turns out, to . . . an engineer. All that is of secondary importance."

"And have you never gone to see Alexandra Petrovna?"

Romashov practically whispered these words, but both officers shuddered upon hearing them and could not look away from one another's faces for some time. During these few seconds, all the human barriers of deceit, pretension, and impenetrability vanished, and the two could see straight into one another's hearts. Immediately, they understood a hundred things that they had been hiding from each other up to that moment, and their entire previous conversation suddenly took on a sort of singular, deep, almost tragic dimension.

"You too? How . . . ?" Nazanski said finally, an expression of mad suffering in his eyes.

Only a moment later, however, he came to himself and cried out, with a drawn smile:

"Pah—what a misunderstanding! You've deviated from our theme. The letter I showed you was written a hundred years ago; the woman who wrote it now lives somewhere far away, in Transcaucasia . . . Anyway, where were we?"

"It's time for me to go home, Vasily Nilich. It's late," said Romashov, standing.

Nazanski did not try to stop him. They said goodbye, neither coldly nor dryly, but still with a certain amount of embarrassment. Romashov was now even more convinced that the letter had been written by Shurochka. He thought about it the entire walk home, and could not understand what kind of feelings it was causing him to feel. Envy towards Nazanski—an envy for the past, and a sort of evilly triumphant pity for Nikolaev; but at the same time a sort of new hope—an indistinct feeling, cloudy, but at the same time sweet and alluring. As if the letter had handed him some sort of secret and invisible thread, leading into the future.

The wind died down.

The night was full of a deep quiet, and the darkness seemed velvety and warm. But a secret creative force was making itself felt in the dreamless air, in the calm of the invisible forest, in the smell of the earth. Romashov walked on without seeing the road, and it felt to him at that moment as if something powerful, masterful and gentle were going to breathe its hot breath against his face. In his heart he felt a jealous sadness of the bright and irretrievable springs that had already gone by, his childhood: a quiet and good-natured envy for his innocent and tender past . . .

When he got home, he found a second letter from Raisa Alexandrovna Peterson. She wrote, in a ridiculous and bombastic style, about treacherous deception, that topic that she understood so well, and about all the terrible ways that the broken heart of a woman can take its revenge.

I know what I have to do! If I do not die of consumption as a result of your despicable behavior, then, believe me, I will pay you back with interest. Maybe you think that no one knows where you go every evening? You're blind! The walls themselves have ears. I know every step you take. But, all the same, even someone as irresistibly handsome—and posessing such godlike eloquence too!—will get nothing *there*, other than 'N' throwing you out the door like a pup. As for me, I advise you to be careful. I am not one of those women, who forgive an insult.

I, who was born near Kafkaz,
Know how to wield a knife!!!

Once yours, now nobody's,

Raisa.

P.S. Without fail, be at the officers' club this Saturday. We must talk. I will save the third quadrille for you, though now *it means nothing*.

R.P.

The stupidity, the pretension of the provincial bog and its base gossip displayed by this ungrammatical and senseless letter overwhelmed Romashov. He felt soiled from head to foot by a heavy and indelible mud, which had been applied to him by his connection with this unloved woman—a connection that had gone on now for almost half a year. He lay on his bed, despondent, as if crushed by the entire day's events, and, with his covers already pulled up, repeated Nazanski's words to himself:

"His thoughts were gray, like a soldier's uniform."

He soon fell into a deep sleep. And as always happened to him after a period of great distress, he pictured himself in his dreams as a child. Then his life was not dirty, melancholy, or monotonous; his body felt cheerful and his heart was light and clear, and playing with an unthinking joy. And all the world was light and clear, and at its very center the dear, familiar streets of Moscow sparkled with those beautiful lights that it is possible to see only in dreams. But somewhere in the paradise of this happy-go-lucky world, far off toward the horizon, a dark and ominous pall hung: a gray, despondent city was hiding there—a city full of heavy and boring military service, with company schools, with drunken parties, with weighty and nasty romantic connections, with suffering and loneliness. All of life rang and shone with joy, but the dark, menacing spot lay in wait for Romashov, secretly, like a black ghost. It knew its turn would come. And only the young Romashov—pure, unworried, innocent—cried passionately for his elder twin, who was swimming towards that evil-looking darkness.

In the middle of the night he woke up and saw that his pillow was wet from tears. He could not immediately hold them back, and they continued to run down his cheek for a long time, in warm, wet, quick-moving streams.

VI

Save for a few careerists and men of ambition, the majority of the officers treated their military service as if it were a period of enforced labor, loathsome and unwanted, which they suffered through without any joy. The junior officers acted like schoolboys, showing up late to their classes or secretly avoiding them if they felt they could get away with it. The company commanders, most of whom had large families and were therefore overwhelmed by domestic squabbles and their wives' romances, not to mention the crushing weight of their poverty and a life lived beyond their means, groaned beneath the weight of countless expenses and promissary notes. They sewed patch onto patch, snatching up money from one place in order to pay their debts in another; many of them decided—frequently at their wives' insistence—to borrow from the coffers or from the salaries that were due to the soldiers for voluntary labor. Others stole money that had been sent to the soldiers via letters, which they opened as was their right, often over a period of months and even years. A few managed to live solely off the money they made in card games like Vint, Shtoss, and Landsknet; some of these men cheated, but this fact was well known, and people looked the other way. All of them drank heavily when they got together at the officers' club or while visiting one another. A few, like Sliva, drank alone.

Because of this, officers had no time to take their duties seriously. For the most part, the inner workings of the regiment were handled by the sergeant major, who kept all the books, and whose veined and callused hands had a subtle but powerful grip on the regiment commander. The company heads, who held their service in the same disgust as the subaltern officers did, "squeezed the men" mostly in order to keep up appearances, and only occasionally because of the petty tyrant's love for power.

Battallion commanders were useless for the most part, especially during the winter. There are two intermediary ranks in the army, batallion commander and brigadeer commander, and officers in these positions frequently found themselves without specific duties or responsibilities. In summer, despite this fact, they conducted the Batallion training, took part in regimental and divisional activities, and suffered through maneuvers. In their free time they gathered together, read the *Invalid* diligently and asked about promotions, played cards, allowed the younger officers to buy them drinks, hosted parties at their houses, and attempted to marry off their many daughters.

Before the big inspection, however, everyone, from the lowest rank to the highest, tightened their belts and helped one another do the same. During this time no one had any rest; they made up for their hours of idleness with effort and study, although most of this was just wasted energy. Without any consideration of physical limits, they pushed their soldiers past the point of exhaustion. The company commanders beleaguered the junior officers with harsh reprimands; the junior officers swore awkwardly, clumsily, and unnaturally; while the non-commissioned officers, hoarse from all their cursing, fought fiercely among themselves. However, it was not just the non-commissioned officers that fought.

It was a hard time of year, truly, and the entire regiment, from the commander down to the last worn-out batboy in his little cell, dreamed about his Sunday break and the free time that it would bring with it, as if the whole thing were a sort of blissful idyll.

That spring, the regiment was devoting all its strength towards preparing for the May parade. It had become widely known that the review would be conducted by the corps commander: a demanding combat general, whose name was famous in the international military literature for his notes on the Karilist war and on the Franco-Prussian campaign of 1870, in which he participated as a volunteer. Even more famous were the orders that he sent, which were written in a style whose elegance and concision were reminiscent of Suvorov. In these orders, he used his characteristically biting and unforgiving sarcasm (which the officers feared much more than any sort of disciplinary punshment) to make short work of unruly subordinates. For this reason, a hurried, feverish industry had possessed the company for two weeks already, to the point that the exhausted officers awaited the day off with the same expectation as the like worn-out soldiers.

For Romashov, however, the sweet charm of this interlude was soured by his confinement to quarters. He woke up very early and could not get back to sleep no matter how hard he tried. He dressed sluggishly, drank his tea with disgust, and once in a while even called roughly for Gainan, who, as always, was happy, lively, and clumsy, like a puppy.

Romashov walked around his tiny room in his gray greatcoat, which was unbuttoned. His legs brushed against the legs of the bed and his elbows skirted the wobbly, dust-covered bookcase. For the first time all year—and this thanks to unlucky circumstances that were out of his control—he had been left alone with himself. This had been prevented, up until now, by his service, duties, the officers' club, card games, his courting of Raisa, his evenings at the Nikolaevs'. On those rare occasions when a free, unoccupied hour did happen to come his way, Romashov (who was filled at these times with boredom and idleness, almost to the point of being afraid of himself) would hurry to the club, or to someone's house, or simply out onto the street to meet up with one of his unmarried friends—which meeting would always end in a drinking bout. Now he thought with anguish about the day of solitude that lay before him, and strange, uncomfortable, pointless thoughts clambored into his head.

The late service bells were ringing in town. Romashov listened as the enchantingly deep and springlike peals, each of which seemed to give rise to its successor just as its own sound was about to die, reached him through the second layer of insulating glass. Beneath the window, the garden was starting to bloom. The sweet cherry trees were round and bushy and covered all over with white blossoms, like a flock of snow-white sheep, or a crowd of girls wearing white dresses. Here and there strong, straight-backed poplars towered above them, their branches raised high into the sky, as if in prayer; alongside them rose narrow old chestnuts, with their powerful, cupola-like tops thrust out. The trees were still bare and the naked twigs black, but already the first, furry, joyful buds had begun to give them a yellowish tint. The morning was turning out to be bright, clear, and wet. The trees quivered quietly and shook slowly. It seemed as if a tender and cool wind were playing among them, and joking, and, bending their flowers down, kissing them.

To the right of his window, Romashov could see the section of muddy black road through the gates, as well as the fence running along its other side. People were walking slowly along this fence, placing their feet carefully on the dry spots in the road. "They have the whole day in front of them," Romashov thought, following them enviously with his eyes. "Why should they hurry? An entire free day!"

All of a sudden he wanted—impatiently, passionately, and to the point of tears—to get dressed and leave his room. He felt compelled, not by the officers' club, as was usually the case, but simply by the street, the air. He had never put any value on his freedom, and was now surprised by how much happiness could lie in the simple ability to go wherever one wished: to visit a favorite side street, enter a square, or go to a church, without once fearing or even thinking of the consequences. That kind of possibility suddenly seemed to him like some kind of fantastic holiday of the spirit.

He remembered also how, when he was very young, before he had gone off to the military academy, his mother used to punish him by tying his leg to the bed with a thin string, and then leaving. Little Romashov had sat there obediently for hours. At any other time he wouldn't have thought twice about leaving the house for the entire day, even though he had to slide down the drainpipe from the second-floor window in order to do so. Frequently, after slipping out this way, he would tag along across Moscow with a military musician or funeral procession, boldly stealing some sugar, jam, or cigarettes from his mother for his friends. But the string! It had a strange, hypnotic effect on him. He was afraid to pull on it with even the least amount of strength, lest it somehow break. This was not the horror of punishment, nor, of course, conscience and repentance, but just plain hypnotism: no more than a superstitious horror before the powerful and inscrutible acts of adults, or the respectful terror of the savage before the shaman's magic circle.

"And now here I am, sitting like a schoolboy, like a kid again, my leg tied," Romashov thought, as he lumbered around the room. "The door is open, I have the desire to leave, to go where I want, to do what I want, to speak, to laugh—but I sit tied to the string. This 'I' sits. I. This is truly all I am! But he is the one who decides, that I must sit. I have not given my consent."

"I!" Romashov stopped in the middle of the room and, with his legs apart and his head lowered, began thinking deeply. "I! I! I!" he shouted suddenly, and loudly, with surprise, as if he had only now understood this sharp word. "Who is standing here looking at the black crack in the floor? I am. How strange—I-yeeee"—he drew the word out slowly, plumbing the sound for whatever sense it held.

Romashov's smile was exhausted and awkward, and soon after it appeared he frowned, paling under the strain of his thoughts. Similar ones had occurred to him frequently over the last five or six years, as so often happens with young people during the period of their heart's maturation. A simple truth, a proverb, a well-known saying, whose words he had known by rote for years, would, thanks to some kind of inner illumination, suddenly take on a deep philosophical meaning, and then it would seem to him that he was hearing it for the first time—practically as if he himself had discovered it. He even remembered the first time "this" had happened. In school, in seminary class, the priest had been talking about the parable of the builders and the stones. One builder had begun with the smallest stones, so that by the time he had reached the heavier ones, he was unable to lift them. Another had proceeded in the opposite manner and had finished his work completely. For Romashov, it was as if the wealth of practical wisdom hidden in that simple parable—which he had known and remembered since he had learned how to read—had suddenly opened up to him. Soon, the same thing had happened to another well-known proverb: "Measure seven times, cut once." In a single happy, penetrating moment he understood everything: prudence, foresight, the economy of care, measurement. A huge amount of lived experience lay in those five words. And in that same way, now, he was stunned and shaken by the sudden and unexpectedly bright awareness of his own individuality . . .

"Me—that's interior," Romashov thought. "And all the weariness—that's extraneous, that's not me. There's the room, the street, the trees, the sky, the regimental commander, Lieutenant Andrusevich, the service, my friends, the soldiers—none of them are me. No, no, none of it is me. Here are my hands and my feet." Romashov held his hands in front of his face and looked at them with surprise, as if for the first time. "No. None of it is me. And if I pinch myself on the hand . . . like so . . . that's me. I see my hand, I hold it up—that's me. This, that I'm thinking right now, that's also me. And if I decide to go for a walk, that's me. And the person who stops—that's me too.

"How strange, how simple, and how incredible. Maybe everyone has such an I? And maybe not everyone has one? Maybe I'm the only person who has one? And if that were really the case? Say I were standing in front of a hundred soldiers, and I cried out to them: 'Eyes to the right!' and a hundred men, each of whom had their own I, and who saw in me something strange, something outside of themselves—all of them turned their heads to the right simultaneously. But I can't distinguish them from one another—to me, they're a mass. And for Colonel Shulgovich, maybe, I myself, and Vetkin, and Lubov, and all the lieutenants, and the captain too all slide together into a single face, and we appear strange to him, and he is unable to tell any of us apart?"

The door creaked, and Gainan flew into the room, hopping from foot to foot and jerking up his shoulders, as if he had been tripped. He shouted:

"The commissary will not give me any more cigarettes, sir. They say that lieutenant Skriabin has told them not to extend you any more on credit."

"Devil take it!" Romashov barked. "All right, then, go, be on your way . . . But how will I survive without cigarettes? . . . Never mind, you can go, Gainan."

"What was I thinking about just now," Romashov asked himself, once he was alone again. He had lost the thread of his thought and, being unused to thinking in a straight line, was not immediately able to find it again. "What was it? Something important, something vital . . . Come: I've got to start at the beginning . . . Here I am, under house arrest . . . People are walking along the street . . . When I was a child, Mama tied my leg to the bed . . . She tied 'me' to the bed . . . Yes, yes . . . Soldiers also have an 'I' . . . Colonel Shuglovich . . . I remember . . . But come, we must go further back, further . . .

"I'm sitting in my room. The door is unlocked. I want to leave, but I can't. Why can't I? Did I commit a crime? Did I steal something? Kill someone? No; while talking with someone, someone who was facing me, I failed to keep my feet together, and made some remark. Maybe I should have kept my feet together? Why? Is that really important? Is that really a matter of life or death? Twenty years—no, thirty—are still only a second in the huge span of time that was after all there before me, and will still be there after me. Only a second! My 'I' will be put out, like a lamp whose wick is pinched. But a lamp is relit again, and again, and again, while I won't be. And this room won't be either, nor the sky, nor the regiment, nor the army itself, nor the stars, nor this green ball, nor my hands and feet . . . Because there will be no more Me . . .

"Yes, yes . . . That's it . . . Very good . . . Wait . . . You have to go slowly . . . A little further . . . There will be no Me. It was dark, and then someone lit my life and then after that it was extinguished, and there was darkness again, forever and ever . . . What did I do in that tiny moment? I put my hands on my pants seam and my heels together and kept my toes stretched out while marching, and cried out, as loudly as I could, 'Shoulder arms!' I swore and cursed because the men were holding their rifles the wrong way, trembled in front of the entire company . . . And why? These ghosts, which die with my I, made me do a hundred inconvenient and unnecessary things, and in this way they insulted and humiliated 'me.' Me!!! Why should I have to take orders from ghosts?"

Romashov sat at his desk, leaning his elbows on it and cutching his head in his hands. He was trying hard to hold on to the unusual thoughts that were racing around in his head.

"Hmmm . . . But what about all that you're forgetting? Your country? The cradle of the race? The fatherland? The sacrifice on the altar? . . . And what about military honor and discipline? Who is going to protect your home if it's invaded by foreign enemies? . . . Well, yes, but I'm going to die, and then I won't have a home anymore, or enemies, or honor. They exist only so long as my consciousness exists. But take away homeland, and honor, and uniforms, and all those mighty words, and my I will still be here, inviolable. Could it be then that, at the end of the day, my I is more important than all those thoughts about necessity and honor and love? Here I am, doing my duty . . . when suddenly my I says, 'I don't want to!' No, not my I—bigger than that, the entire army full of I's or even bigger, all the I's of the world might say 'I don't want to!' And then all of a sudden the war becomes senseless, and the 'Forward march!' and 'About face!' cease to exist—because there is no longer any necessity for them. Yes, yes, yes! It's true—it's true," a kind of joyful shout arose inside Romashov. "All that military valor, and discipline, and bureaucracy, and the the honor of the uniform, and all the military science—all of it is founded only on the fact that men are unwilling, or unable, or don't dare to say 'I don't want to!'

"What is this whole cunningly constructed building called warcraft, after all? Nothing. A puffball, a castle in the clouds, founded not even on the four distinct words 'I don't want to,' but simply on the fact that for some reason, so far, these words have remained unspoken. My I never says 'I don't want to eat, I don't want to breathe, I don't want to see.' But if someone proposes that it die, it says without fail—without fail—'I don't want to.' So then what is war, with its unavoidable slaughter and military arts, which we study only so we can kill better. The world's mistake? Blindness?

"But wait, hold on . . . Could it be that I'm the one who's made a mistake? I must be mistaken—this 'I don't want to' is so simple, so natural, that it must be something that enters everyone's heads. Well, all right, then; let's disperse. Let's say that tomorrow, let's just say that this idea came into the heads of everyone at exactly the same time: Russians, Germans, the English, the Japanese . . . Then there would be no more war, no officers or soldiers, everyone would go home. What would happen then? Really, what would happen? I don't know, but Shuglovich would probably say something like, 'Then they would attack by surprise and take our land and our houses, raze our crops, steal our wives and sisters.' And the rebels? The socialists? The revolutionaries? . . . No, it's not true. For everybody, all of humanity has said: I don't want bloodshed. Who then would come with their weapons and force? Nobody. What would happen? Is it possible, maybe, that then 'everyone would get along'? Would everybody give way to everybody else? Help one another? Forgive? Oh God, oh God, what would happen?"

Romashov was so occupied with his thoughts that he did not notice that Gainan had quietly come up behind him to hand him something over his shoulder. Romashov jumped and gave a small frightened shout:

"What the devil do you want? . . ."

Gainan lay a brown paper package on the desk.

"For you!" he said in his familiar and affectionate way. Romashov felt that he was smiling affectionately at him behind his back. "Cigarettes, for you. Go ahead and smoke!"

Romashov looked at the packet. The phrase "'Trubach' cigarettes, price 3 k for 20 p" was written on it.

"What is this? Why?" he asked with surprise. "Where did you get them?"

"I noticed that you didn't have any cigarettes, so I bought them with my own money. Smoke them, please, smoke them. It's nothing. I'm giving them to you."

Gainan, who was growing flustered now, bolted out of the room, banging the door shut behind him. The sub-lieutenant lit a cigarette. The smell of sealing wax and burnt feathers spread through the room.

"What a dear fellow!" Romashov thought affectionately. "I rage and bellow at him; every night I order him to take off not only my boots but my socks and pants too. And here he buys me cigarettes with his last few kopecks. 'Please, smoke them!' But why? . . ."

He stood up again and, placing his hand behind his back, began to pace around the room.

"One hundred men in our regiment. And each of these is a person with thoughts, feelings, his own character and experience of the world, with unique preferences and antipathies. Do I know anything about them? No—nothing, except their physiognomies. Here they are, from right to left: Soltis, Ryaboshapka, Vedeneyevs, Egorov, Yashishin . . . gray, monotonous faces. How have I tried to touch their hearts with my heart, their Me with my Me? Nothing."

Suddenly, Romashov recalled an unbearable night that had happened late last fall. A few of the officers, he among them, had been sitting around drinking vodka, when the sergeant major of the ninth company, a man named Gumenyuk, had run up and, breathing heavily, cried out to their company commander:

"Sir, they're driving in some fresh meat! . . ."

They were indeed "driving in some fresh meat." The new recruits stood in the regimental yard, in a single heap in the rain, like a herd of frightened and obedient animals, glancing around timidly and mistrustfully. Still, it was clear that every one of them had a face that was completely his own. Perhaps it only seemed that way because of how variously they were dressed? "That one there is probably a metal worker," Romashov had thought, staring at his face as he passed. "And that one over there's a good fellow, no doubt, who can play the harmonica.

That one's well read, he's quick and a little sly, with a silver tongue—maybe a waiter before?" It was clear that they really had been driven, or rather dragged, only a few days earlier, away from their moaning women and wailing children, and that they themselves had put on a brave face and acted tough in order to not start crying in the middle of their drunken stupor . . . A year later, however, and here they were standing in a long, lifeless line, gray, wooden, indistinguishable: soldiers, in other words! They had not wanted to come. "They did not want." Good God, what was the cause of this terrible senselessness? When had this knot first gotten tied? Or was it just like what happened with roosters? Put a rooster's head on a block and he'll run away. But draw a chalk line on his beak, and then after that onto the block, and he will think that he and the block are tied together, and sit, not moving a muscle, his eyes open wide, as if on some terror hovering in front of him.

Romashov went over to his bed and collapsed onto it.

"Well, what else can I do?" he asked himself sternly, almost spitefully. "Really, what other options do I have? Leave the service? But what do you know how to do? First boarding school, then the corps of cadets, then the academy . . . Locked into the life of an officer . . . Have you ever experienced struggle? Want? No, you've had everything you needed; French rolls might as well grow on trees, so far as you're concerned. Just try and leave. They'll finish you off, you'll become a drunkard, you will fall with your first step into civilian life. Wait. Who among the officers that you know left the service willingly? No one. All of them put a high price on what they themselves do, simply because they've never been suited for anything else and don't know how to do anything anyway. And if they do leave, they go about afterward in their soiled uniform jacket and cap: *'Ayez la bonte . . . comprenez vous . . .'* Ah, what can I do! What can I do! . . ."

"Hey there, little jailbird!" a female voice said clearly from below the window.

Romashov jumped up from the bed and ran to the window. Shurochka was standing in the yard. She held a hand up over her eyes to shield them from the light, pressed her fresh, smiling face against the glass, and said in a singsong:

"Pity the poor prisoner . . ."

Romashov was about to turn the handle, but then he remembered that the second pane of glass had not yet been removed from the window for spring. So, seized by a sudden rush of joyful determination, he grabbed hold of the frame and pulled it toward him. It opened with a crack and raining bits of lime and dry putty onto Romashov's head. A cool breeze, full of the sweet, subtle and joyful fragrance of white flowers, streamed into the room.

"That's it! That's how one finds a way out!" cried a jubillant, laughing voice in Romashov's heart.

"Rommy! You lunatic! What are you doing?"

He took the small hand that she held out to him through the window (it was covered in a tight brown glove), and boldly kissed, first the top of it and then, turning it over, the palm, in the little square hole right above the button. He had never done this before, but despite herself, she didn't resist but only looked at him with confused surprise, as if submitting herself to his passionate daring.

"Alexandra Petrovna! How can I ever thank you! My dear!"

"What's come over you, Rommy? Why are you so happy all of a sudden?" she asked, smiling, but still without lowering her intense and curious gaze from Romashov's face. "Your eyes are shining. Hold on—I've brought you a *kalatch*, as if you were a real prisoner. Today we have some wonderful apple pastries, sweet ones . . . Give me the basket, Stepan."

He looked at her with bright, loving eyes, but didn't let her hand go. She still wasn't resisting this. He said quickly:

"Ah! If you only knew, what I'd been thinking about all morning . . . If you only knew! But maybe later . . ."

"Yes, later . . . Here comes my lord and master . . . Let go my hand. You're surprising me today, Yuri Aleksevich. I'd even say you look better."

Nikolaev approached the window. He frowned, greeting Romashov indifferently.

"Let's go, Shurochka," he said. "God only knows what's going on. You're both mad, as far as I'm concerned. What if the commander gets wind of it—what good will that do? Then they'll arrest him for sure. Goodbye, Romashov. Stop by sometime."

"Stop by, Yuri Alexevich," Shurochka repeated.

She left the window, but returned quickly after and said in a quick whisper:

"Listen, Rommy: really, don't forget us. I have only one person I can be myself around—that's you. Do you understand? Only, don't you dare make those sheeps' eyes at me again. Because then I won't want to see you. Please, Rommy, don't even think of it. You're barely even a man."

VII

The regimental adjutant, one Captain Fedorovsky, came to see Romashov at three thirty. He was a tall and *imposing* young man, as the regimental wives put it, with cold eyes and a mustache that drooped down practically to his shoulders, like a long cord. He had excellent manners, but was strictly formal with the young officers, whom he kept at arm's length due to the high opinion he held of his own office. The company commanders constantly sought his company.

Upon entering the room, he cast his narrowed eyes over Romashov's pitiful decor. The sub-lieutenant, who was lying on his bed, quickly jumped up and, blushing, began hurriedly buttoning up his jacket.

"I've got a summons for you from the regimental commander," Fedorovsky said dryly. "Do get dressed and come with me."

"My apologies . . . I'll be quick . . . Should I wear my uniform as usual? I'm sorry, I'm in my house clothes at the moment."

"Don't be embarrassed. A frock coat will be acceptable. May I sit?"

"Oh, excuse me. Please do. Would you like some tea?" Romashov said.

"No, thank you. If you could pick up the pace a little, please."

He sat down at the desk without removing his coat or gloves; meanwhile, Romashov got dressed, his mind whirling as he fumbled confusedly over his shirt, which was not particularly clean. Meanwhile, Fedorovsky sat without moving, his straight back and his face made of stone, as he rested his hands on the hilt of his sword.

"You don't have any idea why they summoned me, do you?"

The adjutant shrugged.

"A strange question. How would I know that? You, no doubt, have a much better idea about it than I do . . . Ready? I suggest that you put your sword belt under your shoulder strap, and not the other way around. You know how much the regimental commander hates that. There we are . . . all right, come along."

A carriage stood at the gate, harnessed to a pair of strapping regimental horses. The officers got in and set off. Romashov tried politely to keep to his side of the seat, so as not to cramp the adjutant; his efforts, however, went apparently unnoticed. They ran into Vetkin along the way. He and Fedorovsky exchanged formalities; but as soon as the adjutant's back was turned he made a quick gesture at Romashov, as if to say: "You're in for it now, aren't you, my friend?" They passed other officers. Some of these looked at Romashov curiously, others with surprise, and a few with barely concealed grins; he shrunk involuntarily under their stares.

Colonel Shulgovich did not receive Romashov immediately: he had someone else in his office. They were made to wait in a half-lit entrance hall, which smelled of apples, camphor, freshly lacquered furniture, and some other, more peculiar, though not entirely unpleasant scent, such as might be emitted by the clothes and possessions of a wealthy and fastidious German family. As he waited in the entrance hall, Romashov glanced at himself a few times in the cheval glass that was hanging on the wall, enclosed in a frame made of bright ash; every time he did this his face appeared offensively pale, ugly, and somehow unnatural to him; his coat shabby; his sash too baggy.

At first, only the deep monotonous sound of the commander's low bass emanated from inside the office. The words were unintelligible, but one could guess from their angry boom-ing intonations that the colonel was balling someone out with persistent and unwavering rage. This went on for five minutes, after which point Shuglovich suddenly became quiet. A trem-bling, pleading voice could be heard, followed by a brief pause; then Romashov heard (distinctly and to the last syllable) the following words, pronounced with a terrible spirit of arrogance, indignation and contempt:

"What are you trying to pull here? Children? A woman? I don't give a damn about your children! Before you had them you should have thought for a second about how you were going to take care of them. What? Aha, now it's 'I'm to blame, Colonel sir. Colonel sir, you haven't done anything.' You understand, Captain, of course, that if Colonel sir weren't court-marshalling you, then he'd be the one committing the offense? Wha-a-at? Shut your trap! It's not a mistake: it's a crime. You don't belong in this regiment—you belong in another place, you know where. What's that?"

The timid, pleading voice trembled again, so pitifully that it seemed as if it were barely human. "My God, what's going on here?" thought Romashov, who had stopped in front of the mir-ror, and was now staring straight ahead at his pale face without seeing it, feeling how swiftly and painfully his racing heart was wearing itself out. "What a terror! . . . My God . . ."

The mournful voice kept on going for quite some time. When it had said its piece, the commander's deep bass began rolling again, though now more quietly and pallatively, as if Shuglovich had already succeeded in disgorging his rage and sat-isfying his thirst for power through the humiliation of another person.

He began speaking again in the same curt manner.

"Very good. The last time. But un-der-stand, this is the last time. Do you hear me? Cut this into your red, drunken nose. If it reaches my ears that you've been seen carousing again . . . What's that? All right, all right, I know what your promises are worth. Get your regiment ready for my inspection. Not your regiment—your brothel! I'm going to come see for myself in a week . . . So, here's what I suggest: before you do anything else, return the soldiers' money and the regimental funds. Do you hear me? Do it tomorrow. What? Why should I care about that . . . You can pull it out of your nose, for all I care, Captain . . . Goodbye . . ."

Whoever was inside slipped hesitatingly toward the office door, on tiptoes, his boots scraping. But the commander's voice, which had suddenly grown so harsh that it was obvious now that it was exaggerated, stopped him.

"Stop, come here, you devil . . . Running back to your Jewish moneylender, I daresay? Huh? To write a promissary note? You stupid, stupid, stupid fool . . . But then again, you can't help it, you've got a devil in your liver. One, two . . . One, two, three, four . . . Three hundred. I can't give you any more. Pay me back when you can. Good Lord, what filth you're dabbling in, Captain!" The colonel began to yell, raising his voice to the top of the scale. "Don't you dare do it again—ever! It's low! March, march, march! To the devil, to the devil. Well, give him my compliments!"

The diminutive Captain Svetlovidov exited into the hall; he was red all over, his nose was dripping and his temple beaded; he looked humiliated. His right hand, which was in his pocket, rustled the new bills spasmodically. Catching sight of Romashov, he shifted uneasily from foot to foot, laughed with affected gaiety, and thrust his warm, damp, shivering palm into the sub-lieutenant's hand. His strained and confused eyes ran over Romashov's face, as if trying to decide for themselves: had he heard, or not?

"Fierce as a tiger!" he whispered, nodding toward the office with a mixture of embarrassment and familiarity. "But it's nothing!" Svetlovidov crossed himself twice quickly. "Nothing at all. Good luck, gentlemen, good luck, gentlemen!"

"Bon-da-ren-ko!" the regimental commander shouted from behind the wall. The sound of his huge voice immediately filled every nook and cranny of the house and, shaking, so it seemed, the hallway's thin partitions. He never used a bell to ask for anything, preferring to rely instead on his remarkable voice. "Bondarenko! Who else have we got? Send him in."

"What a lion!" Svetlovidov whispered with a crooked smile. "Goodbye, lieutenant. Enjoy your steam bath."

The orderly darted out from between the doors. He was a typical commander's orderly, with a good-looking and impudent face, oily hair parted to one side, and white cotton gloves. He spoke in a voice that was respectful, but at the same time cheeky; he even screwed his eyes up slightly when he looked at the sub-lieutenant:

"His excellency will see you now."

He opened the office door, stood to one side, and then stood aside. Romashov went in.

Colonel Shulgovich was sitting at his desk, in the corner to the left of the entrance. He was wearing a gray jacket, beneath which flashes of brilliant white could be seen. His meaty red hands lay on the arms of his wooden armchair. His large, ancient face, with its head of bristly gray hair, and gray, wedge-shaped beard was cold and severe. His colorless bright eyes stared aggressively straight ahead. At the sub-lieutenant's bow he gave a sharp nod. Romashov noticed suddenly that there was a silver earring in his ear, in the shape of a full moon with a cross on it. "I hadn't seen that before," he thought.

"It's no good, sir," the commander began in the growling bass that seemed to emerge from the depths of his stomach. He paused for a long time. "It is shameful, sir!" he continued, raising his voice. "You've been in the service for barely a minute, and all of a sudden you're wagging your tail. I have many things to be upset with you about. And what is this latest example all about, if you'll pardon my asking? His regimental commander tells him off, and he, the damned ensign allows himself to spout off some sort of nonsense. It's an outrage!" the colonel shouted this so loudly that Romashov flinched. "It's unthinkble! Depravity!"

Romashov stared gloomily to one side. It seemed to him that no power in the world could have compelled him to move his eyes and look at the colonel's face. "Where has my I gone?" he heard something say, suddenly, in his head. "All you can do is stand quietly at attention."

"It's come to my attention—I'm not going to say how, exactly, but I know it for a fact—that you've been drinking. That's despicable. A young man, a greenhorn, barely out of the academy, and here he is drinking with his fellows like the oldest hand in the regiment. Believe me, my boy, I know everything; you can't hide any of it from me. I know many things you can't even guess at. If you want to go down that slippery slope, that's your business. But I'm going to tell you for the last time: think about what I'm saying to you. This is the way it always happens, my friend: first one little glass, then another, and after that, you see, you end up in a ditch. Get it into your skull. More could happen to you than just that, you know: we're patient, but even an angel's patience can break . . . Look, don't make it come to that. You're only one man, but the officers you run with form a family. One can always grab a troublemaker by his tail, and toss him from the company . . . you see what I'm saying?"

"Here I am standing still. I'm keeping quiet," Romashov thought drearily, as he stared without turning his head at the earring in the colonel's ear. "But what I really need to say is that I don't care a fig for his 'family' and am ready this very minute to throw myself out, to resign. Do I dare say it?"

Romashov's heart skipped a beat and then resumed its racing; he swallowed his saliva with a weak movement of his lips. But he continued to stand there without moving.

"As for your behavior as a whole . . ." Suglovich continued severely. "To take one example, you hadn't even been in the regiment for a year when you requested a leave. You mentioned as a reason something about your mother's poor health, and even presented some kind of letter from her. Now, I would never dare, you understand—I would *never* dare—to doubt one of my officers. As soon as you said the word 'mother,' it was your mother as far as I'm concerned. But you know, when something like this happens . . ."

For a long time now Romashov had been conscious of the trembling (scarcely perceptible at first, but stronger and stronger as the conversation went on) of his right knee. Finally this involuntary nervous movement became so overt that it caused his entire body to shake. This was very awkward and very unpleasant, and Romashov had at first been humiliated by the thought that Shuglovich must surely be taking this trembling as a sign of fear. But when the colonel began talking about his mother, his blood suddenly began to heat up; a powerful stream of it rushed to his head, and the shaking stopped, momentarily. For the first time, he raised his eyes and stared point-blank at the bridge of Shuglovich's nose, with a hard, hateful, and (he could sense that his face betrayed this as well) impertinent expression. Immediately, it was as if the wall that normally stood between the lowly officer and the terrifying commander had been spanned by a gigantic bridge. The whole room seemed to darken, as if the curtains had been drawn. The commander's thick voice grew so deep that it became practically inaudible. A span of monstrous darkness and silence opened beneath them—a space without ideas, without will, without all those interior impressions, almost without consciousness, other than the single conviction that now, this very minute, something absurd, unforgivable, and awful was happening. A strange, almost alien voice from somewhere outside of Romashov whispered in his ear: "Now, I am going to hit him." His eyes slid slowly across the large, old, oily cheek, to the silver earring in its ear with the cross and half moon.

Then he saw, as if in a dream and without yet understanding it completely, that glints of surprise, horror, alarm, and pity were all flashing by turns through Shuglovich's eyes. A crazy, unshakable desire took hold of Romashov with a menacing and elemental force; it receded suddenly, dispersed, and then faded into the distance. Romashov took a deep, strong breath, as if he had just woken up. Everything immediately became simple and ordinary in his eyes. Shuglovich motioned fussily toward a chair and said with unexpectedly artless attentiveness:

"Good heavens . . . How touchy you are . . . Go ahead, sit down, you look posessed! You're all like that, of course. You look at me as if I were an animal. He's ranting and raging, a mole, an old fogey without any sense, with no brain, devil take him. As for me," the deep voice began to flutter with warm, worried tones, "God knows that I love you all as if you were my own children. What—you think I don't suffer for you? That it doesn't hurt? Oh, my boy, my boy, you don't know a thing about it. Granted, I get worked up, I have to catch myself from going overboard—is it really right for such an old man to get so furious? Oh-ho, you are young. But all right, that's done. Give me your hand. It's time for lunch."

Romashov bowed quietly and grasped the large, cold, fragrant hand that had been extended to him. His resentment at having been insulted had passed, but he didn't feel any better. After the weighty and high-minded thoughts of this morning, his current behavior made him feel like a small, pitiful, pale schoolboy, a somewhat unloved, shy, and neglected little fellow, and this discrepancy was shameful to him. Therefore, as he followed the colonel to the table, he thought to himself, using his usual third person: *"Dark thoughts furrowed his forehead."*

Shuglovich had no children. His wife came to the table, a full-bodied, weighty, imposing and taciturn woman, with no neck and many chins. Regardless of its pince-nez and haughty expression, her simple-looking face gave the impression that it had been hastily sculpted out of dough, with a pair of raisins stuck on as eyes. Behind her, the colonel's elderly mother walked with rapid, shuffling steps. She was small and deaf, but still cheerful, venomous, and influential nonetheless. She appraised Romashov unceremoniously over the top's of her glasses and then thrust a dark, tiny, wrinkled hand (it looked like a religious relic) straight at his lips. Then she turned to the colonel and asked him, in a tone of voice that implied they were the only two people in the room:

"Who's this? I don't remember him."

Shuglovich cupped a hand around his mouth like a trumpet and shouted into the old woman's ear:

"Sub-lieutenant Romashov, Mother. An excellent officer . . . one of our up-and-coming front-liners . . . From the corps of cadets . . . Ah yes!" he said suddenly. "You hail from Penza province, don't you, lieutenant?"

"Yes, Colonel sir, from Penza."

"Of course, of course . . . Now I remember. You and I are countrymen—Narovchatsky district, correct?"

"Exactly, sir. Narovchatsky."

"Well, yes . . . How could I have forgotten that? We're from Insarsky ourselves. Mother!" He cupped his hands toward his mother's ear again. "Sub-lieutenant Romashov is from the Penza province, like us! From Narovchatsky! He's a countryman!"

"Ah!" The old woman raised her eyebrows significantly. "Ah yes, yes, yes . . . I think . . . Now I see: you're Sergei Petrovich Shishkin's son, aren't you?"

"No, mother—the sub-lieutenant's last name is Romashov, not Shishkin!"

"Of course, of course . . . That's what I'm saying . . . I didn't know Sergei Petrovich myself . . . though I knew him by reputation. His brother, on the other hand, Peter Petrovich—I saw him often. Our estates were right next to each other. I am very, very pleased to make your acquaintance, young man . . . You've done well for yourself."

"Looks like the old girl's off again," the colonel whispered affectionately. "Have a seat, Sub-lieutenant . . . Lieutenant

Fedorovsky!" he cried through the door. "Finish up in there and come have some vodka!"

The adjutant, who always dined with the commander, as was the case in most regiments, came in quickly. His spurs jingled softly and gently as he approached the majolica coffee table, with its array of hors d'oeuvres, poured himself a vodka, and calmly began eating. Romashov felt envy, and a sort of distant, superficial respect for him.

"How about you?" Shuglovich asked him. "Aren't you going to have a drink?"

"No, thank you. I don't really feel like it," Romashov answered in a hoarse voice, and coughed.

"Ex-ce-lent. That's the way to do it. Keep it up."

The lunch was both delicious and filling. It was clear that the childless colonel and his wife had preserved a single innocent passion: to eat well. A balmy soup made out of young roots was served, a roasted bream with kasha, as well as a wonderful fattened duck from their own flock, which they served with asparagus. Three bottles stood on the table—one of white wine, one of red wine, one of Madera—they'd been opened already, true, and were now plugged up tight with figured silver stoppers, but they were good: of an expensive foreign make. The colonel—whose recent fury seemed to have had an excellent effect on his appetite—ate with such relish that it was pleasant just to watch him. He joked, affably and crudely, the entire time. When the asparagus came he thrust a stiff and blindingly white napkin deep into the collar of his double-breasted jacked, and remarked happily:

"If I were the tsar, I would eat asparagus every day!"

Earlier, however, while the fish was being served, he did not restrain himself and shouted at Romashov in a commanding tone:

"Sub-lieutenant! Put that knife down. Fish and cutlets are eaten exclusively with the fork. To do otherwise is unacceptable! Officers must know how to eat. Every officer might be invited to sit at a refined table. Remember that."

Romashov sat awkwardly through lunch; he felt constrained, he didn't know where to put his hands and so for the most part kept them under the table, plaiting the fringes of the tablecloth into little braids. It had taken him only a year in the service to grow unaccustomed to good family décor: to excellent and comfortable furniture and a well-set table. A single thought tormented him throughout the entire meal: "This is awful, such weakness and cowardice on my part, that I can't, that I don't dare remove myself from this wretched lunch. I'm going to stand up right now, give the usual bow and leave. Then they can think whatever they want. Anyway, he won't bite me. He can't eat my soul, my thoughts, my consciousness. Why don't I leave?" And again, his heart paralyzed with shyness, he paled from inner agitation, annoyed with himself, he knew that he would never do it.

It was evening already when the coffee was brought out. The red, slanting rays of the sun burst through the window, throwing bright, honey-colored spots on the dark wallpaper, the tablecloth, the crystal, the faces of the diners. Everything grew quiet in the melancholy charm of the evening hour.

"When I was still an ensign," Shulgovich said suddenly. "The commander of our brigade was a General Fonarov. An old salt, in uniform since birth, no doubt. I remember, he would go up to the drummers—he loved drums terribly—and say: 'Well, shir, play me shomething shad.' Just like that. This was the general who, whenever guests came to visit him at home, would always retire exactly at eleven o'clock. He would turn to his guests and say, 'Well, shirs, go on, drink, enjoy yourshelvesh. Ash for me, I shleep tonight in Neptunesh embrashe.' 'You mean Morpheus, sir?' we said. 'Shame minerology . . .' he said. So now, sirs," Shuglovich stood, hanging his napkin on the back of the chair, "I am off to sleep in Neptune's embrace. You are free to go."

The officers rose and stood at attention.

"A hideous and ironic smile flashed across his thin lips," Romashov thought: only thought, however, since his face in that minute was pitiful, pale, and unpleasantly deferential.

Romashov headed home again feeling lonely, anguished—lost in some sort of strange, dark, and menacing country. The blue-gray east was burning once again with layers of amber-red dawn, and once again Romashov wondered from afar at the line of the horizon, its houses and fields: the fantastic, magical city, with its graceful, beautiful, happy inhabitants.

The street grew dark quickly. Jewish children ran screeching past him. Somewhere—from the walls of the houses, from the gate, from the wicket fence and the garden—a woman's laugh resounded, continuously and enthusiastically, with the kind of hot, lively, happy tremble that can only be heard in early spring. And beside the soft and pensive melancholy in Romashov's heart there began to grow a strange, confusing recollection and regret for a happiness that had never existed, and about a past spring, which had been even more beautiful than this one, and in his heart there began to grow a vague and sweet presentiment of coming love stirred . . .

When he got home Gainan was in his darkened storeroom with the bust of Pushkin. The great poet was smeared all over with grease, and the lamp that was burning in front of him threw glossy spots on his nose, plump lips, and sinewy neck. Gainan himself, sitting Turkish-style on the three boards that he had exchanged for his bed, swayed back and forth muttering something in a monotonous and leisurely singsong.

"Gainan!" Romashov called to him.

The orderly shuddered and, leaping from the bed, stretched. His face displayed an expression of fear and confusion.

"Allah?" Romashov inquired kindly.

The Cheremis's tiny, earless face broke into a wide smile. The lamplight glistened over his extraordinarily white teeth.

"Allah, sir!"

"All right, all right . . . Sit down, sit down now." Romashov gave the orderly a friendly pat on the shoulder. "No matter, Gainan, you have Allah, I have Allah. One Allah, my friend, for every man."

"Good old Gainan," the sub-lieutenant thought, as he went into his room. "And I won't even shake his hand. It's true, I can't—I don't dare. Devil take it! From this day forward, I must dress and undress myself. Only a pig lets someone do that for him."

That night, instead of going out, he opened his desk drawer and removed a fat notebook, the pages of which were overflowing with tiny erratic handwriting, and proceeded to write deep into the night. It was the third story that Romashov had ever written, entitled "The Fatal First Finale." The sub-lieutenant himself was ashamed of his literary attempts and would have never admitted them to anyone in the world.

VIII

The construction of the regimental barracks, which was taking place near the railway tracks on the outskirts of town, in a spot known as the Pasture, had only barely begun. Until it was completed, the entire regiment and all of its offices were being housed in private residences. The officers' club was located in a small, single-story building, each of whose rooms was devoted to a different activity. On the long side, which ran parallel to the street, there was a dancing hall and living room, and on the short side, which extended into a dark and dirty alley, the dining room and the kitchen were located, not to mention various "numbered" rooms for officers who were passing through. The house's two halves were connected by a sort of narrow, twisting, crooked corridor; each crook revealed a different door, and because of this it was possible to visit, one after the other, a buffet, a billiard room, a cloakroom, and a ladies' powder room. All of these rooms, save the dining room, were empty most of the time; no one ever aired them out, and because of this they were filled with a greasy, sour, and unlived-in air, as well as the peculiar smell of the old heavily upholstered furniture.

Romashov arrived at the club at nine o'clock. Five or six of the single officers were already there, but the regimental wives had not yet shown up. A strange and endless competition existed among these women: a battle of good form, which dictated that it was shabby to be among the first to arrive at a ball. The musicians had already taken their places in the glass gallery, which connected to the hall by way of a glass double door. Triple-armed candelabra hung in the hall between the windows, and a chandelier with trembling crystals dangled from the ceiling. The bright light made the large room, with its unadorned walls covered in white wallpaper, its stacked Viennese chairs, and its tulle window curtains, seem especially empty.

In the billiard room, two battalion adjutants, lieutenants Bek-Agamatov and Olizar (whom everyone in the regiment called Count Olizar) were playing five-ball for beer. Olizar—tall and thin, with a head full of slicked-back, heavily pomaded hair: a young old man, with a plain but wrinkled and foppish face—kept dropping various billiard-related witticisms. Bek-Agamatov was losing and angry. Captain Leshenko, a melancholy man of forty-five years, whose every glance suggested anguish, was watching their game from his seat on the windowsill. His entire body seemed to be drooping under the weight of utter hopelessness: a long, meaty, flabby red nose dangled from the top of his face like a pepper pod; two thin brown strings of mustache drooped down his chin; his eyebrows descended from the bridge of his nose to his temples, giving his eyes a sort of eternal whimper; even the old frock coat he carried around hung on his sloping shoulders and hollow chest as if he were a coat rack. Leshenko never drank, never played cards or even smoked. But it gave him a strange pleasure (which no one could figure out) to hang around in the card or billiard rooms, somewhere behind the action, or in the dining room when things got especially exciting. He would sit there for hours, silent and downcast, without saying a single word. Everyone in the regiment had grown accustomed to this, to the point that now no game or drinking bout seemed to be fully under way unless the silent Leshenko was present.

After greeting the three officers, Romashov sat next to Leshenko, who scooted courteously over, sighed, and looked at the young officer with his sad and doggedly devoted eyes.

"How is Maria Victorovna doing these days?" Romashov asked in a familiar and deliberately loud voice, as one might speak to someone who was deaf or slow to understand (this was how everyone in the regiment spoke to Leshenko—even ensigns).

"Thank you for asking, my friend," Leshenko answered with a heavy sigh. "Her nerves are acting up as usual . . . She hasn't been having a very good time."

"And why isn't she here? Or maybe Maria Victorovna isn't coming out tonight?"

"No, no—she'll be here. She's coming, my friend. It's only that, you see, there wasn't a place for me in the carriage. She and Raisa Alexandrovna rented an equipage together. They told me: 'Your boots are dirty, you'll ruin our dresses.'"

"One down the middle! A perfect cut. Take your balls out of your pockets, Bek!" Olizar shouted.

"First get them in, then I'll take them out," Bek-Agamatov retorted.

Leshenko took the little brown ends of his mustache into his mouth and began chewing at them attentively.

"My dear Yuri Alexevich, I have a favor to ask you," he said in a halting and pleading tone. "You're master of ceremonies tonight, right?"

"Yes. Devil take them. They made me master of ceremonies. I prostrated myself in front of the adjutant—I wanted to call in sick, even. But you know what he said? 'All right, then: show me a doctor's report.'"

Leshenko continued ingratiatingly. "Here's my request, my friend: I wonder if you could arrange it so that she doesn't spend too much time sitting on the sidelines. I would consider it a personal favor."

"Maria Victorovna, you mean?"

"I do. Of course I do."

"Yellow ball, corner pocket," Bek-Agamatov announced. "Clean and simple—I might as well be ordering something at the pharmacy."

It was unpleasant for him to play because of his height, and he had to stretch himself out on his stomach in order to reach across the billiard table. His face was red from the effort of this, and a pair of veins like a V had swollen on his forehead.

"*Jamais!*" Olizar mocked confidently. "Not even I could pull that off."

Bek-Agamatov's cue nicked the ball with a dry crack, but it didn't move.

"A whiff!" Olizar shouted happily. He began dancing a can-can around the billiard table. "Caught you sleeping, my love."

Bek-Agamatov banged the heavy end of his cue against the floor.

"How dare you speak while I'm shooting!" he cried, his black eyes flashing. "I'm done here."

"Don't throw stones, my dove, your blood's boiling, it's the milliner in his corner all over again! . . ."

One of the orderlies whose job it was to help the women in the entrance hall take their coats off ran up to Romashov.

"A woman is asking for you in the hall, sir."

Three women, who had just arrived, were already walking back and forth in the entrance hall. All of them were elderly. The oldest, Anna Ivanovna Migunova, who was the wife of the chief supply officer, turned to Romashov and addressed him in a stern tone, drawing her words out affectedly as she nodded with worldly gravity.

"Sub-lieutenant Romashov, if you would, please tell them to play something for us."

"Yes, ma'am." Romashov bowed and went over to the musicians' window. "Zisserman!" he shouted at the old conductor. "Go ahead and play something already!"

The opening measure of the overture from the "Long Live the Tsar" crashed through the open windows. The candle flames trembled back and forth in time to the music.

Little by little, the women began to arrive. A year earlier Romashov had loved these minutes before the ball began, when, in his capacity as master of ceremonies, he greeted the women as they passed through the entrance hall. How secretive and charming they had seemed to him, as, excited by the lights, music, and the promise of dancing, they cast off their bonnets, boas and fur coats in a whirl of happy activity. Along with their laughter and chatter they brought a smell of frost, perfume, powder, and kid gloves into the narrow entry hall: the elusive, deeply moving odor of a beautiful and well-dressed woman before a ball. How sparkling and love-drunk their eyes looked in the mirror, as they briskly adjusted their hair! What music their rustling skirts made! How wonderful it felt to touch their small hands, their scarves, their fans! . . .

By now, however, this delight had vanished, and Romashov knew it wasn't coming back. These days he understood, with no small amount of shame, that much of that charm had been lifted from bad French novels, in which heroes with names like Gustav and Arman were invariably making the same pass through the vestibules of this or that Russian embassy ball. Likewise he knew that, year after year, if they thought the night was going to be particularly splendid, the women of the regiment hauled out the same "chic" dress, and scrubbed their gloves with benzene, in a pitiful attempt to gussy it up. Their shared passion for scarves, oversized fake jewelry, feathers, and too many ribbons seemed funny and pretentious to him: evidence of a kind of ragged, tasteless, homegrown luxuriousness. They put on greasy-looking ceruse and blush, but the effect was clumsy and crudely naïve: their faces were shadowed an ominous blue color. But the most disgusting thing of all for Romashov was the fact that he, like everyone else in the regiment, was privy to the secret history of each dress and ball, down to the last coquettish remark. He knew what all these efforts were hiding: the pitiful poverty, the pains, artfulness, scandals, the reciprocated hatred, the slavish provincial game of good manners, and, finally, the boring, insipid liasons . . .

Captain Talman and his wife came in. Both were tall and plump; she was gentle and somewhat flabby-looking, with blonde hair, while he had a sly and dark-complexioned face, a constant cough, and a hoarse voice. Before Talman had even opened his mouth, Romashov knew that he was going to utter his stock phrase; he did, of course, after winking one of his Gypsy eyes:

"So, Sub-lieutenant, is the poker table all sewed up yet?"

"Not yet. Everyone's in the dining room."

"Not yet? You know, Sonyichka, I think I'm going to . . . make my way to the dining room. I want to run through the latest Invalid. You, my dear Romashov—put her out to pasture . . . see if you can arrange a quadrille for her somehow."

After this the Likachevich girls fluttered into the entry hall. They were a happy brood, with their guffaws and mispronunciations, led by their mother: a tiny, lively woman, who had been dancing and giving birth to children for the majority of her forty years without showing any signs of fatigue—the latter "between the second and third quadrille," as Archakovsky, the regiment wit, liked to put it.

The girls, who were continually mixing up their R's and W's, fell on Romashov with a burst of smiles and interruptions:

"Weally, Wommy, why haven't you come to visit us?"

"Bad, bad, bad Womashov!"

"Eviw eviw eviw!"

"Bad bad bad!"

"You weally must dance the fiwst quwadwille with me."

"Mesdames! . . . Mesdames!" Romashov said, playing the gentleman despite himself, as he bowed to all sides.

At that moment he chanced to look over at the front door and see, through its window, the thin face and full lips of Raisa Alexandra Peterson, whose hat looked like a box that she had tied to her head with a white scarf. Romashov darted toward the living room in a childish rush. But no matter how short his glimpse had been, or how much the sub-lieutenant tried to convince himself that Raisa hadn't noticed him, he still felt alarmed—for he had seen something new and troubling in the tiny eyes of his onetime beloved: something sharp, malicious, and menacing.

He went into the dining room. Many people had already gathered there; almost every place at the long, oilcloth-covered table had been taken. A blue tobacco cloud swayed in the air above them. The smell of cooking oil was coming from the kitchen. Two or three groups of officers had already begun to eat and drink. Someone was reading a newspaper. The thick and motley sound of voices mingled with the stomping of feet, the cracking of billiard balls and banging of the kitchen doors. A cold ankle-high draft was drifting in from the hall.

Romashov looked around for Lieutenant Bobetinsky. Bobetinsky was standing near the table, his hands thrust in his pants pockets, rocking back and forth from his heels to his toes and squinting through his cigarette smoke. Romashov touched his sleeve.

"What?" he said, turning his head and removing one hand from its pocket without unscrewing his eyes. He gave Romashov a refined look and then tweaked his long red mustache, squinting into the sub-lieutenant's eyes as he raised his elbow. "Ah! It's you? *Neyz to zee you . . .*"

He always spoke this way, imitating, by his stilted and mannered tone (or so he thought), the young "Golden Guards." He had a high opinion of his abilities; he considered himself quite knowledgeable on the topics of horses and women, an excellent dancer who was moreover cultured and elegant, though already, despite his twenty-four years, a worldly and disillusioned individual. Because of this he held his shoulders back theatrically, imitated the French poorly, dallied through marches and made tired, careless gestures while speaking.

"Peter Fadeyevich, my friend, I beg you: relieve me," Romashov asked.

"Mais, mon ami!" Bobetinsky threw his shoulders back and raised his eyebrows, googling his eyes as if he had no idea what

Romashov was talking about. "But, my friend," he translated. "Whatever for? *Pourqoui?* Really, you're . . . How does one put it? . . . You're shoocking me! . . ."

"Please, old boy, I'm begging you . . ."

"Stop it . . . First of all, a little less fa-mi-liar, if you please. What is this 'old boy,' *et cetera?*"

"But I beg you, Peter Fadevich . . . My head hurts . . . My throat too . . . I'm positively disabled."

Romashov pleaded persuasively and for some time with his friend. Eventually he even resorted to flattery. For truly, no one in the regiment could dance as beautifully, and with such facility, as Peter Fadeyevich, and anyway, it had been a woman who asked . . .

"A woman?" Bobetinsky assumed a distracted and melancholy expression. "A woman? My friend, in my time . . ." He gave Romashov a disappointed and bitterly world-weary smile. "What is a woman to me? Ha-ha . . . *Une enigma!* But all right, I suppose I might . . . I suppose."

Suddenly he added, in the same disappointed voice:

"*Mon cher ami*, you don't happen to have on you . . . How to put it . . . Three rubles?"

"If only!" Romashov sighed.

"How about one ruble?"

"Mmm!"

"*Disagreable* . . . Never mind. In any case let's have a drink of vodka together."

"Unfortunately, I haven't got any credit, Peter Fadeyevich."

"Really? *Pauvre enfant!* . . . Nevertheless." Bobetinsky made a sharp and careless gesture of generosity. "I will treat you myself."

Meanwhile, the conversation in the dining room had grown louder, and at the same time more interesting for everybody. They were talking about officers' duels: a topic about which opinions varied.

The most influential of these opinions belonged to Lieutenant Archakovsky, who was a somewhat shady character—perhaps even a cardshark. It was whispered that during his time in the reserves, before he joined the regiment, he had been the stationmaster of a postal outpost, and had been tried for kicking a coachman so hard with his heel that he died.

"It's easy enough for those louts and sons of bitches in the Guards to duel," Archakovsky said crudely, "but for us . . . Well, sure, I'm single . . . But let's assume that Vasily Vasiliyevich Lipskin and I went out for a few beers, and that, after a few cold ones, I knocked him around a little bit. What could we do? If he didn't want to shoot me he'd have to leave the regiment—but in that case I ask you, what would his children eat? Then again, if he decided to challenge me to a duel, I'd put a bullet in his stomach, and there again, his children starve . . . It's all rubbish."

"Hold on a second . . . Ahem . . . Just wait a minute," interrupted Lekh, a drunken old sub-lieutenant who was holding a glass in one hand, while gesturing weakly in the air in front of him with the other. "You understand what the words 'for the honor of the uniform' mean, don't you? . . . Ahem, brother, there's the rub . . . Honor . . . You know, I remember once when I was still in the Temruski regiment—eighteen hundred and sixty two, that must have been . . ."

"No one wants to hear about your Temruski regiment," Archakovsky said sharply. "Tell us another one about what life was like under King Herod."

"Ahem, brother . . . How rude! You're just a stripling, while I, I'm . . . ahem . . . As I was saying, once in the Temruski regiment . . ."

"Only blood can wash away a stain on one's honor," Lieutenant Bobetinsky interjected in a pompous tone, throwing his shoulders back like a rooster.

"We had an ensign at the time, Soluha was his name," Lekh said, persevering.

Captain Osadchin, a commander of the first company, detached himself from the buffet table and approached the group.

"I've been listening to your conversation about dueling. Very interesting," he said, in a deep, roaring bass that seemed to extinguish all the other voices. "Good evening, Sub-lieutenant. Good evening, everyone."

"Ah, the Colossus of Rhodes," Lekh fawned. "Sit down over here, ahem. A living monument! Have a vodka with me?"

"Absolutely," Osadchin answered in his deep bass.

This officer always produced a strange and irritating impression on Romashov, arousing in him a feeling somewhere between terror and curiosity. Like Lieutenant Shuglovich, Osadchin was famous, not just in the regiment, but throughout the division, for the particular quality of his voice—to say nothing of his gigantic body and incredible physical strength. His remarkable knowledge of military protocol was also well known. He was transferred periodically from unit to unit; in less than half a year he could transform the most undisciplined, run-down organization into something possessing the efficiency and utility of a gigantic machine, and instilled with an unhuman fear of its commanding officer. His fascination and influence were even less understood by his peers given the fact that he not only never fought, but never even got into arguments, except in the rarest and most exceptional circumstances. Romashov was always struck by the way that his handsome and gloomy face, whose strange paleness was emphasized even more distinctly by his black, almost bluish hair, seemed to possess a kind of intense, self-possessed, and cruel quality: something that seemed less characteristic of a human being than of a huge and powerful beast. Frequently, while surreptitiously observing him from a distance, Romashov imagined what a man like that must look like when enraged; thinking about it he paled in terror and wrung his chilly palms. So now he observed, as if in a trance, how this self-assured, strong man calmly accepted the chair next to the wall that had been so courteously offered him.

Osadchin downed a vodka, cracked a radish with a crunch, and asked disinterestedly:

"So, what have we decided so far?"

"Well, brother, I'll tell you . . . It happened like this, when I was in the Temyurski regiment. Lieutenant von Zoon—the soldiers called him 'Zoon the Loon'—one day he was at a party like this one . . ."

But here he was interrupted by Lipsky, a forty-year-old staff captain, red-faced and fat, who despite his years loved to play the part of the joker among his fellow officers, imitating, for some reason, the strange and hysterical tone of a spoiled but still beloved blockhead.

"If I may, Captain? I'll keep my report short. Lieutenant Archakovsky here began by saying that duels are rubbish. 'Bam! Give him one right between the eyes, then you're set.' After him Lieutenant Bobetinsky piped up demanding blood. At about this point, the good sub-lieutenant began trying to relate an anecdote from his previous life; so far, it seems, he has had no success. Just as he was about to begin, in fact, Sub-lieutenant Mihin launched his own personal opinion into the hustle and bustle, but due to the insufficient volume of his voice, and the bashfulness that comes so naturally to him, this opinion went unheard."

Sub-lieutenant Mihin, a small, weak-chested youth with an embarassed, servile, and freckled face, out of which a pair of soft dark eyes stared shyly, almost fearfully, blushed suddenly.

"I only, sirs . . . Sirs, perhaps I'm mistakened," he began to stammer, rubbing his face with embarrassment. "But, in my opinion, that is to say that it seems to me . . . one must look at each situation individually. Sometimes a duel can be pragmatic, that's for certain, something that any of us would be willing to go through. That's for certain. But sometimes, you know, it's . . . perhaps, the greatest honor comes from . . . It's . . . to forgive . . . Still, I don't know, what other kinds of duels there are . . . now . . ."

Archakovsky waved his hand at the young sub-lieutenant dismissively. "Tut tut, Decadent Ivanovich."

"Ahem! If I might be allowed to speak!"

Immediately Osadchin silenced the other voices with his own powerful bellow:

"A duel, my dear sirs, must invariably have the gravest consequences—otherwise it is an absurdity! It's a pitiful foolishness, a compromise, a condescention, a comedy. Single shots traded at fifty paces! I will say this to you now: an arrangement like that leads only to the sort of Frenchified foolishness that we read about in the newspapers. The duelists arrive and take their shots; when it's all over they communicate the particulars to the dailies: 'Fortunately, the duel ended favorably. The rivals exchanged shots without wounding one another, demonstrating in this way their outstanding bravery. Later, over breakfast, the onetime enemies decided to exchange friendly handshakes instead.' This sort of duel, my friends, is rubbish indeed. Introducing it into our society won't improve anything."

A number of voices immediately rose up to answer him. Lekh, who had attempted several times while Osadchin was talking to finish his speech, began again: "As I, ahem, was saying, my friends . . . Here we are, listen up, you young bucks." But no one was listening. He looked at each officer in turn, searching for a sympathetic glance; but they were excited by their argument and so avoided his eyes, as he bobbed his heavy head mournfully. Finally his gaze found Romashov's. The young officer knew from his own experience how hard it was to suffer through those moments when words that have been repeated over and over again seemed to hang in the air, compelling you, somehow, to reiterate them with hopeless persistence. Therefore he did not avoid the sub-lieutenant, who now pulled him happily to the table by the sleeve.

"At least you'll hear me out, ensign," Lekh said sadly. "Here, sit down, let's have a vodka together . . . They're loafers, the lot of them." Lekh shook his fist impotently at the arguing officers. "Gab, gab, gab, but they don't have any experience. Let me tell you what happened to us one time . . ."

With a glass in one hand, gesturing with the other like a choir conductor, his crestfallen head dangling, Lekh began to tell one of the countless tales, with which he was stuffed like a sausage with sausage meat, but which he could never manage to finish due to their constant digressions, asides, comparisons, and riddlings. His current story boiled down to one officer challenging another—this, of course, was a tremendously long time ago—to an American-style duel, which would be decided based on whether one of them pulled an even- or odd-numbered bill out of his pocket. One of the officers—it was difficult to remember which one it was, Zoon the Loon or Soluha—resorted to cheating: "So you see, ahem, he glued two bills together, so that there was an even number on one side, and on the other, an odd one. So then he pulls the bills out—here we go . . . And he says . . ."

The sub-lieutenant was, however, unable as usual to finish his story, this time because Raisa Alexandrovna Peterson was making her way playfully through the buffet. Standing at the doorway of the dining room, but without entering (since to do so would have been inappropriate), she called out in a happy and capricious voice, the way a woman calls when she is spoiled but beloved by everyone:

"Gentlemen! What's this? The women are waiting, and you sit here entertaining yourselves! We want to dance!"

Two or three young officers stood and made for the hall; others continued to sit and smoke and talk, not paying the coquette any attention; old Lekh, however, after crossing his arms over his chest in a way that caused some of the vodka to spill from his glass, approached her with short, wavering, steps, and cried out with drunken enthusiasm:

"Goddess! And how do the authorities allow shuch a beauty to ekshisht? If I might kiss your hand!"

"Yuri Alexevich." Miss Peterson giggled. "Aren't you our master of ceremonies tonight? A fine job you're doing, too!"

"*Mille pardonnes, madame. C'est ma faut!* . . . It's my fault," shouted Bobetinsky, as he flew up to her. He shuffled his feet as he approached and then squatted down, keeping his torso perfectly poised; he fluttered his lowered hands as if preparing to launch into some sort of ballet step. "Your hand. *Votre main, madame.* To the hall, gentlemen—the hall!"

He took Miss Peterson by the hand and threw his head back proudly. Once they were in the other room he raised his voice into a fashionable (or so he imagined) lilt, as he gestured to the orchestra:

"Missieurs, invite your partners to waltz! A waltz—musicians!"

"Excuse me, sub-lieutenant, but my duties are calling me," Romashov said.

"All right, brother," Lekh said, with a disappointed nod. "I see that you're from the same tree as the rest of them. How about the great field marshall . . . ahem, of Moltik, the military strategist who took the vow of silence?"

"If you'll just excuse me, sir . . ."

"Now don't fidget . . . A short tale, really . . . When the great strategist dined with his officers . . . ahem . . . he put before him on the table a purse, full, my brother, of gold. He had decided beforehand to give this purse to whichever officer uttered even a single intelligent word over the course of the evening. But when the old man died—after having lived one hundred and ninety years on this earth—the entire purse remained uncollected. Well? You've cracked it, eh? Well, okay, then, go ahead, my brother. Go on, go, little sparrow . . . Hop about as you wish . . ."

IX

Out in the hall, which was shaking under the enormous noise of the waltz, two couples were already dancing. Bobetinsky, his elbows spread out like a pair of wings, minced rapidly around the taller figure of Mrs. Talman, who danced with the impressive serenity of a stone statue. The strapping, long-haired Archakovsky orbited one of the small, pink Likachev girls, his body bent lightly above hers as he stared at the part in her hair, shifting laconically and carelessly from foot to foot without executing any real steps, the way one would dance with a child. Fifteen other women sat along the wall trying to make it look as if they were completely untroubled by their solitude. As was always the case at the regimental parties, there seemed to be four times as many women present as there were men. The beginning of the evening, at least, promised to be a bore.

Raisa Peterson, who had opened the ball (always a matter of special pride among the women), took her first dance with the thin, well-built Olizar. He held her hand as if he were pinning it to his left hip; she leaned her chin languidly on his shoulder, on top of her other hand, with her head turned back toward the hall, in a mannered and unnatural position. After they finished their turn, she puposefully sat down close to Romashov, who was standing near the door of the ladies' powder room. She fanned herself quickly and, glancing at Olizar, who was leaning toward her, said in a singsong drawl:

"No, tell me, Count, why am I always so hot? I beg you—tell me! . . ."

Olizar executed a half bow, jingled his spurs, and pinched first one and then the other end of his mustache.

"My dear, not even Martin Zadek could tell you that."

As Olizar's eyes began to settle on her flat décolleté, she shot to her feet and took an unnaturally deep breath.

"Ah, why is my temperature always rising!" Raisa Alexandrovna kept on, hinting by her smile that her words contained some sort of special, indecent meaning. "I must have a firey temperament! . . ."

Olizar let out a brief and indistinct neigh.

Romashov stood in annoyance, glancing sideays at Ms. Peterson as he thought: "How disgusting she is!" The memory of his previous physical intimacy with that woman made him feel suddenly as if he hadn't washed or put on a fresh pair of undergarments in weeks.

"Yes, yes, yes, don't laugh at me, Count. You have no idea—my mother was Greek!"

"She speaks like an idiot," Romashov thought. "Strange, that I hadn't realized it until now. She sounds as if she had a cold or was congested. *'By budder wuz Geek.'* "

At that point Ms. Peterson turned to Romashov and stared at him provocatively with screwed-up eyes.

"His expression had become impenetrable, like a mask," Romashov thought to himself, as was his wont.

"Hello, Yuri Alexandrovich! Why haven't you come to greet me?" Raisa Alexandrovna sang.

Romashov walked up to her. Her malicious pupils had become unusually small and sharp.

She squeezed his hand tightly.

"I've kept the third quadrille for you, as you asked. I hope you didn't forget?"

Romashov bowed.

"How awkward you are," Ms. Peterson said, making a face. "You're supposed to say: *Enchanté, madame*" ("Adshadte, badab," Romashov heard.) "Isn't he a cad, count?"

"Well, of course I remembered," Romashov muttered hesitantly. "The honor is all mine."

Bobetinsky had done little to keep the party's spirits up. He directed everyone with a disappointed and exhaustedly patronizing look, as if performing a duty that was terribly important to other people, but somehow excrutiating for him. At the start of the third quadrille, however, he grew more animated. Flying into the hall with quick, fluid steps, as if on skates, he began shouting in an especially loud voice:

"Le quadrille! Cavallieri, engage vos dammes!"

Romashov and Raisa Alexandrovna stood next to one another near the musicians' window. There was Mihin and Leshenko's wife, who barely reached her partner's shoulder. A number of dancers had been added for the third quadrille, so that now the pairs were spread out over both the length and breadth of the hall. Each person danced in turn, and so every measure was played twice.

"I have to explain myself, I have to end this," Romashov thought, as the deafening din of the drum and the orchestra's brass section roared from the window. "Enough!"

"His face hardened into an expression of unshakable decision."

It was an old tradition for the master of ceremonies to sneak a few special tricks and harmless jokes into the evening's entertainment. During the third quadrille, for example, it had always been considered essential to mix the figures up, and to make a few "accidental" mistakes, which invariably roused the crowd to laughter and guffawing. So, after unexpectedly beginning the quadrille on the second measure, Bobetinsky forced the men to dance solo and then, as if he had only just realized his mistake, reunited them with the women for a *grande ronde*.

"*Madam, avance* . . . Now back, *requilles. Solo, cavallier! Pardon, back, balance avec vos dammes!* Now back again!"

Raisa Alexandrovna continued to speak in a sarcastic tone, panting from anger, but smiling in a way that made it look as if she were uttering the most agreeable pleasantries:

"I will not allow you to treat me this way. Do you hear me? I am not your kept girl. Yes. And civilized people do not act this way. Yes."

"Let's not get angry, Raisa Alexandrovna," Romashov said, gently and firmly.

"Oh, how honorable—you're not worth getting angry at! All I can do is despise you. But I won't allow anyone to laugh at me. Why didn't you answer my letter?"

"But I didn't get any letter from you, I swear."

"Ha! What do you take me for? As if I didn't know where you go . . . But rest assured . . ."

"*Cavallieri, en avance! Ronde de Cavale. Au gauche!* To the left, the left! Yes, the left, gentlemen! Ah, nobody understands a thing! *Plus de la vie, messiuers!*" Bobetinsky tapped his foot in despair as he tried to keep the pairs dancing regularly.

"I know all the intrigues of that woman, that lilliputian," Raisa continued, when Romashov had returned to his place. "All her vain obsession—and for what! The daughter of an embezzling lawyer . . ."

"Please don't speak to me about my friends that way," Romashov said sternly.

At this point a disagreeable scene occurred. Ms. Peterson let fly a series of crude remarks about Shurochka. She completely forgot about her fake smile and, enraged, attempted to shout down the music with her hoarse voice. Romashov blushed, humiliated by his weakness and confusion, the pain of embarrassing Shurochka, and the fact that he could not manage to get a single word in over the deafening sound of the quadrille. Most of all he blushed because already people were beginning to look at them.

"Yes, yes, her father was caught stealing—who's she to look down her nose at me?" Ms. Peterson cried. "You tell me, she is *negliger*ing us. I know a little something about her! I do!"

"Please," Romashov begged.

"The two of you have yet to see my claws—but you will. I'll open that idiot Nikolaev's eyes, the one she's been trying to foist on the academy for three years. But how's he supposed to get in, when the fool can't even see what's happening under his very nose . . . ? Still, what an admirer she's managed to attract! . . ."

"Now the mazurka! *Promenade!*" Bobetinsky cried, leaning forward like a soaring archangel as he led them down the length of the hall.

The floor began to shake and sway beneath the heavy tramping, the chandelier crystals shook in time to the mazurka, casting a multicolored fire, and the tulle window curtains swayed rhythmically.

"Why don't we go our separate ways quietly and peacefully?" Romashov asked mildly. This woman filled his heart with disgust, as well as a sort of petty, vile, yet still indomitable cowardice. "You don't love me anymore . . . Let's part as dear friends."

"A-a! You think I'll fall for that? Don't worry, my dear," (she pronounced this "*by dear*") "I'm not the kind of girl you just get rid of. I get rid of men, when I want to. But I cannot praise your cheek enough . . ."

"Let's wrap this up, shall we?" Romashov said impatiently, his voice muffled behind his clenched teeth.

"A five minute *entre-act. Cavallieri, occupe vos damme!*" the master of ceremonies shouted.

"Yes—when *I* want to. You have deceived me wretchedly. I sacrificed everything for you, gave you everything that an honorable woman can give . . . I didn't dare look my husband in the eye—that worthy and excellent man. For you, I forgot my obligations as wife and mother. Oh, why, why didn't I remain faithful to him?"

"Oh, come now!"

Romashov couldn't help but smile. The serialized romances she undertook with new recruits were famous—as, no doubt, all romances which took place between the seventy-five regimental officers and their wives were. Certain expressions that she had used to describe her husband to Romashov's face and in letters, came to his mind—phrases like "my fool," "that awful man," "that blockhead, who torments me," as well as others that were no less damning.

"Ah! You dare keep smiling? Very well!" Raisa flared up. "Let's go!" She remembered herself suddenly and, taking her cavalier by the hand, minced forward, giving her torso a gratifying little shake as she smiled tensely.

When they finished the figure, her face again immediately assumed an angry expression—"like an angry insect," Romashov thought.

"I'll never forgive you for that. Never! Do you hear me? I know why you're so mean, why you desire so basely to flee from me. But it won't work—it won't, it won't, it won't! Instead of telling me honorably and straight out that you don't love me

125

THE DUEL

anymore, you try to deceive me and use me like a kept woman, like a whore . . . but you won't succeed. Ha! . . ."

"All right, then, let's speak truthfully," Romashov said, barely able now to contain his fury. He was growing paler and paler as he clenched his teeth more and more. "You want to hear it? All right, you're right: I don't love you."

"Oh no! And that's supposed to hurt me now?"

"I never loved you. Nor did you love me, by the way. We were both playing a repulsive, false, and dirty game—a sort of ridiculous lovers' farce. I understood you completely, Raisa Alexandrovna. You didn't need kindness, love—not even simple attachment. You're too small and insignificant for that. Because"—and here Romashov remembered Nazanski's words—"because only elevated and refined natures are capable of love!"

"Ha! You're talking about yourself, of course—an elevated nature?"

The music began to roar again. Romashov stared wrathfully through the window at the trombone's copper-colored mouth, which was spitting its barks and rasps into the hall as if indifferent to their effect. The soldier who was playing this instrument puffed out his cheeks, googling his glazed-over eyes as he went blue from the strain. Looking at him, Romashov felt repulsed.

"Let's not argue. Maybe I'm not capable of truly loving either, but that's not the point. The point is that you, with your narrow provincial opinions and your backwater ambitions, invariably need someone to 'orbit' you, and others to see this. Or maybe you think that I didn't understand why you were being so familiar with me during these parties—the soft glances, the imperious and intimate tone, all delivered at exactly those moments when other people were watching us? That's it, of course: it's essential that someone be watching. Otherwise the game doesn't mean anything to you. You don't need love from me; you simply want people to see you being compromised again."

"I could have found someone better and more interesting than you to do that with," Peterson objected with pompous pide.

"Don't get upset—you won't hurt me that way. I repeat: all you want is that someone be considered your slave, one more slave to your irresistible beauty. But time flies, and slaves grow rarer and rarer. And in order not to lose your most recent lover, you coldly, calculatingly, haul both your duties as a mother and your marriage vows onto the sacrificial altar."

"Oh, you'll be hearing more from me!" Raisa whispered maliciously.

Raisa's husband, Captain Peterson, weaved his way toward them through the galloping pairs. He was a sickly, feeble-looking man, with a bald yellow skull, and black eyes that were moist and and gentle, but with a secret twinkle of rage in them. It was said of him that he was madly in love with his wife—so in love, in fact, that he cultivated a bantering, sweet, but completely fake friendship with all his wife's worshipers. It was also well known that he paid these men back with hatred, treachery, and ruthlessly dirty tricks as soon as they had escaped, joyful and relieved, from his wife's service.

His blue lips twisted into a smile before he had made it halfway across the hall.

"Raisy, you're dancing! Hello, George, old boy. We haven't seen you for a while! We'd gotten used to you—we were even starting to miss you."

"I've . . . Well . . . I've had my studies," Romashov muttered.

"We know all about your studies," Peterson smiled, raising his hand in a mock blow. But his black eyes with their jaundiced whites skittered back and forth between his wife's and Romashov's faces with tormented alarm.

"I must confess, I thought the two of you were having an argument. I looked over and there you are sitting down and getting heated about something. What's going on?"

Romashov kept quiet, staring awkwardly at Peterson's sallow, wrinkled, unhealthy-looking neck. But Raisa spoke up with the same imputent confidence that she always displayed while lying:

"Yuri Alexandrovich philosophizes about everything. He says that dancing is a waste of time and that to dance is stupid and ridiculous."

"But he's been dancing regardless," Peterson remarked with venomous goodwill. "Well, then, go on, dance, my children, dance, don't let me stop you."

He had barely left when Raisa said, with affected feeling:

"And to think that I have deceived that excellent, extraordinary man! . . . And for whom? Oh, if only he knew—if only he could know . . ."

"The mazurka!" Bobetinsky cried. "Cavallieri, you must charm your women!"

The air in the hall had grown thick from the movement of the bodies and the heat that rose from the parquet floors, to the point that now the candle flames had shrunk to hazy yellow specks. There were many pairs dancing, and since the floor was barely big enough to hold all of them, each had to trample around their own limited space, crowding and shoving up against their neighbors. In the dance that Bobetinsky had just suggested, the free cavaliers were supposed to follow along behind one or another of the dancing pairs. As he circled around them, while at the same time performing the steps of the mazurka (which came out funny and awkward), the free cavalier waited expectantly for the exact moment when the woman and he stood face to face in front of one another. When this happened, he clapped his hands quickly in order to indicate that he had "taken" her; meanwhile the other cavalier tried to prevent him from doing this by turning continually and moving his woman back and forth: he backed away himself, jumped to one side and even threw his left elbow out in a sweeping motion, which he aimed at his rival's chest. Uncomfortable, crude, and unseemly situations always arose from these types of dances.

"What an actress!" Romashov whispered hoarsely, bending his head close to Raisa's. "It is pitiful and hilarious to hear you speak like that."

"You, apparently, are drunk!" Raisa shouted squeamishly, as she leveled the sort of gaze at Romashov that the heroine of a novel might use to measure a villain from head to toe.

"Tell me, really—why did you deceive me?" Romashov exclaimed angrily. "You give yourself to me only so that I might not leave you. Oh, if only you had done that out of love, or even not out of love, but only with some sort of feeling, I would have understood. But it was only from dissipation, from shabby vanity. Could you really not be horrified by the thought of how terrible it was for the two of us to give ourselves to one another without love, out of boredom, distraction, without even curiosity, and then . . . to . . . like a maid on break eating sunflower seeds. You have to understand: this is worse than when a woman gives herself away for money. Then at least there is a need, there's seduction . . . Understand, it's shameful to me, it's awful to think about that coldness, idleness, that degrading depravity!"

Romashov watched the dancers with bored and lifeless eyes, his forehead bathed in cold sweat. Mrs. Talman swam majestically past him, looking sensitive and severe, her feet barely moving, not even glancing at Epifanov, her cavallier, who pranced joyfully around her, like a goat. There was the little Likacheva girl, flushed, with shining eyes and a white, innocent, naked, but still girlish neck . . . There was Olizar on his thin legs, which were straight and well formed, like the needles of two south-pointing compasses. Watching them all, Romashov felt a headache and the desire to cry. Meanwhile, Raisa spoke on, pale with rage, lathering her words with an exaggerated and theatrical sarcasm:

"How charming! An officer strutting around in the role of Joseph!"

"A role, yes, that's just it . . ." Romashov sighed. "I know how ridiculous and pretentious it all is . . . but I haven't stopped grieving over my lost purity, the lost purity of my body. We both willingly lay together in the gutter, and now I feel that I'll never be able to have a good, wholesome love. And the blame for that is yours—do you hear me? You, you, you! You're older and more experienced than me. You knew perfectly how this worked."

Ms. Peterson rose from her seat with exaggerated displeasure.

"Enough!" she said dramatically. "You've gotten what you wanted. I loathe you! I hope that from this day forth you will stop visiting our house, where we received you like a member of our family, gave you food and drink—only to find out now that you are a blackguard. I only regret that I can't tell my husband everything. That blessed man! I pray for him and would confess it all if I thought he would survive the shock. But believe me, he would be perfectly capable of taking revenge for insults towards a defenseless woman."

Romashov stood in front of her and, squinting painfully through his glasses, watched her large, thin, withered mouth twist itself into a paroxysm of rage. The roar of the music, with the continual, persistent coughs of the wretched trombone, and the urgent beats of the bass drum seemed to be pounding their way inside his head from beyond the window. He heard Raisa's words only in snatches and did not understand them. But it seemed to him that they, like the drumming itself, were striking him directly on the head and causing his brain to shake.

Raisa closed her fan with a crack.

"Villainous swine!" she whispered tragically, and made her way across the hall toward the ladies' room.

It was all over, but the relief that Romashov had expected to feel was still missing from his heart, and the dirty, sad heaviness had not been put to sleep, as he previously thought it would. Instead, he felt a lingering sense of wrong at the cowardice and insincerity he had displayed by placing all the blame for his actions on a narrow-minded and pitiful woman. He imagined her there, in the ladies' room, with puffy red eyes and bitter tears, filled with resentment, confusion, and impotent rage.

"How the mighty have fallen," he thought with disgust and boredom. "What a life! Gray, grimy, and narrow. This depraved and useless relationship, drunkenness, anguish, the deathly monotonous service, and not a single living word, not a single moment of real happiness. Books, music, art—where did they all go?"

He returned to the dining room. There, Osadchin and Vetkin (who was in the same company as Romashov) were carrying a soused Lekh towards the door. His head dangled weakly as he babbled on about his responsibilities as an archbishop. The straight-faced Osadchin chimed in with his deep bass, like a deacon:

"Bless us, O Father. Let the service begin . . ."

The closer the dancing came to being over, the noisier it became in the dining room. The air was saturated with tobacco smoke, to the point that two people sitting at opposite ends of the table would have barely been able to see one another. In one corner people were singing; by the window, a handful of others were telling dirty jokes: the usual garnish to the officers' club meals.

"No no, gentlemen . . . Allow me!" Archakovsky shouted. "One day a soldier came to lodge with a Ukrainian. And wouldn't you know it, this Ukrainian has himself a gor-ge-ous wife. So the soldier thinks to himself: how do I go about this . . ."

The moment he finished his story, Vasily Vasilyevich Lipsky broke in excitedly.

"No, no, gentlemen . . . Here, I've got one for you."

But he too was barely able to finish before the next man butted in.

"It happened in Odessa, gentlemen. Picture this . . ."

The jokes were all foul, smutty, and dull-witted. As usual, it was always the most confident and crude storyteller who garnered the most laughs.

Vetkin, who had just come back from the yard, where he'd deposited Lekh in a carriage, invited Romashov to sit down with him.

"Come, Georgie . . . Let's have a drink. I'm rich as a Jew today. I won last night and am planning to break the bank again."

Romashov was desperate to speak to someone—to pour his heart out with all its despair and disgust at life. He drank glass after glass, looking at Vetkin with pleading eyes, and speaking in a warm, trembling voice.

"We forget, Pavel Pavlovich, all of us, that there's another life out there. I don't know where, but somewhere people live, and the lives they lead are so full, so joyful and true. Somewhere people struggle, suffer, love broadly and deeply . . . My friend, the life we lead! The life we lead!"

"All right . . . Yes, of course, my friend. Life, like you say," Pavel Pavlovich answered sluggishly. "But you know, that's just natural philosophy and energy fields. Speaking of which, what do you think—do you believe in auras?"

"Oh, what are we doing!" Romashov said in torment. "Today we drink to the point of drunkenness, tomorrow it's one, two, left, right, then at night we drink ourselves silly again—then back to the drill. Could this really be all there is to life? No, you only think that that's everything."

Vetkin gave him a confused look, as if he were regarding him through some kind of film, hiccupped, and suddenly began singing, in a thin and trembling tenor:

> She lived in peace and quiet,
> She lived in the forest,
> Spinning at her wheel . . .
> Give it up, angel, take care of yourself.
> But with all her heart
> She loved her spinning wheel.

"Let's go play some cards, Romashov Romashovsky. I'll lend you ten rubles."

"Nobody understands. I don't have anyone to talk to," Romashov thought sadly. For a moment he thought of Shurochka—so strong, so bold and beautiful—and something languid, sweet, and hopeless began to ache in the area of his heart.

He remained at the club until it began to grow light outside, watching them play cards and even playing a few hands himself, though without pleasure or enthusiasm. At one point he noticed that Archakovsky, having lured a pair of clean-shaven sub-ensigns to a separate table, was cheating clumsily, dealing himself two cards at a time instead of one. Romashov wanted to do something about this, to call him out, but then he decided to let things be. "Eh, it's all the same. I can't do anything about it," he thought passively.

Vetkin, who had lost his millions in five minutes, sat sleeping in his chair, pale and with his mouth wide open. Next to Romashov, Leshenko was watching the game despondently. It was hard to understand how he managed to sit there hour after hour with such a melancholy expression on his face. Then, dawn. The swollen lights winked their long yellow flames. The faces of the players were pale and exhausted. Romashov stared at the cards, the pile of silver and paper bills and the green cloth smudged with chalk, while in his heavy, foggy head a single thought circled sluggishly, about his fall, and about the dirtiness of his boring, monotonous life.

X

It was bright but chilly: a true spring morning. The cherry trees were in bloom.

Romashov, who had only barely managed to rouse himself, was late as usual for morning maneuvers; so he made his way, with an uncomfortable feeling of shame, to the plaza where his company was practicing. This familiar situation was degrading to the young officer, and the presence of Captain Sliva, the unit commander, only made it keener and more painful.

He was a rude and stern remnant of the old guard, who believed in the relentless enforcement of discipline through physical intimidation, petty formalities, marches executed in triple time and punishment doled out with one's fists. Even in a regiment that, thanks to its uncultivated provinciality, didn't care much about humanitarian values, he stood out as a sort of wild holdover from the ferocious military past, about whom people told many curious and practically unbelievable stories. He dismissively referred to everything not having to do with rules, regulations, and the regimental order as foolishness and playacting: none of it existed for him. He had spent his entire life toiling in the military, and had read neither a single book nor a single newspaper, save the official sections of the *Invalid*. He loathed entertainments like dancing and shows with all his callous heart, and there was no foul and dirty expression from the soldier's lexicon that he would not use when talking about them. It was said of him—and it was very possible that this was true—that one spring night, while he was sitting next to an open window looking over the regimental ledgers, a nightingale had begun singing in a nearby bush. Sliva listened for a while and then shouted suddenly at his manservant:

"Zakharchuk! Throw a rock at that fu-cking bird. Shut him up . . ."

This flabby and cheap-looking individual was terribly strict with his soldiers. He not only allowed the sergeants to beat them, but even did so himself—harshly, until blood had been shed, or the offender collapsed under his wounds. At the same time, he was attentive to his soldier's needs: he didn't hold back the money sent them from home, and he personally sat every day at the company registrar (though he requisitioned the sum allotted for voluntary work solely for himself). Only the men in the fifth regiment looked happier and more satisfied than his.

Still, Sliva scolded and harassed his young officers, using raw and humiliating techniques, to which his native Ukrainian sense of humor added a special bite. If, for example, a subaltern officer began to march out of step during drill, Sliva cried, with his usual slight stammer.

"Ho-hold up there, boys! The entire re-egiment, devil take her, is marching wrong. Only this sub-lieutenant is do-ooing it right."

Other times, after having told the company off in the foulest language, he would quickly, but pungently, add:

"Excepting the officers and sub-lieutenants, of course."

He was particularly harsh and insistent on those occasions when a young officer was late—a situation that Romashov had plenty of experience with. Upon spotting the sub-lieutenant at a distance, Sliva would call the regiment to attention, turn precisely and with an ironically polite flourish to the latecomer, and, remaining motionless himself, watch in his hand, observe quietly as a humiliated Romashov stumbled over his sword, searching for his place in line. Sometimes he asked, with furious courtesy, belting the words out so that the soldiers could hear: "Is it all right with you if we continue, Sub-lieutenant?" Other mornings he inquired, with courteous concern, but in a deliberately loud voice, how the sub-lieutenant had slept and what kind of dreams he had had. Only after having humiliated him publicly in one of these ways would he take Romashov aside and, looking at him point-blank with his square fishy eyes, let him have it.

"Well, it's all the same, after all," Romashov thought despondently, as he approached the regiment. "It's bad here, it's bad there—what's the difference? My life is over with!"

The regimental commander, Lieutenant Vetkin, Lyubov, and the sergeant major, who were standing in the center of the plazza, turned in unison to watch Romashov's approach. The soldiers likewise turned their heads in his direction. At that moment Romashov imagined that he was watching himself—a confused figure—make his clumsy approach under these strange men's gaze, and the whole thing became even more disagreeable to him.

"But who knows, maybe there's nothing to be ashamed of?" he consoled himself, following a line of reasoning that is typical of shy people. "Maybe it only seems humiliating to me, while to everyone else it's business as usual. For example, let's say Lyubov was the one who was late, instead of me, and I was standing in my place watching him approach. Well, what's so remarkable about that: there's Lyubov, he's Lyubov. It's ridiculous," he decided finally, and was suddenly calm. "All right, it's embarrassing . . . but it won't last a month—it won't even last a week, a day. Anyway, life's short: you forget about everything in the end."

Strangely enough, Sliva seemed to pay no attention to his approach. Only when Romashov had stopped in front of him to salute respectfully and knock his heels together, did Sliva extend his sweaty palm, which looked like a bundle of five cold sausages, and say:

"Let me remind you, sub-lieutenant, that you are required to show up for drills five minutes before the arrival of the eldest subaltern-officer and ten minutes before the company commander."

"It's my fault, Captain," Romashov answered expressionlessly.

"Oh, it's your fault! Well, then, excuse me! No doubt you were sleeping—well, dreams won't sew you a new fur coat. Will the officers please attend to their platoons."

The company divided up into its constituent parts and spread out over the plaza. The platoon began their morning gymnastics. The soldiers stood in columns, separated from one another by a step, with their uniforms unbuttoned to give them room to move. Bobilyev, an efficient sergeant in Romashov's half-company, shouted out his commands while glancing respectfully at the passing officers. He thrust his jaw out and crossed his eyes:

"On your toes! Squat smoothly! Ha-a-ands . . . to the sides!"

And then, in a low and drawn-out singsong:

"Be-e-e-e-gin!"

"One!" the soldiers sang in unison, as they squatted slowly. Bobilyev, who was also squatting, ran his strict and self-satisfied gaze down the column.

Meanwhile, next to him the small fidgety lance corporal Seroshtan cried out in a thin voice, sharply and suddenly, like a young bird:

"Right arm with left leg, left arm with right leg. Like this! One, two, one, two!" Ten healthy young voices cried out sharply and dilligently: "One, two, one, two!"

"Halt!" Seroshtan cried piercingly. "La-ap-shin! You there, playing the fool! You use your fists like a Riasan woman handling a pair of tongs—hou, hou! Do the movements the way you're supposed to, damn it!"

After this the sergeants led their platoons at double march to the exercise equipment located in the various corners of the plaza. Sub-lieutenant Lyubov, who was strong and agile and an excellent gymnast, quickly removed his overcoat and uniform jacket and, wearing only his light-blue cotton undershirt, attacked the parallel bars first. He hoisted himself up on one end of the equipment, rocking his body back and forth three times before suddenly executing a full twist, so that his feet suddenly found themselves directly over his head, after which he pushed off so vigorously that he soared a full three yards into the air, turning once before landing gracefully, like a cat, on the ground.

"More fooling around, Sub-lieutenant Lyubov!" Sliva shouted, with mock severity. In the depths of his heart, the old "Bourbon" nourished a weakness for this sub-lieutenant, who was an excellent fighter with a thorough knowledge of military regulations. "This isn't the county fair, you know. Show us how it's done in the manual."

"I hear you, Captain!" Lyubov barked happily. "But that doesn't mean I'm going to obey you," he added under his breath, winking at Romashov.

The fourth platoon was exercising on the inclined ladder. One after another, the men approached the device, threw themselves on the first bar, and then began pulling themselves across it hand over hand. Sergeant Shapovalenko stood underneath them making remarks.

"Don't danlge! Keep those tootsies up!"

Soon it was the left-flank infantryman Khlebnikov's turn. He was the regimental laughingstock; frequently while looking at him, Romashov had to wonder how they could have possibly enlisted such a pitiful, underfed individual—a dwarf almost, with his dirty beardless face, which looked like a scrunched-up fist. As soon as the sub-lieutenant's gaze met his idiotic eyes, in which a sort of blunt and submissive terror had been calcifying, most likely, since he was born, a strange mixture of guilt and depression began tugging at his conscience.

Khlebnikov dangled by his hands, awkwardly, clumsily, like a hanged man.

"Pull yourself up, you dog-faced cretin—pull your-self up!" shouted the sergeant. "Up!"

Khlebnikov tried to pull himself up, but all he managed to do was kick his feet helplessly and shake himself back and forth. He turned his gray little face, from which his dirty, jerked-up nose stood out laughably, to one side. Suddenly he tore his hands from the bar and fell like a sack onto the ground.

"Ah-ha! So you don't feel like doing gymnastics today?" the sergeant began to yell. "You, lout, you're holding everybody up! I'm talking to you!"

"Don't you dare strike him, Shapovalenko!" Romashov cried, burning all over with shame and rage. "Don't you dare do that—ever!" he cried. He ran up to the sergeant and grabbed him by the shoulders.

Shapovalenko stood at attention and saluted. In his eyes, which assumed immediately the usual soldier's blankness, a barely perceptible smile glinted.

"Yes, sir. Only, if I may say so, we simply can't do anything with him."

Khlebnikov was standing right next to them, shaking all over; he stared at the officers dim-wittedly, whipping his nose with the edge of his palm. With a sharp and helpless feeling of pity, Romashov turned from him and continued on to the third plattoon.

After gymnastics, while the soldiers were enjoying their ten-minute break, the officers met once more in the center of the plaza, around the parallel bars. The conversation turned to the upcoming May parade.

"Just think of what we're up against!" Sliva said, spreading his hands as his eyes welled with watery amazement. "I'll tell you one thing: every general wants things a different way. I remember we had one of them, General Lieutenant Lvovich, the corps commander. He had come to us from the engineers; so, naturally, all we did under his watch was dig. Regulations, maneuvers, marching—he didn't care about any of it. From morning to night we built every kind of shelter, lodge—you name it. In the summer we used earth, in the winter, snow. The whole company became covered with clay from head to toe. He saw to it that the commander of the tenth company, Captain Aleinikov, God rest his soul, was presented the Medal of Anna for his construction of some kind of rampart, which he managed to do in two hours."

"Well done!" Lyubov put in.

"How about General Aragon and his rifle drills—you remember that, Pavel Pavlich?"

"Ah yes! 'The perfect shot.'"

"What's that mean?" Romashov asked.

Sliva waved his hand contemptuously.

"Just that the only thing we ever thought about during that time were his shooting instructions. A soldier answered 'I believe' during inspection, exactly as the general himself liked to say, and instead of 'By Pontius Pilate,' one would swear on 'The perfect shot.' That got into one's head! They didn't call the index finger an index finger, but a trigger, and instead of your right eye, it was your 'sight.'"

"And do you remember, Afanasy Kirilich, how we stuffed those theories into them?" Vetkin said. "Trajectory, derivation . . . Good God, I didn't understand any of it myself. You were supposed to say to the soldiers, 'Here's your rifle, look down the barrel. What do you see?' And they were supposed to answer, 'The line of sight.' But they could shoot. You remember that, Afanasy Kirilich?"

"Of course. Our division was mentioned in the foreign papers for our shooting. Ten percent better than the highest mark—how about that? But then, did we ever cheat! The good shots would be passed along from company to company to bring up the average. Sometimes during regimental rifle exams, the junior officers would pepper the targets with revolver shots from the dugout. One company shot so well that when they examined the targets, they found five more bullets in the target than the soldiers had fired. One hundred and five percent accuracy. Thankfully, the sergeant major was able to paste over the holes."

"And do you remember Slesarev's Shreiverobsky gymnastics routines?"

"Do I! I had it up to here with them. Real ballet, that. Yes, there have always been plenty of such generals around, devil take them! But I'll tell you, none of it is half as bad as the way things go nowadays. Kiss and make up—that's how we prefer it. In the old days they knew how to talk to you—but now? Now it's,

'Oh please, Mr. Soldier, forgive me—hey there, neighbor, show a little compassion.' A beating is what he needs—that'd knock the foolishness out of him! Ah, yes: we must 'develop his mental capacity, quickness, and ability to think.' Whatever that means. 'Here, pardon me, let's try something new, I call it the 'billiard attack'!'

"It won't do," Vetkin said, nodding his head sympathetically.

"You stand there like an idiot, as the Kazakhs bear down on you at full speed. Down on you and then over you! Well, all right, why don't we try getting out of the way? But if you do that, here comes the communiqué: 'Apparently, the captain has developed a case of nerves. Please inform him that his services will no longer be required.' "

"Sly old devil," Vetkin said. "He pulled quite a trick on the K regiment. He had his company stand in the middle of a gigantic puddle and then shouted 'Lie down!' at the company commander. The commander hesitated for a second, before shouting to his men: 'Lie down!' The soldiers had no idea what he was talking about, they thought they'd heard him wrong. Then the general began to dress down the commander as if he were an orderly: 'Is that what your regiment's made of! A bunch of stuffed shirts! If they're afraid to lie down in this puddle, how are you going to get them to stand up when they're lying in some ditch, under enemy fire? You don't have soldiers here—you've got old women. And their commander's the oldest one of them all! You're under house arrest!'

"And what's the use of that? To humiliate the commander in public, and then later talk about 'discipline'? Who'll care about your discipline after that? And to hit a man, to lay him out—don't you dare. No-o-o . . . Excuse me—that's a human being you're talking about, an individual! No, in the old days, there were none of these 'individuals': we'd have peeled their hides off, the swine. But back then there was Sevastopol to worry about, and the Italian campaign, and those kinds of things. Demote me if you want: all the same, when a fool acts up, I'll give him what he deserves!"

"Hitting soldiers is dishonorable," Romashov objected in a muffled voice. He had been trying hard up to this point to keep quiet. "One mustn't hit a man who not only can't answer back, but isn't even allowed to put a hand in front of his face to ward off the blow. He can't even move his head and dodge. That's shameful!"

Sliva scrunched his eyes up wrathfully. He thrust his lower lip out beneath his clipped gray mustache and looked Romashov up and down.

"What the hell did you say?" he drawled contemptuously.

Romashov paled. A cold feeling began to spread in his chest and stomach, and his heart started beating as if it were somehow in every part of his body at once.

"I said that it's wrong . . . I did—and I'll say it again . . . precisely," he said, with incoherent persistence.

"Well, then, by all means—enlighten me!" Sliva said in a dainty singsong. "Don't worry: we've seen plenty of weeping willows like yourself. You'll be taking cracks at their ugly mugs yourself before the year's out, if they don't run you out of the regiment. You're no better than me."

Romashov stared at him with hatred and said almost in a whisper:

"If you lay a finger on any of these soldiers, I will report you to the regimental commander."

"What did you say?" Sliva shouted menacingly; but then he pulled up short. "All right, then, suit yourself," he said dryly. "You're still young, Sub-lieutenant; I suggest you don't try to educate a veteran combat officer who has served his government with honor for twenty-five years. Now, if you would all kindly return to your units."

He turned his back sharply on the officers.

"Are you poking your nose into this on purpose?" Vetkin said as he walked next to Romashov. "You can see for yourself that Sliva's no weakling. You don't know him yet the way that I know him. He'll slander you so badly, you won't know where to hide. And if you try to answer him, he'll put you under house arrest."

"But if that's the case, Pavel Pavlich, this isn't military service—it's slavery!" Romashov shouted, with tears of rage and injured pride in his voice. "These selfish old barbarians insult us! They purposefully try to cultivate rudeness, hatred, and crude self-aggrandizing among the officers."

"Yes, yes, of course you're right," Vetkin acknowledged passively. He yawned.

Romashov had begun to get heated:

"But why does it have to be this way, what's the purpose of all this calling out and beating and rude shouting? Ah! I didn't expect it to be this way at all when I became an officer. I'll never forget my first impression. I had only been in the company for three days, and I was called out by that redheaded bastard Archakovsky. During a conversation at a party I addressed him as 'lieutenant,' since he had already called me 'sub-lieutenant.' And then, even though he was sitting next to me and we were drinking beer together, he began shouting at me: 'First of all, it's not 'lieutenant' to you, it's 'lieutenant sir,' and second . . . second, be so good as to stand up when you're addressing a higher ranking officer!' And I got out of my chair and stood in front of him, humiliated, until Sub-lieutenant Lekh bawled him out. No, no, that's enough, Pavel Pavlich. All of it has become so loathsome and despicable to me—I can't stand it! . . ."

XI

They were teaching terminology in the company schoolhouse. The soldiers of the third platoon sat in the narrow room, on benches which had been arranged into a square—in the center of which Lance-Corporal Seroshtan was walking back and forth. Next to him, in an identical square, Sergeant Shapovalenko was walking back and forth the same way.

"Bondarenko!" Seroshtan shouted in a stentorian voice.

Bondarenko struck both his feet against the floor, springing up quickly and rigidly, like a jack-in-the-box.

"All right, Bondarenko, let's say you're standing in line with your rifle, and your commanding officer comes up to you and asks: 'What's that in your hand, Bondarenko?' What do you answer?"

"A rifle?" Bondarenko guessed.

"A rifle—is that a fact? Why don't you just say 'gun,' like the bumpkin you are. At home it's a rifle, but in the service we call it, simply, a small-caliber rapid-fire Berdan-style infantry rifle number two, with a sliding lock. Say it, you son of a bitch!"

Bondarenko fired back the words which, of course, he already knew.

"Sit down!" Seroshtan commanded. "And why were you given this rifle? Answer me that . . ." His stern eyes went around the room, settling on each of his subordinates in turn.

"Shevchuk!"

Shevchuk stood up with a sullen look and answered in a thick bass, slowly and nasally, cutting his phrases short in a way that made it sound like he was putting periods at the ends of them:

"This rifle was given to me because. Because in times of peace I do things with her. And times of war. I protect the throne and fatherland from its enemies." He became quiet, sniffed his nose, and then added ominously: "Internal as well as external."

"Very good. You know your stuff, Shevchuk—only don't mumble. A soldier must be joyous, like an eagle. Sit down. Now tell me, Ovechkin, who are these external enemies?"

Ovechkin, a grocer from Orel, answered quickly and loquaciously, veritably choking with pleasure.

"External enemies are all those governments with which we are at war. The French, the German, the Italians, the Turks, the Europeans, the Indians . . ."

"That's enough," Seroshtan interrupted him. "Regulations don't cover them all. Sit down, Ovechkin. Now tell me— Arhipov! Who do we designate as in-ter-nal e-ne-mies?"

He pronounced the last two words with particular emphasis, throwing a significant glance toward Markuson the conscript.

The awkward, pock-marked Arhipov remained doggedly silent as he looked out the schoolhouse window. A sensible, intelligent, and crafty fellow outside of the service, he performed his military duties like a complete idiot. Clearly, this was because his healthy mind, which was used to observing and considering the simple and clear practices of country living, and was therefore unable to perceive the connections between the terminology he studied and actual life. Because of this, he did not understand and was unable to learn the simplest things, to the great surprise and dissatisfaction of his platoon commander.

"Well! Should I wait here while you gather your thoughts?" Seroshtan said, beginning to get angry.

"Internal enemies . . . enemies . . ."

"You don't know," Seroshtan shouted threateningly. He made a step toward Arhipov but then, glancing sidewise at the officer, decided to only shake his head. He gave Arhipov a terrible look. "Listen up! 'Internal enemies' is a term used to designate those who act against the law. For example . . . ?" He met the searching eyes of Ovechkin. "Give us an example, Ovechkin."

Ovechkin leapt up and cried happily:

"Rebels, students, thieves, Jews and Poles!"

Shapovalenko's class was being conducted in the square next to theirs. He read off the questions he held in his hand in a singsong voice, pacing from bench to bench as the soldiers answered from memory.

"Soltys, what's a sentry?'

Soltys, a Lithuanian, whose eyes blinked and strained under the effort, shouted:

"A sentry is invisible."

"Well all right, and what else?"

"A sentry is a soldier, who has been sent to guard a designated post."

"True. I see, Soltys, that you have really started to apply yourself. And what does that mean, Pahorukov: 'Established at your post'?"

"It means you don't sleep, don't nap, don't smoke, and no matter what the circumstances, do not accept any presents or things."

"And what about saluting?"

"You show your respect by saluting any officer that passes you."

"All right, sit down."

Shapovalenko, who had been observing an ironic smile on the volunteer Fokin's face for some time now, shouted at him with special severity:

"Volunteer! Why are you standing like that? If your commanding officer gives you the command you have to pop up like you're doing a jumping jack. What's a banner?"

Fokin, an ex-student with a university insignia on his breast, stood in front of the sergeant in a respectful pose. But his young gray eyes sparkled gleefully.

"A banner is a sacred battle emblem, under which . . ."

"Incorrect!" Shapovalenko cuts him off angrily, banging his notebook with his hand.

"No, I've got it right," Fokin said, in a quiet but direct voice.

"Wha-at's that?! If a superior officer tells you you're wrong, that means you're wrong!"

"Look it up for yourself in the regulations."

"I'm a non-commissioned officer, therefore I know the regulations better than you do. Tell me what a banner is! All of you volunteers have mush for brains. Maybe I should enlist myself in cadets' school to learn something? What do you know? What's this em-be-lem? It's an *em-blem*! Not an em-be-lem. It's a sacred military emblem, like a sign."

"Shapovalenko, don't argue," Romashov interjected. "Just get on with your lesson."

"Yes, sir, sub-lieutenant sir!" Shapovalenko said, drawing his words out. "Only, if I may, sir—this student is constantly talking back.'

"All right, all right, continue!"

"Yes, sir . . . Khlebnikov! Who is our corps commander?"

Khlebnikov looked at the non-com with confused eyes. A single, sibilant sound, like a raven's hoarse caw, tore itself from his mouth.

"Pull yourself together!" the non-com shouted at him angrily. "He . . ."

"Well, 'he,' yes—what else do you have for us?"

Romashov, who turned away at exactly that moment, heard Shapovalenko add in a hoarse whisper:

"Don't you worry: after class I'll continue the examination on your ugly snout!"

But then when he turned back to him, Shapovalenko said, loudly and indifferently:

"His excellency . . . Well, what about it, Khlebnikov, go on!"

"His . . . infantry . . . lieutenant," Khlebnikov muttered in fearful bursts.

"A-a-a!" Shapovalenko wheezed, grinding his teeth together. "Now what, Khlebnikov, am I going to do with you? I try, I take pains with you, but it doesn't make any difference: you're such a camel, the only thing you have plenty of is water. Zero effort. Stand like that until the end of the philology class. After supper present yourself to me, and I'll deal with you separately. Grechenko! Who is our corps commander?"

"Same today as it will be tomorrow and the day after tomorrow. Same as it will be until the end of my life," Romashov thought, as he walked from platoon to platoon. "And what if I did just leave, throw it all away? . . . What torment! . . ."

After philology the men went out to the yard to prepare for shooting instruction. In one section the men were told to aim using a mirror, while another shot pellets at a target. In the third section they were screwballing the target with a Livchak device. In the second platoon, sergeant Master Lyubov had begun shouting over the entire plaza in a satisfied tenor:

"Eyes forward . . . one column at a time . . . company fire . . . and again! Com-pa-nyyyy . . ."—he stretched out the last sound, pausing before he shouted suddenly, "Fire!"

Shots sounded. Lyubov continued, clearly reveling in the sound of his own voice.

"Order aaaa-rms!"

Sliva, whose back was hunched, was walking sluggishly from platoon to platoon, setting things straight and making brief, harsh remarks.

"Suck in your stomach—you look pregnant! Why are you holding your rifle like that? You're not a church deacon! What are you gaping at, Kartashov? Want some kasha? Where's your drill instructor? Sergeant-Major, keep Kartashov and his rifle here for an hour after class. What an idiot! How did you roll up your overcoat, Vedeneyev? There's no beginning, no end, no middle even. Nincompoop!"

After shooting practice the men put their rifles up and lay around on the young spring grass, which had been trampled flat by their boots. It was warm and bright. In the air you could smell the young leaves of the poplars growing in two rows along either side of the road. Vetkin approached Romashov again.

"Cheer up, Yuri Alexeyevich," he said, taking his hand. "It's not worth it. Let's finish these classes and have a glass, and everything will be better . . . What do you think about that?"

"Frankly it bores me, my dear Pavel Pavlich," Romashov said wearily.

"So you're not happy," Vetkin said. "But how could you be? Men need to learn how to do these things. What if a war breaks out?"

"A war—of course," Romashov agreed despondently. "But what's the use of wars? What if it's all some kind of gigantic mistake, a worldwide delusion, a madness? Can it really be in our nature to kill one another?"

"There's your philosophy again. The devil with it! And if the Germans fall on us suddenly? Who will protect Russia?"

"I have absolutely no idea and am not saying that I do, Pavel Pavlich," Romashov objected, shortly and plaintively. "I know nothing, nothing. But take the North American war, for example, or the Italian war of independence, or the Spanish guerrillas . . . or the Choans during the revolution . . . They fought when they had to! Simple ploughmen, herders."

"Well, yes, the Americans . . . How can we compare . . . It's impossible. In my opinion, if you think that way, then it's better not to be in the service. In our line of work, one's generally not supposed to think. Only, allow me to ask you one question: how would we spend our days if we weren't in the service? What are we good for, when the only words we know are 'Right!' and 'Left!'? We can die, that's for sure. And die when they God-damn tell us to. Finally, if I may, bread isn't free. And that's about it, Mr. Philosopher. Come with me to the club after drills?"

"Sure," Romashov agreed unenthusiastically. "Strictly speaking, it's swinish to spend every day that way. But you're right, at least: if one thinks about it, it's better not to serve at all."

They continued their talk as they walked back and forward along the plaza, stopping finally in front of the fourth platoon. The soldiers sat and lay on the ground near their stacked rifles. A few were eating bread, which soldiers eat every day, from morning to night, and in every circumstance: on inspection, when they halt during maneuvers, in the church before the confessional—even when they're about to receive corporal punishment.

Romashov heard a sort of lazily aggressive voice call out: "Khlebnikov, hey, Khlebnikov! . . ."

"What?" Klebnikhov responded with nasal gloominess.

"What did you do back home?"

"I worked," Khlebnikov answered sleepily.

"What kind of work, piss-for-brains?'

"All kinds. I ploughed land, herded livestock."

"What makes you so curious?" piped Uncle Shpinev, one of the regiment old-timers. "Everyone knows what he did: he was a wet nurse."

Romashov glanced as he passed at Khlebnikov's grayhaired, pitiful, unbearded face, and again an uncomfortable and painful feeling seemed to scrape across his heart.

"Fall in!" Sliva shouted from the center of the plaza. "Officers, to your places!"

The bayonets clattered against one another. The soldiers bustlingly adjusted their uniforms and then stood still once they had made it to their places.

"Even yourselves out!" Sliva commanded. "Attention!"

Then, moving closer to the company, he cried in a singsong:

"Rifle drill, by division, count off . . . Company, mount guard!"

"One," the soldiers barked, raising their rifles sharply.

Sliva slowly inspected the formation, making his usual sharp remarks: "Rotate the butt"; "Hold your bayonet higher"; "Put the butt against you." Then he turned again toward the company and commanded:

"And . . . Two!'

"Two!" the soldiers shouted.

And again Sliva went around checking the precision and correctness of their formation.

After the rifle drill by numbers, there was a drill without numbers, then turns, the division of rows, combinations and dispersals and various other formations. Romashov did everything that the rules demanded of him, like a machine, but he couldn't shake Vetkin's words: "If you think that way, then it's better not even to be in the service. You must leave the military." And all the intricacies of military regulation: the adroitness of a turn, the spirit of rifle formation, the firm positioning of the legs in a march, and in addition to all these tactics and fortifications, on which nine of the best years of his life had been broken, and which would necessarily fill all of his remaning years and which furthermore had seemed so important and meaningful not long ago—all this suddenly seemed boring, unnatural, fake; an aimless and idle thing, which served only to perpetuate a shared international delusion—a sort of absurd delirium.

When the practice was over, he went with Vetkin to the officers' club, and drank quite a bit of vodka with him. While hovering on the verge of passing out, Romashov covered Vetkin with kisses, cried loud, hysterical tears on his shoulder, filled with pity for the emptiness and melancholy of his life, and for the fact that no one understood him, and that "a certain woman" did not love him, though who she was—that, no one would ever discover. Vetkin downed glass after glass, opening his mouth from time to time to remark with distaste:

"The only thing that's regrettable about your situation, Romashov, is how poorly you hold your liquor. One glass and you're done."

Later, he banged his fist suddenly against the table and shouted menacingly:

"And if they order us to die—we'll die!"

"We'll die," Romashov said pitifully. "What does that mean? Death is a joke . . . My heart hurts . . ."

Romashov didn't remember how he got home or who put him to bed. It seemed to him that he was swimming in a thick blue cloud filled with millions of tiny sparks. This cloud rocked slowly back and forth, lifting and dropping his body as it did so—and under the influence of this rhythmic rocking the sub-lieutenant's heart began to calm; it grew peaceful and tired in the midst of its persistent nausea. His head seemed to have inflated to gigantic proportions; inside it someone was shouting, in a tenacious and pitiless voice that caused Romashov terrible pain:

"One! Two! One! Two!"

XII

The 23rd of April was a very busy and a very strange day for Romashov. At ten in the morning, while the sub-lieutenant was still lying in bed, the Nikolaevs' batman Stepan came to him with a letter from Alexandra Petrovna.

> Rommy, my dear, I wouldn't be at all surprised to find out that you had forgotten that today is both your and my saint's day. So I'm reminding you about it. <u>No matter what</u>, I want to see you! Only don't come during the day, but at five o'clock sharp. We're going to have a picnic at The Oaks.
>
> Yours,
>
> A.N.

The letter trembled in Romashov's hand as he read it. An entire week had passed already since he had seen Shurochka's sweet face, which could be affectionate, funny, friendly, and attentive by turn, or felt her tender and powerful charm. "Today!" whispered something joyous and exultant within him.

"Today!" Romashov cried loudly, jumping sideways out of bed onto the floor. "Gainan, I need to wash up!"

Gainan came in.

"Your excellency, the batman is waiting outside. He wants to know if you wish to send a reply or not."

"Of course, of course!" Romashov stared at him as he slowly sat down. "He wants a tip. But I don't have anything for him now." He looked at his servant with bewilderment.

Gainan gave him a wide and happy smile.

"I don't have anything either! You don't have anything, and I don't have anything. How about that!"

The memory of that black spring night, muddy and wet, when he pressed himself against the slippery fence and listened to Stepan's indifferent voice in the darkness lashed through Romashov's head. *He comes, he comes: every day he comes. But only the devil knows why.* He came to himself with a feeling of unbearable shame. Oh, what future bliss the sub-lieutenant would have given for a kopek, a single kopek!

Romashov rubbed his face vigorously and even let out an agitated quack.

"Gainan," he whispered, glancing fearfully towards the door. "Gainan, tell him that the sub-lieutenant will tip him this evening without fail. You hear? Without fail."

Romashov was currently suffering through a period of great financial difficulty. His credit had been stopped everywhere: in the bar, in the commissary, at the officers' lending house . . . The only place he could get lunch or dinner was at the officers' club, where he was forced to eat his meal without vodka or side dishes. He didn't even have any tea or sugar. The only thing that was left, by a sort of hilarious cosmic joke, was a huge can of coffee, which he drank regularly every morning without sugar. When he was finished he gave Gainan a cup, so that Gainan could make coffee for himself out of what was left.

The sub-lieutenant gulped down the black, strong, bitter swill with a grimace of distaste, as he thought about his situation. "Hm . . . for starters, how could I possibly show up without a gift? And should it be candy or a pair of gloves? Then again, I don't know what size she wears. Candy? The best thing would be to bring her perfume: the candy around here is terrible . . . A fan maybe? Hm . . . ! Of course perfume is better, yes. She loves Bouquet S. Afterwards there'll be a picnic: the cab ride there and back, let's say: that's five, plus Stepan's tea, there goes another ruble! Yes sir, Sub-lietutenant Romashov, there's no way you'll get away with spending anything less than ten rubles."

He reviewed his assets. His salary? But just yesterday he had signed the wage schedule. All of his salary had been there, in precise columns, including a section for promissory notes; a sublieutenant was not allowed to receive even a kopek from these. Maybe he could ask for an advance? He had tried that at least thirty times already, without success. The treasurer was the staff captain Doroshenko—a strict and ill-tempered man, especially with "newbies." He'd been wounded in the Turkish war, but in a most uncomfortable and disreputable place: the heel. The wound (which, however, he had received not while running away, but while turning towards his plattoon to order an attack) had provoked so much teasing and mockery that, though he had set out for the war a carefree ensign, he'd returned from it a bilious and irritable hypochondriac. No, Doroshenko wouldn't give out any money, especially to a sub-lieutenant who had already signed over three straight months' wage to the payment of past debts.

"But we won't let that get us down!" Romashov said to himself. "Let's go through the officers—company by company. In order. First company: Osadchin!"

Osadchin's handsome and excellent face, with its rough, beast-like eyes, appeared before Romashov. "No—anyone other than him. Not him. Second company—Talman. Dear Talman: he borrows money from everybody, even from sub-ensigns. Khutinsky?"

Romashov thought it over. A crazy and childish idea flashed through his head: to request a loan from the regiment commander. "Imagine it! No doubt he'd be horrorstricken first, then start trembling with rage—and then he'd kick me out of his offce. 'What's this? Silence! Four days in the guardroom!'"

The sub-lieutenant chuckled to himself. No, he could come up with something better than that! The day, which had begun under such happy auspices, could not fail to deliver. He wasn't sure why he felt this way: the reason was elusive, incomprehensible even, but he felt it nonetheless, incontrovertibly, somewhere deep inside him.

"How about Captain Dyeverena? The one whom the soldiers call 'Dim-manure' as a joke. But wasn't there also a General Budberg Von Shaufus, who the soldiers called 'Bugbear Von Shithouse.' No, Dyeverena is a miser and doesn't like me—that I know . . ."

He went through all the commanders this way, from the first company to the sixteenth, including non-coms; then with a sigh, he turned to the junior officers. He still hadn't lost faith in his success, but he was starting to grow agitated, when suddenly a single name glittered in his mind: Sub-lieutenant Rafalski!

"Rafalski, of course. My brain must be broken . . . Gainan! My jacket, gloves, coat—look alive!"

Sub-lieutenant Rafalski, the commander of the fourth batallion, was a strange old bachelor, whom the men of the regiment referred to as Lieutenant Burden"—jokingly and behind his back, of course. He spent little time with his fellow officers, visiting with them only on Easter and New Year's, and paid such superficial attention to his military duties that he received continual rebukes from commanding officers and serious abuse during training exercises. Meanwhile, he devoted all his care, not to mention the reservoir of affection that lay unfulfilled within his heart, towards the love and friendship of his little animals:

birds, fish, and four-footed creatures, of which he possessed quite a large and unique menagerie. The women of the regiment, who were secretly hurt by his inattention, said that they could not understand how anyone could spend time with him. "Akh, those animals—what horrors! Not to mention the stink, if you'll pardon the expression! Phew!"

The fact that all of Lieutenant Burden's savings went into his little zoo limited his own possessions to the barest of necessities. God only knew how old his uniform and coat were; he slept in his own dilapidated quarters and ate at the fifteenth company's mess hall, for whose rations he unfailingly paid more than the usual amount. To his peers, however—especially the junior officers—he rarely refused to lend small sums, at least when he had any money to give. Paying him back was frowned upon, even considered somewhat naïve—after all, his nickname was "Lieutenant Burden."

Dissolute ensigns like Lyubov, when they went to ask him for a loan of a couple rubles, would say: "I've come to see your zoo." This was the way to the old bachelor's heart and pockets. "Are there any new beasties, Ivan Antonich? Please show me. You talk about them all so wonderfully . . ."

Romashov visited him often, though without a mercenary goal—for to be honest, animals themselves aroused in him a particular, tender, and intense sort of love. In Moscow, when he had been a cadet and then a junker, he had gone to the circus more frequently than the theater, and the zoo even more than both of them, not to mention the various little menageries around the city. His boyhood dream had been to own a St. Bernard; now he secretly dreamed of being made a battallion adjutant, so that he would receive a horse. Neither of these dreams, however, were destined to become realities: the first due to the poverty in which his family lived, and the second thanks to the fact that he did not "cut a good enough figure" to be an adjutant.

He left his house. The warm spring air brushed his cheeks with soothing caresses. The earth, which had only recently dried after the rain, squished beneath his feet with a pleasant resilience. The white caps of the bird cherry and lilacs twisted over the fences, spilling onto the road in thick bunches. Romashov felt something expand suddenly inside his chest, as if he were about to take flight. After glancing around briefly to see if there was anyone else on the road, he removed Shurochka's letter from his pocket, reread it, and pressed his lips passionately to her signature.

"Oh, what a sky! Oh, what trees!" he whispered, his eyes wet.

Lieutenant Burden lived in the middle of a huge yard, in a house surrounded by a tall green lattice. A brief message was written on the wicker gate: DOGS! DO NOT ENTER WITHOUT RINGING! Romashov rang. From behind the gate a disheveled, sleepy, and lazy-looking servant appeared.

"Is the lieutenant home?"

"Come on in if you'd like, sir."

"Announce me first."

"No need, sir." The servant sleepily scratched his thigh. "They don't like it, you know, when you announce people."

Romashov walked down the brick-lined path towards the house. From around a corner jumped two gigantic, mouse-colored Great Dane pups. One of these began barking, loudly but playfully. Romashov thumped him with his hand, at which point the dog began to pivot his front legs back and forth, first to the right and then to the left, and to bark even louder. His companion stepped on Romashov's heels and stuck his muzzle curiously into the lining of his coat. A young donkey stood in the center of the yard, on the new green grass. He was dozing peacefully in the spring sun, frowning and tossing his ears with pleasure. Chickens strutted around, as well as multicolored roosters, ducks, and Chinese geese with scales on their noses; guinea fowl cried out distressingly, and a wonderful turkey, with his tail spread and his wings against the ground, circled a slender turkey-hen with arrogant lust. By a nearby trough, an enormous, pink Yorkshire pig lay on his side in the dirt.

Lieutenant Burden, who was standing at the window with his back to the door, dressed in a leather Swedish jacket, did not notice when Romashov came in. He was fiddling with a glass aquarium, into whose water he had sunk his arm up to the elbow. Romashov had to cough loudly twice before Burden turned his long, lean, bearded face with its old tortoise-shell glasses towards him.

"Ah—Sub-lieutenant Romashov! What a pleasure, what a pleasure . . ." Rafalski said welcomingly. "Excuse me for not giving you my hand—I'm all wet, don't you know. As you can see, I'm installing a new siphon. I simplified the old one, and now it works like a charm. Would you like some tea?"

"Thank you, no. I've had some already. Lieutenant, sir: I have come . . ."

"No doubt you've heard the rumor that the regiment is going to move to another town?" Rafalski said, as if continuing a momentarily interrupted conversation. "Naturally, you can see why this news would drive me to despair. Think about it— how am I supposed to transport my fish? Half of them will die. And the aquarium? The glass is almost four meters long—see for yourself. Ah, my boy!" he said, jumping suddenly to another topic. "What an aquarium I saw at Sevastapol! A reservoir, by god . . . the size of this room, made of stone, with running sea-water. Electricity! You can stand over it and see how the fish live. Balugas, sharks, skates, sea roosters—ah, such darlings! Several different types of ray: imagine a kind of pancake, a meter and a half long, wiggling its sides, you see, completely freely, and at the back, a tail like a gun . . . I stood there for two hours . . . What are you smiling about?"

"Forgive me . . . I only just noticed that there's a white mouse sitting on your shoulder."

"Ah, you, you little rogue, what are you getting into?" Rafalski turned his head and made a sound with his teeth like a kiss, only unusually dainty, so that it came out like a mouse's squeak. The small, white, red-eyed animal came right up to his face and, shivering his whole body, began to poke his little snout fussily against the man's beard and mouth.

"They're so familiar with you!" Romashov said.

"Yes . . . familiar," Rafalski sighed, and shook his head. "And what a shame that we're not more familiar with them. Men train dogs, tame horses, domesticate cats, but as for what an existence like this can teach us—we're not even curious. A scientist dedicates his entire life, devil take him, to explaining this or that silly antidiluvian word, and people consider it honorable—they practically canonize him there and then. But take the dog—just the dog. These lively, thoughtful, intelligent animals live side by side with us, and not a single university professor has spent any time at all examining their psychology!"

"Perhaps there are works that examine these questions, only we don't know about them?" Romashov suggested timidly.

"Works? Hm . . . of course there are, and of the greatest importance. Take my collection, for example—it's a veritable library." The sub-lieutenant pointed to a row of bookcases that ran along the wall. "These men write intelligently and probingly. Immense learning! What ambition, what sharp-sighted methods . . . But that's not what I'm talking about—not at all! None of them think about the purpose of their studies in any way . . . If they only directed their attention for a single day on dogs or cats. Think about it, just try and think about how a dog lives, what she thinks, how she makes her way around with her passions, her joys. Listen: I've seen clowns train dogs. It's staggering! . . . It's hypnosis, in so many words: genuine hypnosis! What one clown showed me in a hotel in Kiev—it was remarkable, simply unbelievable! But then you think—a clown, a clown! And what if a serious natural scientist devoted himself to this, armed with his knowledge, with his remarkable ability to marry experience and intelligence, with his learned capacities. What startling things we'd hear about dogs' intellectual abilities, about their characters, about their ability to count—you'd better believe there would be something about that! A whole world—an enormous, fascinating world! For example, say what you want, but I for one am convinced that dogs have their own language and that it's quite an extensive one—to say the least."

"Then why hasn't anyone occupied themselves with this yet, Ivan Antonovich?" Romashov asked. "It's so simple!"

Rafalski smiled sarcastically.

"Simply because it is so simple. Simply that. A knot is simply a piece of string. First of all, think about what a dog is to this kind of man . . . A vertebrate, a mammal, a predator of a certain breed, and so on. All that is true. On the other hand, approach a dog as you would a person, or a child, or like a thinking being . . . Truly, despite all their pride of learning, people like that are no different from your everyday muzhik, who thinks that instead of souls dogs have, so to speak, just airy vapor."

He stopped talking and began working again, breathing heavily and angrily, and grunting, as he perched himself above the gutta-percha chimney that he was fitting to the bottom of the aquarium. Romashov gathered himself to speak.

"Ivan Antonovich, I have a great, great favor to ask of you . . ."

"Money?"

"I'm truly ashamed to bother you about it—truly. Just a little: ten rubles maybe. I can't promise to pay you back soon, but . . ."

Ivan Antonovich pulled his hands out of the water and began drying them off with a towel.

"Ten I can do. No more, but I can do ten with great pleasure. I dare say it's for some stupid thing or another? No, no, no, I'm joking. Come with me."

He led him across the length of the house, which consisted of five or six rooms. There was not a single piece of furniture, nor a single curtain anywhere. The air reeked with the characteristically acrid smell of small carnivorous life. The floors were so soiled that one's feet slipped on them.

In every corner there were little burrows and lairs that looked like tiny kennels, as well as hollow stumps, and barrels whose ends had been knocked out. A pair of branchy trees had been set up in two of the rooms—one for birds, the other for martens and squirrels, with cleverly designed hollows and nests. Examining these, one sensed (as with so many of the animal accomodations) how much thoughtful care and love, not to mention keen observation, had gone into their making.

"See this beast here?" Rafalski said, pointing to a small kennel that was surrounded by a fence of prickly barbed wire. From its round opening, which was the size of the bottom of a glass, two bright black dots sparkled. "This is the most rapacious, the most ferocious animal in the entire world. The polecat. You wouldn't think it, but next to him all those lions and panthers are nothing more than meek little calfs. The lion eats his pound of meat and takes off—then watches equably as the jackals finish it up. But if this pretty little scoundrel makes his way into your chicken pen, not a single bird will be left—he bites, without fail, right here, in the cerebellum. He remains undomesticatable, the scoundrel. He's the wildest, the least tame of all my beasts. Hey, you—rascal!"

He plunged his hand into the enclosure. From the circular door he pulled a small raging face with wide open jaws, in which sharp white teeth sparkled. The polecat quickly showed himself, then hid again, making noises that sounded like angry coughs.

"See what I mean? And I've been feeding him for a year . . ."

The sub-lieutenant had apparently forgotten all about Romashov's request. He led him from den to den, showing him his favorites, which he described with such sweetness and enthusiasm, and with such an understanding of their habits and characters, that it was almost as if he were talking about good, close friends. To be fair, he had an excellent collection for a provincial enthusiast: white mice, hares, guinea pigs, hedgehogs, marmots, some poisonous snakes in glass boxes, a couple varieties of lizards, two marmosets, a black Australian rabbit, and a rare, extraordinarily beautiful angora cat.

"What do you think? Not bad, eh?" Rafalski said, as he showed him the cat. "Charming, even, wouldn't you say? But don't give him too much credit. He's stupid. The stupidest of all the cats. There again!" He grew suddenly animated. "Again, you see how unfamiliar we are with the mental lives of our domesticated animals. What do we know about the cat? About horses? About cows? Pigs? Do you know who else is quite smart? The pig. Yes, yes, don't laugh"—Romashov had not even thought of laughing— "Pigs are terribly bright. Last year I had a wild boar who played a real trick on me. They used to bring me runoff from the sugar refinery, which I used for my vegetable garden and for the pigs. But he didn't have the patience to wait, you see. The delivery boy left to get my servant, and he grabbed the stopper with his teeth and pulled it out of the barrel. The runoff poured out, you see, and he helped himself. Another time—we'd discovered his previous theft—he didn't just take the stopper out, but buried it in the garden. That's pigs for you. I confess," Rafalski winked and made a sly face, "I confess, I'm writing a little article about my pigs . . . Only shh! . . . It's a secret . . . Don't tell anyone. It's frowned upon: a sub-lieutenant in the holy Russian army, and then suddenly he writes an article on pigs. Now I have Yorkshires. You've seen them? Do you want to go have a look? There in the yard I also have a young badger, a sweet little badger . . . Shall we go?"

"I'm sorry, Ivan Antonovich," Romashov said. "I would, gladly. Only, God knows, I have no time."

Rafalski smacked his head with his hand.

"Of course, my boy! Excuse me. I'm old, I natter on . . . All right, yes, yes, let's move along."

They went to a bare little room, which was literally empty save for a narrow cot, the linen of which sagged like the bottom of a boat, and a night table with a stool. Rafalski took a box off the night table and removed some money.

"I'm very happy to be of service to you, Sub-lieutenant— very happy. Well, still . . . What else can I say . . . I'm babbling . . . Very happy . . . Come back when you have a moment. We'll talk more."

As he was making his way towards the street, Romashov ran into Vetkin. His mustache was terribly disheveled, and his cap flattened on one side, so that it sat tilted on his head in a raffish manner.

"Ah-hah! Prince Hamlet!" Vetkin cried happily. "From where and to where? Devil take it, you're glowing, like a saint."

"Well—I am a saint today," Romashov smiled.

"Is that so? Ah yes, truly: Gregory and Alexandra. Divine. Allow me to give you a hug."

They embraced fiercely, right there in the middle of the road.

"In that case, maybe we should stop by the officers' club? Let's toast to the most, as our good friend Archakovsky says," Vetkin suggested.

"I can't, Pavel Pavlich. I'm late. Anyway, it looks like you're in fine form already."

"Oh-ho-ho!" Vetkin tipped his chin up proudly and knowingly. "Today I executed a maneuver that would make the minister of finance's stomach turn with envy."

"Really?"

Vetkin's maneuver was completely simple, though not particularly sharp-witted; moreover, its success had to do with the regimental tailor Haim. Vetkin had given him a receipt for a pair of uniforms; but instead of the uniforms, the crafty Pavel Pavlich had gotten him to dole out thirty rubles of ready money.

"All things considered, we both ended up satisfied," Vetkin said triumphantly. "The Jew's satisfied, because in exchange for his thirty rubles he gets forty-five back from the uniform dispensary, and I'm satisfied, since I'll be taking all those little cheats to the cleaners at the officers' club tonight. How about that? Nicely done, wouldn't you say?

"Very nice," Romashov agreed. "I'll keep it in mind for next time. However, you must excuse me, Pavel Pavlich. Good luck tonight."

They went their separate ways. But after a minute Vetkin called out to his friend. Romashov turned around.

"You got a tour of the menagerie?" Vetkin asked slyly, gesturing with a large hand over his shoulder at Rafalski's house.

Romashov nodded his head and said with conviction:

"That Rafalski of ours is a holy man. A darling!"

"You said it!" Vetkin agreed. "Only nuts!"

XIII

When he got to the Nikolaevs' house at around five o'clock, Romashov was surprised to find that the happy self-confidence he'd been feeling all morning had transformed, over the course of the day, into a sort of strange and groundless anxiety. It seemed to him that this change had occurred, not suddenly, at that very moment, but rather some time much earlier; clearly, the apprehension had grown in his heart, steadily and imperceptibly, from some specific moment. This type of thing had happened to him even during his earliest childhood; so he knew that in order to combat his panic he had to find its source. However, it was not until evening, after spending an entire day trying to do this, that he remembered how, at noontime, while walking towards the station along the rails, he had been deafened by the unexpected whistle of a train—had been frightened even, and so found himself in a bad mood without really realizing it. But then soon after this, he recalled, he had become light and even happy again.

He reviewed the day's impressions in reverse order. Svidersky's shop; the perfume; renting Leiba's cab—what a wonderful cabman he is; asking the time at the post office; a perfect morning, really; Stepan . . . had it been Stepan? But no: he was keeping a ruble separate in his pocket for Stepan. What was it, then? What?

Three horse-drawn carriages were already waiting at the fence. Two servants held the reins of the saddled horses: an old brown gelding, which Olizar had bought recently from the cavalry remainders, and Bek-Agamalov's beautiful, frisky golden mare, with her fierce and flashing eyes.

A thought flashed through Romashov's mind. "Ah: the letter! That strange phrase: 'No matter what' . . . underlined, too . . . What was that supposed to mean? Perhaps Nikolaev is angry at me? Jealous? Perhaps there's been gossip of some kind? Nikolaev has been dry with me lately. No, no, I'll let it go."

"Keep going!" he shouted at the driver.

But just then—without seeing or hearing, but just feeling that the door had opened—he felt his heart begin to beat sweetly and stormily.

"Rommy! Where are you going?" he heard behind him. It was the happy, melodic voice of Alexandra Petrovna.

He tugged on Leib's coat and jumped out of the carriage. Shurochka stood in the black doorframe. She was wearing a plain white dress with red flowers on her belt, on her right hip; similar flowers sat, with bright warmth, in her hair. Strange: Romashov recognized her immediately—and yet, at the same it was as if he were seeing her for the first time. He sensed that there was something bright, new, and festive inside her.

He muttered his congratulations with unceremonious warmth. As he was doing so she said quickly and under her voice:

"Thank you for coming, Rommy. Ah, I was so afraid you would refuse. Listen: be gentle and glad today. Don't pay attention to anything. You're funny: you wither if someone touches you. You're such a shrinking violet."

"Alexandra Petrovna . . . the letter you sent today troubled me. There was a phrase in it . . ."

"Don't worry about it, my dear, my dear . . ." Looking straight into his eyes, she took both his hands and pressed them strongly. Once again, Romashov found something completely unfamiliar in her gaze: a kind of affectionate tenderness, as well as an intensity, anxiety, and, even deeper in the mysterious depths of her blue irises, a strange, secret, inaccessible understanding, which seemed to be speaking in the most hidden and dark language of the soul . . .

"Please, you don't need to worry. Don't think about it today . . . Doesn't the fact that I stood here watching the whole time as your carriage approached make you happy? What a scaredy-cat you are. Don't you dare look at me like that!"

She smiled in embarrassment and shook her head.

"Well, all right . . . Rommy, my awkward one, as usual, you won't kiss my hand. That's better. And now another one. There. Good boy. Let's go now—and don't forget," she said in a rushed, intense whisper, "today is our day. Alexandra and George her knight. Do you hear me? Go."

"Here, if you would . . . a modest gift . . ."

"What's this? Perfume? How silly of you! No, no, I'm joking. Thank you, my dear Rommy. Volodya!" she said, loudly and naturally, as she entered the living room. "Here's another one for the picnic. And it's his name day too."

The living room was loud and disorderly, as was always the case before group outings. The thick cloud of tobacco smoke took on a sky-blue color in those spots where it was intersected by the sloping shafts of spring sunlight that were streaming in through the window. In the middle of the living room, seven or eight officers stood talking heatedly; the loudest shouts were coming from the tall figure of Talman, whose braying voice was punctuated every few seconds by coughs. The group consisted of Captain Osadchi, the inseperable adjutants Olizar and Bek-Agamatov, Lieutenant Andrusevich, a small, bold man with a sharp and rat-like face, and someone else, who Romashov could not immediately make out. Sophia Pavlovna Talman, smiling, powdered and rouged like a large, dressed-up doll, sat on the divan with Sub-lieutenant Mikhin's two sisters. Both women were wearing identical white dresses with green ribbons, which were plain and homemade but still gratifying; both were pink-skinned, black-haired, dark-eyed and freckled; both had remarkably white but slightly crooked teeth that, nevertheless, gave their saucy mouths a distinct and unique charm; and both were good-natured and cheerful, and in this way they resembled both one another and their brother as well, who was very ugly. Other regimental women had been invited: the wife of

Lieutenant Andrusevich, who was small, pale, fat, stupid, and hilarious, and who loved above all else puns and bawdy jokes, and the friendly, talkative, lisping Likavech girls.

As was frequently the case at officers' get-togethers, the women kept apart from the men, in a separate group. Only Captain Dietz sat with them, lain carelessly and foppishly across the sofa. This officer, who, with his long figure and worn-out but self-assured face, resembled a member of the Prussian service as they were drawn in German caricatures, had been transferred to the infantry regiment from the guards due to some sort of dark and scandalous incident. He was remarkable for his unshakable ablomb in conversations with men, and for his impudent forwardness with women. He was also a great card player, who met with continual success: he never played at the officers' club but only at the civilian card parties that met in the houses of town officials and local Polish landowners. He was not well liked in the regiment, though he was feared, and everyone somehow vaguely expected him to come to some sort of loud and messy end. It was said that he had some sort of connection to the young wife of a decrepit brigadeer commander who lived in the town. In the same way, there were rumors about his closeness to Madame Talman: it was on her account that he was usually invited places—a circumstance demanded by the unique laws of regimental courtesy and consideration.

"Good to see you, very good," Nikolaev said as he met Romashov. "Much better now that you're here. Why didn't you come this morning to have pirogis with us?"

He spoke happily, with an affectionate smile, but in his voice and eyes Romashov clearly caught that same estranged, forced, dry expression that he felt every time he met Nikolaev these days.

"He doesn't like me," Romashov thought quickly. "Why? Is he angry? Jealous? Do I annoy him?"

"We've been having weapons inspection in the regiment, you know . . ." Romashov lied bravely. "The preparation has left us no free time, even on holidays . . . However, I confess, I'm quite confused . . . I had no idea that you were having a picnic—I simply came, thrusting myself on you as usual. To be honest, I'm a little embarrassed . . ."

Nikolaev smiled broadly and gave Romashov's shoulder a condescending pat.

"No, no—don't worry, my friend . . . You're like family— the more the merrier . . . What's with this Mandarin formality? Only, I don't know if there's a place in the carriage. Well, we'll manage somehow."

"I brought a carriage," Romashov reassured him, shaking his shoulder out almost imperceptibly from under Nikolaev's hands. "Actually, it would be my pleasure if you'd make use of it as you wish."

He glanced up quickly and met Shurochka's eyes.

"Thank you, my dear!" she said with the same warm and strangely attentive glance that she'd given him earlier.

"How amazing she is today!" Romashov thought.

"Wonderful," Nikolaev said, looking at his watch. "What do you think, gentlemen?" he inquired, "Shall we go?"

"Let's go, let's go, as the parrot said when Vashka the cat grabbed his tail through the birdcage," Olizar shouted jokingly.

They rose with exclamations and smiles; the women looked around for their umbrellas and hats and put on their gloves;

Mr. Talman, who was suffering from bronchitis, shouted to the entire room that they should not forget to bring along warm shawls; a lively hubbub ensued.

The tiny Mikhin took Romashov aside.

"Yuri Alexceich, I have a favor to ask you," he said. "It is very important to me. Please accompany my sisters, otherwise Deitz will sit with them, which would be simply unbearable to me. He always speaks so . . . crudely to them—it brings them to the point of tears. I mean, I despise violence as much as the next man—but God knows I'm going to punch him in his ugly mug one of these days! . . ."

Romashov wanted very much to travel with Shurochka, but Mikhin—whose clear, bright eyes were looking at him pleadingly—was always so nice to him, and anyway Romashov's heart was filled at that moment with such an overwhelming joy, that there was no way he could refuse.

The party lingered noisily for some time on the porch trying to work out who would ride with whom. Romashov found a place with the two Mikhin women. Staff Captain Leshenko, whom Romashov had not noticed before, and who no one, apparently, wanted to ride with, was shifting from one foot to another between the carriages with the same depressed and abject look that he always wore. Romashov called him over and offered him a place next to his on the front seat. Leshenko looked at the sub-lieutenant with his usual doglike devotion, and took his place in the carriage with a sigh.

At last, everyone was seated. Somewhere in the front Olizar was wheeling around on his old, sluggish gelding, clowning about as he sung lines from an operetta:

> Come sit with me in the carriage quick,
> Come sit with me in the carriage soon.

"Forward, at a trot!" Osadchin commanded loudly.

The carriages set off.

XIV

The picnic turned out to be louder and rowdier than it was pleasant. They traveled four miles into The Oaks: a forty-five-acre grove that ranged over a long, gently sloping incline, to where it was skirted at its base by a bright and narrow river. The grove itself was made up of a sparse but beautiful copse of hundred-year-old oaks, whose strong trunks had been obscured by a thick and unbroken layer of shrubbery. Despite this covering, there were still plenty of charming, sizable clearings to be found, which were fresh, pleasant, and covered with sweet new grass. In one of these clearings, servants that they had sent ahead with samovars and baskets were waiting for them.

They spread the tablecloth on the ground immediately and began arranging themselves. The women set out the dishes and plates, while the men assisted them with exaggeratedly polite gestures. Olizar tied one of the napkins into an apron, put another on his head like a chef's hat, and did an impression of Lukich, the cook from the officers' club. A long time was spent shuffling the seats around so that the women alternated with their cavaliers. Necessity forced them to half-sit, half-lie in uncomfortable positions, which was not something most of them did regularly, and which caused the silent Leshenko to remark suddenly, in a bombastic tone, and with a look of exaggerated stupidity:

"Look at us—lying around like the ancient Greeks."

Shurochka sat across from him, with Mr. Talman on one side of her and on the other—Romashov. She was being unusually talkative and gay, and was so animated that many of the guests could not help but notice her excitement. For his part, Romashov had never found her so enchantingly beautiful. A large, feverish feeling of a kind he hadn't seen before was streaming, trembling, and pleading its way through her. Every once in a while she turned to Romashov and stared at him wordlessly, for perhaps only a half-second more than normal, but still long enough for him to perceive an enigmantic and irresistible flame in her eyes.

Osadchin, who was sitting alone at the head of the table, got to his knees. After striking his glass with a fork and requesting silence, he began talking in a low, chesty voice, which rolled out over the crisp air of the forest in rich waves.

"Ladies and gentlemen . . . Let us drink our first glass to the health of our beautiful hostess, whose name day it is today. May God give her every happiness in the world, and make her a general's wife."

And, raising his large glass high, he roared at the top of his incredibly powerful lungs:

"Hoorah!"

The entire grove seemed to perk up at this lion's roar, as the resounding echoes ran amongst the trees. Andrusevich, who was sitting beside Osadchin, fell on his back in mock horror, as if deafened. The others cried out amicably. The men pushed their glasses towards Shurochka. Romashov purposefully waited until everyone else had taken their turn, and she noticed this. She smiled with quiet intensity, holding out her glass of white wine as she turned towards him. Her eyes in that moment dilated, growing darker; her lips moved expressively but without a sound, as if talking to themselves. But then she turned and, smiling, returned to her conversation with Mr. Talman. "What did she say?" Romashov thought. "But—what did she say?" The question excited and alarmed him. When no one was looking he tried to find the answer by covering his face with his hand and repeating the same movements that Shurochka had made with her own lips. But it was no use. "My dear?" "I love you?" "Rommy?"—no, none of these. The only thing he could say for certain was that there had been three syllables.

Afterwards they gave a toast to Nikolaev's health, and to his future success on the general's staff; they drank enthusiastically, as if his admission into the academy were beyond doubt. Then, at Shurochka's suggestion, they gave a rather underwhelming toast to Romashov's Saint's day. They drank to the women present, then to everyone present, then to all other women whether present or not, and to the sacred name of their regiment, and to the undefeatable Russian army . . .

Talman, who was already drunk enough, raised his glass and cried out hoarsely, but movingly:

"Gentlemen, I propose that we drink a toast to the health of our beloved, our blessed monarch, for whom each of us is prepared to spill his own blood to the last drop!"

He delivered the last words of this in an unexpectedly thin and whistling falsetto, for he had run out of breath. His black

Gypsy's eyes, with their jaundiced whites, blinked suddenly in pitiful helplessness, as tears rolled down his swarthy cheeks.

"The anthem, the anthem!" fat little Andruchev demanded excitedly.

They stood up. The officers saluted. The dissonant but rousing sound of the anthem spread over the grove, and the louder it grew, the more melancholy and out of tune the sensitive staff captain Leshenko's voice began to sound.

They drank a lot, as usual—as people always drink in the military, whether visiting, at parties, lunches, or picnics. They all spoke at once, making it hard to understand what one another were saying. Shurochka, who had already drunk quite a bit of white wine, and whose face was flushed, with moist red lips and eyes made entirely black by her dilated pupils, suddenly leaned in close towards Romashov.

"I don't like these provincial picnics, there's something shallow and pretentious about them," she said. "I know I have to do this for my husband before he leaves, but good Lord—how stupid it all is. We could have done this at home, in the garden—you know how wonderfully ancient and shady our garden is. All the same, I seem to be absolutely mad with happiness today. Good heavens, how happy I am! No, Rommy, my dear, I know why, I'll tell you later, later . . . yes . . . Ah no, no, Rommy, I don't understand it—not at all."

The lids of her beautiful eyes were half-shut, giving her face an alluring, promising, agonizingly impatient look. She'd become shamelessly beautiful over the course of the evening, and Romashov, who still did not understand how this had happened, nonetheless could sense the passionate excitement that had possessed her—could sense it by the sweet shivering that was shooting up through his arms and legs and chest.

"There's something special about you today. What's going on?" he asked in a whisper.

She answered him with a sort of naïve and mild surprise.

"I'm telling you, I don't know. I don't know. Look: the sky is blue, the light is blue . . . And inside me there's the most wonderful blue-colored feeling—a sort of blue joy! Pour me some more wine, Rommy, my dear boy . . ."

At the other end of the tablecloth a conversation had started up about preparations for the war with Germany, which many thought was practically a foregone conclusion at that point. The cries and arguments, which arose from several different directions at once, blurred together nonsensically. Suddenly, Osadchin's angry, confident voice rose above the clamor. He was a little drunk, but in his case that only meant that his red face had become terribly pale, and that the heavy look in his large black eyes had become even gloomier.

"Nonsense!" he shouted sharply. "Every word of it is nonsense, I say. War has degenerated. Everything in the world has degenerated. Children are born idiots, women are lopsided and men have bad nerves. 'Oh, blood! Oh, I'm fainting!'" he said, in a sort of nasal tone. "And all of this is because the time of true, fierce, merciless war has passed. How can you call this a real war? Someone shoots at you from fifteen miles away and you go home a hero. You call that gallantry, for Christ's sake? They take a prisoner, and it's all, 'Ah, my dear, er, I mean, my friend, would you perhaps like a smoke? Or maybe some tea? Poor thing . . . Are you warm? Is the bed soft enough?' Oo-ooh," Ocadchin began to growl terribly, pulling his head up like a bull about to gore someone. "In the Middle Ages they could fight—no one will dispute that. Night attacks. Whole cities on fire. 'For three days the soldiers plundered the village!' Burst to pieces. Blood and fire. Knocking the bottoms out of barrels. Blood and wine in the street. Imagine how joyful those feasts in the ruins were! Women—naked, beautiful, tears streaming down their cheeks—dragged through the streets by their hair. No pity. They were the sweet spoils of the victors! . . ."

"We, on the other hand, would rather you don't overexert yourself," Sophia Talman remarked jokingly.

"At night the houses burned, and the wind rocked the charred bodies over which the ravens cawed. And underneath the hanged men: raging bonfires, the feasts of the conquerors. There were no prisoners. Why would there be prisoners? Why waste unnecessary energy? Ah!" Ocadchin groaned in rage and gnashed his teeth. "That was a brave time—a time of wonders! And the warriors! They fought face-to-face for hours, cold-blooded and mad, brutally and with staggering skill. What men, what terrible physical strength! Gentlemen!" He rose to his feet and drew himself up to his full, imposing height, his voice ringing with passion and daring. "Gentlemen, I know your classes have taught you that contemporary warfare is something humane. But let's drink—and if no one else will join me, I'll drink alone—to the glory of warriors past, and to joyous and bloodthirsty brutality!"

Everyone was silent—overcome, it seemed, by the unexpected ecstacy of this usually morose and reserved man. They looked at him with curiosity and fear. But then suddenly Bek-Agamatov jumped up from where he was sitting. He did this quickly, and so unexpectedly that many of the other guests started, and one of the women leapt back in alarm. His eyes skitted around, shining wildly. His clenched white teeth were bared like fangs. His breathing was heavy, but he couldn't seem to find the words for what he wanted to say.

"O-o! That's it . . . That, I understand! Ah!" With frantic strength, as if in rage, he grabbed at Osadchin's hand and began tugging on it. "To hell with these whiners! To hell with pity! Ah! To the fight!"

His barbaric heart, whose ancestral bloodlust lay dormant most of the time, had roused itself now and needed to move. He looked around him with bloodshot eyes and, removing his sword suddenly from its sheath, fell furiously on an oak sapling. Branches and young leaves flew onto the tablecloth, falling like rain on everyone who was sitting down.

"Bek! You madman! What a savage!" the women shouted.

Bek-Agamatov came to his senses immediately and sat down. He seemed visibly upset by his frenzied spasm, but his thin nostrils quivered with every wheezing breath, and his black eyes, which stared out from beneath their brows with disfigured rage, loped challengingly around the circle.

Romashov had heard, and at the same time not heard Osadchin's speech. He was experiencing a strange state, a sort of waking dream, like the one that descends upon men in stories when they drink strange, unworldly potions. It seemed to him that a warm, tender web had wrapped itself, softly and lazily, around his entire body, and was now tickling him tenderly and filling his soul to its depths with an exultant happiness. His hands touched Shurochka's frequently, as if under their own direction, but neither he nor she looked at one another anymore. Romashov felt like he was sleeping. The voices of Bek-Agamatov and Osadchin reached him from a kind of distant, unbelievable cloud: he could understand what they were saying, but their words meant absolutely nothing to him.

"Osadchin is . . . a cruel man. He doesn't like me," Romashov thought, though by this point, the person he was thinking about was no longer the Osadchin that had just been speaking but a new figure: a caricature that had been projected on a sort of interior screen, where it could be examined and manipulated, like a moving photograph. "Osadchin has a small, thin, pitiful wife who's always pregnant . . . He never takes her anywhere . . . A young soldier in his company killed himself last year . . . Osadchin . . . Yes . . . What is an Osadchin? Here, now Bek's shouting . . . Who is this fellow, anyway? Do I know him – is that possible? Yes, I know him, but then why the devil is he so strange, alien, and unintelligible to me? And this someone sitting next to me . . . Who are you? Joy is streaming from you—a joy that's making me drunk. 'Blue joy!' . . . There's Nikolaev sitting across from me. He's not happy. He's kept quiet this whole time. He looks over here, but only every once in a while—as if he didn't want anyone to notice. So what, let him be jealous—it's all the same. Oh, blue joy!"

It was getting dark. The soft purple shadows of the trees lay on the clearing. Little Mikhin seemed to suddenly remember something:

"Gentlemen, what about the violets? I was told there were violets around here. Let's gather some."

"It's too late," someone remarked. "At this point you won't be able to see anything in the grass."

"At this point, it's easier to lose something in the grass than to find it," Deitz said. He flashed a nasty smile.

"Well, then let's start the bonfire," Andrusevich suggested.

They gathered a huge pile of brushwood and dry, year-old leaves, which they then lit. A thick column of bright flame rose into the sky. As if frightened, the last remnants of the day ceded their places to the darkness, which, having ventured out of the grove, began gathering now around the bonfire. Crimson spots trembled fearfully on the tops of the oaks, and it seemed as if the trees had begun to stir, to rock back and forth, now gazing down at the red circle of light, now hiding themselves back in the darkness.

Everyone stood up. The servants lit lanterns. The young officers were joking around like schoolboys. Olizar wrestled Mikhin; to everyone's surprise, the small, awkward Mikhin threw his much taller and better-built opponent to the ground twice in a row. After this they began jumping over the fire. Andrusevich imitated a fly beating against a window and an old woman catching a chicken, mimicking the sounds of a saw or knife being sharpened on a whetstone—he was a real master at these types of things. Even Deitz juggled some empty bottles, with real agility.

"Ladies and gentlemen, if you please, I'll show you an amazing trick!" Talman shouted suddenly. "There's no magic here, no wizardry: just sleight of hand. If my esteemed audience would kindly direct its attention to the fact that I have nothing up either of my sleeves. Let us begin. *Ein, zvei, drei* . . . Alley-oop! . . ."

Quickly, and to a chorus of general laughter, he removed a pair of new decks from his pockets and cracked their seals open, one after the other.

"Cards, anyone?" he suggested. "In the open air? Ah?"

Osadchi, Nikolaev, and Andrusevich all sat down to play. Leshenko took his place behind them with a deep sigh. Nikolaev, who was clearly upset about something, resisted for a while—but eventually they talked him into it. As he took his place, he glanced around anxiously, over and over again, searching for Shurochka's eyes, but the low light of the bonfire meant that he had to squint, contorting his face with a pitiful, tortured, and unattractive look.

The rest of the party dispersed gradually into the field, staying for the most part near the bonfire. They tried to organize a game of tag, but the fun ended after the eldest Mikhin, whom Deitz caught, blushed suddenly to the tips of her ears and quit the game point-blank. When she spoke, her voice trembled with indignation and resentment, the cause of which—however, she did not explain.

Romashov walked deeper into the grove along a narrow path. He himself had no idea what he expected to come from this, but his heart beat sweetly and languorously with a vague and blissful premonition. He stopped. He heard the light crack of twigs behind him, then quick steps and the rustling of a silk slip. Shurochka walked quickly up to him—she was light and well built and fine, like the forest air, with her white dress moving between the dark trunks of the huge trees. Romashov went to meet her and embraced her without a word. She was breathing heavily from her quick pace. Her breath touched Romashov's cheeks and lips in warm little bursts, and he felt her heart beating under his palm.

"Let's sit down," Shurochka said.

She lowered herself onto the grass and began putting her hair up at the back of her head with both hands. Romashov lay down by her feet and looked up at her, but since the ground in that spot was slightly lower than where he was, he could only make out the vague and delicate outline of her neck and chin.

Suddenly she asked him, in a soft and trembling voice:

"Rommy, do you feel good?"

"I do feel good," he answered. After he had said this, he thought about it for a second. He remembered what his day had been like, and repeated warmly: "Yes, today I feel very good! But what's come over you?"

"What do you mean?"

She bent closer to him, staring into his eyes. All of a sudden Romashov could see her entire face.

"You're strange, different. You've never been this beautiful before. Something inside you is shining, singing. There's something new in you, something mysterious, I don't know what . . . but . . . You're not angry with me, are you Alexandra Petrovna . . . ? You're not afraid that they're missing us back at the bonfire?"

She laughed quietly, and her deep, affectionate laughter was answered in Romashov's breast by a shudder of joy.

"Oh, Rommy . . . My dear, good, cowardly, dear Rommy! I told you, this is our day. Don't think about anything, Rommy. You know why I'm so brave today? No? You really don't know? It's because today, I'm in love with you. No, no, don't even think it: things won't be the same tomorrow . . ."

Romashov held his hands out towards her, searching for her body.

"Alexandra Petrovna . . . Shurochka . . . Sasha!" he said reverently.

"Don't call me Shurochka, I don't wan't that. Anything else, only not that . . . By the way," she said suddenly, as if only just remembering it, "you know you have a very nice name. George. Much better than Yuri . . . Georg-ie," she said, drawing it out slowly, as if to listen to each sound of the word. "A proud name."

"Oh, my darling!" Romashov said passionately.

"Wait a second . . . Listen: I'm about to tell you the most important part. I saw you today, in a dream. It was incredibly beautiful. I dreamt that you and I were dancing a waltz in some sort of special room. Oh, I'd recognize that room right now down to its last detail. There were carpets all over the place, but only a single red lantern; a new piano was glittering, there were two windows, with red curtains—everything was red, you see. Music was coming from somewhere I couldn't make out, and we were dancing . . . No, no, that kind of sweet, sincere closeness is only possible in dreams. We spun around faster and faster, but our feet weren't touching the floor, and I twirled, twirled, twirled—as if I were swimming in the air. Ah, it went on for so long and was so continually wonderful . . . Tell me, Rommy, do you ever fly in dreams?"

Romashov didn't answer this at first. He felt as if he had stepped into a strange and irresistable fairy tale, which was both unreal and lifelike at the same time. Yes, that was it: the warmth and the darkness of this spring night were like a fairy tale, and the attentive, subdued circle of trees was part of the spell too, and the strange, sweet woman in the white dress sitting close to him, so close. He had to make a willful effort to speak.

"Of course I fly," he answered. "Though less and less each year. Before, when I was a child, I flew around on the ceiling. It was terribly funny to look down at the people below me—they looked like they were walking upside down. They tried to knock me off with a broom, but they couldn't. I kept flying around and laughing. Now it's different—now I only jump," Romashov said with a sigh. "I push off with my feet and fly along the ground. For twenty paces maybe, and not very high—no more than a yard."

Shurochka lay down completely, leaning back on her elbows and putting her hands behind her head. After keeping quiet for a while, she continued thoughtfully:

"And then after the dream, the next morning, I wanted to see you. I wanted to see you so much . . . so much. If you hadn't come tonight, I don't know what I would have done—probably run to see you. That's why I asked you not to come before four o'clock. I was afraid of myself. Do you understand, my darling?"

Her feet lay a half yard away from Romashov's face, crossed one over the other: two small feet in tight slippers and black, white-patterned stockings. Suddenly, with a cloudy head and noise roaring in his ears, Romashov pressed his lips through the stockings against that cold, lively, supple body.

"No . . . Rommy . . . don't," he heard her say above him, in a voice that was weak and drawling, almost lazy.

He lifted his head up. And again, for a second everything around him seemed to be part of a wonderful and hidden fairy-tale forest. The grove climbed evenly along the slope, with its dark leaves, and the scattered, quiet trees whose black bodies seemed to be listening to something through their drowse, keenly and motionlessly. Past the thick branches and the distant trunks at the top of this rise, above the straight, high line of the horizon, a narrow stripe of sunset was burning neither red nor crimson, but a dark purple, an extraordinary color that resembled extinguished coals, or a flame observed through a glass of thick red wine. And on that same mountain, in the dark and fragrant grass, among the black trees, the unfathomable, beautiful white woman lay resting, like a forest goddess.

Romashov moved his body closer to her. Her face seemed to be radiating pale light. Her eyes were like a pair of dark spots—he couldn't make them out, but he felt nonetheless that she was looking at him.

"It's a fairy tale," he whispered quietly, only his lips moving.

"Yes, my darling, a fairy tale . . ."

He began to kiss her dress; he found her hand and pressed his face into her thin, warm, fragrant palm, and said, in a searching voice that was gasping for breath:

"Sasha . . . I love you . . . I love you . . ."

As he lifted his head up higher, he began to make out her eyes, which had grown huge and black, and were now narrowing, now widening—and because of this her whole familiar yet unfamiliar face changed for him in the darkness. His parched lips searched greedily for her mouth, but she bent away from him, shook her head quietly, and repeated, in a slow whisper:

"No, no, no . . . no, my darling . . ."

"Beloved . . . what happiness . . . I love you," Romashov said, in a kind of blissful delirium. "I love you. Look around: the night, and the quiet, and no one else but us. Oh, my joy, how I love you!"

But she whispered, "No, no," breathing heavily, laying her entire body out on the ground. Finally, she started to speak, in a barely audible voice—as if just saying the words was difficult for her.

"Why, Rommy? . . . Why are you so—so weak! Enough with hiding it—I'm drawn to you, everything about you is dear to me: your clumsiness, your purity, your kindness. I'm not saying that I love you, but I think about you all the time, I see you in my dreams, I . . . I feel you . . . Being close to you excites me. But why are you so pitiful? For pity is the sister of contempt. Think about it, I can't respect you—but if only you were strong!" She grabbed Romashov's hat, and began to softly pet and examine his soft hair. "If only you could make a name for yourself—work your way into a grand situation!"

"I'll do it, I'll do it!" Romashov said quietly. "Only, be mine. Come to me. My whole life, I've . . ."

She interrupted him, with a tender and melancholy smile, which he heard in her tone:

"I know you want to, my dear, I do, but you'll never do it. I know you won't. Oh, if only I could believe in you a little bit, I would throw off everything and come to you. Ah, Rommy, my beloved. In some legend or other it was written that God first decided to make every human being whole, and then for some reason split them all into two pieces and cast them out into the world. So for the rest of their lives, each half searches for its partner—and none ever finds it. My dear, you know that you and I are two halves; we have everything in common: our likes, our dislikes, our thoughts, dreams, desires. We understand one another given only half hints and half words—without words even, with our hearts only. And yet I have to reject you. Ah, this is already the second time in my life such a thing has happened to me."

"Yes, I know."

"He told you?" Shurochka said quickly.

"No, it happened by accident. But I know."

They grew quiet. Up in the sky, the first stars were burning their shivering green dots. The rest of the grove, which was submersed in thick shadow, was suffused with a light, thoughtful silence. The bonfire, wherever it was, could not be seen from where they were, but every once in a while, a red light flickered over the tops of the closest oaks, like the reflection of distant summer lightning. Shurochka stroked Romashov's head and face quietly; when his lips found her hands, she pressed her palm to his mouth herself.

"I don't love my husband," she said slowly, as if thinking out loud. "He's rude, dull, indelicate. Ah—I'm ashamed to say it—but we women never forget the first time we fall under a man's power. Also, he's wildly jealous. He's pestered me about poor Nazanski ever since it happened. He wormed every little thing out of me, made the craziest assumptions, too . . . He asked me such disgusting questions. Good Lord! An innocent adolescent romance! But just saying the name would send him flying into a rage."

As she spoke, her voice trembled just a little bit, and her hands shook when she stroked his face.

"Are you cold?" Romashov asked.

"No, my dear, I'm fine," she said gently.

And with a sudden, unexpected, uncontrollable passion she cried:

"Ah, it feels so good being to be with you, my love!"

After this he took her hand and began softly stroking her thin palm.

"Tell me, I beg you. You said yourself that you don't love him . . . Why are you together? . . ." he asked.

But she sat up sharply and nervously pressed her forhead and cheeks, as if to wipe them dry.

"It's late. Let's go. Please—they'll start talking," she said, in a different, completely calm voice.

They rose from the grass and stood facing one another without speaking, listening to one another's breathing, looking into one another's eyes without really seeing them.

"Farewell!" she cried suddenly in a voice like an animal. "Farewell, my joy, my fleeting joy!"

She threw her arms around his neck and pressed her hot moist mouth to his lips, her teeth clenched, pouring her whole body from feet to breast into his with a groan of passion. To Romashov, it was as if the black trunks of the oaks swung to one side, and the earth floated to the other, and that time stood still.

Afterwards she gradually removed herself from his grasp, and said sternly:

"Farewell. That's enough. Now we must go back."

Romashov fell on the grass in front of her—prone almost. He embraced her legs and began giving her knees long, hard kisses.

"Sasha, Sashenka!" he babbled senselessly. "Why won't you give yourself to me? Why? Give yourself to me!"

"Come on, come on," she hurried him. "Stand up, George Alexandrovich. They'll be looking for us. Let's go!"

They walked in the direction of the distant voices. Romashov's legs were giving way and his temple throbbing. He shook as he walked.

"I don't want any lies," Shurochka said, hurriedly and still with heavy breathing. "No: lies are beneath me—what I don't want is cowardice, and with lies, there is always cowardice. I told you the truth: I have never betrayed my husband, and the only way I ever will is if I cast him off completely. But his caresses and kisses are unbearable to me, they fill me with revulsion. Listen, only now—no, even earlier, when I thought of you, of your lips—only now do I understand the treacherous delight, the blissfulness a lover can give me. But I don't want cowardice, I don't want secret theft. And I don't want a child. Foo, what filth! An officer of the guard's wife, forty-eight rubles' wage, six children, diapers, poverty . . . How horrible!"

Romashov looked at her, bewildered.

"But if you have a husband . . . there's no getting out of it," he said hesitantly.

Shurochka let out a huge laugh. In that laugh was something that he found instinctively unpleasant, which sent a chill into his heart.

"Rommy . . . oh, oi, oi, how styooo-pid you are!" she said, drawing out her words in the childish way that Romashov was so familiar with. "Really, don't you understand these things? No, tell me the truth—don't you really?"

He shrugged his shoulders in confusion. His inexperience was beginning to make him feel uncomfortable.

"Excuse me . . . but I must confess . . . truly . . ."

"Well, bless you, don't worry. How pure and dear you are, Rommy! Well, when you get older, you'll remember my words, I'm sure: one does different things with a husband than one does with a lover. Ah, don't think about it—please. It's disgusting—but what to do . . ."

They were approaching the spot where the picnic had been. The bonfire's flames were clearly visible through the trees. The rough columns, lit with fire, seemed to stand out from the black metal, and on their side flickered a red inconstant light.

"Well, and what if I pushed myself?" Romashov asked. "If I achieved what your husband wants to achieve, or even more? What would happen then?"

She pressed her cheek hard against his shoulder

"Then—yes. Yes, yes, yes . . ."

They had already entered the clearing. Now they could see the entire bonfire and the small black figures of the people surrounding it.

"Rommy, this is the last time I'm going to say this." Alexandra Petrovna spoke hurriedly, though with fear and sadness in her voice. "I didn't want to spoil it: that's why I didn't mention anything before. Listen, you must not come visit us again."

He stood there, dumbfounded, confused.

"But why? Oh Sasha! . . ."

"Let's go, let's go . . . Someone, I don't know who, is sending my husband anonymous letters. He mentioned it in passing, but didn't show it to me. They wrote some kind of dirty invented filth about me and about you. In short, I beg you: do not visit us anymore."

"Sasha!" Romashov pleaded, tugging at her hands.

"Ah, my dear, my beloved, my darling—it hurts me to see you this way! But this is how it has to be. Listen to me: I'm afraid he'll speak to you about it himself. If he does, please, for the love of God, keep control of yourself. Promise me that."

"All right," Romashov said sadly.

"All right, then, that's everything. Farewell, my poor one. My forsaken! Give me your hand. Hold me tightly, until it hurts. Like that . . . Oi! . . . Now farewell. Farewell, my joy!"

They parted before they reached the bonfire. Shurochka walked along the top of the slope, and Romashov went down, taking the long way back beside the river. The card game wasn't over yet, but their absence had been noticed. Deitz, at least, stared insolently at Romashov as he passed by the fire, and gave an insinuating cough. Romashov wanted to throw one of the burning logs at him.

After that he watched as Nikolaev stood up from the card table and took Shurochka aside, where he spoke to her for a long time, his face twisted and his gestures furious. All at once, she stood up straight and spoke a few words with an incredible expression of indignation and contempt—and then all of a sudden that large, strong man shriveled meekly and slunk off, like a wild animal that had been tamed, but which nurtured within itself a barely subdued hatred.

The picnic ended soon after that. The night had grown colder, and a dampness was blowing off the river. Whatever reserves of happiness the party had been feeding off of had long exhausted themselves, and now everyone was letting out tired, blatantly discontented yawns. Romashov rode back with Mikhin's sisters again, keeping quiet all the way home. His mind returned obsessively to the memory of the silent black forest, and the dark mountain and the blood-colored stripe of sunset above it, and the white body of a woman lying in the black and fragrant grass. But despite his deep, intense, and earnest sadness, he still thought to himself, in his usual pathetic manner:

"His handsome face was clouded with sorrow."

XV

On May 1, the regiment relocated to a camp two miles outside of town, on the other side of the railway tracks. It was the same facility they used every year. Regulations concerning this period stated that junior officers had to be housed with their regiments, in wooden barracks; due, however, to the awful disrepair and dangerous state of the buildings that were supposed to house the sixth regiment (for whose maintenance the necessary sum could not be found), Romashov had to stay in his room in town. He made four trips a day: to classes in the morning, then back to the officers' club for lunch, then to evening classes and once more into town. This irritated and exhausted him. During the first two weeks at the barracks he grew thinner and darker, and his eyes sunk in their sockets.

It was hard on everyone, officers and soldiers alike. There was no relief from the fatigue of preparing for the May inspection. The regimental commanders wore their regiments down with two or three superfluous hours in the plaza. The sound of uninterrupted ear-boxing resounded in every class of every platoon of every regiment. Often, while standing at a distance (say two hundred paces or so away) Romashov was able to observe the methodical thoroughness with which a frenzied regiment managed to beat each of its soldiers in turn, from the left flank to the right. First the noiseless movement of the hand and then—it took barely a second—the dry crack of the blow; and then again, and again, and again . . . There was much about this behavior that was awful and sickening. The non-coms beat their subordinates savagely for paltry errors of terminology, for missteps in marching—they beat them until they bled, knocked their teeth out, burst their eardrums, forced them to the ground. It never occurred to anyone to feel pity for themselves; the entire regiment seemed to have been possessed by a sort of spell, an ominous nightmare, an absurd hypnosis. And all of it was made even worse by the terrible heat. May that year was unusually sultry.

Everyone's nerves were stretched to the utmost. At the officers' club, during lunch or dinner, ridiculous arguments flared up more and more often: groundless fights, tussles. The soldiers grew thin and idiotic-looking. During those rare periods when they were allowed to relax, not a joke, not a laugh emerged from the barracks. However, in the evening, after roll call, they were forced to get together and pretend to enjoy themselves. Their indifferent faces formed a circle and began barking disaffectedly:

> For the Russian
> Bullets and bombs are nothing,
> He's drunk on them,
> They're just trifles to him.

Afterwards someone played a jig on the harmonica, and the field marshall commanded:

"Gregorash, Skvortsov, get in a circle. Dance, you idiots! Be merry!"

They danced, but there was something wooden and dead about their dancing, as with their songs. Something that made you want to cry.

The fifth regiment was the only place where the men had any freedom or ease. They started their lessons later than everyone else and finished them earlier. The men in that regiment were well matched, well fed, and spry; they met the gazes of the commanding officers thoughtfully and bravely; even their uniforms and shirts looked livelier on them than they did on the rest of the regiment. Their commander was Captain Stelkovsky. He was a strange man, a bachelor, quite rich compared to the rest of the regiment (he received a monthly sum of around two hundred rubles from somewhere or other) and of a very independent character: dryly self-possessed, reserved and distant with his peers, and a libertine to boot. He lured young, often underaged village girls into his service and then dismissed them after a month, rewarding them according to his usual generosity; he did this with inscrutable regularity, year after year. He never fought with or swore at his men, although he didn't exactly coddle them either, and the soldiers in his regiment were as good in both appearance and ability as the members of the much vaunted guard units. He was patient, level-headed, and certainly quite dogged, very much so, even: qualities that he successfully transmitted to his non-coms. Because of all this, he was able to achieve quietly, and in a single day, results that it took other regiments a week to get using beatings, punishments, tirades, and turmoil. He was sparing with his words and rarely raised his voice, but when he spoke, his soldiers stood at complete attention. His peers were hostile towards him, but his soldiers loved him sincerely: he was, perhaps, the lone example in the Russian army.

The fifteenth of May—which day, by order of the corps commander, was devoted entirely to the inspection—arrived at last. That morning, in every regiment except the fifth, the non-coms woke everyone up at four o'clock. The poorly rested, yawning soldiers shivered in their linen shirts despite how warm the morning was. In the gay, rose-colored light of the cloudless day their faces looked gray, glossy, and pitiful.

At six o'clock the officers appeared before their regiments. The hour of assembly was set for ten o'clock, but not a single regiment commander, with the exception of Stelkovsky, thought that it might be a good idea to let their men sleep and relax before the drill. On the contrary, that morning they hammered away at terminology and shooting practice even more fervently and pedantically than usual, peppering the air with exceptionally bad language and dishing out an extraordinary amount of thrashings and jaw-sockings.

At nine o'clock the regiments assembled in the plaza, five hundred paces in front of the barracks. A long straight line, made up of the sixteen regimental standard bearers with the colors of their various regiments attached to their rifles, was already in their positions, along a line that stretched out over a mile. Lieutenant Kovako, a standard bearer, and one of the ceremony's most important participants, was riding up and down the line smoothing it out, shouting fervently as he galloped along, letting his reins out, his cap turned backwards, wet and red all over from the effort. His sword beat grimly against his horse's ribs; the worn white beast, which was speckled all over with liverspots, and had a cataract in its right eye, twirled his short tail frantically, producing short, abrupt noises, like gunshots, with each step of his ragged gallop. A lot depended on Lieutenant Kovako today: the entire order of the company's sixteen regiments derived from the impeccable thread of his standard bearers.

At exactly ten minutes to ten o'clock, the fifth regiment emerged from the barracks. Emphatically, with long rapid strides that made the ground shake, these hundred men (all of whom were so adroit, capable, straight-backed, and possessed such fresh, clean-washed faces, and caps tilted rakishly over their right ears, that it seemed as if they'd been picked for exactly these qualities) came into sight of the rest of the company. Captain Stelkovsky, a small, thin man in baggy trousers, walked five feet off the right flank, indifferent, apparently, to the fact that he was out of pace; he narrowed his eyes happily, inclined his head first to one side, then to the other, inspecting the alignment. The batallion commander, Sub-lieutenant Lekh, who, like all the officers, had been in a nervous and senseless state all morning, swooped down to berate him on his late arrival, but Stelkovsky coolly took out his watch, examined it, and then answered dryly, almost with scorn:

"In the order it said to gather at ten o'clock. Right now it's three minutes before ten. I do not consider it my right to deprive the men of sleep."

"No dis-cussion!" Lekh cried, waving his hands as he reigned in his horse. "As for your remarks on the service, please, just keep them to yourself!"

Despite his vehemence, he knew he was in the wrong, and because of this he went off immediately to take his peevishness out on the eighth regiment, where the officers were inspecting the soldiers' backpacks.

"What's this mess? Are we setting up a bazaar? A little shop? No one feeds his dogs before a hunt—what were you thinking? Suit up!"

At ten fifteen they began evening out the regiments. This was a long, elaborate, and painstaking process. Long ropes were stretched tight along a series of pegs from marker to marker. Each soldier in the first line had to place the tips of their toes against the rope: high military style dictated that this had to be done without fail, using the utmost mathematical precision. But there was more: the space created by the parted toes had to be large enough so that the rifle butt could be placed therein; likewise, the posture of every soldier's body had to be identical. And the regimental commander was beside himself, crying: "Ivanov, move your body forward! Burchenko, drop your right shoulder! Your left toe back! Further! . . ."

At ten thirty the regimental commander arrived. He was riding a huge bay-colored gelding, which was dappled with dark spots, its four legs white to the knees. Lieutenant Shuglovich cut an impressive, almost majestic figure on horseback; he sat solidly in the saddle, although his too-short stirrups betrayed the fact that he was an infantry man. Greeting the regiment, he cried out exuberantly and with affected vigor:

"Aren't you a handsome bunch! . . ."

Romashov thought of his fourth platoon—particularly the puny, infantile figure of Khlebnikov, and could not stop himself from smiling. "Oh, yes—handsome indeed!"

The banners were brought out to the accompaniment of a regimental march, and the tedious waiting began. A chain of lookouts, whose purpose it was to send up the signal as soon the corps commander arrived, stretched all the way from the plaza to the train station. A couple of false alarms had already been raised: when this happened, the pegs with the ropes attached were hastily pulled out as the regiment evened itself out, drew itself up, and stood frozen in expectation. After a few tense minutes had passed, the men were allowed to stand at ease again, though they couldn't change the position of their feet. In front of them, three hundred feet from the formation, the bright, multicolored dots of women's dresses, parasols, and hats could be seen: these were the regimental women, who had gathered together to watch the parade. Romashov was well aware that Shurochka was not a member of that colorful and even festive group, but when he looked over in its direction he felt a sort of continual sweet ache around his heart, and had to exhale frequently for some strange reason that was beyond his control.

Suddenly a single short and hurriedly pronounced phrase passed through the rows like a wind: "He's here, he's here!" All at once, they had come to the conclusion that something truly momentous was about to happen. Full of a morning's worth of pent-up excitement and nervousness, the soldiers began to busily smooth themselves out, straighten themselves up, and cough nervously. No one had even had to give them the order.

"A-ten-shun! Standard bearers, to your places," Shuglovich commanded.

Shifting his eyes to the right, Romashov spotted a handful of tiny figures riding along the distant edge of the field, kicking up clouds of light yellowish dust as they came closer and closer. Shuglovich, whose face was stern and ecstatic-looking, rode out from the middle of the regiment, at least four times further than he had to. Strutting around with motions that were quite elegant, holding his silver beard high and staring into the black motionless mass of men with his terrible, joyful, and despairing eyes, he rolled his voice out over the entire field:

"Re-gi-ment, listen up! Pree-sen-n-n-t . . ."

He paused here, as if to savor the enormous power he had over these hundreds of men—until, red from the effort, the tendons of his neck straning, he barked out suddenly and at the top of his lungs:

"Arms!"

One-two! Hands splashed against holsters, bolts clacked against belt buckles. From over the right flank floated the sharp, merry, and distinct sounds of the welcoming march. The throng of playful clarinets dashed around like snickering children, the great golden trumpets shouted in victorious celebration, the dense drumbeats hurried them along, and the heavy trombones, who seemed to be having trouble keeping up with the rest of the group, affectionately added their deep, quiet, velvety voices. The train in its station let out a series of long, thin, rapid whistles, and this gentle new sound merged with the orchestra's honeyed chords, blending with them into a single sublime and joyful harmony. All at once, Romashov found himself seized by a sort of bold and merry emotion, which snapped him to his senses and infused him with a feeling of wholesome lightness. With heartfelt and happy clarity he noticed the sky's blue, which was pale from the intense heat, and the sun's gold, trembling in the air, and the warm green of the distant field (it was if he had never seen any of these things before)—and then suddenly he felt young, strong, shrewd, and proud in the knowledge that he belonged to that orderly, motionless, powerful mass of men, which was being directed, secretly, by a single invisible will . . .

Shuglovich held his unsheathed sword up to his face, and then rode out at a heavy gallop to meet them.

The general's calm, rich voice resounded over the boisterous music.

"Greetings, first regiment!"

The soldiers returned his cry warmly. The train whistled once again—sharply and quickly this time, as if excited. The corps commander moved slowly down the front line, greeting each regiment in turn. Romashov had already gotten a good look at his bulky, swollen figure with its breast and fatty stomach squeezed into a cross-studded jacket; his large square face, turned towards the soldiers; his strapping gray horse with its red, dandified, monogrammed saddle and bone-chain harness; his small feet in their shabby varnished boots.

"Greetings, sixth!"

The soldiers standing near Romashov began shouting extraordinarily loudly, like men overwhelmed by the pent-up strength of their own cries. The general sat confidently and easily on his horse; her eyes were beautiful and bloodshot, and her neck strained splendidly as she chomped the iron bit in her mouth, drooling a light white foam and taking lithe, even, ballettic steps. A thought flashed through Romashov's head: "He has white hair at his temples, but a black mustache: it must be dyed."

The corps commander's dark, youthful, intelligent, and humorous eyes stared attentively through their gold-colored glasses into each pair of eyes that was watching him. As he pulled alongside Romashov, he touched the brim of his cap. Romashov stood at full attention, his leg muscles tensed to the point of pain, squeezing the handle of his raised saber. A loyal, joyful rapture ran like a chill down his hand and arm, coating them with goose bumps. And as he gazed continually into the face of the corps commander, he thought to himself, in his naïve and childish way: *"The eyes of the war general lingered with satisfaction on the well-formed, lean figure of the young sub-lieutenant."*

The corps commander gave each of the regiments as he passed them the same greeting. A flashing retinue followed raggedly behind him: around fifteen staff officers on excellent, well-groomed horses. Romashov watched them with the same devoted gaze that he gave to the commander, but none of the retinue paid the sub-lieutenant any attention: all of these parades with their welcoming bands, all these excited little foot soldiers were nothing more than the usual, even boring routine to them. So Romashov, with a confused mixture of envy and malice, decided that these arrogant men must live a special, beautiful, elevated life, which he himself was unable to reach.

Someone in the distance signaled for the music to stop. The corps commander trotted briskly down the front line, from the left flank to the right, followed by the uniformly spirited, brightly colored, and smartly dressed line of his retinue. Lieutenant Shuglovich rode up to the first regiment. He pulled up his bay gelding, leaned his corpulent body back, and shouted, with the same sort of unnaturally ferocious, terrified, and hoarse voice that a fireman uses to shout at a fire:

"Captain Osadchin! Lead the regiments out! Live-ly! . . ."

When it came to shouting out directions, the regimental commander and Osadchin carried on a continual friendly competition. So now, Osadchin's foppish and mechanical commands were heard even in the sixteenth regiment.

"Regiment, shoulder arms! Eyes forward, march!"

The regiment had developed, by means of lengthy and sustained practice sessions, a special march, remarkably quick and with very hard steps, which required that the soldiers raise their legs high and strike them against the ground hard. The sound produced by this motion, which was loud and impressive, was the envy of all the other regimental commanders.

But the first regiment hadn't gone fifty steps when the corps commander cried out impatiently.

"What the hell is that? Regiment, halt. Regiment commander, report to me, please. What are you showing me here? What is this—a coronation ceremony? A torchlight procession? Marching in triple time? We are no longer, Captain, in the time of Nicholas the First, when men remained in the service for twenty-five years. How many extra days have you wasted on this ballet? Precious days!"

Osadchin stood in front of him, tall, motionless, mortified, with his unsheathed saber lowered in disappointment. The general paused for a second, assuming a sad and sarcastic expression and then continuing in a calmer voice:

"These men look marched to death. Hey, you there, William Wallace. Let me ask you . . . Let's try him. What's this young man's name?"

The general pointed at the second man over from the right flank.

"Ignati Mihailov, your excellency," Osadchin answered in his indifferent wooden soldier's bass.

"Good. And what do you know about him? Is he a bachlor? Is he married? Does he have any children? Maybe he's having a hard time of it out here in the woods? Maybe he has problems? Needs? What about it?"

"Your excellency, I have no idea. There are a hundred men. It's difficult to remember each of them."

"It's difficult to remember!" the general repeated heatedly. "Oh, gentlemen, gentlemen! The Scriptures say, *Do not extinguish the spirit*—but what are you doing here? For this is the great gray beast himself, who, when the war comes, will shield you with his own breast, and carry you from the fire on his shoulders. When the frost descends, his threadbare overcoat will protect you. But you find it 'difficult to remember.' "

And, momentarily irritated, fiddling nervously and for no apparent reason with his reins, the general shouted over Osadchin's head towards the regimental commander:

"Lieutenant, lead this company away. There will be no inspection. Away, away, now! Paper dolls! Cardboard clowns with cast-iron heads!"

After this, the inspection took a turn for the worse. The fear and fatigue of the soldiers, the brainless severity of the non-coms, the souless, routine, and negligent attitude that the officers displayed towards their duties: all this was clearly and disgracefully revealed by the inspection. In the second company, the men didn't know "Our Fatherland"; in the third, the officers themselves became confused about the order of dismissal; in the fourth, one of the soldiers fainted during rifle practice. But the most damning thing of all was that not a single company knew what to do during an unexpected cavalry attack, even though they had prepared for this situation and were aware of its importance. The corps commander himself had invented and introduced this particular countermeasure into the general lexicon; it consisted of a series of quick reorganizations, which depended on the commanding officer's resourcefulness, quick wits, and broad personal initiative. Every company failed it in turn, save the fifth.

After inspecting the individual companies, the general removed all the officers and non-coms from the ranks; he then proceeded to ask the men if they were satisfied with things, whether they were treated according to regulations, and whether there were any complaints or claims. But the soldiers barked in unison that they were "completely satisfied" and that "everything is fine." When it was the first regiment's turn to answer these questions, Romashov heard Rydna, his company's sergeant-major, who was standing behind him, say in a sibilant and menacing voice:

"Anyone makes a claim, I'll make one right back to him when the inspection's over!"

The fifth company, on the other hand, put on an excellent performance. The dashing, invigorated-looking men executed their maneuvers with such bold, light, and lively steps, with such dexterity and freedom, that it seemed as if, for them, the inspection was not a horrible examination at all, but a sort of fun and simple game. The general's mood, though still gloomy, improved significantly when he saw them. "Good, boys, good," he said, for the first time in the inspection.

Stelkovsky's real coup came during the simulated cavalry attack. The general wasted no time describing the situation: "Cavalry, right, eight hundred paces"; at which point Stelkovsky calmly halted his company and, using precise movements and without wasting a single second, turned to face the imaginary enemy that was barreling down on them. He closed ranks with great economy: first line to their knees, second standing; gave the order to fire, let fly two or three imaginary volleys and then commanded, "Take up arms!"

"Excellent, brothers! Thank you, young men!" the general praised.

After the men were questioned, the fifth company fell in again. But the general hesitated to dismiss them. He rode quietly back and forth along the front line, observing the soldiers' faces with special interest. A thin, satisfied smile lit up his intelligent eyes through his glasses, beneath their heavy, puffy eyelids. Suddenly he stopped his horse and turned to his chief of staff:

"Look at those mugs, Lieutenant! You feed them pirogis, Captain? Hey, you there, chubby cheeks," he gestured with his chin towards one soldier, "I bet they call you Smitty, don't they?"

"You got it, your excellency—I mean no, your excellency: Mihail Boriychuck!" the soldier shouted, with a satisfied, child-like smile.

"I see. Well, you look like a Smitty. I could be mistakened," the general said. "It happens, I guess. Unless . . ." He cheerfully reeled off a bawdy phrase.

The soldier's face broke completely into a stupid and happy grin.

"Nothing of the sort, your excellency!" he shouted, even more loudly. "Although back home, I did practice the blacksmith's trade. I was a smith."

"There—you see!" the general nodded amicably. He took great pride in his knowledge of soldiers. "Well, Captain, has he been a good soldier?"

"A very good soldier. All of my soldiers are good," Stelkovsky answered, with his usual self-assurance.

The general's brows frowned, but his lips smiled, and because of this his entire face became good-natured and lovable.

"Well, perhaps that's how it seems to you, Captain . . . Any demerits?"

"Not a one, your excellency. Not a single one in five years."

The general shifted himself weightily in his saddle and extended his chubby hand with its white unbuttoned glove to Stelkovsky.

"Thank you, brother," he said in a trembling voice, and his eyes suddenly started to glisten with tears. Like most eccentric war generals, he enjoyed a good cry every now and then. "Thank you, your soldiers have brought an old man comfort. Thank you, soldiers!" he shouted vehemently to the company.

Thanks to the good impression made by Stelkovsky, the inspection of the sixth company went comparatively well. The general wasn't praised, but he wasn't dressed-down either. When it came to bayonetting the straw dummies, however, their performance was a disaster.

"No no no no no!" the corps commander said feverishly, thrusting himself forward on his saddle. "Not that way! Brothers, listen to me. Aim at the heart, the very center of the heart, and thrust to the hilt. Get mad! You're not putting bread in an oven; you're skewering your enemy . . ."

After that, each successive regiment incurred the corps commander's wrath. He even stopped getting upset about it and making his characteristic biting remarks, but only sat on his horse, quietly hunched and with a bored look on his face. He didn't even look at the fifteenth and sixteen companies, but only waved his hand exhaustedly and said with disgust:

"Well, that's . . . that's just a total abomination."

There was still the ceremonial march to get through. The entire regiment arranged itself by company into a series of narrow, closed-off columns. Once more, the standard bearers rode ahead and extended themselves along the right flank in a long, moving line. By now it had grown unbearably hot. The men were exhausted from the stuffiness and from their bodies' heavy perspiration, not to mention the boredom of keeping in close quarters for so long, and the smell of boots, cheap tobacco, dirty human skin, and black bread.

But when it came time for the ceremonial march, everyone cheered up. The officers practically told the soldiers, "Look, you must try to perform well in front of the corps. Don't disgrace us." Their appeal made, a sort of ingratiating, hesitant, guilty attitude seemed to creep into the faces of the higher-ranking men—as if the wrath of such an unimaginably powerful figure as the corps commander had suddenly placed the same on them that was on the soldiers, leveling and equaling both groups and instilling an equal amount of fear, agitation, and wretchedness.

Shuglovich's order reached them from a great distance. "Regiment, a-ten-shun! . . . Musicians, li-i-ine up!"

The five hundred men began to move as one, with a muffled and hurried murmur, before suddenly going quiet and standing at a nervous and apprehensive attention.

Shuglovich was nowhere to be seen. Again his booming, overflowing voice rolled towards them:

"Regiment, shoulder arms!"

The four batallion commanders turned their horses towards their sections, and commanded:

"Batallions, shoulder . . ." at which point they stared tensely at the regiment commander.

From somewhere far ahead of the regiment a cavalry sword flashed in the air, and was lowered. This was the signal for the general order, and the four batallion commanders shouted together:

". . . arms!"

The regiment took up their rifles clumsily, and with a muffled tinkling sound. Somewhere bayonets clanked together.

Then Shuglovich, theatrically drawing out his words, commanded—artfully, sternly, joyously, and as loudly as his huge lungs were capable:

"The ce-re-mo-ni-al ma-a-a-arch!"

Now all the sixteen company commanders sang out, in distinct and inharmonious voices:

"The ceremonial march!"

And somewhere, at the tail of the column, a lone remaning commander cried out, after the others, and in a wobbly and embarrassed voice:

"The ceremonial . . ." and then quietly broke off.

"By platoon!" Shuglovich's voice rolled.

"By platoon!" the regimental commanders immediately repeated.

"To the second mark!" Shuglovich's voice boomed.

"To the second mark!"

"Look right!"

"Look right!" echoed the many voices.

Shuglovich waited two or three seconds before commanding sharply:

"First platoon—quick march!"

Osadchin's thick and muffled command seemed to roll over the earth itself and then penetrate the dense columns:

"First platoon. Look right . . . ick . . . arch!"

The regimental drums crashed simultaniously in front of them.

From behind this, one could have watched as a long, straight line detached itself from the forest of raised bayonets and began rolling evenly forward.

"Second platoon, forward!" Romashov heard Archakovsky's high, womanly voice.

A second line of bayonets rocked back and forth and then detached itself. The drumming had grown significantly duller and more muted by this point, as if sunk under pounds of dirt; but all of a sudden the orchestra's gleeful, shining, strikingly beautiful breeze swooped down on it, causing the tempo to pick up immediately and the entire regiment to come to life and stand at attention. Their heads were held higher, their bodies became straighter, and their gray, tired faces grew clearer.

The platoons marched off one after the other—and with each departure the music became brighter, more delighted, happier. The last platoon of the first batallion hurried off. Sub-lieutenant Lekh spurred his bony black horse forward, accompanied by Olizar. Both held their sabers "aloft," meaning with the hilts level with their faces. They heard Stelkovsky's calm and, as always, easy command. The banner poles swung fluidly into position above the bayonets. Captain Sliva was in front: he was hunchbacked, flabby, and kept looking from side to side with bulging and watery eyes and his long dangling arms, like a bored old monkey.

"F-first platoon . . . f-forward!"

Romashov leads his platoon with quick and agile steps. Something blissful, beautiful, and proud is growing in his heart. He slides his eyes quickly over the faces of the first column; as he does this, the splendid phrase "*The veteran swordsman regarded them with his eagle-eye*" flashes through his head, and he sings out jauntily:

"Se-cond pla-toon . . ."

"One, two!" Romashov counts mentally, tapping a toe inside his boot to keep time. "Start on the left. *Left*, right." And with a happy face, his head thrown back, he shouts in a high tenor that can be heard across the entire field:

"Forward!"

And then, turning already on one leg, as if on a spring, he adds without turning around, in a singsong that is two tones lower:

"Lo-ok right!"

The sheer beauty of the moment is making him drunk. He feels as if the music is filling his heart with a burning, dazzling light, and that the honeyed, jubilant cries are falling on him from somewhere high above—from the sky maybe, the sun. As happened when they first met the inspection, a sweet, trembling chill runs down the length of his body, tightening his skin to the point of goose bumps and lifting the hair on his head until it shivers.

All together, and in time with the music, the fifth company answers the general's praise with a chorus of shouts. The bright sounds of the march, which seem to be exulting in their freedom from the physical container of the human body, sound even louder and deeper as they rush towards Romashov. There, in front of him and little to his right, the sub-lieutenant can clearly make out the motley group of womens' dresses, which seem in the blinding noon light like burning flowers in a fairy tale. Off to his left the golden trumpets of the orchestra flash, and Romashov feels that there is an invisible magic line connecting the music with the general himself—the crossing of which will be a matter of joy and awe.

But the first platoon has already joined their line.

"Excellent, children!" comes the satisfied voice of the corps commander—and "A-a-a-a!" the soldiers respond in their deliriously high-pitched voices. The music bursts out even more loudly in front of them. "Superb," Romashov thinks as he watches the general. "Brilliant!"

Romashov is alone now. With fluid, elastic steps—his feet barely touching the ground—he approaches the target line. His head is thrown back audaciously, held proudly to the left. A sensation of lightness and freedom suffuses his entire body: it is as if he has unexpectedly been given the ability to fly. Imagining himself to be the object of the general delight, the excellent center of the whole world, he talks to himself, in a kind of irridescent, delighted dream:

"*Look, look—there's Romashov.*" "*The ladies' eyes glistened with passion.*" One, two, left! . . . "*Out in front of the platoon of elegant marchers went the handsome young sub-lieutenant.*" Left, right! . . ." *'Lieutenant Shuglovich, that Romashov of yours is singularly capable,' said the corps commander. 'I would like to make him my adjutant.'* "Left . . .

One more second, one more instant—and Romashov will cross the magic thread. The music blares its mindless, heroic, firey celebration. "Here comes the applause," Romashov thinks, his heart full of festive brightness. He can hear the voice of the corps comander; there's Shuglovich's voice, and someone else . . . "The general praised them of course, but why haven't the soldiers answered? Someone behind me is shouting . . . What's going on?"

Romashov turned around, and paled. Instead of maintaining two straight and even lines, his platoon had devolved into a knotted, shapeless mass, which curled in every direction like a flock of sheep. This was because the sub-lieutenant, flushed with rapture and dreams of glory, had not paid attention to the fact that he was listing gradually further and further right, to the point that now he was practically pressed against the platoon's flank, and so disturbing the movement of the entire group. In the same moment that Romashov realized all this, he also saw Private Khlebnikov, who was toddling along by himself twenty feet behind the rest of the platoon, right in the general's line of sight. He had fallen along the way and was now trying to catch up; his dust-coated body was so bogged down beneath the weight of his ammunition that he was practically running on all fours, holding his rifle by its barrel in one hand, and with the other, picking ineffectively at his nose.

Romashov felt suddenly that the shining May day had turned dark, that a morbid, alien weight had settled on his shoulders like a mountain of sand, and that the music had started playing wearily and morosely. And he felt that he himself was small, weak, and ugly, with wilted movements and dirty, awkward, unsteady legs.

The regimental adjutant galloped up to him. Fedorovsky's face, with its jumping lower jaw, was red and twisted with rage. He was breathing hard, from anger, and from how fast he'd been riding. He had started shouting furiously while still a ways away, swallowing his words as he repeated them obsessively:

"Sub-lieutenant . . . Romashov . . . The regiment commander orders you . . . the strongest rebuke . . . In seven days . . . on house arrest . . . in staff headquarters . . . The disorder, a scandal . . . The entire regiment, ooooh . . . and furthermore! . . . You little fool!"

Romashov didn't answer him—he didn't even turn his head. The man had every right to bawl him out, of course! The soldiers listened on as the adjutant screamed—"Well, then, let them listen, as it must be, let them," Romashov thought to himself with a feeling of acute disgust. "Everything's over for me. I'll shoot myself. I am shamed forever. Everything, everything's over. I'm ridiculous, I'm small, I have a pale, ugly face, an absurd kind of face, the ugliest face in the world. It's all over! The soldiers walking behind me are watching at my back, smiling and nudging one another. Maybe they feel sorry for me? No: I am definitely, definitely going to shoot myself!"

The platoon, which was now quite distant from where the corps commander was standing, turned their shoulders to the left one after the other and returned to the position that they'd originally been in before the maneuvers had started. The companies were reorganized into their regular order. While the last of the lines walked past them, the men were permitted to stand at ease, and the officers left their places in order to stretch and smoke the cigarettes that they'd been hiding in their sleeves all day. Only Romashov remained where he was, in the middle of the front line, on the right flank of his platoon. With the end of his unsheathed bayonet he picked strenuously at the ground around his feet. Despite the fact that he kept his head lowered, he still felt that curious, amused, disdainful looks were being cast at him from every side.

Captain Sliva walked past Romashov, muttering hoarsely at him through clenched teeth, but without stopping or looking up, as if he were speaking to himself:

"P-please h-have your application for transfer to another regiment on my desk by the end of the day."

Vetkin was the next to approach. Romashov saw that both his pale, good-natured eyes and the corners of his downturned lips had assumed the fastidious and pitying expression that people usually use while examining a dog that's been run over. And in that moment, to his own disgust, the sub-lieutenant realized that his own face had likewise put on a sort of dull, brainless smile.

"Come on, Yuri Alexandrovich," Vetkin said. "Let's have a smoke."

And then, clicking his tongue and shaking his head in exasperation, he added:

"Jesus, kid!"

Romashov's chin began to tremble; his throat felt bitter-tasting and constricted. He was barely holding back his tears; he answered in the jerky and breathless voice of an upset child:

"No . . . What for? . . . I don't want . . ."

Vetkin went back to his place. "Now I'll walk up to Sliva and strike him on the cheek," Romashov thought. "Or I'll go up to the corps commander and say: 'It's shameful of you, an old man, to play the soldier and torture men. Let them have their rest. Because of you they've been beaten for two weeks.' "

But suddenly he remembered his proud dreams about the well-built and handsome sub-lieutenant, and the women's passion, and the satisfaction of the war general—and he felt so ashamed that he blushed for a moment, not just on his face, but on his chest and back even.

"You are a laughable, despicable, repulsive man!" he shouted mentally. "I'll shoot myself today, then everyone will know it."

The inspection ended. The companies marched for the corps commander a few more times: first in double time, then at a run, then in closed ranks with their rifles held horizontally. The general, who appeared to have softened a little, praised the soldiers a few more times. It was almost four o'clock already. Finally the regiment stopped and allowed the men to stand at ease. The staff bugler played the "officers' call," as a summons moved down the rows.

"Officers, report to the corps commander."

The officers left their formations and formed a closed circle around the commander. He sat on his horse, hunched over and quite exhausted, apparently, though his intelligent, screwed-up, bugged-out eyes peered through his gold glasses with alert amusement.

"I'll be brief," he began, weightily and abruptly. "The regiment's performance was completely unsatisfactory. I don't blame the men: I blame the officers. If the driver is bad, the horses will not pull. As far as I can tell, you have no concern for your men or their troubles. Remember well: *'Blessed is he who lays down his life for his friend.'* Instead of which, you have a single thought in your heads—namely, how to satisfy your commanding officer during an inspection. You've lathered your men up as if they were cabhorses. The officers look unkempt and neglected, like sextons in uniforms. All this, by the way, will be available for your perusal in my report. One sub-lieutenant of the sixth or seventh company lost his alignment and made a hash of his company. Shameful! I do not demand marches at triple time, but clearsightedness and calm under pressure are a must."

"That's me he's talking about!" Romashov thought with horror, and it seemed to him that everyone in the circle simultaneously turned their attention towards him now. But no one moved. Everyone stood quietly, heads hanging, motionless, without raising their eyes to the general's face.

"My warmest thanks to the commander of the fifth company!" the corps commander continued. "Where are you, Captain? Ah, there!" The general took his cap off with both his hands, somewhat theatrically, revealing his bald powerful skull with a bump above its forehead, and bowed low to Stelkovsky. "Once more I thank you and shake your hand with pleasure. If it pleases God that this corps remain under my command during wartime, the first assignment of any importance will be given to you. And now, gentlemen, my respects. You are free to go. I'll be glad to see you again—though in a different light, I hope. And now, I'll be off."

"Your excellency." Shuglovich stepped forward. "Might I be so bold as to invite you, on behalf of my fellow officers, to dine with us tonight. We will be . . ."

"No, I'm afraid not!" the general interrupted him dryly. "I'm very grateful, but I've been invited to Count Ledohovsky's tonight."

He set off at full speed over the wide path, which had been cleared by the officers. When he reached the regiment the men rose up by themselves, without having been ordered to, and stood quietly at attention.

"Thank you, Regiment N!" the general said, in a strong and friendly voice. "I give you two days of rest. And now . . ." he shouted gayly, "quick march to your tents! Hooray!"

It was as if he had nudged the entire regiment with these brief shouts. With a deafening joyful roar a half a thousand men went their different ways, and the earth shook and groaned beneath their feet.

Romashov broke off from the other officers, who were going into town together, choosing instead to take a longer road past the camp. He felt like some kind of pitiful outcast from the regimental family: not even an adult, but a contrary, wayward, and deformed child.

While he passed his company's officers' tents, his attention was caught by a constrained but enraged shout. He stood still for a minute: in the half light between the tents he could make out his sergeant-major Rinda, a small, red-faced, apoplectic lout, who was growing more wildly and more visciously enraged as he pounded his fists into Khlebnikov's face. Khlebnikov looked bruised, stupid, and bewildered; his senseless eyes shone with vivid terror and his head shook pitifully from side to side with each blow, causing the two halves of his jaw to knock audibly against one another.

Romashov hurried past, practically running. He didn't have the strength to help Khlebnikov. As he did this, however, he had the sick realization that, in some strange, fateful, unpleasant way the day had intertwined his own fate with that of the unhappy, cowed, tormented soldier. It was as if they were two cripples, suffering from a disease that caused the same disgust in whomever they met. And despite the fact that his awareness of this similarity instilled in Romashov a prick of shame and repugnance, still, he had to admit that there was something strangely, deeply, sincerely human about it as well.

XVI

The one road that led from the camp to town crossed the railroad tracks in a steep ravine. Romashov ran quickly down the narrow and thickly trampled slope, which was so steep as to be practically sheer, and then began arduously climbing up the other side. About halfway up, he noitced that someone was standing above him, in a jacket with his overcoat thrown over his shoulder. He stopped for a second and squinted until he recognized Nikolaev.

"Here it comes," Romashov thought. His heart began to ache wearily with anxious foreboding. But he continued climbing anyway.

The two officers had not seen one another for about five days, but they didn't say hello now, and for some reason this didn't seem strange to Romashov: as if it could not have been otherwise on this difficult, unlucky day. Neither saluted.

"I have been waiting for you here on purpose, Yuri Alexich," Nikolaev said, staring over Romashov's shoulder at something in the distance, towards the camp.

"At your service, Vladimir Efimich," Romashov answered, in a falsely mellow yet shaky voice. He bent over, plucked a stalk of last year's dry brown grass and began chewing on it absent-mindedly. As he did this he stared fixedly at the tiny figure of himself that was reflected in the buttons on Nikolaev's coat. Its head was tiny and narrow and its legs were miniscule, but it bulged out awkwardly on its sides.

"I won't keep you long, I only have a few things to say," Nikolaev said.

He spoke especially softly, with the pronounced courtesy of a hot-tempered and angry man who had decided to restrain himself. But the more they spoke, never once looking one another in the eyes, the more awkward it became, to the point that eventually Romashov inquired:

"Shall we take a walk?"

The winding path, which had been trampled down by walkers, crossed a big beet field. In the distance the officers could see the little white houses and the red tile roofs of the town. They walked next to one another, keeping their distance as they walked across through thick and fleshy undergrowth. For a while, they were both quiet. Finally Nikolaev, who was breathing deeply and loudly, and with visible difficulty, started to speak:

"Before anything, I have to ask you one question: do you display the necessary respect towards my wife . . . towards Alexandra Petrovna?"

"What do you mean, Vladimir Efimich . . ." Romashov interrupted. "I should ask you . . ."

"Excuse me!" Nikolaev said, flaring up suddenly. "We are going to take turns asking our questions: I will go first, then you. Otherwise we will get in each other's way. We will speak honestly and openly. Before anything, answer me: does the gossip they've been spreading about her interest you in the least? That is to say . . . The devil! . . . Don't you care about her reputation? No, no, wait, don't interrupt me . . . For you won't deny, I hope, that you've had nothing but good from both her and me, and that you have always been welcomed in our home as a close friend, practically a member of our family."

Romashov tripped over some loose earth, stumbled clumsily, and muttered embarrassedly:

"Believe me, I always will be grateful to you and Alexandra Petrovna . . ."

"Ah, no, not quite—not like that. I'm not looking for your thanks," Nikolaev said, growing more and more angry. "I want to talk about the filthy, slanderous gossip they've been spreading about my wife, which . . . that is to say . . ." Nikolaev took a few deep breaths and covered his face with his hands. "In a word, you are mixed up in this. Both of us—she and I, I mean—both of us receive these nasty, boorish, annonymous letters almost daily. I am not going to show them to you . . . They are despicable. And in these letters, they say," Nikolaev faltered for a second. "Well, devil take it! . . . They say that you are Alexandra Petrovna's lover and that . . . Oh, the meanness! . . . And so on . . . That every day you have some sort of secret meeting, which the entire regiment knows about. It's despicable!"

He ground his teeth angrily and spat.

"I know who wrote those letters," Romashov said quietly, turning to the side.

"You know who?"

Nikolaev stopped walking and grabbed Romashov roughly by the hand. It was clear, that a sudden jerk of rage had robbed him momentarily of his calculated self-control. His cowlike eyes grew wide and his face flushed; a thick saliva trickled from the corner of his trembling lips. He cried out fiercely and bent forward, thrusting his face point-blank at Romashov:

"How can you keep quiet, then, if you know! In your situation even the least honorable of men would understand—would shut the bastards' mouths. Listen to you . . . you military Don Juan! If you have any honor at all, and are not some sort of . . ."

Romashov, who had grown pale, looked hatefully into Nikolaev's eyes. His legs and arms felt suddenly heavy, and his head light, as if empty; his heart, which had fallen down somewhere deep inside him, beat with huge, painful strokes that shook his entire body.

"Please, do not shout at me," he said, in a confused drawl. "Have some manners—I will not allow you to shout at me."

"I am not shouting at you," Nikolaev said, still rudely, though in a softer tone. "I am only trying to persuade you—though I have the right to demand. Our past relationship gives me that right. If you value Alexandra Petrovna's clean, unsullied name even a little, then you must find a way to stop this badgering."

"All right, I'll do what I can," Romashov answered dryly.

He turned and walked back towards the center of the path. Nikolaev caught up to him.

"And then . . . only you, if you please, don't get angry . . ." Nikolaev said, palitating, with a shadow of embarrassment. "For once you start talking about these things, it's better to get it all out . . . don't you think so?"

"Yes," Romashov said, half-questioningly.

"You saw yourself how sympathetically we treated you— that is to say, myself and Alexandra Petrovna. And if I was compelled . . . No . . . Well, I mean, you yourself know that there's nothing more terrible than gossip in a backwater town like this one!"

"All right," Romashov answered sadly. "I'll stop visiting you. Is that really what you wanted to ask me? Well, then, fine. By the way, I myself had decided to stop my visits. A few days ago I went there for all of five minutes, to give Alexandra Petrovna back her books, and, I dare confess to you, it was the last time."

"Yes . . . there it is . . ." Nikolaev said vaguely, and went embarrassedly silent.

At that minute the officers turned off the path onto the main road. There were still three hundred steps remaining to the town, and because there was nothing more to talk about, they walked side by side, keeping quiet and not looking at one another. Neither one could decide whether to stay or to turn back. The situation was becoming more false and strained with each minute.

Finally, somewhere around the first houses of the town they met a cabby. Nikolaev stopped him.

"All right, then . . . That's it," he said again awkwardly, turning to Romashov. "So goodbye, Yuri Alekceyevich."

Instead of shaking hands, they saluted one another. But as Romashov watched Nikolaev's strong back fade into the white dust, he felt suddenly that the most important part of his life had been torn from him, leaving him alone, abandoned by the entire world.

He walked slowly home. Gainan, who met him in the yard, had begun grinning amicably and happily while Romashov was still in the distance. He took the sub-lieutenant's coat from him, smiling at how much fun he was having and dancing his usual little in-place jig.

"Did you eat lunch?" he asked with sympathetic concern. "Are you hungry? I can run to the club for you, bring back some food."

"Go to hell!" Romashov screeched at him. "Get out of here, go away and don't you dare enter my room. And no matter who asks—I'm not home. Even if the holy emperor himself drops in."

He lay on his bed and buried his head in his pillow, gnawing the fabric between his teeth. His eyes were on fire; something prickly and alien simultaneously stung and gripped his throat, so that he wanted to cry. He longed desperately for these hot, sweet tears: these long, bitter, cathartic sobs. Over and over again, he went over the day that had just ended, exaggerating everything shameful and painful that had happened to him in the hope of demonstrating to himself, as he would have to a stranger, how humbled, unhappy, meek, and disgarded he was. But the tears didn't come.

After this something strange happened. Romashov had been lying in the darkness for a couple of minutes with his eyes closed, not thinking about anything but not falling asleep either, or even just dozing off temporarily, when suddenly he found himself awake for some reason, gripped by the familiar feeling of sadness. Looking around, he saw that the room had already grown dark. Apparently more than five hours had passed during his mysterious period of mental numbness.

All of a sudden he was hungry. He stood up, buttoned his saber, threw his overcoat on his shoulders and set off for the officers' club. It wasn't far away—barely two hundred yards. Romashov always walked there, not along the street, but on the darkened path, a sort of vacant plot of land, with vegetable gardens and fences.

The lamps were burning brightly in the living room, and the billiard room, and the kitchen—and because of this the club's dirty, cluttered yard seemed especially dark, as if flooded with ink. The windows were all wide open. Romashov could hear the sounds of conversation, laughter, singing, and the sharp clack of billiard balls.

He was about to go in through the back entrance when he heard the irritating and ridiculous voice of Captain Sliva coming from the window two steps away, and stopped. Romashov looked carefully through it, and saw the stooped back of his regiment commander

"The entire regiment is marching, l-like a single m-man—bap! Bap! Bap!" Sliva said, neatly chopping the side of one hand against the palm of the other. "And then that thing comes along, like a sort of joke—o! o!—a yak, a billy-goat." He threw his hands up in artless frustration. "I t-told it t-to him straight: b-beat it, I said, with all due res-respect, f-find another regiment. And wouldn't it be better for him if he left the company? What makes you think you're a fucking officer? Nothing but a dis-dis-distraction . . ."

Romashov narrowed his eyes as he shrunk back. He felt that if he were to move, everyone sitting at the table would notice him and rush to the window. He stood as he was for a minute or two. Then, trying to breathe as quietly as possible, bending his back and sinking his head into his shoulders, he tiptoed along the wall, walked quickly to the gate and then, after dashing across the moonlit road, hid himself in the deep shadows cast by the fence on the other side of the road.

Romashov walked the town for a long time that night, keeping to the shadows, never knowing quite where he was headed. At one point he stopped across from the Nikolaev's house, which was bright white in the moonlight, beneath the strange, lustrous shine of its green metal roof. The street was deathly quiet, deserted, and, it seemed, forgotten about. The straight lines of the shadows cast by the house and fence divided it into two distinct halves—one of which was completely black, and the other of which shone slickly with its smooth round cobblestones.

A lamp was making a large warm spot behind the thick red curtains. "My darling, could you really not be feeling how terrible I feel—how much I suffer, how I love you!" Romashov whispered, grimacing pitifully as he gripped his chest with both hands.

All at once it occurred to him that he could communicate his suffering to Shurochka through the house's walls. He gritted his teeth and strained his mind, compelling her with a feverish will as he clenched his fists so tightly that his fingernails began to dig into them. He felt the cold sensation of goose bumps creeping over his body:

"Look out the window . . . Go up to the curtains. Get up from the divan and go to the curtains. Look out, look out, look out. Listen to me, I'm ordering you right now to go to the window."

The curtains didn't move. "You aren't listening to me!" Romashov whispered bitterly. "You're sitting next to him right now, by the lamp, calm, indifferent, beautiful. Ah, God, my God, how unhappy I am!"

He sighed and, with tired steps, his head sunk low, plodded on.

He walked past Nazanski's house, but it was dark inside. Romashov did think he saw a figure in white flashing past the window of the unlit room; but for some reason this was awful to him, and he decided not to call out.

Days later Romashov would remember this fantastic, practically delirious stroll as if it had been a kind of distant and unforgettable dream. He himself couldn't have said how he ended up at the Jewish cemetery. It was located on the outskirts of town, on a hill, to whose side its white walls clung quietly and secretively. The cold headstones rose naked and identical from the bright sleeping grass, casting their thin shadows sadly before them. Above the cemetery, a simple but hallowed solitude ruled, silently and sternly.

After this, he had found himself on the other side of town— and then maybe it really had been a dream? He'd stood for a while in the middle of the long, rolling, flashing dam that loosely circumscribed the Bug River. The mud squelched melodiously and the sleepy water heaved thickly and lazily around his legs, as the moonlight trembled through the rippling surface like the shaft of a gigantic punter's pole. Millions of silver fishes seemed to be swimming through this water, winding along their proscribed paths to the far shore, which hung above them, dark, silent and empty. And then Romashov remembered that everywhere, at the outskirts of town as well as on the street, the sweet, gently suggestive aroma of the white acacia flowers had followed him.

Strange thoughts had entered his head that night—lonely thoughts, sometimes sad, sometimes terrifying, sometimes hilariously trivial, like the thoughts he'd had during his childhood. More often than not, he found himself daydreaming like an inexperienced gambler who'd lost everything he owned in a single night, and who had been gripped, suddenly, by the alluring idea that nothing at all had happened: that the dashing Sub-lieutenant Romashov had performed wonderfully before the general during the ceremonial march, winning special commendation, and that he was sitting now, along with his friends, in the well-lit dining room of the officers' club, laughing and drinking red wine. Again and again, however, these dreams were shattered by the memory of his quarrel with Fedorovksy, or the scathing words of the regiment commander, or his conversation with Nikolaev, at which point Romashov again felt himself to be irredeemably unhappy and ashamed.

Some secret instinct led him to the place where, earlier that day, he and Nikolaev had gone their separate ways. As he stood there, Romashov had turned the idea of killing himself over in his mind; but his thoughts were indecisive and fearless: suffused instead by a hidden and delicious self-satisfaction. His usual, irrepressible habit of fantasizing rid the idea of all its terror, gussying it up with bright and beautiful colors:

"Gainan rushes out of Romashov's room. His face distorted by fear. Pale and trembling, he runs into the packed dining room of the officers' club. Everyone rises from their chairs involuntarily at his appearance. 'Sirs . . . the sub-lieutenant . . . has shot himself!' Gainan has trouble getting the words out. General confusion. Their faces pale. Horror in their eyes. 'Who shot himself? Where? Which sub-lieutenant?' Someone recognizes Gainan. 'Why, that's Romashov's

batman!' 'That's his Cheremiss.' They run into the room, some without their hats on. Romashov is lying on the bed. On the floor, a Smith and Wesson revolver with a government-issue seal on it lies in a pool of blood . . . Doctor Znoiko, the regimental physician, shoves his way through the crowd of officers that have packed the tiny room. 'In the temple,' he says quietly, amid the general silence. 'It's over.' Someone remarks under his breath: 'Gentlemen, remove your hats!' Many cross themselves. Vetkin finds a note on the desk, written in pencil, in a firm hand. He reads it out loud: 'I forgive everyone, I die of my own free will, life is so difficult and sad! Promise to break the news of my death gently to my mother. George Romashov.' Everybody looks around, reading in one another's eyes the same disquieting, unspeakable thought: 'We are his killers!'

"The coffin beneath its golden brocaded shroud rocks rhythmically in the hands of his eight friends. All the officers follow, and behind them, the sixth regiment. Captain Sliva is scowling sternly. The good face of Vetkin is puffy from crying, but now, in public, he contains himself. Lyubov cries openly, unashamed of his grief—the dear, good boy! The deep, mournful sobs of the funeral march mingle in the spring air. Here, too, are the regimental women and Shurochka. 'I kissed him,' she thinks despairingly. 'I loved him! I could have stopped him—saved him!' 'Too late!' Romashov answers her mentally, and with a bitter smile.

"The officers talked quietly amongst themselves as they walked behind the coffin. 'Ah, what a tragedy. For how kind our friend was, how handsome, what a capable officer! . . . No, it's true . . . We did not understand him!' The funeral march's sobs grow stronger: Beethoven's 'Funeral March for a Hero.' And Romashov lies in his coffin, still and cold, with an eternal smile on his lips. A modest bouquet of violets has been secretly laid on his breast—no one knows who put them there.

He forgave everyone: Shurochka, and Sliva, and Fedorovsky, and the corps commander. May they not cry for him. He was too pure and fine for this life. It will be better for him there!"

Tears came to his eyes, but Romashov did not hold them back. It was so pleasant to imagine himself mourned and unfairly offended!

After this, he had walked across the beetfield. The low, fat leaves of the beet-stalks were a muddle of white and black spots around his feet. The broad expanse of the moonlit field overwhelmed him. Romashov clambered up the ridge and stood looking down at the railway tracks.

The slope he was standing on was engulfed entirely in black shadow, while on the other side of the tracks a light fell that was so pale and bright that it seemed as if one could make out each individual grass blade there. The ravine ran below, like a dark abyss, in which the washed rails glistened weakly, like water in a trough. Far in the distance, in the middle of a large field, the straight rows of camp tents stood paling in white light.

A narrow shelf of land stuck out a little further down the ridge from where Romashov stood. He walked over to it and sat down on the grass. His hunger and exhaustion were making him nauseous, and his legs felt shaky and weak. The large, deserted field—the dark half, the light half, the dim, translucent air, the growing grass—all of this was immersed in a clear, hushed quiet, which rang in Romashov's ears. The only thing interrupting this quiet was the occasional passing train, whose piercing whistles, in the silence of that strange night, sounded lively, alarmed, and threatening.

Romashov lay on his back. The gauzy white clouds stood still, as the round moon ran above them. The heavens were

232

ALEXANDER KUPRIN

cold, enormous, and empty, and it seemed as if the entire space between the earth and the sky was suffused with an ancient terror and anguish. "There—is God!" Romashov thought. Suddenly, and with a stab of self-pity, he began to speak in a fierce and bitter whisper:

"God! Why did you turn away from me? I'm small, I'm weak, I'm a grain of sand—what have I done to make you mad, God? For you can do anything, you're good, you see all—why have you set yourself against me, God?"

But his own words became terrible to him, and he began whispering hurriedly and feverishly:

"No, no, good one, dear one, forgive me, forgive me! I won't puff myself up." And he added with a clipped defenseless humility: "Do whatever you want with me. I'll do anything, gratefully."

As he said this, a half-crafty, half-innocent thought stirred in the depths of his heart: that his patient submission would touch and soften this omniscient god, and that then something wonderful would happen, causing everything in his current life—all its difficulties and unpleasantness—to be revealed as nothing more than a foolish dream.

"Where are you-ou-ou?" the steam engine cried impatiently. And a second thin note stretched itself out menacingly: "You-ou-ou!'

Something began rustling and flickering over on the bright side of the ravine, at the very top of the ridge. Romashov tilted his head up in order to get a better look at it. A gray and formless figure, which only barely stood out from the grass in the transparent and dull moonlight, was descending the slope. Only the movements of its body and the light rustle of the disturbed earth made it possible to follow this figure's progress.

It crossed the rails. "A soldier maybe?" Romashov thought anxiously. "At least, it's definitely a person. Probably only a lunatic or a drunk. But who could it be?"

The gray figure crossed the rails and entered the shadow side. Clearly, it was a soldier. He made his way up the slope slowly and clumsily, disappearing once from Romashov's sight. But then two or three minutes later, a round, short-haired head without a hat came back into view.

The mottled light fell directly on the figure's face, and Romashov saw that it was a soldier from the left flank of his platoon: Khlebnikov. He was walking with his head bowed, holding his hat in his hand, eyes fixed lifelessly on the ground in front of him. He seemed to be moving under the influence of some kind of strange, internal, hidden strength. He walked so close by the officer, that he almost touched his overcoat. The bright, sharp dots of his pupils reflected the moonlight.

"Khlebnikov? Is that you?" Romashov called out to him.

The soldier cried out and, stopping suddenly, began shivering where he stood from fright.

Romashov stood up quickly. He saw before him a deathly, ragged face, with cut, swollen, bloody lips, and one eye almost swollen shut. In the unreliable night light the marks of his beating had an ominous, exaggerated look. And, looking at Khlebnikov, Romashov thought: "This is the same man who today with me won the displeasure of the entire regiment. We are similarly unhappy."

"Where are you going, my good man? What are you doing?" Romashov asked pleasantly and, without knowing why himself, lay both of his hands on the soldier's shoulders.

Khlebnikov stared at him with a wild and confused expression, but then he turned quickly away. His lips smacked together and slowly parted, and from them emerged a short, senseless wheeze. A dull, irritating feeling, like the one that precedes a faint, which felt like a sickly sweet tickle, slowly spread through Romashov's chest and stomach.

"They beat you? Yes? Go ahead, tell me. Yes? Sit here, sit with me."

He pulled Khlebnikov down by the hands. The soldier, like a folding mannequin, somehow lightly, absurdly, and obediently collapsed on the wet grass, next to the sub-lieutenant.

"Where were you going?" Romashov asked.

Khebnikov remained quiet, sitting in an awkward pose with his legs stuck out unnaturally. Romashov saw that his head continually, with barely noticeable pushes, lowered onto his breast. Once more the sub-lieutenant heard the short wheezing sound, and in his heart moved an awful pity.

"You wanted to run away? Put your hat on. Listen, Khlebnikov, right now I am not your commanding officer, I am myself: an unhappy, lonely man, dead to the world. Things are hard for you? Painful? Tell me about it, openly. Maybe, you have wanted to kill yourself?" Romashov asked in a whisper incoherently.

Something clicked and began grumbling in Khlebnikov's throat, but he continued to keep quiet. At that moment Romashov remarked that the soldier was shuddering with frequent, swift shudders: his head shuddered, his jaws shuddered, with quiet little taps. For a second the officer was scared. This dreamless feverish night, the feeling of loneliness, the even, matte, lifeless moonlight, the black depths of the cut down below, and next to him the silent soldier, who had been beaten senseless—all of it, all of it seemed to him to be some kind of ridiculous, during the very last days of the world. But suddenly, a tide of warm, self-forgetting, endless sympathy enveloped his soul. And, feeling his own sorrow to be small and negligible, feeling himself grown up and intelligent in relation to this worried, persecuted man, he affectionately and strongly embraced Khlebnikov by the neck, pulled him towards himself and began speaking heatedly, with a passionate conviction:

"Khlebnikov, you've got it bad, haven't you? It's bad for me too, my friend, it's bad for me too, believe me. I have no idea about what to do in the world. Everything is some kind of bestial, meaningless, burdensome nonsense! But you must endure, my friend, you must endure . . . That's what has to be done."

Bending his head low, Khlebnikov suddenly fell to Romashov's knees. And the soldier, tenaciously grasping with his hands the officer's legs, pressed his face to them, his entire body beginning to shake, sighing and writhing from the suppressed sobs.

"No more . . ." Khlebnikov babbled incoherently. "I can't, barin, take no more . . . Oh, lord . . . they beat me, they laugh . . . the platoon commander wants money, the squad commander shouts . . . But where to get it? My stomach is torn up . . . It was already torn up when I was a kid . . . I have a hernia, barin . . . Oh Lord, oh Lord!"

Romashov bent close above the head that was reeling frenziedly around his knees. He smelled the dirty, unhealthy body and unwashed hair and the sour-smelling overcoat that covered this man when he slept. An infinite sorrow, horror, not-understanding, and deep, guilty pity filled the officer's heart, clenching it and constraining it to the point of pain. And, quietly bending towards the short-haired, prickly, dirty head, he whispered, almost inaudibly:

"My brother!"

Khlebnikov grabbed the officer's hand, and Romashov felt on it in addition to the hot teardrops the cold and sticky touch of another person's lips. But he did not take his hand away and spoke simple, touching, quieting words, like those with which an adult speaks to an upset child.

Afterwards he himself brought Khlebnikov back to the camp. He sent for Shapovalenko, who was the non-commissioned officer on duty in the regiment that night. He showed up in his underclothes, yawning, screwing his eyes up and scratching himself here on the back, here on the stomach.

Romashov ordered him to relieve Khlebnikov of his guard duty.

"But sir, his shift isn't over yet!"

"Don't argue!" Romashov shouted at him. "Tomorrow you will tell the company commander that I ordered it . . . You'll come to me tomorrow?" he asked Khlebnikov, who answered him quietly with a shy, thankful gaze.

Romashov walked slowly through the camp, returning home. A whisper in one of the tents made him stop and listen. Someone was telling a story in a subdued and breathy voice:

"So-o, the devil himself sends his most greatest wizard to a soldier. The wizard comes and says, 'Soldier, hey, soldier, I'm going to eat you!' And the soldier answers him and says, 'No, you can't eat me, for I myself am a wizard!'"

Once more Romashov went to the cutting. He was oppressed by a feeling of the absurdity, chaos, and unintelligibility of life. Stopping at the top of the slope, he raised his eyes up, towards the sky. There as before was the cold space and the endless terror. And almost unexpected, for he himself, having raised his fists above his head and shaking them, Romashov cried out madly:

"You! Old cheat! If you can and dare do something, then . . . Well how about this: make it, so that right now I break my leg."

He headlong, closing his eyes, threw himself down the steep slope, in two leaps jumped across the rails, and, without stopping, with a single breath clambered up the other side. His nostrils swelled, his breast inhaled by fits. But in his heart, a proud, daring, and wicked courage flared suddenly to life.

XVII

From that night on, a crack began to form in the depths of Romashov's heart. He avoided the company of the other officers, ate most of his meals in his room, never went out dancing at night, and stopped drinking. He was maturing, somewhat; he himself noticed that he'd been acting older and more serious over the last few days, and that he displayed a sadder and more imperturbable calm in his dealings with other people. Often, the realization of this brought to mind an idea that he'd read about somewhere (and that he'd found funny at the time): namely, that a man's life was divided up into "lusters," each of which consisted of seven years, and that over the course of a single of these lusters one's blood, body, thoughts, feelings, and character all changed completely. And here Romashov had just recently come to the end of his twenty-first year.

The soldier Khlebnikov did come and see him, but only after Romashov reminded him. After that he began to visit more and more often.

The first time he came he had the same look about him, of a naked, mangy, much-beaten dog that shied timidly from any hand that reached out to pet him. But little by little, the attention and kindness that the officer showed him warmed and emboldened his heart. In a fit of remorseful and cringing fellow-feeling, he confessed his entire life story to Romashov. His family consisted of a mother, a drunken father, their half-idiotic son, and four young daughters. What land they owned had been unfairly seized by the village commune; now they lived crammed together in a state-owned hut, designated to them by that very same commune. The parents worked in strangers' houses, while the children begged. Khlebnikov received no money from home; his general frailness meant that he was never allotted any voluntary work either. Without at least a little money a soldier's life is hard: he had no tea or sugar and could not afford to buy soap, let alone treat the plattoon commander and squad commander to a sip of vodka at the buffet. His entire salary—twenty-two and a half kopeks a week—went to this kind of little favor to his commanding officers. They beat him daily, mocked him, insulted him, and gave him the hardest and most unpleasant jobs available, whether it was his turn to do them or not.

Romashov realized, to his surprise, and with a feeling of anguish and horror, that the narrow course of his day brought him into contact with hundreds of these gray Khlebnikovs, each of whom sufferend his own pains and rejoiced over his own pleasure, but all of which had been homogenized and degraded by their slavery, the indifference of their commanding officers, and the arbitrary punishments that they had to endure. And the most horrible part of all was that none of the officers—including Romashov himself, until now at least—had any idea that this gray mass, with its thoughtless, unceasingly obedient faces, was actually made up of living people, rather than a bunch of gears that could be fit into the gigantic mechanisms of companies, batallions, regiments . . .

Romashov pulled what strings he could in order to find Khlebnikov some voluntary work. The rest of the company noticed this unusual patronage. Frequently, Romashov saw that when he was around, the non-coms treated Khlebnikov with an exaggerated and sarcastic politeness, speaking to him in purposely over-sweet singsong. Captain Sliva was in on the joke too, apparently. Sometimes he even turned towards the air and began grumbling:

"Oh, ex-cuse me! The liberals are coming, I tell you. They've corrupted the regiment. Better a smack on the head than a kiss on the lips is what I say, but they prefer to coddle the little darlings."

Now that Romashov had more freedom and time alone, he found himself visited more and more often by strange and complicated thoughts, like the ones that had so disturbed him during his house arrest a month earlier. Usually this happened at dusk, after his duties were over for the day, as he walked quietly under the garden's thick sleeping trees and listened, all alone, his heart aching, to the buzz of the evening insects, while the rose-colored sky quietly darkened.

The variety of his new interior life amazed him. Before this, he had never guessed how much happiness, power, and profound interest lay hidden in such a simple and ordinary thing as human thought.

It was already very clear to him that he would leave the army and join the reserves without fail as soon as he had completed his three years of service, which he needed to do in order to pay for his time at the military academy. He had no idea, however, what he was going to do once he had become a civilian. He turned possible jobs over in his mind one by one: tax collector, railroad worker, merchant. He thought about becoming an estate manager, or signing up with some department or other. At first he was overwhelmed by all the various occupations and professions that a man could busy himself with. "Why would anyone get involved with such ridiculous, strange, filthy lines of work?" he thought. "Why devote one's life to being a jailor, for example, or an acrobat, or a callus-remover, an executioner, a cesspool cleaner, a dog barber, a gendarme, a magician, a prostitute, a bathhouse attendant, a horse doctor, a gravedigger, or the principal of a school? Then again, doesn't this just go to show that even the stupidest, most random, capricious, violent, and depraved human idea will find people to be its slaves and masters?"

The more and more deeply he thought about this, the more it struck him as true that the great majority of educated professions were founded solely on the disavowal of human honor, which capacity allowed them to pander to all possible defects and insufficiencies. After all, if human nature were perfect, would we need all these contortionists, accountants, bureaucrats, policemen, customs officials, checkpoint officers, inspectors, and overseers?

His mind moved on to priests, doctors, pedagogues, advocates, and judges—to those people whose jobs forced them to deal with the hearts, minds, and passions of their fellow men. However, it seemed to Romashov that the individuals in these lines of work were often even more hardened and corrupt: full of a profound cold-bloodedness, lifeless formality, and habitual, if shameful, disinterest. And what about the architects of one's daily happiness—the engineers, architects, inventors, manufacturers, and factory owners of the world? But these men (who, with their special abilities, might have been able to craft human life into pleasing and beautiful shapes) worked only for rich people. They were weighed down by fear for their own hides, a deep love of their young and lairs, a terror of life, and, because of this, a cowardly dependence on money. It was this type of person who inevitably fashioned the fate of poor, harried Khlebnikov—who cared for him and educated him and told him "Give me your hand, brother."

Romashov continued thinking in this vein, hesitantly, and with remarkable slowness, but still deeper and deeper into the phenomena of life. Before it had all seemed so simple. The world was divided into two unequal parts. One—the smaller— was made up of officers, who walked around swathed in honor, strength, influence, the wizardly virtue of a uniform, and, in addition to this uniform, a sort of inherited sense of bravery, physical strength, and unmatchable pride. The other part—which was huge and faceless—was made up of civilians, otherwise known as putty, the masses, the dregs. They were despised, to the point that one was considered a good lad for cursing at or beating this or that civilian, for putting out one's cigarette on his nose, for pulling his top hat down over his ears, or any other such sophomoric prank. And then, stepping back from reality like someone observing it from the side, looking on it from something like a hidden corner, a tiny chink in the wall, Romashov began to understand, little by little, that military service and its illusory gallantry was a result of a cruel and disgraceful misunderstanding, common to all men. "How is it possible that a class of people is allowed to exist," Romashov asked himself, "who, during peacetime, and without doing the least bit of good, eats other people's bread and other people's butter, dresses in other people's clothes, lives in other people's houses—and then in wartime goes out and thoughtlessly murders and mutilates men just like themselves?"

It became more and more clear to him that there were only three vocations that a man could be proud of: science, art, and unforced physical labor. His dreams of doing some literary work returned. Sometimes, when he happened to read a good book, one full of sincere inspiration, he thought: "My God, but it's so simple, I've thought and felt that way myself. I could have written this exactly!" He was seized by the desire to write a novella, or a large novel: a canvas in which the terror and boredom of military life might be put to good use. It all held together wonderfully in his mind—the scenes were bright, the figures lively, the plot unwound and accumulated in an intricately shapely pattern, and it was exceptionally pleasurable and interesting to think about it. But when he sat himself down to write, it came out pale, childishly flaccid and awkward, pompous and banal. While he was writing—quickly and heatedly—he himself did not notice these defects, but when he set next to his pages to read even a small sample from the great Russian creators, he was overcome by a helpless despair, shame, and disgust with his art.

With these thoughts in his head he frequently wandered these days in the town in the warm nights at the end of May. He himself didn't remark that he chose always one and the same road: from the Jewish cemetery to the dam and then to the embankment near the railroad. Sometimes it happened that, consumed by the passion for the work of the mind, which was new to him, he paid no attention to where he was going, and then suddenly, coming to himself and waking up, he saw with surprise, that he was on the other end of the town.

And every night he walked past Shurochka's window, he walked along the other side of the street, stealthily, holding his breath, his heart beating, feeling like he was undertaking some sort of secret, shameful piece of thievery. When the lamp in the Nikolaevs' living room went out and the black glass of the window glistened opaquely from the moon light, he tapped his heels near the fence, clasped his hands tightly against his chest, and said in a pleading whisper:

"Sleep, my beautiful, sleep, my love. I'm nearby, I'm watching over you!"

In these minutes he felt tears in his eyes, but in his heart, in addition to tenderness and emotion and to a self-assured loyalty, turned a blind, living jealousy of the mature male.

One day Nikolaev was invited to the commanding regiment to play cards. Romashov knew this. That night, walking along the street, he smelled from behind some kind of fence, from the palisades, the heady and ardent smell of narcissus. He jumped over the fence and in the shadows picked from the bed, dirtying his hands in the moist earth, an entire armful of those white, delicate, wet flowers.

The window of Shurochka's bedroom was open; it looked out onto the yard and was not lit. With a daring that he had not expected of himself, Romashov slipped through the creaking gate, walked up to the wall, and threw the flowers through the window. Nothing stirred within the room. Romshov stood there for three minutes and waited, and the beating of his heart could be heard down the entire street. Afterwards, as he was leaving, blushing from shame, he walked on tiptoes out to the street.

Another day he received a short and angry note from Shurochka.

"Never do that again. Tenderness in the style of Romeo and Juliet is ridiculous, especially in a backwater amry regiment."

During the day Romashov tried even from a distance to see her on the street, but for some reason this didn't happen. Frequently, catching sight, from a distance, of a woman whose figure, gait, and hat reminded him of Shurochka, he ran to her with beating heart, gasping for breath, feeling how his hands had become cold and damp from the agitation. And every time he recognized his mistake he experienced a deep feeling of loneliness, boredom, and a kind of killing hollowness.

XVIII

During the last days of May a young soldier in Captain Osadchin's company hanged himself; strangely enough, he did so on exactly the same date that an identical event had occurred the year before. Romashov was the officer on duty at the time, and so, against his will, had to be present during the autopsy. The soldier had still not had time to decompose. The thick smell of raw meat emanating from the pieces of his cut-up body reminded Romashov of the stench given off by the carcasses hanging in a butcher's window. He saw the gray and blue slime of the man's glossy intestines, saw the contents of his stomach, saw his brain—a convulsing, red-gray mound, which quivered on the table every time someone stepped in the room, like a jelly taken out of its mold. All of this was new, terrible, and offensive. The entire scene was so novel, horrible, and offensive that it caused Romashov to feel a sort of disgusted contempt for the man.

Every once in a while, a period of general, acute, and chaotic drunkenness erupted in the regiment. Perhaps these periods began in those strange moments when men who had been brought together by circumstance, but who were condemned as one to a life of pointless idleness and senseless brutality, looked suddenly into one another's eyes and saw, there, deep behind their tangled and oppressed minds, a hidden spark of horror, anguish, and insanity. At which point, with a life as sated and full as a pedigree bull's, they burst the bounds of their regulations.

Something like this happened after the suicide. Osadchin started it. The regiment had just enjoyed a few consecutive days off, which he had spent at the officers' club, gambling desperately and drinking ungodly amounts. Strangely enough, this huge, strong, rapacious man bent the entire regiment to his own powerful will, whipping them into a sort of frenzy as he heaped abuse upon the suicide's name, and stared at his audience with cynical impatience, as if daring them to rebuke him.

It was six o'clock in the evening. Romashov was sitting with his feet on the windowsill, softly whistling the waltz from *Faust*. The crows in the garden were cawing and the magpies chattering. Night had not yet fallen completely, but light and thoughtful shadows were already roaming between the trees.

Suddenly a voice began to sing loudly and enthusiastically, though off-key, from Romashov's porch:

> "The raging horses snort and froth;
> They tear against the heavy bi-i-it . . ."

The doors flew open, and Vetkin hurled himself into the room. He continued to sing, keeping his balance with difficulty:

> "With weary eyes, the girls and madams
> Watch their loved ones depart."

He was drunk, powerfully, to the point of stupor, and had been since the day before. His eyelids were red and swollen from sleepless nights. His cap sat tilted on the back of his head. His mustache, still wet, was dark, and weighed down as if by thick icicles like a pair of walrus tusks.

"Romulus! You Syrian Anchorite, let me kiss you!" he cried out. "Why are you so sour tonight? Come on, everyone's having fun except you. They're playing cards, drinking. Come on!"

He gave Romashov a fierce and prolonged kiss on the lips, wetting his face with his mustache hair.

"All right, Pavel Pavlovich, calm down, calm down," Romashov protested weakly. "What's got you so excited?"

"Give me your hand, my friend! You little schoolgirl. In you, I love my former passion and vanished youth. Right now at the officers' club Osadchin's going at it so hard, the mirrors are starting to rattle. Rommstein, I love you—my brother! Let me kiss you really, like a true Russian, on the lips!"

Vetkin's swollen face and glazed-over eyes disgusted Romashov; the terrible stink of his breath had coated his wet lips and mustache. But he was helpless as always to resist this kind of request, and so only smiled, artificially and flaccidly.

"Wait—why did I come to see you again?" Vetkin shouted, hiccupping and staggering. "It was something important . . . Ah, now I remember. Well, my brother, I took Bobetinsky to the cleaners. You understand—utterly, to the last kopek. It got to the point where he asked to pay with a promissory note. So I said to him: 'Nothing doing, old boy, *entendez*, can't you sweeten it just a little?' So he put his revolver in. Here, have a look, Romatosky." Vetkin turned his pocket inside out, removing finally a small, elegant revolver in a gray suede holster. "That, my friend, is a Mervin. So I ask him: 'How much did you pay for this?' 'Twenty-five.' 'Ten.' 'Fifteen.' 'All right then, and fuck you!' He put a ruble down on a color and a suit. Bang, bang, bang, bang! Five games later he's out. Hel-lo, a hundred geese! And he still hasn't paid me everything. An excellent revolver and a cartridge to go with it. Here—take it, Romossetti. As a souvenir and a sign of my sincere friendship I give you this revolver, and ask you to always remember diligently what kind of person this Vetkin is: a brave officer. There! Now that's poetry!"

"But why are you doing this, Pavel Pavlovich? Put it away."

"What? You think it's a bad revolver? It could kill an elephant. Wait a second, we'll try it now. Where do you keep your servant? I'll go and ask him for a board of some kind. Hey, boy! Arm-bearer!"

He wobbled into the vestibule, where Gainan could usually be found and then romped around there a little, before returning a minute later with the bust of Pushkin under his right arm.

"Stop, Pavel Pavlovich—it's not worth the effort," Romashov protested half-heartedly.

"Nonsense! It's just putty of some kind. Here, we'll put it on the stool. Stand up straight, you rascal!" Vetkin threatened the bust with his hand. "Are you listening to me? I'm going to teach you a lesson!"

He stepped to one side, leaned against the windowsill next to Romashov, and cocked the revolver. He waved the gun around in the air with such jerky and drunken movements that Romashov, who had screwed up his eyes in fright, was sure he would shoot something accidentally.

The distance was no more than eight paces. Vetkin took a long time aiming, whirling the barrel in various directions. Finally he took his shot; it hit the bust on the right cheek, leaving a large, jagged black hole. Romashov's ears rang from the noise.

"See that? A little almond!" Vetkin cried out. "Well, then, there you are, that's yours: a souvenir of my affection. Now put on your jacket and let's go to the club. We'll drink to the glory of Russian weapons."

"It's not worth it, Pavel Pavlich—really, it would be better if we didn't," Romashov pleaded feebly.

But he was unable to refuse. He couldn't express himself decisively enough, or pitch his voice with a strong enough intonation. So, reproving himself mentally for this spineless lack of will, he dragged himself along behind Vetkin as he zigzagged unsteadily through the kitchen garden, between the cucumbers and the cabbages.

It was a truly crazy night: messy, loud, intoxicated. They began by drinking at the officers' club; then they went to the train station to have some mulled wine, after which they returned to the party again. At first, Romashov held back; he was annoyed with himself for giving in and was experiencing the tedious feeling of squeamishness and awkwardness that every sober person feels in the company of drunks. Their laughter seemed unnatural to him, their witticisms flat, and their singing off-key. But then all of a sudden the hot red wine that they had drunk at the train station began to make his head reel, filling it with a noisy and convulsive happiness. A gray film, made out of a million specks of sand, grew up over his eyes, and everything became comfortable, funny, and comprehensible.

The hours flew by like seconds, and only afterwards, when the lamps in the dining room were being extinguished, did Romashov understand vaguely that a significant amount of time had elapsed, and that it was now night.

"Well, gentlemen, let's find some girls," someone suggested. "To the Shleifers'!"

"To the Shlefers,' the Shleifers'! Hooray!"

The men bustled about, crashing their chairs back and laughing. Everything that night seemed to be happening of its own volition. Carriages stood ready in the yard—but no one knew where they had come from. Romashov had been experiencing periodic blackouts all night, each of which was presaged by a moment of especially clear and heightened understanding. At one point, he found himself sitting in an equipage next to Vetkin. Some third person sat across from them, but Romashov couldn't make out his face in the darkness—although he did bob his torso towards him in a half-bow. This person's face was swathed in darkness; it appeared to be alternately shrinking into a fist and stretching out in various directions. At the same time, it seemed surprisingly familiar. Suddenly Romashov heard a blunt, wooden laugh, which he realized after a second was his own.

"Vetkin, Vetkin—ha ha, my friend. I know where we're going," he said, with drunken slyness. "You, my friend, are taking me to see the women. I know, my friend."

A second carriage passed them, clattering deafeningly over the cobblestones. A flash of lantern-light illuminated bay horses charging forward at a disorderly gallop, a coachman waving his whip above his head, and four officers, shouting and whistling as they rocked in their seats.

For a minute, Romashov's mind became unusually luminous and clear. Yes, here they were, on the way to a certain place, where some women would offer up their bodies, their caresses, and the great secret of their sex to whomever desired them. For money? For a minute? What difference did it make? "Women! Women!" a wild and sweet voice cried impatiently inside him. The thought of Shurochka came to him like a distant, barely audible voice—but there was nothing vulgar or insulting about that association. On the contrary, Romashov found his heart stirring quietly and pleasantly under its gratifying and strangely exciting influence.

He was here, on his way there, to that unknown place he had never even seen, not even once—to that strange, secret, captivating essence: to women! And then his secret dream would become a reality, and he would watch them, take them in his arms, listen to their affectionate laughter and singing, and there would be a mysterious but joyous quieting of the passionate thirst that had driven him towards the one woman in the world, to her, to Shurochka! And yet he still had no distinct goal in mind—he, who had been rejected by a single woman, and so was now compelled, imperiously, elementally, by that sphere of undisguised, open, simple love, which he circled the way that, on a cold night, a tired and chilled migrating bird would circle a lighthouse flame. And really, that was all it was.

The horses took a right turn. Immediately the wheels stopped knocking and the axles stopped rattling. The equipage rocked with gentle firmness over the ruts and potholes as it glided down the hill. Romashov opened his eyes. A scatter of tiny fires lay spread out below him. They dove behind trees and invisible houses and then jumped out again, so that it looked like a large dispersed crowd, like a fantastic torchlight procession, was wandering through the valley. For a moment, the warm and fragrant smell of wormwood wafted up from somewhere; a large dark branch rustled above their heads, and a damp chill touched them, like a breath from an old grave.

"Where are we going?" Romashov asked again.

"To Zavalie's!" shouted the person sitting across from them. Romashov was surprised by this. He thought: "Ah, must be Lieutenant Epifanov. We're going to Shleifers'."

"Have you really never been there?" Vetkin asked.

"You can both go to hell!" Romshov shouted.

Epifanov laughed and said:

"Listen, Yuri Aleksevich, please, just let us drop a hint that it's your first time. Ah? Well, they're darlings there, real sweethearts. They love that kind of thing. Please let us?"

Once again, Romashov's mind was swallowed by a thick and impenetrable murk. Immediately after this, as if without any break in time at all, he found himself in a large hall, with a parquet floor and Venetian chairs lining the walls. Long red curtains with yellow bouquets on them hung above the main doorway, as well as the three other doors that led into dark and tiny rooms. These curtains billowed lazily and fluttered over the windows, which opened onto the black darkness of the yard. Lamps burnt on the walls. The room was bright and smoky and smelled distinctly like Jewish cooking, but every once in a while the refreshing smell of grass, flowering white acacia, and spring air came in through the open window.

There were around ten officers there. It seemed as if all of them were singing, shouting, and laughing in unison. Romashov wandered around with a beneficent and naïve smile on his face; recognizing the faces of Bek-Agamalov, Lyubov, Vetkin, Epifanov, Archakovsky, Olizar, and all the others, he felt, to his surprise and satisfaction, as if he were seeing them for the first time. Staff Captain Leshenko was there too; he sat under the window with his usual look of unassuming melancholy. Bottles of beer and thick cherry liqueur appeared on the table as if on their own (as everything happened that night). Romashov drank a shot with someone, clinking his glass and exchanging kisses, then feeling how sticky and sweet his hands and lips had become.

There were five or six women there by now. One of them, who looked like a fourteen-year-old girl, dressed like a page-boy, with pink stocking on her legs, was sitting on Bek-Agamalov's lap and playing with his aiguillette. Another, a large blonde in a red silk blouse and dark skirt, with a big, red, makeup-covered face and thick, black, rounded eyebrows, approached Romashov.

She sat sideways on the chair, casually and with her legs crossed. Romashov noticed how well her dress defined her perfect and powerful thigh. His hands started trembling, and his mouth grew cold. He asked, shyly:

"And what is your name, madame?"

"My name? Malvina." She turned her back indifferently on the officer, dangling her legs back and forth. "Give me a cigarette."

A pair of Jewish musicians appeared from somewhere: one played the violin, and the other, the tambourine. A predictable and off-key polka melody was struck up, and Olizar and Archakovsky started dancing the cancan, to the accompaniment of repeated, rattling thumps. They capered around by turns, on one leg and then the other, slapping one another's outstretched arms, then retreating again, bending their knees and sticking their thumbs under their armpits, as they twirled their thighs around outrageously and thrust their torsos back and forth. Suddenly, Bek-Agamalov leapt on the table and shouted, in a high, frenzied voice:

"Civilians can go to hell! I want them out! Get out now!"

Two civilians were standing in the doorway—all of the officers in the regiment knew them, since they came to the officers' club every night. One was an official in the treasury department and the other was the brother of a local judge, a minor landowner. Both were very nice young men.

The treasury official, who had a bloodless and strained-looking smile on his face, spoke searchingly, while still trying to keep his tone free and easy.

"Why, I'm Dubetsky, sir—you know me . . . Allow us, if you will, to share in your company . . . After all, sir, we aren't in any way hindering you."

"It may be crowded in here, but nobody seems to be bothered," the judge's brother said, laughing tensely.

"Out!" Bek-Agamalov cried. "March!"

"Gentlemen, bring them forward," Archakovsky said, laughing.

The room erupted. Everyone began spinning, groaning, laughing, stamping their feet. The lamps' smoking tongues jumped up. The cool night air burst through the window, breathing anxiously on their faces. The civilians, who were already out in the yard, wailed dolefully, loudly, tearfully:

"This doesn't end here! We're going to complain to the regimental commander. I will write to the governor. Usurpers!"

"Yoo-loo-loo-loo-loo! Sic 'em!" cried a thin falsetto. It was Vetkin, who had stuck his head out one of the windows.

To Romashov, all this was just another deformed, absurd, nightmarish picture on the motley ribbon that had been unraveling in front of him all day, without either interruptions or connections between its shrieking segments. Once more, the violins struck up their monotonous squeal, and the tambourines began to shake and buzz. Someone without a uniform, in only a white shirt, was squatting in the middle of the room, dancing, resting his hands back against the floor every minute or so. A beautiful and emaciated woman (Romashov had not noticed her before) with wild black hair and an unconcealed collarbone that stuck out prominently, clasped her naked hands around the melancholy Leshenko's neck, singing loudly into his ear, as if she were trying to shout down the music:

> "When consumption sets in
> You grow pale and thin
> And the doctors begin
> To surround you . . ."

Bobetinsky splashed some of his beer over the partition of one of the unlit side rooms, causing a sleepy, deep, and unsatisfied voice to shout querulously:

"For the love of . . . Who did that? What a swinish thing to do!"

"Have you been here long?" Romashov asked the woman in the red blouse, laying his hand furtively on her warm and sturdy leg, as if he himself were barely paying attention to what he was doing.

He didn't catch her answer, however, for his attention was distracted by a wild scene. Sub-lieutenant Lyubov was chasing one of the musicians around the room, beating him over the head as hard as he could with his own tambourine. The Jew let out a series of brief and unintelligible cries, shooting terrified glances over his shoulder and tucking in the long tails of his frock coat as he dashed from corner to corner. The whole room was laughing. Archakovsky laughed so hard he fell on the ground and began rolling from side to side, tears streaming from his eyes. Then came the piercing wail of the second musician. Someone grabbed the violin from his hand and hurled it furiously to the ground. Its sounding board emitted a melodic crack as it shattered, which sound harmonized strangely with the Jew's despairing cries. After this, Romashov experienced a few minutes of dark oblivion. Coming to himself again, he felt like a man in the middle of a violent dream; he watched as everyone in the room began to cry and run around, waving their hands. A handful of people closed quickly and tightly around Bek-Agamalov, but then they retreated to their rooms, granting him a wide berth.

"Get out! Everybody!" Bek-Agamalov shouted rabidly.

He gnashed his teeth, shaking his fist above his head and stamping his feet. His face was flushed crimson and a pair of veins ran like cables down his aggressively lowered forehead, all the way to his nose. Large round pupils gleamed terribly in his widened eyes.

He appeared to have lost the capacity for human speech, for he began roaring like a crazed animal, in a frightful and quivering voice.

"*A-a-a-a!*"

All of a sudden his body shifted to the left, and he pulled his saber from its sheath. It rattled, flashing above his head with a sharp whistle. Everyone in the room immediately dove for the windows and doors. The women screamed hysterically. The men shoved each other. In the midst of being swept towards the exit, Romashov felt a painful prick on his cheek as someone's epaulet or button gashed him, drawing blood. Once they were out in the yard people started shouting at one another in agitated and hurried voices. Only Romashov remained in the doorway. His heart was beating fast and hard, but in addition to his fear he felt a sort of sweet, tempestuous, happy expectation.

"I'll cut them to shreds!" Bek-Agamalov shouted, gnashing his teeth.

He had been completely overwhelmed by an intense fear. With the strength of a man possessed, and using only a couple blows, he split the table in two; then he waved his saber vigorously at the mirror, sending the splinters flying left and right like a spray of iridescent rain. He swept all the bottles and glasses off another table with a single slash.

Suddenly, however, a piercing, and insolent cry arose from somewhere:

"Fool! Boor!"

The woman who shouted this (who Romashov only now noticed) had bare arms and loose dark hair; only minutes earlier, she had been hanging on Leshenko. She was standing in a niche behind the stove, leaning far forward with her arms akimbo as she cried over and over again, like a market woman who had been short changed.

"Fool! Boor! Lackey! No one's afraid of you! Fool, fool, fool, fool! . . ."

Bek-Agamalov knit his brows in confusion and lowered his saber. Romashov watched as his face grew slowly pale and his eyes flared with ominous yellow sparks. And at the same time, he began bending his legs lower and lower, tensing up and pulling his head into his neck, like an animal preparing to lunge.

"Quiet!" he barked hoarsely, as if spitting the words out.

"Fool! Blockhead! Armenian goat-fucker! I will not be quiet! Fool! Fool!" the woman shouted, her entire body shaking with each cry.

Romashov knew that he himself was growing paler by the second. In his mind, he felt a familiar sensation of weightlessness, emptiness, and freedom. A strange mixture of fear and happiness, like a light and intoxicating foam, buoyed his heart suddenly upwards. He watched as Bek-Agamalov raised the saber above his head without taking his eyes off the woman. And then suddenly a hot stream of un-self-conscious rapture, fear, physical cold, laughter and courage surged through Romashov. As he threw himself forward he heard Bek-Agamalov whisper furiously:

"You won't be quiet? I'm telling you for the last . . ."

Romashov grabbed Bek-Agamalov's hand firmly, with a strength that even he had not expected. The two officers, who were standing barely a foot apart, stared unblinkingly at one another for a few seconds. Romashov heard Bek-Agamalov's rapid, horse-like snorts; he saw the fearsome whites and flashing pupils of his eyes, his gnashing jaw—but despite all this he could tell that the mad fire was being slowly extinguished from that twisted face. Standing there, he felt the wonderful and inexpressible joy of a man poised between life and death, who knew already that he was going to win this game. The scene's terrible significance must have been clear to all those observing them, for outside the windows the yard had grown quiet—so quiet in fact that somewhere about two paces away in the darkness, a nightingale suddenly poured out its loud, carefree trill.

"Out of the way!" Bek-Agamalov sputtered.

"Bek, you do not hit women," Romashov said calmly. "Bek, you will be ashamed for the rest of your life. Do not hit her."

The last sparks of frenzy in Bek-Agamalov's eyes had gone out. Romashov quickly closed his eyelids and exhaled deeply, like a man about to faint. His heart began to beat quickly and wildly, as if in fear, and his head felt heavy and warm again.

"Out of the way!" Bek-Agamalov repeated, tearing his hand away angrily.

Romashov no longer felt that he had the strength to resist him, but he wasn't afraid of him either. He touched his friend's shoulder lightly and spoke compassionately and affectionately.

"Forgive me . . . But you really will thank me for this later."

Bek-Agamalov slammed his saber into its holster with a sharp crack.

"Very well! To the devil!" he shouted angrily, though already with a certain amount of pretense and embarrassment. "This isn't over. You have no right! . . ."

To those people observing them from the yard, it was clear that the most terrible part of the scene was over. With strained and exaggerated laughter, the crowd threw itself back into the room. Now that everyone had decided to calm down, they spoke to Bek-Agamalov easily and with the usual friendly familiarity. But he was weak and put out, and his darkened face soon took on an exhausted and shrinking expression.

Shleifer—a fat woman with gelatinous breasts and dark rings under her hard, lashless eyes—ran up. She threw herself on one officer after another, grabbing at their hands and coat buttons and shouting tearfully:

"But sirs, well, just look at the mirror, the table, the food, the women! Who's going to pay for all this?"

In keeping with the way things had been going that night, some unknown person stayed behind to settle up with her. The other officers crowded out. The fresh, tender air of the May night touched Romashov's chest lightly and pleasantly, filling his entire body with a fresh, joyful trembling. It seemed to him that every last trace of the day's drunkenness had been erased from his brain in an instant, as if at the touch of wet sponge.

Bek-Agamalov came up to him and took him by the hand.

"Ride back with me, Romashov," he said. "All right?"

And then, when they sat down next to one another and Romashov, leaning to his right, watched the horses toss their broad hindquarters as they galloped awkwardly forward, escorting the equipage to the town, Bek-Agamalov's groping hand found his, and pressed it, tightly, painfully, and for a long time. Nothing more was said between them.

XIX

Still, the excitement that they had all just been through began to make itself felt in a general nervous excitement. On the way back to the officers' club they raised hell. When they passed a Jew on the road they flagged him down and then, after ripping the hat from his head, spurred the driver on again. Later they threw the hat onto a fence or in a tree. Bobetinsky beat up the carriage driver. The rest of them sang loudly and shouted senselessly. Only Bek-Agamalov, who was snuffling angrily next to Romashov, kept quiet the entire time.

Despite the fact that it was late, the officers' club was brightly lit and full of people. In the card room and dining room, at the buffet and the billiard table flaccid, sour-eyed men in unbuttoned jackets jostled one another ineffectively, incensed by the wine, tobacco, and reckless gambling. As he was drinking a toast with some of these officers, Romashov was surprised to suddenly recognize Nikolaev's face among the crowd. He was sitting next to Osadchin, flushed bright red and drunk, though trying hard to keep control of himself. When Romashov left the table to approach him, Nikolaev glanced quickly at him and then turned away in order not to give him his hand. He began talking with exaggerated interest to his neighbor.

"Give us a song, Vetkin!" Osadchin shouted over everyone else's voices.

"Let's *sing* some-*thing*!" Vetkin sang, mimicking a melody from the church antiphone.

"Sing some-*thing*. Sing some-*thing*!" the others intoned.

"When the pope's away, the priests will play," Vetkin said. "Pope, deacon, sexton, governmental erections. Come forth, Nikifor, come forth."

"Come forth, Nikifor, come fo-o-orth," the choir answered him softly, in perfect harmony with Osadchin's warm mild octaves.

Vetkin conducted the singers, standing in the center of the table and waving his hands over them. His eyes were fearsome one minute and tenderly approving the next; he hissed at those who were singing off-key, holding his fascinated singers together with a minute tremble of his extended palms.

"You're sharp, Staff Captain Leshenko! A bear must have boxed in your eardrums! Quiet!" Osadchin shouted. "Gentlemen, please! We're trying to sing here!"

"Like a rich man eating ice cre-e-eam," Vetkin said, lowering his hands.

The tobacco smoke was making Romashov's eyes water. The oilcloth covering the table was sticky, and touching it, he remembered that he had not yet washed his hands that evening. He walked across the courtyard to the officers' lounge, where he knew there was a washbasin set up. This was a cold and empty little room with a single window. A series of lockers stood along the wall, as well as two cots set up like hospital beds. The linen on these had never been changed, nor had the floor been washed, or the room itself aired out. Because of this, the lounge always smelled like dirty sheets, old tobacco smoke, and greasy boots. It was meant as a place to stay for officers who had been temporarily assigned to the regimental staff from elsewhere; but it was more often used as a place for the especially drunken officers to lie down for a night—sometimes two or even three to a bed. Because of this, it was called "The Tomb," "The Morgue," or the "Burial Ground." There was an unconscious but terribly pungent irony in these nicknames due to the fact that, from the time the regiment had moved into town, several officers and one batboy had already shot themselves in this Officers Lounge—indeed, on these same two beds. But then there hadn't been a single year during which at least one officer hadn't shot himself.

When Romashov entered the Tomb he found two men sitting on one of the beds, at the head, underneath the window. They were sitting in the dark, without a fire, and it was only by their barely audible breathing that Romashov realized they were there. He had to practically bend over them before he recognized who they were: Staff Captain Klodt, a thief and alcoholic, who had been dismissed from the command of his company, and Sub-lieutenant Zolotuhin, a lanky, older, already balding gambler and scandal-monger, who was also a foul-mouthed and inveterate drunk. Four 250-gram bottles of vodka glistened dully on the table between them; there was an empty dish too, with some kind of swill in it, and two full glasses. He didn't see a single trace of food. The two drunks kept quiet, as if they wanted to stay hidden from their newly arrived friend. When Romashov bent over them they looked up at him and smiled craftily in the half-light.

"Good heavens, what are you doing?" he asked fearfully.

"Tsss!" Zolotuhin raised his hand in cryptic warning. "Hold on—you'll ruin it."

"Quiet now!" Klodt whispered shortly.

Suddenly a cart began to rumble somewhere in the distance. The two men snatched up their glasses, banged them against the table, and drank simultaneously.

"And what's that supposed to be?!" Romashov exclaimed

"That, sweetheart," Klodt answered in a pregnant whisper, "that's our signal. A cart knocking. Greenhorn," he turned to Zolotuhin, "what should we drink to this time? How about when a wolf howls?"

"We drank to that already," Zolotuhin said, looking seriously out the window at the moon's thin sickle standing low and bored above the town. "Just wait. Maybe a dog will start barking. Keep quiet."

They kept on whispering this way, with their heads bowed towards one another, gripped by a dark, drunken, insane hilarity. And at just that moment, a song that was muffled and softened by the walls, and which was therefore had the harmoniously sad sound of a funeral service, reached them from the dining room.

Romashov threw up his hands and shook his head.

"Gentlemen, stop it, for the love of God: that's terrible," he said, with anguish.

"Fuck off!" Zolotuhin bawled suddenly. "No, wait, stay, brother! Where are you going? Before you take off, have a drink with us upright gentlemen. No, no, don't try to get the drop on us, brother. Grab him, Staff Captain, and I'll lock the door."

They jumped off the bed, giggling crazily as they grabbed Romashov. And then suddenly everything—the dark, stinking room, the mad, secret, midnight drunkenness, the lack of light, the two men out of their minds—all of it suddenly blew on Romashov an unendurable terror of death and madness.

Trembling all over, he pushed Zolotuhin aside with a piercing cry and leaped out of the Tomb.

He knew that he needed to go home, but a mysterious attraction made him return to the dining room. Many of the people there were sleeping, in their chairs or on the windowsills. The room was insufferably hot, and despite the open windows the lamps and candles weren't wavering at all. The exhausted servants and the soldiers who were serving that night as waiters stood dozing on their feet, yawning continuously through clenched jaws, with their nostrils only. But the general debauch continued.

Vetkin was standing on the table now, singing in his high, earnest tenor:

"Swi-ift like the wi-ind,
'Til we co-ome to the e-end."

Many of the officers in the regiment had attended religious schools, which meant that they sang well even when drunk. The song's simple, sad, touching melody ennobled its pretentious lyrics, so that for a second everyone grew melancholy and close under the low ceiling of that musty room, in the midst of their blind, confused, circumscribed lives.

"You die, they dig a grave,
It's as if you never lived . . ."

Vetkin sang expressively, and the sound of his own high, pleading voice combined with the physical feeling of singing in harmony with the choir brought tears to his good, dumb eyes.

Archakovsky accompanied him cautiously. In order to make his voice vibrate he toggled his Adam's apple with two fingers. Osadchin added his deep, ductile notes, and soon it seemed that the other voices were swimming in these low, organ-like sounds as if on a dark wind.

Afterwards there was a short silence as each man felt a moment of quiet contemplation open in the middle of his drunken intoxication. Suddenly Osadchin, staring with bloodshot eyes at the table in front of him, began singing under his breath:

"On the narrow road we walk, everything is lamentable: life is like a yoke . . ."

"Oh please!" someone remarked in a bored-sounding voice. "We've heard enough of this dirge already. More than enough."

But the others had already begun to take up the funereal melody—and then suddenly, into the foul, spattered, smoke-filled dining room came the pure, bright chords of John of Damascus's requiem, suffused with intense and heartfelt sadness, and a passionate lament for his departing life:

"And I believe that those who follow me will come to delight, for trophies have been prepared for you and the crowns of heaven . . ."

Then Archakovsky, who knew the mass as well as any deacon, cried out:

"Let us speak now with all our souls . . ."

They went through the whole service this way; and when they came at last to the final appeal, Osadchin bent his head on its sinewy neck and, with a strangely awful, despairing, and malevolent look in his eyes, began singing in his low voice, which thrummed like the string of a double bass.

"In the blessed passing of life and the eternal quiet you await, oh Lord, your dead servant Nikifor . . ." Osadchin broke out suddenly with a crude and terrible oath, "And make for him an eternal . . ."

Romashov jumped up and struck the table furiously with all his strength.

"Quiet! I won't let you go on like this!" he cried, in a piercing and impassioned voice. "Why do you have to make it all a joke? Captain Osadchin, you act like it's all fun and games to you, but I know it's not! It's painful and terrible—I know, I can see that you feel it in your heart!"

A moment of general silence followed, punctuated only by an anonymous annoyed voice:

"Is he drunk?"

After this, however (as had just happened at the Shleiffers'), the world began to hum and groan, jumping out of its seat and rolling itself up into a sort of motley, moving, shrieking ball. Vetkin leaped up, hitting his head on one of the hanging lamps and sending it rocking back and forth in huge fluid swings, which in turn blew the shadows of the raucous men up until they looked like giants, or shrunk them down until they disappeared into the floorboards, before scattering them in ominous confusion over the walls and ceiling.

Everything that happened next to these unbalanced, hallucinating, drunk, and unhappy men at the officers' club happened quickly, absurdly, and irrevocably. It was as if they had been possessed by some kind of evil, chaotic, stupid, impishly riotous demon, who forced them to curse and throw themselves into the most disorderly contortions.

In the middle of this madness, Romashov suddenly saw someone's face and wrenched, crying mouth thrust towards him. It was so distorted and disfigured by rage that at first he didn't recognize it—but then Nikolaev shouted at him, splattering him with slobber as the muscles under his left eye began jerking nervously:

"How dare you? You're the one who's disgraced the regiment! You—and others like you, like Nazanski! You're here for just a little while . . ."

Someone pulled Romashov back protectively. He saw that it was Bek-Agamalov; but after a second he shook him off and turned away. Paling from what had just happened, he spoke in a hoarse and quiet voice, a pitiful and exhausted smile on his face:

"Why mention Nazanski? Perhaps you have some sort of secret reason to be unhappy with him?"

"Fool—scum!" Nikolaev barked at the top of his voice. "Just give me one crack at that lousy snout of yours!"

He shook his fist menacingly at Romashov and narrowed his eyes, but did not hit him. A miserable fainting feeling began to sink through Romashov's chest and stomach. Until now he had not noticed—in fact, he had practically forgotten about it—that he was holding an object of some kind in his right hand. Suddenly, with a quick flick of his arm, he splashed his remaining beer onto Nikolaev's face.

A dull pain accompanied by a flash of white lightning burst in his left eye. With a long, bestial howl he threw himself on Nikolaev, sending them both crashing down in a tangle of legs. The two tore across the floor, knocking over chairs and gulping down mouthfuls of dirty, stinking sweat, as they squeezed, gashed, and pressed one another, panting and snarling. One thing Romashov did remember later was how by sheer luck his hand had hit Nikolaev's cheek, and he had torn into that slippery, disgusting, hot mouth . . . And yet he hadn't felt any pain when his head and elbows knocked against the ground.

He had no idea how it ended. He found himself standing in a corner, which was where they had driven him after tearing him off of Nikolaev. Bek-Agamalov forced him to drink some water, but Romashov's lips knocked so convulsively against the rim that he was afraid that he might bite off a piece of the glass. His jacket was torn under one arm, and one of the torn-off shoulder straps was dangling from it like a piece of ribbon. Romashov had lost his voice, but he shouted soundlessly, with only his lips.

"I've got more of that . . . to show him! . . . I challenge . . . !"

Old Lekh, who had now woken up and was acting sober and serious after sleeping through the whole thing in his place at the other end of the table, assumed an unusually stern and authoritative tone:

"As the oldest person here, I order you gentlemen to disperse immediately. I mean it, gentlemen—this instant. I'll give the regiment commander a full report on everything that happened here in the morning."

At which point they all went their separate ways, depressed and embarrassed and intent on avoiding one another's eyes—for each of them was afraid to see his own fear and guilty sadness reflected there: the fear and sadness of a poor and dirty little animal, whose dark mind had been momentarily illuminated by a flash of human consciousness.

It was dawn. The sky was bright and innocent-looking and the air still and cool. The damp trees, which stood wrapped in a barely visible mist, were waking up quietly from their dark and mysterious dreams—and then as Romashov made his way home he looked at them, and the sky, and the wet, gray, dewy grass, and felt that he was low, loathsome, misshapen, and forever alien from such a charming morning, with its childlike, half-awake smile.

XX

That same day—this was a Wednesday—Romashov received a brief official note:

> The Officers' Court of the N infantry regiment hereby requests that Sub-lieutenant Romashov appear before them at six o'clock in the main hall of the officers' club. Formal attire is mandatory.
>
> Sub-lieutenant Migunov
> Chairman of the Court

Romashov could not hold back a melancholy smile: this "mandatory formal attire" (which consisted of a uniform with shoulder strap and colored sash) was worn only on the most special occasions, in front of a court, for example, or for public reproof, or for any unpleasant appearance before the authorities.

At six o'clock he went to the club and asked that his presence be announced to the Chairman of the Court. He was told to wait. After taking a seat in the dining room under an open window, he opened a newspaper and, without any interest or even understanding, began running his eyes over the letters printed there. The three officers who were already in the dining room hailed him dryly and then started talking amongst themselves in low voices, as if to make sure that he wouldn't hear them. Sub-lieutenant Mihin was the only one of them who gave his hand a long, hard shake. His eyes were wet, but he blushed wordlessly, fumbled into his jacket, and left.

Soon after this, Nikolaev came into the dining room and approached the bar. He was pale, the lids of his eyes were dark, his left cheek twitched continually, and there was a large, fat bruise on his temple. Memories of the previous night's fight flashed through Romashov's head with painful clarity as, shaking under the dull unbearable weight of that shameful encounter, he slunk down behind his newspaper and screwed his eyes up tightly.

He heard Nikolaev ask for a glass of cognac at the bar, and then thank someone. Then he felt Nikolaev's steps passing in front of him. A door slammed against its frame. And then suddenly, after a few seconds, he heard a sharp whisper coming from behind his back, from the yard outside the window.

"Don't look behind you! Sit still. Listen."

It was Nikolaev. The newspaper trembled in Romashov's hands.

"Strictly speaking, I'm not allowed to be talking with you. But to hell with these French niceties. What's done is done. Despite everything, I still consider you a decent human being. I ask you—are you listening—I ask you to not say a word about my wife or the anonymous letters. Do you understand?"

Romashov, who was screening himself from the other officers behind his newspaper, nodded slowly. He heard the sound of feet crunching over pebbles in the yard. Only after five minutes had passed did he turn and look outside. Nikolaev had already gone.

"Sir," interrupted an orderly in front of him. "Their honors request your presence."

The hall's long, narrow walls were lined with several card tables covered in green cloth. The judges sat here with their backs to the windows, which meant that their faces were dark. Sub-lieutenant Migunov, the chairman—a plump, arrogant man with no neck and rounded, hunched shoulders—sat in an armchair in the middle of the row; sub-lieutenants Rafalski and Lekh sat to either side of him, followed by captains Osadchin and Peterson on the right, and on the left, Captain Dyeverena and Staff Captain Doroshenko, the regimental book-keeper. The table was completely clear of objects, except for a folder of papers in front of Doroshenko, the court clerk. The large, empty hall was chilly and dark, regardless of the fact that in the yard it was a hot and sunny day. The air reeked of old wood and ancient molding upholstery.

The chief lay both of his large white, plump hands palms up on the tablecloth and, looking at each in turn, began speaking in a wooden tone:

"Sub-lieutenant Romashov, the officers' court assembled here today by order of the regimental commander, has been asked to clarify the circumstances of the regrettable and intolerable conflict that took place yesterday in the officers' club between yourself and Lieutenant Nikolaev. I ask that you tell us what happened, in as great detail as possible."

Romashov tugged at his cap band and then stood there before them with his arms at his sides. The only other time he had felt so intimidated, bewildered, and awkward was during his school years, when he had failed an exam. He began his testimony in a halting voice and continued at a mumble, full of confused and irrelevant phrases, to which he added a series of ridiculous interjections. As he was doing this, he stared in turn at each of the judges, mentally reckoning up their feelings towards him. "Migunov: indifferent, like a rock—though he's flattered to be the chief and proud of having such terrible influence and responsibility. Sub-lieutenant Burden is looking at me with pity and something like a woman's gaze. Ah, my dear Burden—do you remember the time you lent me ten rubles? Old Lekh is acting seriously. He's sober today, and he has bags under his eyes like deep scars. He's not my enemy, but like many of them he's acted badly himself at the club on multiple occasions and now relishes the opportunity to play the stern and unbending zealot of official honor. Then there's Osadchin and Peterson: these two are my real enemies. By law, of course, I could get rid of Osadchin—the entire fight began because of his requiem—but what difference would that make? Peterson's got a little smile in the corner of his mouth—there's something foul, base, cunning in that smile. Could he know about the anonymous leters? Dyeverena's got a sleepy face, and his eyes are like bits of cloudy balls. Dyeverena does not like me. Doroshenko doesn't either. A sub-lieutenant who only signs his paychecks over to pay his debts. Ah, you've drawn a bad hand, my dear Yuri Alexeyevich."

"Excuse me for just one minute," Osadchin said, suddenly interrupting him. "Your honor, will you allow me to ask a question?"

"Please." Migunov nodded self-importantly.

"Tell us, Sub-lieutenant Romashov," Osadchin began, as if straining under the weight of his words, "where had you been before you arrived at the officers' club in such an impossible state?"

Romashov blushed, as he became instantly aware of the copious sweat droplets that had broken out all over his forehead.

"I was . . . I was . . . Well, I was in a certain place," he said. And then he added, almost in a whisper, "I was in a brothel."

"A-ha—so you were in a brothel?" Osadchin took this up in a purposefully loud voice, which dripped with implication. "No doubt, you had a little something to drink at this establishment?"

"Y-yes, I did," Romashov answered jerkily.

"Very good. I have no further questions," Osadchin said, turning to the chairman.

"Please, the court requests that you continue with your testimony," Migunov said. "Let's see here: you left off at the point where you were throwing your beer in Lieutenant Nikolaev's face . . . What happened next?"

Romashov's version of his night was disconnected, but sincere and very detailed. He had just started to speak, awkwardly and with great embarrassment, about the repentance that he had felt for his behavior, when he was interrupted by Captain Peterson. Rubbing his bony yellow hands with their long deathly palms and blue nails together as if to wash them, this man began speaking firmly and courteously, almost tenderly, in a thin and insinuating voice:

"Well, of course, all of that is naturally a credit to your excellent fellow-feeling. But tell us, Sub-lieutenant Romashov— before this unlucky and deplorable event occurred, had you ever been to Lieutenant Nikolaev's house?"

Romashov's guard went up; he answered curtly, staring not at Peterson, but at the rest of the judges.

"I had, yes, but I don't understand what this has to do with what we're talking about."

"Just a minute—I ask that you answer only the questions asked," Peterson said. "What I want to know is whether you had any special cause for disliking Nikolaev—a cause of not a military nature, but rather a domestic, or even family one?"

Romashov drew himself up and, his gaze clear, looked straight into Peterson's dark and consumptive eyes.

"I visited the Nikolaev house no more frequently than I visited other people I knew," he said, loudly and sharply. "And no: before this happened there was no sort of enmity between us. Everything happened accidentally and unexpectedly, because we were both drunk."

"He-he-he, we have already heard quite a bit about your drunkenness," Peterson cut him off once more. "But I'm curious: did you and he have any sort of confrontation before this? I don't mean a fight, you understand: just any sort of misunderstanding, or tension perhaps, due to some sort of private matter. A disagreement of beliefs, let's say, or some other kind of intrigue? Ah?"

"Honorable chairman, may I refuse to answer any of the questions put to me?" Romashov asked suddenly.

"Yes, you may," Migunov answered coldly. "You may, if you wish, give no testimony at all, or give it in writing. It is your right."

"In that case I declare that I will not answer a single one of Captain Peterson's questions," Romashov said. "It will be better for both him and myself that way."

He was asked to elaborate on a few more meaningless details, after which the chairman said that he was free to go. However, he was called in two more times to give additional testimony: once that same night, and once on Thursday morning. Even someone like Romashov—who was very inexperienced in these practical matters—understood how negligently and clumsily the court conducted its affairs, and with what extreme carelessness it committed its huge amount of mistakes and faux pas. And the largest blunder of all was that, despite the precise and clear regulation outlined in Article 149 of the disciplinary code, which strictly prohibited anyone from divulging court proceedings, the honorable members of the jury all gossiped freely about what had taken place. They talked about the results of the judgment with their wives, their mistresses—the women in town they knew, and further: to tailors, midwives, even their servants. For twenty-four hours Romashov was being talked about by the entire town—for a whole day, he was a celebrity. When he walked down the street, people watched him from their windows, or behind their gates, their palisades, the cracks in their fences. Woman raised a hand to him in the distance, and he was constantly hearing his name spoken behind his back, in a quick whisper. No one doubted that there would be a duel between Nikolaev and himself. They were even making bets on the outcome.

On Thursday morning, as he was walking past the Lykachevys' house on his way to the officers' club, he heard someone suddenly call out his name.

"Yuri Alexandrovich, Yuri Alexandrovich—over here!"

He stopped and looked up. Katya Lykachevy was standing on the other side of the fence on a little garden bench. She was in a light Japanese bathrobe, the triangular opening of which left her thin and charmingly girlish neck bare. And she was so rosy, fresh, and delicious all over that Romashov became momentarily happy.

She leaned over the fence in order to give him her hand, which was still cold and damp from washing. As she did so she chattered away:

"Oh, wieutenant, why haven't you come to thee uth? Ith thameful to negwect your fwiendth. Eviw, eviw, eviw . . . Tss, I know aw, aw about you!" She made her eyes suddenly big and frightened. "Take thith, and weaw it always, always awound youw neck."

She pulled a kind of amulet on a light silk cord from her kimono, straight between her breasts, and hurriedly thrust it into his hand. The amulet was still warm from her body.

"This is supposed to help me?" Romashov asked jokingly. "What is it anyway?"

"Ith a theecwet, don't you dawe waff! Atheist! Eviw!"

"Apparently I am now in fashion. Wonderful girl," Romashov thought, as he said goodbye to Katya. But he could not hold himself back from thinking of himself here, and for the last time, in the third person of his beautiful phrases:

"A kindly smile shone through the stern mask of the grizzled duelist."

That night he was summoned once again to the court—this time along with Nikolaev. The enemies stood in front of the table, side by side practically. They didn't look at one another, but even at a distance, each of them could feel the other's mood. They stared continuously at the chairman as he read them the court's judgment:

"The Officers' Court of the N infantry regiment, consisting of" (here followed the ranks and names of the judges) "Under the chairmanship of Sub-lieutenant Migunov, and having reviewed the details of the conflict that took place at the officers' club between Lieutenant Nikolaev and Sub-lieutenant Romashov, has decided that, given the extreme mutual hostility existing between these officers, a resolution is impossible, and that a duel between them therefore appears to be the only means of satisfying the offended honor of the parties involved. This is the opinion of the court, seconded by the commander of the regiment."

When he finished reading, Sub-lieutenant Migunov removed his glasses and returned them to their case.

"It remains for you, gentlemen," he said, with stony ceremony, "to choose your seconds, two for each side, and to send them here, to the officers' club, at nine o'clock tonight, at which time, together with us, they will chose the conditions of the duel. By the way," he added, standing as he tucked his glasses case into his back pocket, "by the way, the judgment rendered here today is not the final word for either of you. You remain absolutely free either to go through with the duel or," he parted his hands here and paused, "or to leave the service. Therefore . . . you are free, gentlemen . . . A few words more. I would advise you—not as the chairman of this court, but simply as your old comrade—to refrain from appearing at the club until after the duel itself. Doing so might lead to complications. Now, good day."

Nikolaev turned sharply and left the hall with quick steps. Romashov followed slowly behind him. He was not afraid, but he felt incredibly lonely all of a sudden, and strangely removed—as if he had been cut off from the rest of the world. Stepping outside, he stared long and with focused attention at the sky, the trees, a cow grazing by the fence opposite him, the sparrows bathing in the dust in the middle of the road, and thought: "There you have it: everything is alive, busy, bustling about, growing and shining, while to me nothing is vital or even interesting anymore. I've been sentenced. I'm alone."

Halfheartedly, and with a feeling almost of boredom, he went to find Bek-Agamalov and Vetkin, who he had decided to ask to be his seconds. Both readily agreed: Bek-Agamalov with brooding composure, Vetkin with an affectionate and worldly handshake.

Romashov did not want to go back home: it was awful and tedious there. At a time like this, with the minutes pressing down on him, and his spirit wilting beneath life's harsh and unyielding surface, he longed for the sympathetic understanding of a kind, tender, subtle heart.

Suddenly, he remembered Nazanski.

XXI

Nazanski was at home, as usual. He had just woken up from a heavy drunken sleep and now lay on his bed in only his long johns, with his hands beneath his head. His eyes were clouded over with a haze of weary indifference. The sleepy expression on his face had not yet completely disappeared when Romashov leaned over him and said, with hesitant agitation:

"Hello, Vasily Nilich. I'm not disturbing you, am I?"

"Hello," Nazanski answered in a weak and husky voice. "What's the good word? Go on—take a seat."

He extended a warm moist hand to Romashov, regarding him as if he were, not his favorite, most interesting friend, but rather a familiar phantom from a dream that he'd already tired of a long time ago.

"You're not well?" Romashov asked shyly, sitting down cross-legged on the bed. "Well, then, I won't disturb you. I'll go."

Nazanski lifted his head up slightly from the pillow and, squinting, gave Romashov a concerted stare.

"No . . . wait a second. Ah, how my head hurts! Listen, George Alekseevich . . . There's something about you today . . . something unusual. Help me, I can't seem to get my thoughts in order. What's going on with you?"

Romashov stared at him with silent compassion. Nazanski's entire face had undergone a strange alteration since the two officers had last seen one another. His eyes, which were rimmed now with black circles, had sunk deeply into their sockets; his temples had yellowed; and his saggy, swollen cheeks, with their splotchy and dirty skin, had been overgrown by an unattractive layer of curly hair.

"Nothing special. I just wanted to see you," Romashov said offhandedly. "I'm fighting a duel tomorrow with Nikolaev, and the idea of going back to my room repulses me. But I suppose it doesn't matter. Goodbye. It's just, you know, I have no one to talk to . . . and my heart feels heavy."

Nazanski closed his eyes, sending his face into a series of agonized spasms. Clearly, it was costing him an unnatural effort of will to return to full consciousness. When he did finally open his eyes, sparks of extraordinary warmth were shining in them.

"No, wait . . . this is what we'll do." Nazansky turned laboriously onto his side, propping himself up on an elbow. "Go over there, in the chest . . . You know where I mean . . . No, I don't want an apple . . . There are some mint tablets. Thank you, my friend. This is what we're going to do . . . Foo, what foolishness! . . . Help me get some air—it's disgusting in here, and I'm afraid of it . . . All the time, these terrible hallucinations. Let's go out, we'll go for a ride in the boat and have a little talk. What do you think of that?"

He drank a series of shots, knitting his brow each time, and pinching his face into a look of extreme disgust. Romashov watched as, slowly but surely, his blue eyes began to burn with life and brightness, growing handsome again.

They left the house and hired a driver to take them to the end of town, to the river. A Jewish flour-mill stood in a gigantic red building on one side of the dam; the other side was spotted all over with swimming holes, at some of which it was also possible to hire a boat. Romashov rowed, while Nazanski in the stern half-lay, half-sat under his overcoat.

The river that fed the dam was broad and still, like a huge pond. The banks on either side of it sloped steadily and gently upwards. The grass growing on these banks was so even, bright, and sunny that one wanted to run one's fingers through it. The weeds in the shore-water had turned green: in the center of their thick, dark, circular clumps, the huge heads of water lilies bloomed.

Romashov told a detailed version of his fight with Nikolaev; meanwhile, Nazanski listened to him thoughtfully, tilting his head and staring at the water, which was expanding out from the boat's prow, lazily, and in thick streams that sparkled in the light like ribbons of melted glass.

"Tell me the truth, Romashov—are you scared?" Nazanski asked quietly.

"Of the duel? No, I'm not scared," Romashov answered quickly. But then he fell silent, imagining for a second what it would be like to stand that close to Nikolaev, and look down to see the lowered black barrel of a revolver in his extended hand. "No, no," he said. "I'm not going to pretend that I'm not afraid. Of course, it's terrifying. But I know that I'm not going to get cold feet. I'm not going to run away, or ask for forgiveness."

Nazanski dropped the ends of his fingers into the warm evening water, which seemed to be practically murmuring beneath them. He coughed slightly and then began speaking in a slow, weakened voice:

"Ah, my dear, dear Romashov . . . Why do you want to do this? I mean, think about it: if you know in your heart that you aren't going to behave like a coward—if you are completely sure—then isn't it a hundred times braver to refuse to go through with it?"

"He struck me—in the face!" Romashov said stubbornly, as the burning rage rose powerfully within him again.

"Well, all right, he struck you," Nazanski conceded, staring at Romashov with his sorrowful, affectionate eyes. "Does that really have to lead to this? Everything in the world passes away—both your pain and your hatred will pass. And you yourself will forget about what happened. But you'll never forget about a man that you've killed. He'll be with you in your bed, at your table, when you're alone or in a crowd. The idle chatter that filters down to us from fools, sop-heads, and caged parrots all tries to assure you that killing someone in a duel is not murder. What idiocy! But they persist in the sentimental belief that robbers have nightmares about the brains and blood of their victims. No, a murderer is a murderer. And the important thing isn't the pain, or the death, or the power, or the squeamish disgust towards blood and corpses—no, more terrible than any of that is taking from a man the joy of his life. The great joy of his life!" Nazanski repeated this suddenly, loudly, with tears in his voice. "For no one—neither you, nor me, ah, no, not anyone in the entire world believes that there is any kind of afterlife. Because of that everyone is afraid of death, though tiny-souled fools deceive themselves with the prospect of radiant gardens and sweet songs sung by castrati. As for the strong ones? They quietly step across the border of necessity. You and I—we're not the strong ones. When we think about what's going to happen to us after our death, we imagine empty cold and a dark cellar. No, my friend, it's all nonsense: a cellar would be a welcome deception—a joyful consolation. But try to realize the full horror of the idea that there will be nothing, absolutely nothing, neither darkness, nor emptiness, nor cold . . . there won't even be a thought of these things—even the fear of them won't be left to us! Not even fear! Think of it!"

Romashov put up his oar. The boat was barely moving on the water, and its motion was only perceptible by the way the green banks on either side of them were sliding quietly past.

"Yes—there won't be anything," Romashov repeated thoughtfully.

"But look, no, really, just look at it: how beautiful, how captivating life is!" Nazanski cried, raising his arms wide on either side of him. "Oh, what joy, life, what a blessed beauty! Look at it. The blue sky, the evening sun, the quiet water—one can't help but tremble with passion looking at them. In the distance over there the windmill is waving its wings at us; there's the short green grass, and the water on the banks—which is pink, pink from the sunset. Ah, how wonderful it is—how happy and tender!"

Nazanski suddenly covered his eyes with his hand and began to sob; but then he regained control of himself and began talking again, unashamed of his tears, staring at Romashov with wet shining eyes:

"No, if I fall beneath a train, and my life is cut short, and my guts mix with the sand and are wound on a wheel, and if in that last moment someone asks me, 'Well then, is life beautiful now?,' I'll say thankfully, 'Ah, how beautiful it is!' How much joy we are given, with only a single sight! And what about music, the smell of flowers, the sweet love of women! And then, the immeasurable delights—human thought, the golden sun of life itself! Yurochka—my brother! . . . Forgive me, if I call you this." Nazanski held a trembling hand out to him from far away, as if asking for forgiveness. "Look, let's say you're stuck in a prison for centuries, forever, and your entire life you only get to see what you can through the cracks of two old, well-worn bricks . . . No, let's say that there isn't even a single spark of light in your cell, not a single sound—nothing! And yet, can you really compare that to the alien terror of death? You still have your mind, your imagination, your memory, your ability to create—a man can live with these things. And more than that: you'll have minutes full of passion and joy."

"Yes, life is beautiful," Romashov said.

"Beautiful!" Nazanski repeated feverishly. "And here are two men who—because one hit the other, or kissed his wife, or looked at him impolitely, or simply squinted and twisted his mustache while walking past him—here are two men who are prepared to shoot one another, to kill one another. As for their wounds, their suffering, their deaths—to the devil with all that! But what's really being destroyed here: this pitiful, shuffling clump that calls himself 'man,' perhaps? No! What's being destroyed is the sun, the hot, friendly sun, the bright sky, nature—the entire diverse beauty of life and the highest pleasure and pride: a human mind! The man who destroys that kills something which will never, never, never come again! Ah, fools, fools!"

Nazanski shook his head sadly and let it fall with a long sigh. The boat entered the reeds. Romashov took up the oars again. The tall green moving stems rustling around the boat bowed slowly and weightily before them. It was darker and cooler here than it had been at the start of the river.

"What am I going to do?" Romashov asked darkly and rudely. "Leave for the reserves? Where will I go?"

Nazanski smiled affectionately.

"Wait, Romashov. Look me in the eyes. Like this. No, don't look away, look straight and answer on your honor. Do you really find your work in the army interesting, good, useful? I know you better than anyone, and I can tell how you really feel: you don't believe in any of it."

"No, I don't," Romashov answered forcefully. "But where will I go?"

"Stop, slow down for a second. Think about our officers. I don't mean the guardsmen who dance at balls, speak French, and live off their parents or lawfully wedded wives. No, think about all us unhappy officers out here in the infantry: the backbone of the brave and glorious Russian army. But it's all used goods, riff-raff, garbage. The sons of crippled captains—at best. Most of us are just products of the gymnasium, secondary-school graduates, who weren't able to complete the seminary. Look at our regiment, for example. Who do we have who's served well and for a long time? Paupers, onerous family men, beggars prepared to make any compromise, to perform any cruelty, to kill, even, or steal a soldier's kopek—and all of it for a little bowl of food to bring home. They order him to shoot, and he shoots—but at whom? For what? Maybe for nothing. It's all the same to him, he doesn't think about it. He knows that his house is creaking, his children have rickets, and so he bugs his eyes out like a woodpecker for no reason and repeats the same word over and over again: '*The oath!*' Everything about him that's talented or capable, he drinks away. Seventy-five percent of our officers contract syphilis. One lucky man—that's one man in five years—makes it to the academy, and people spit when they talk about him. The smoother ones, or those with some kind of patronage, invariably leave for the gendarmes, or shoot for a job as a police officer in a big city. Noblemen and those with small fortunes want to be local officials. We'll say the remainder of the men are sharp, with good hearts—but what are they supposed to do? For them the service is a matter of unbroken disgust, a burden, a despicable yoke. They try to work up some sort of side interest for themselves, something that can absorb them completely and leave nothing else left over. One takes an interest in collecting, many of them just wait and wait for the evenings when, after having eaten at home, they can take up a little needle under the lamplight and cross-stitch some kind of mangy unnecessary little carpet, or use their fretsaw to cut the tracery for a self-portrait. In the service little dreams like these become the very heart of joy. Cards, the pursuit of women—there's that, of course. But worst of all are the ones that fall in love with honor, that petty, cruel military honor. I mean Osadchin and the like, who beat their soldier's teeth and eyes in. Do you know that I once saw Archakovsky begin beating his batboy so badly that I had to hold him back? Afterwards there was blood not just on the walls, but on the ceiling too. And do you want to know what happened? Just this: the batman ran to complain to the company commander, and the company commander sent him with a note to the sergeant major, and then the sergeant major beat him for another half hour, until his face was blue, bug-eyed, and bloody. That soldier took his complaint to the inspector general twice, but without any results."

Nazanski fell silent and began rubbing his temples with his palms.

"Wait . . . Ah, how my mind is running . . ." he said anxiously. "This is how it is when your thoughts drive you, instead of the other way around. Yes, now I remember! There's more. Look at the rest of the officers—Staff Captain Plavsky, for example. The devil only knows what kind of trash he eats. He cooks up any old rubbish on his kerosene lamp, goes around practically in rags, in order to save twenty-five rubles out of his forty-eight-ruble salary every month. Ho-ho! He's already put about two thousand in the bank, which he lends out secretly to his friends at a ghastly interest rate. Is miserliness like this innate? No, not at all: it's only one more way to escape the misery, to hide oneself from the cruel and unfathomable mindlessness of military service . . . Captain Stelkovsky—an intelligent man, strong and brave. But what keeps him going? Seducing inexperienced village girls. Or Sub-Lieutenant Burden, at last. A holy fool, kind and with a good soul—singularly charming even—and yet even he escapes completely into the management of his little menagerie. What does the army mean to him, or parades, banners, reprimands, honor? They're all just shallow and unnecessary details."

"Burden is wonderful, I love him," Romashov put in.

"Of course he is," Nazanski agreed limpidly. "But do you know what I saw?" He frowned suddenly. "Do you know what kind of trick I saw him play one day during maneuvers? After evening marches we went on attack. By that point we were all beaten down, tired—everyone was on edge, officers and soldiers alike. Burden told the bugler to sound the attack, but for God only knows what reason he played the call to summon the reserves instead. He did it once, then he did it twice, and then a third time. And then suddenly Burden—the same kind, good, wonderful Burden—galloped up to the bugler, who was still trumpeting, and banged his fist against the bugle with all his strength. It's true—I myself saw the bugler spit not just blood but his smashed teeth out on the ground."

"Oh my God!" Romashov groaned in disgust.

"That's how they all are, even the best of them, even the kindest, the good fathers and wonderful husbands—military life lowers them all, turning them into cowardly, evil, stupid beasts. And do you want to know why? I'll tell you: because there isn't a single person serving who actually believes in the military's brainless objectives. You know how children love to play war, right? Well, history had a turbulent childhood of her own—a time of violence, which was ruled by a young and happy generation. Men at that time traveled in mercenary bands, and war was a joyful intoxication—a bold and bloody pleasure. The elders chose the bravest, strongest, most cunning man they could find, and his word—so long as he avoided being killed by his subordinates—became as true as God's to the people. But mankind has gotten wiser and wiser every year, to the point that now the intelligence playing those children's games is deeper and more serious. Fearless adventurers have become card sharks. A soldier no longer enters into military service like a man starting out on a great and noble path. Instead they toss a lasso around him and string him up; he curses and starts to cry. As for the elders, they've changed, from wild, fascinating, merciless, and worshipful chiefs into cowardly bureaucrats living off their pitiful salaries. Their bravery has become damaged goods. Military discipline—that is, discipline through fear—causes mutual loathing. The beautiful pheasants have molted. I know of only one other example of this in human history: the monasteries. At first they were bold, beautiful, delightful. Perhaps—who knows exactly why—they were called into being from a worldly necessity? But a hundred years have passed, and now what's left of them? A hundred thousand do-nothings, corrupt, well-fed idlers, despised even by those who from time to time find themselves with spiritual needs. And all of this is disguised by outward forms, the charlatan ritual of castes, and manic, hilarious ceremonies. Yes—now that I think about it, my comparison with the monasteries was a completely logical one. Just think how much the two have in common. In one, cassocks; in the other, cedar: a uniform, and the clattering of arms, sighs, holy words; in the other, fake bravado and proud honor, which continually rolls its eyes and thrusts its chest out, tucking its elbows in and pulling its shoulders back as it asks itself 'Am I being insulted?' People from both these professions, and others too, live like parasites and know it, really know it deep in their souls, but are afraid to admit it to themselves consciously—and more importantly, in their guts. The more they try to hide this by clothing themselves in strange costumes, the more they are forced to lie."

Nazanski snorted angrily and fell silent.

"Keep talking, keep talking," Romashov pleaded.

"But the time will come, you know. Things are already turning. A time of great disappointment and frightening re-evaluation. You remember when I told you about humanity's unseen but relentless genius? Its laws are clear, unstoppable. And the wiser humanity grows, the more deeply it is infused with these laws. I have no doubt that, given this, everything in the world will sooner or later balance out. If enslavement lasts for centuries, then its fall will be terrible. The more powerful the power, the more bloody its destruction. And I am deeply, utterly sure that the time is coming when all of us dyed-in-the-wool dandies, incubi, and one-of-a-kind fops, will get what we deserve. Women will be ashamed of our company and soldiers will stop listening to us—not because we beat people who aren't able to protect themselves, or because we abuse women and then hide behind our uniform to avoid punishment; nor because we chop up anyone who bumps into us at a tavern into little soup cubes when we're drunk. Of course, for that too, but we have much more to answer for than just that right now: we're blind and deaf to everything. A gigantic and completely new life has been dawning for some time now, far away from our dirty, stinking station. A new, brave, proud people has appeared, their minds on fire with free thought. It's like the final act in a melodrama, when the old towers and dungeons collapse, revealing a daz-zling brightness behind them. But we just puff ourselves up like turkeys, google our eyes, and start blabbering haughtily: 'What? Where? Silence! Mutiny! I'll shoot!' And it's for this cluck-ing scorn of the freedom of the human soul that they'll never forgive us."

The boat entered a quiet, flooded glade. A tight green wall of high and unmoving reeds encircled them on all sides. The boat was practically surrounded: shut off from the entire world. Seagulls flew above them, so close sometimes that they almost batted Romashov with their wings, and he felt the puff of air from their powerful movement. Their nests must have been somewhere in the thicket of reeds. Nazanski lay in the stern on his back and stared for a long time at the sky, where motionless gold clouds were already being tinted with a blush of rose.

Romashov said shyly:

"You aren't tired, are you? Please go on."

And Nazanski, as if resuming his own train of thought out loud, began to speak again:

"Yes, it's true: an utterly different, wonderful new era is upon us. I've spent some time as a free man, you know: I've read a lot, experienced and seen a lot. For years the old ravens and jack-daws have been beating the same thing into our heads from the moment we start school: 'Love your neighbor like yourself, and know that meekness, attentiveness, and patience are the goal of all humanity.' The more honorable, stronger, more rapacious ones say: 'Take our hands, we'll go down in flames—but at least we'll make an enlightened and easy life for future genera-tions to enjoy.' But I have never have understood this. Who can tell me, clearly and persuasively, what I have in common with these slavish fools—devil take them all!—with these diseased and contaminated idiots? Oh, the legend that I hate above all others—with all my heart, with every particle of loathing in my soul—is the legend of Julian the Hospitalor. The leper says: 'I'm shaking, lie next to me in my bed. I'm frozen, press your lips to my contaminated mouth and breath on me.' Ooh, I detest this! I detest lepers and neighbors. What reward, then, could possi-bly make me bash my head in for the men of the thirty-second century? Oh, I know—I've heard the hen's argument about some sort of a world soul, about religious duty. But even when I believed that with my mind, I didn't once feel it in my heart. Are you following me, Romashov?"

Romashov looked at Nazanski with shamefaced gratitude.

"I understand you completely, completely," he said. "When I am no more, then the whole world will expire? Is that what you meant?"

"Exactly. And with that, I say, love for humanity is smoked completely from the human heart. When this happens, a new and godly belief will be born—one which will remain deathless until the end of the world. A love for one's self, for one's own wonderful body, for one's all-powerful mind, and for the endless richness of one's emotions. Think about it—just think about it, Romashov: who is dearer and more intimate to you than yourself? No one. You are the tsar of the world, its pride and ornament. You are the god of all living things. Everything you see, hear, feel, belongs only to you. Do what you want. Take whatever you want. Don't be afraid of anyone in the entire universe, for there is no one greater than you and no one will ever be your equal. A time will come when the great belief in one's own self will burn, like tongues of fire sent from the Holy Ghost, in the heads of all men, and then there will be no slaves, no masters, no cripples, no pity, no vice, no evil, no envy. Then men will become gods. And just think: how will I dare to insult, push, or deceive a man who I feel to be a holy god like myself? Then life will be beautiful. A bright dawn will spread over the entire earth; nothing vulgar or pretentious will assault our eyes, life will become a sweet labor, a free study, divine music, a happy, easy, endless holiday. Love, freedom from the dark way of property, will become the holy religion of the world, and not a secret shameful sin to be indulged in a dark corner, while looking over one's shoulder in disgust. And then our bodies themselves will become luminous, strong, and beautiful, clothed in bright and extraordinary garments. I believe in this as strongly as I believe in the night sky above us," Nazanski cried out, triumphantly raising his arm above him. "This is how I truly believe that divine future life will be!"

Romashov was shocked and excited. He began babbling with pale lips.

"Nazanski, this is a dream—a fantasy!"

Nazanski smiled with quiet condescension.

"Yes," he said, a hint of amusement in his voice. "Some professor of dogmatic theology or classical philology sets his legs, spreads his hands, and says, with a tilt of the head, 'Come now, that's a manifestation of extreme individualism!' But that's not because of fearsome words, my dear Romashov: it's because nothing in this world is more practical than these fantasies, which these days are dreamt by only a few. And it's these men, these fantasists, who serve as our most faithful and hopeful supports. Let's forget that we are soldiers. We are civilians. Out on the street stands a monster: a great, two-headed monster. Whenever anyone walks past him, he socks them in the mug, straight in the mug. He still hasn't hit me, but even the thought that he can hit me, or insult my beloved wife, or deprive me of my freedom—this idea demolishes my pride. It's the one thing I cannot overcome. But then next to me stands a brave and proud man, like me, and I say to him: 'Let's go and do this together in a way that it will leave neither of us defeated.' And we do it. Oh, of course, this is a crude example, a joke, but in the face of that two-headed monster I see everything that binds my soul, that constrains my will, that makes me ashamed of my own personality. And this is not foolish pity for an intimate, but a blessed self-love, which unites my strength with the strength of another man who, as a human soul, is my equal."

Nazanski fell silent. He had grown weary from this unusually strong state of nervous elevation. After a few minutes had passed he continued sluggishly, his voice lowered:

"That's how it is, my dear Georgie Alekseyevich. An enormous and complex life is swimming past us, bubbling throughout. Gods are being born, and passionate thoughts; the old gilded idols are crumbling. Meanwhile we stand in our stalls with our arms akimbo, and roar: 'Ah, you idiots! You putty! I will beat you!' And life will never forgive us . . ."

He stopped, huddled further into his coat, and said exhaustedly:

"It's cold . . . Let's go back home . . ."

Romashov raked them past the reeds. The sun sat on the distant roofs of the city, which were cast in lines of clear and black relief by the red rays of the sunset. Here and there a flash of reflected fire played in a window pane. The water was rose colored where the sunset struck it, smooth and happy-looking; but as soon as it passed the boat it thickened, becoming blue and wrinkled.

Romashov answered himself with a sudden statement:

"You're right. I'll go to the reserves. I don't know how to do this, but I've been giving it some thought for a while now."

Nazanski wrapped himself in his jacket and shivered from the cold.

"Well, then, go—go," he said, with affectionate sadness. "There's something inside you, some kind of inner light . . . I don't know what to call it. But in a swamp like ours, it will be extinguished. They'll simply spit on it, and it will go out. The most important thing is to not be afraid. Don't be afraid of life: it's a pleasant, amusing, wonderful joke. That's what life is. Well, okay, so they're not going to carry you along; you'll fall, tramp around a little, maybe try some carousing. But for god's sake, my friend, any tramp lives ten thousand times fuller and more interesting life than Adam Ivanovich Zergzht or Captain Sliva. Walk the earth, see the city, the country, become familiar with strange, carefree, funny people, see, smell, listen, sleep on dewy grass, freeze in the frost, not tied down to anything, afraid of no one, devoted to a free life with every ounce of purity you've got . . . Ah, how little most people understand about it! It's all the same: to be a cockroach or to saddle a wild horse, to drink vodka or champagne, to die beneath a canopy or in a police station. Those are all just details, small particulars, changing habits. All they can do is throw shadows on the most important and gigantic ideas in life. That's how I like to look at these opulent funerals. In that silver box with its idiotic plume lies nothing more than a dead monkey, and the other living monkeys walk behind him with their snouts in the air, emitting, stickiplastering themselves front and back with their ridiculous stars and rattles . . . And then all these visits, talks, meetings . . . No, my friend, there's only one thing that's inalterable, beautiful, and indispensable: a free soul, and, along with that, creative thought and a happy thirst for life. Truffles come and go—that's a capricious and exceedingly florid game. The conductor, so long as he's not completely stupid, will learn within a year to govern his little kingdom well and with no small satisfaction. But the fattened, self-important, stupid monkey, sitting in his carriage, with glass beads on his fat paunch, will never cry sweet tears of passion at the sight of fleece silvering a willow branch!"

Nazanski fell into a long coughing fit. Afterwards he spat over the side, and continued:

"Leave, Romashov. I say this because I tried to do so myself, of my own free will, and the only reason I returned to this retched cell is . . . Well, let it be . . . It's all the same, you know. Dive boldly into life, it won't deceive you. It's like a huge building with a thousand rooms, in which you can find light, food, wonderful pictures, intelligent, elegant people, laughter, dancing, love—everything that is great and formidable in art. And out of this whole palace, you've seen only a dark, shadowy storeroom, full of trash and cobwebs—and you're afraid to leave it."

Romashov moored them to the post and helped Nazanski climb out of the boat. It was dark by the time they arrived at Nazanski's house. Romashov laid his friend in bed, covering him with blankets and his overcoat.

"Oh, how frightened these rooms make me . . . The dreams, the dreams!"

"Do you want me to stay the night?" Romashov asked.

"No, no, there's no need. Send for some bromides, if you will . . . and a little vodka. I don't have any money right now . . ."

Romashov sat with him until eleven o'clock. Little by little Nazanski stopped shaking. At one point, he opened his large, sparkling, feverish eyes and said, in a halting and decisive voice:

"Leave now. Goodbye."

"Goodbye," Romashov said sadly.

He wanted to say, "You've taught me so much," but the phrase embarrassed him and he only managed a tired joke.

"Why 'Goodbye'? Why not 'See you tomorrow'?"

Nazanski laughed a terrible, senseless, unexpected laugh.

"Why not 'See you tomorrow'?" he cried, in the wild voice of a madman.

Romashov felt a shudder of horror pass through his entire body.

XXII

When he got home Romashov was surprised to see a faint light glimmering through the warm darkness from his room's tiny window. "What's this?" he thought with alarm, involuntarily quickening his steps. "Maybe my seconds have returned with the conditions?" In the vestibule he ran unexpectedly into Gainan; he was momentarily frightened; he shuddered and cried out angrily:

"Who the . . . ! Is that you, Gainan? Who's here?"

He had the feeling that, despite the dark, Gainan was hopping in place as usual.

"A lady has come to see you. She's sitting down."

Romashov opened the door. The lamp's kerosene had run out a while ago, and the flame was crackling out its last smoky flashes. A female figure sat motionless on the bed, her outline barely visible in the heavy quivering half-light.

"Shurochka!" Romashov said, sucking his breath in. For some reason, he approached the bed on tiptoe. "Shurochka, is that you?"

"Shhh. Sit down," she said in a quick whisper. "Put the lamp out."

He blew into the top of the lantern. The timid blue flame was extinguished, and immediately the room became dark and quiet—at which point Romashov noticed, for the first time, the alarm clock ticking hurriedly and loudly on his desk. He sat down next to Alexandra Petrovna leaning forward without looking towards her side of the bed. A strange mixture of fear, agitation, and a sort of sinking feeling in his heart overwhelmed him and stopped him from speaking.

"Who's in the room next to you, behind the wall?" Shurochka asked. "Can they hear?"

"No, the room's empty . . . Just some old furniture . . . The owner's a cabinetmaker. We can speak as loudly as we want."

Nevertheless, they both kept whispering, and in thick and heavy darkness their quiet, halting voices were filled with fear, embarrassment, and a desire to remain hidden. They sat side by side, practically rocking against one another. Romashov's blood sounded in his ears with muffled knocks.

"Why, why did you do it?" she said quietly, but with passionate rebuke.

She lay her hand on his knee. Romashov could feel her lively and nervous warmth through his clothes. He inhaled and relaxed his eyes—but instead of making things darker, this caused a pair of shapes to appear before him, like dark ovals surfacing in a fairy-tale lake, surrounded by blue light.

"I asked you to control yourself around him—don't you remember? No, no, I'm not blaming you. You didn't go looking for a fight—I know you didn't. But really, when the beast woke up inside you, why couldn't you stop thinking about yourself for a minute, and think of me? You never loved me!"

"I love you," Romashov said quietly, and lay his shy, trembling palm on her hands.

Shurochka removed her hand, though very slowly—furtively, even, and as if she were remorseful and afraid of offending him.

"Yes, I know that neither of you spoke my name, but your chivalry turned out to be in vain: scandal gripped the town nonetheless."

"Forgive me, I couldn't control myself. Jealousy made me blind," Romashov said laboriously.

She smiled a long, wicked smile.

"Jealousy? And do you think that my husband is so large-souled that after your fight he forbade himself the pleasure of telling me where you were before you came to the officers' club? He told me about Nazanski too."

"Forgive me," Romashov repeated. "I didn't do anything bad there. Forgive me."

She rose her voice suddenly and began speaking in a more serious and decisive whisper.

"Listen, Georgie Alexeyivh, every minute is precious to me. I've been waiting for you for almost an hour. So we have to speak quickly and only about what we're going to do. You know what Volodya is to me. I don't love him, but I have sacrificed a part of my heart for him. I have more self-respect than he does. Two times he's failed the academy exam. This caused me much more pain and suffering than it did him. All that talk about being a member of the general staff comes from me and me alone. I have pulled my husband up with all my strength, whipped him into shape, crammed with him, propped him up, inflated his pride, and comforted him in times of depression. This has been my personal, most loved, and most painful task. I cannot abandon it. No matter what happens, he will go to the academy."

Romashov hung his head low, his face in his palms. Suddenly, he felt Shurochka running her hand slowly and quietly through his hair. He asked with painful confusion:

"What do I do now?"

She hugged him around the neck and pulled his head tenderly to her chest. She was not wearing a corset, and Romashov could feel the pliant resilience of her body beneath his cheek and smell her warm, heady, intoxicatingly sweet scent. When she spoke, he felt her breath on his hair.

"You remember that night, at the picnic. I told you everything. I don't love him. Think about it: three years, three whole years full of hopes, fantasies, plans, and every other kind of boring, revolting work that you can imagine! For you know how I loathe this philistine and beggarly circle. I want to be wonderfully dressed, always; beautiful, radiant—I want worship and influence! And then suddenly there's this stupid, drunken fight, a scandal that ruins everything, and it all flies away like ash. Oh, how terrible it is! I've never been a mother, but it makes me imagine that I have a child, a beloved, cherished child, in whom all my hopes have been placed, who has wrung from me all my worries, tears, sleepless nights—and then suddenly there's an accident, a chance, some stupid, unpredictable disaster. One day he's playing on the window and his nanny turns her back on him, and he falls on the stones below. My love, that kind of maternal despair is the only thing that I think would equal my sorrow and anger. But it's not your fault."

It was uncomfortable for Romashov to sit bent over like this, for he was afraid to hurt her with his weight. Still, he would have gladly sat that way for hours, listening to the quick and precise beating of her tiny heart.

"Are you listening to me?" she asked, leaning over him.

"Yes, yes . . . Keep speaking . . . If only I could, I'd do whatever you wanted."

"No, no. Let me finish. If you kill him or they forbid him to take his exams—well then it's over! On the day I hear that, I'll toss him aside and go, where doesn't matter: Petersburg, Odessa, Kiev. Don't think this is some made-up piece of magazine romance. I don't need to frighten you with cheap effects. But I'm young, smart, good looking—I know this. Not beautiful. But I'm more interesting than many of the beauties who win nickel-plated trays or musical alarm clocks for their looks at the public balls. I may dishonor myself—but for a moment, I'll burn brighter than fireworks!"

Romashov looked at the window. Now that his eyes had become used to the dark, he could make out the dull and hazy outline of the frame.

"Don't talk like that . . . You don't have to say that . . . You're hurting me," he said sadly. "But if you want me to, I'll back out of the duel tomorrow, I'll ask his forgiveness. Is that what you want?"

She was quiet for a little while. The alarm clock's metallic tick filled every corner of the room. Finally she began speaking under her voice, to herself almost, with an inflection which Romashov couldn't decipher.

"I knew you'd suggest that."

He lifted his head and sat up straight, despite the fact that she still had her hand on his neck.

"I'm not afraid!" he said loudly and deeply.

"No, no, no, no," she said in a hot, quick, pleading whisper. "You don't understand. Come closer to me, like before! Come here!"

She hugged him with both her hands and began whispering, tickling his face with her soft hair and breathing warmly against his cheek:

"You don't understand. I meant something completely different. But I'm ashamed in front of you. You're so pure, good, and it's difficult for me to speak to you about it. I'm calculating, I'm vile . . ."

"No, tell me everything. I love you."

"Listen," she began, and he guessed, he knew, what she was going to say before she had even said it. "If you back out, a huge amount of pain, suffering, and shame will fall on you. No, not like that—not again. Ah, my God, I can't lie to you. My beloved. I've thought this all through and considered everything at length. Let's say you back out. My husband's honor will be rehabilitated. But you understand that even when there's a reconciliation, a duel always leaves some sort of . . . how should I say it? . . . Well, something dubious, something more intriguing, incomprehensible, and disappointing . . . Do you understand me?" she asked, kissing his hair carefully and with deep affection.

"Yes. But so what?"

"So what? Just that if that happens my husband will almost certainly not be allowed to complete his exam. The reputation of an officer of the general staff must be absolutely spotless. Meanwhile, if you at least fought, then there would be something heroic or memorable about it. People will forgive a lot of things to a man who stands in the same place for a few minutes while shooting at one another. Then afterwards . . . when the duel was over you could ask his forgiveness, if you wanted to . . . But that's up to you."

They embraced tightly, whispering like conspirators, touching their faces and hands together and listening to the sound of one another's breathing. But Romashov could tell that some secret and awful creature had crept imperceptibly between them and begun breathing its cold breath on his heart. He wanted to free himself from her arms; but she wouldn't let him go. He spoke dryly, trying to hide his deep and incomprehensible irritation.

"For the love of God, just tell me what you want. I promise to do whatever you ask."

She began speaking decisively; her mouth was almost pressed against his, and her words were like quick, hurried kisses:

"You must absolutely go through with the duel tomorrow. But neither one of you will be wounded. Oh, please understand—don't judge me harshly! I loathe cowardice, I'm a woman, after all. But do this for me, Georgie! Don't ask about my husband, he knows. I've arranged everything."

With a firm movement of his head, he succeeded in freeing himself from her soft, strong arms. He got up from the bed and said:

"All right, so be it. I agree."

She stood up too. Even though he couldn't see anything in the pitch-black darkness he sensed that she was putting her hair back up.

"You're leaving?" Romashov asked.

"Forgive me," she said weakly. "Give me one last kiss."

Romashov's heart shuddered with pity and love. Groping through the dark, his hands found her, and he began to kiss her cheeks and eyes. Shurochka's whole face was wet from her silent crying. This moved him and made him sad.

"My darling . . . don't cry . . . Sasha . . . my darling . . ." He repeated the words tenderly and sympathetically.

She threw her arms suddenly around his neck, gripping him ardently as her body trembled and heaved. Her blazing lips were still pressed against his mouth when she began whispering raggedly through her heavy breath:

"I can't leave like this . . . We'll never see each other again. So what's left to be afraid of? . . . I want, I want it. One time . . . Let's grab our happiness . . . My darling, come to me, come, come . . ."

And so the two of them, and the entire room, and the whole world were all flooded with a sort of unbearable blessedness, a sultry delirium. For a brief second, Shurochka's eyes emerged from the haze of white pillows with enchanted clarity, incredibly close and shining from happiness, and Romashov pressed himself greedily to her lips . . ."

"May I walk with you?" he asked, as he led her out into the yard.

"No, for the love of God, my darling . . . Don't do that. I don't even know how long I've spent with you. What time is it?"

"I have no idea—I don't have a watch. I have absolutely no idea."

She lingered awhile, leaning against the door. The air smelled like earth and dry rocks: the avid smell of a hot night. It was dark, but through the darkness Romashov saw that Shurochka's face was shining with a strange white light, like the face of a marble statue, as it had been in the grove.

"Goodbye, then, my darling," she said finally, in an exhausted voice. "Goodbye."

They kissed; her lips now were cold and motionless. She walked quickly towards the gate, and was swallowed once more by the thick darkness of the night.

Romashov stood and listened until the gate had stopped squeaking and the soft sound of Shurochka's footsteps had fallen silent. Then he returned to his room.

A powerful but pleasant weariness swept over him. He was barely able to get undressed, he was so tired. The last thing he remembered sensing before falling asleep was the light, sweet smell coming from his pillow: the smell of Shurochka's hair, her breath, and her beautiful young body.

XXIII

2nd June, 18——. Town of Z.

To His Excellency's, Commander of the N Infantry Regiment

From Staff Captain Deitz, of this same regiment

REPORT

It is my honor to inform your Excellency that on this 2nd day of June, according to the conditions that were reported to You yesterday, the 1st of June, a duel took place between Lieutenant Nikolaev and Sub-Lieutenant Romashov. The adversaries met at five minutes before 6 in the morning, in the grove known as "The Oaks," located 3 1/2 miles from town. The duration of the duel, including the time spent giving the signals, was 1 min, 10 sec. The arrangement of the duelists was decided by a coin toss. At the command of "forward" both adversaries walked to meet one another; Lieutenant Nikolaev took the first shot, wounding Sub-lieutenant Romashov in the upper-right part of his stomach. After he had fired, Lieutenant Nikolaev stopped advancing; he remained standing where he was, waiting for an answering shot. At the end of the half-minute that had been designated to an answering shot, it became clear that Sub-lieutenant Romashov was unable to respond to his adversary. The result of this was that Sub-lieutenant Romashov's seconds decided to conclude the duel. This was done with general agreement. While being transported into town by carriage, Sub-lieutenant Romashov lapsed into a heavy stupor and died, after seven minutes of interior bleeding. The seconds on Lieutenant Nikolaev's side were myself and Lieutenant Vasin; on Sub-lieutenant Romashov's side, lieutenants Bek-Agamalov and Vetkin. The arrangement of the duel, by general consent, was allotted to me. Enclosed is the testimony of Jr. MD. Znoiko.

Staff Captain Deitz